The Flannery O'Connor Award

Selected Stories

The University of Georgia Press   *Athens and London*

The

Flannery O'Connor

Award

Selected Stories

Edited by Charles East

© 1992 by the University of Georgia Press
Athens, Georgia 30602
All rights reserved
Designed by Louise OFarrell
Printed and bound by Braun-Brumfield
The paper in this book meets the guidelines for permanence
and durability of the Committee on Production Guidelines
for Book Longevity of the Council on Library Resources.

Printed in the United States of America

96 95 94 93 92   C   5 4 3 2 1

Library of Congress Cataloging in Publication Data
The Flannery O'Connor Award : selected stories / edited by Charles East.
p. cm.
ISBN 0-8203-1414-5 (alk. paper)
1. Short stories, American. I. East, Charles.
PS648.S5F57 1992
813'.0108—dc20   91-28973
                                                       CIP

British Library Cataloging in Publication Data available

Contents

Acknowledgments

The stories in this anthology are from the following award-winning collections published by the University of Georgia Press.

David Walton, *Evening Out* (1983)
Leigh Allison Wilson, *From the Bottom Up* (1983)
Sandra Thompson, *Close-Ups* (1984)
Susan Neville, *The Invention of Flight* (1984)
Mary Hood, *How Far She Went* (1984)
François Camoin, *Why Men Are Afraid of Women* (1984)
Molly Giles, *Rough Translations* (1985)
Daniel Curley, *Living with Snakes* (1985)
Peter Meinke, *The Piano Tuner* (1986)
Tony Ardizzone, *The Evening News* (1986)
Salvatore La Puma, *The Boys of Bensonhurst* (1987)
Melissa Pritchard, *Spirit Seizures* (1987)
Philip F. Deaver, *Silent Retreats* (1988)
Gail Galloway Adams, *The Purchase of Order* (1988)
Carole L. Glickfeld, *Useful Gifts* (1989)
Antonya Nelson, *The Expendables* (1990)
Nancy Zafris, *The People I Know* (1990)
Debra Monroe, *The Source of Trouble* (1990)
Robert H. Abel, *Ghost Traps* (1991)
T. M. McNally, *Low Flying Aircraft* (1991)
Alfred DePew, *The Melancholy of Departure* (1992)

Introduction

The situation that writers of short fiction faced at the time the Flannery O'Connor Award was established in 1981 has improved—not enough, there is a way to go yet, but attention is now being paid, and I like to think that the award played at least a small part in it.

There have, of course, always been magazines—and magazine editors—that these writers could count on, from the *New Yorker* (that Holy Grail), *Harper's,* and the *Atlantic* to the women's fashion magazines and the quarterlies. And there were the anthologists: Edward J. O'Brien, Herschel Brickell, Martha Foley, and more recently, William Abrahams and Shannon Ravenel. Their efforts in behalf of the short story should not go unnoticed. Yet for too many writers, publication of their stories in the magazines proved a blind alley. What the editors at book publishing houses had in mind was a novel. As a result, there were collections of short fiction—good ones—going unpublished.

The situation was not one that developed in 1980, or even in 1970. At Louisiana State University Press in the mid-1960s, Richard L. Wentworth and I began to publish collections of short fiction for precisely the same reason. That is, we felt that this was an area which to a large extent had been abandoned by the trade publishers and into which university presses could step in order to bring gifted young writers to the attention of readers and reviewers.

The University of Georgia Press's Flannery O'Connor Award for Short Fiction enlarged upon the idea, offering an annual competition in which two (or occasionally more) winners were chosen. From the beginning, it was apparent that the collections we published would also get the attention of the New York editors. Indeed, in the years since the award was established, as I watched those editors rush in to sign up the authors' second books or to publish the paperback editions of their collections, I came to appreciate the importance of the series as a proving ground for new writers.

I must confess I have never understood why the short story would not make its own way in a country that produced fast food, *Cliff's Notes,* and the thirty-minute sitcom—also, and not incidentally, some of the best of the genre ever written. Nevertheless, the bias against collections of stories was so deeply rooted in the mind and psyche of the commercial publishers that I doubt they any longer knew the basis of their preference. Partly of course it resided in the sales figures; partly, I suspect, in the fact that the longer form, the older form, was assumed to be the weightier, the more serious. Yet the best of Flannery O'Connor's work— some would argue, of Faulkner's work, and Eudora Welty's—is the stories.

Miss Welty's encounters with New York editors over her natural inclination to write in the shorter form is well documented in *Author and Agent* by Michael Kreyling. It no doubt came as a surprise to many of Welty's readers that some of her finest stories, "The Wide Net" and "Why I Live at the P.O.," for instance, were roundly rejected when they were first submitted—"no plot" was a frequent complaint—and that the commercial publishers praised her stories perfunctorily while exhorting her to come forth with a novel.

"Please do not tell me that I will have to write a novel," Welty wrote her agent Diarmuid Russell in 1940. "I do not see why if you enjoy writing short stories and cannot even think in the form of a novel you should be driven away from it and made to slave at something you do not like and do badly. Of course I know nothing about publishing. One publisher wrote me that if he could just get me in a restaurant he could persuade me." Russell, a rare one for that time or any time, wrote his client: "As regards writing a novel follow your own desires. . . . Only by following your own path can you get anywhere. The only real value I can see in a novel for you is that a novel is an arduous piece of work that demands concentration and hard work and this is good for everybody."

Those writers fortunate enough to be offered a contract on a first collection of stories, and they were few indeed, usually signed what was known in the trade as the two-book contract. The second book was a novel. If the novel was thought to be inherently a more serious form than the short story, the short story collection was considered publishing poison. "One reason I like to publish short stories," Flannery O'Connor told an interviewer in 1959, "is that nobody pays any attention to them. . . . When you publish a novel," she added, "the racket is like a fox in the hen house."

Publishing is of course an act of faith. The truth is that more than one short story collection fell by the wayside because the editor's faith foretold the marketing department's faith—or lack of it. The advertising budget for a book of stories, even by an established writer, was seldom in a class with that for a novel. Lack of faith became a self-fulfilling prophecy. The trade houses that did publish short story collections usually did so only in the

cases of (1) young writers of such promise that the editors calculated they had to publish the stories in order to lay claim to
the future novel, or (2) name writers who were at the moment
"between novels."

This was the situation when I arrived at the University of
Georgia Press as editor in 1980. The idea for the establishment
of the Flannery O'Connor Award was that of Paul Zimmer, then
director, a writer himself and, as I soon learned, a creative and
innovative publisher. The notion of naming the series for Flannery O'Connor was also his (I thought at the time, and still do, a
stroke of genius). Within a few months after my arrival, the series
was under way and we were into the first round of submissions—
a round that brought forth an interesting group of manuscripts
and two strong winners, David Walton and Leigh Allison Wilson. The first collection to be published, *Evening Out* by Walton,
appeared in the early spring of 1983, followed by Wilson's *From
the Bottom Up* in the fall of that year.

I left the Press at the end of 1983, and Paul Zimmer the year
after. However, the future of the award was never in serious question. The new director, Malcolm Call, decided to continue the
series, which at his invitation I now edit at long distance. His faith
in the program and his keen publishing sense, and I might add
the enthusiastic support of his associate director, Karen Orchard,
have been indispensable to the success of the series.

One risk that we took—I think probably the greatest risk, and
we were aware of it from the beginning—was being stereotyped
as regional ("Only southern writers need apply"), but I am happy
to say we managed to escape that pitfall. The writers whose collections we published over the first ten years of the series come from
all sections of the country. They live in California, Seattle, Salt
Lake City, Pittsburgh, Kentucky, West Virginia, Georgia, Florida,
Massachusetts, Maine, New York, New Mexico, North Carolina,

Indiana, Ohio. Most of them teach in college or university writing programs.

Five of the twenty-one had had books (novels or collections of short fiction) published before they won the award. At least nine have gone on to publish subsequent novels or collections: Leigh Allison Wilson, Sandra Thompson, Mary Hood, François Camoin, Daniel Curley (who died in an accident in 1988), Tony Ardizzone, Salvatore La Puma, Melissa Pritchard, Antonya Nelson. Several others have books under contract.

If there is a discernible pattern to the work itself—to the stories—it is that combination of things which has always distinguished serious fiction, the best of it. Character is of course an important element—the focus, for instance, of "La Bête: A Figure Study" by Melissa Pritchard, the story of the wondrously fat laundress who achieves immortality as an artist's model, but no less important in a number of the other stories. It is the force of character that draws us to the great-grandmother nearing the end of her life in Susan Neville's story "Banquet" and to the title character in Philip F. Deaver's "Wilbur Gray Falls in Love with an Idea," a middle-aged man recalling the lies and secrets of his life while battling depression and night terrors. And to Billy Lee Boaz, a genius at everything but love—"a type," says the narrator of "Inside Dope" by Gail Galloway Adams, "if men don't recognize, at least the women will."

The voice is what one remembers best about many of these stories. The characters speak to us, and it is the way in which they speak that provides the texture, and frequently much of the force and energy, of the story. "First," says the narrator of Adams's story, "a Boaz is not big. Five foot six is about as tall as they get, and they are dark with black hair and eyes, real tanned skin, and bodies just as trim and tight as their lips are wet and loose."

The voice can sing or turn sad, or laconic. "I have many

friends," says the narrator of François Camoin's "Peacock Blue," "but I can't stand to talk to the closest of them for more than twenty minutes. . . ." The aging homosexual grieving over the loss of his young lover in Alfred DePew's "*Voici! Henri!*" reflects on "how delicate, how temporary life is and how in the flick of a wrist it can be snatched away, or it can drain off a little at a time as you stand by and watch, helpless to do anything."

The voice can also suggest the currents that lie just below the surface of the story, as in "The Source of Trouble" by Debra Monroe, where the narrator is fourteen-year-old Devita. In her last summer before entering high school she is about to discover boys, about to witness her parents' breakup, about to become a woman. Monroe never loses sight of the character or control of the story, which is by turns sad and funny.

Place is an important element in several of these stories, most notably perhaps in "A Country Girl" by Mary Hood, with its setting in a kind of enchanted valley where a barefoot girl sings melodies "low and private as lullaby," but also in David Walton's extraordinary story "Skin and Bone," where the locale is Pittsburgh, and in Salvatore La Puma's "The Mouthpiece" and Carole L. Glickfeld's "What My Mother Knows," the former set in the Bensonhurst section of Brooklyn on the eve of World War II and the latter in 1940s Manhattan. The power of place is also at the heart of "South of the Border" by Leigh Allison Wilson, in which the narrator, driving north out of the South she grew up in, fears she will be drawn back once more "and never be able to leave, my present and future eradicated by the vicious tenacity of the past."

The past—recollections of an earlier time, an early love, a childhood fear—is the focus of "Horror Story" by Sandra Thompson and "The Ponoes" by Peter Meinke. Thompson's "Big Goof," the former 230-pound All-State tackle gone soft but still smelling of Old Spice, and Meinke's Murphy brothers, the scourge of

P.S. 245, "extorters of lunch money, fistfighters, hitters of home runs during gym class," are among the most memorable of the characters in these collections.

The range of subjects and themes is a wide one. In Tony Ardizzone's "World Without End," a story about generational differences, Peter, the former altar boy, dodges his mother's questions and his Chicago past by making jokes about the "good clean Catholic girl" she wishes he had married. "Appetizer," Robert H. Abel's wonderfully told tale of an encounter with a bear while fishing for salmon in Alaska, is pure story. So is "The Metal Shredders" by Nancy Zafris, whose narrator spins a tale of wild dogs and man-eating machines amid a landscape of wrecked cars, "fossils of Skylarks and Chryslers from the twentieth century."

In "Trinity" by Daniel Curley a formerly married couple are brought together by the loss of a child and their deep dislike for one another. "Jet Stream" by T. M. McNally is also a story of loss, of separation—"something," the teenage narrator confides, "I already know how to do, something I'm already getting good at." At the end of the story she and the friend who is about to go to live in California are sitting on the top of a baby grand piano that they have just helped her stepfather push into the swimming pool, along with the TV, the microwave, the couch, and a picture of her mother.

It is these writers' ability to handle humor that distinguishes many of the stories in the Flannery O'Connor Award volumes— for instance, Gail Galloway Adams's "Inside Dope," which I have already mentioned, but also Antonya Nelson's "The Expendables," in which a wedding party spills out onto the street and encounters a Gypsy funeral procession, and Molly Giles's "Pie Dance." Who but Giles's narrator could make you believe in a dog who dances with her late at night, when the children are asleep, and who is now deep into reggae?

I believe this anthology demonstrates why the Flannery O'Connor Award and the series have been so warmly received, especially by the writers themselves, and why we have every reason to be optimistic about the future of the genre. There are many other fine stories in these collections that I have not included. The stories I selected are ones that I have particularly enjoyed, ones that I find myself coming back to and that I thought others would enjoy as well.

Charles East

The Flannery O'Connor Award

Selected Stories

Appetizer

Robert H. Abel

I'm fishing this beautiful stream in Alaska, catching salmon, char and steelhead, when this bear lumbers out of the woods and down to the stream bank. He fixes me with this half-amused, half-curious look which says: You are meat.

The bear's eyes are brown and his shiny golden fur is standing up in spikes, which shows me he has been fishing, too, perhaps where the stream curves behind the peninsula of woods he has just trudged through. He's not making any sound I can hear over the rumble of the water in the softball-sized rocks, but his presence is very loud.

I say "his" presence because temporarily I am not interested in or able to assess the creature's sex. I am looking at a head that is bigger around than my steering wheel, a pair of paws awash in river bubbles that could cover half my windshield. I am glad that I am wearing polarized fishing glasses so the bear cannot see the little teardrops of fear that have crept into the corner of my eyes. To assure him/her I am not the least bit intimidated, I make another cast.

Immediately I tie into a fat Chinook. The splashing of the fish in the stream engages the bear's attention, but he/she registers this for the moment only by shifting his/her glance. I play the fish smartly and when it comes gliding in, tired, pinksided, glittering and astonished, I pluck it out of the water by inserting a finger in its gill—something I normally wouldn't do in order not to injure the fish before I set it free, and I do exactly what you would do in the same situation—throw it to the bear.

The bear's eyes widen and she—for I can see now past her huge shoulder and powerful haunches that she is a she—turns and pounces on the fish with such speed and nimbleness that I am numbed. There is no chance in hell that I, in my insulated waders, am going to outrun her, dodge her blows, escape her jaws. While she is occupied devouring the fish—I can hear her teeth clacking together—I do what you or anyone else would do and cast again.

God answers my muttered prayer and I am blessed with the strike of another fat salmon, like the others on its way to spawning grounds upstream. I would like this fish to survive and release its eggs or sperm to perpetuate the salmon kingdom, but Ms. Bear has just licked her whiskers clean and has now moved knee-deep into the water and, to my consternation, leans against me rather like a large and friendly dog, although her ears are at the level of my shoulder and her back is broader than that of any horse I have ever seen. Ms. Bear is intensely interested in the progress of the salmon toward us, and her head twists and twitches as the fish circles, darts, takes line away, shakes head, rolls over, leaps.

With a bear at your side, it is not the simplest thing to play a fish properly, but the presence of this huge animal, and especially her long snout, thick as my thigh, wonderfully concentrates the mind. She smells like the forest floor, like crushed moss and damp leaves, and she is as warm as a radiator back in my Massachusetts home, the thought of which floods me with a terrible nostalgia. Now I debate whether I should just drift the salmon in under the bear's nose and let her take it that way, but I'm afraid she will break off my fly and leader and right now that fly—a Doctor Wilson number eight—is saving my life. So, with much anxiety, I pretend to take charge and bring the fish in on the side away from the bear, gill and quickly unhook it, turn away from the bear and toss the fish behind me to the bank.

The bear wheels and clambers upon it at once, leaving a vortex of water pouring into the vacuum of the space she has left, which almost topples me. As her teeth snack away, I quickly and furtively regard my poor Doctor Wilson, which is fish-mauled now, bedraggled, almost unrecognizable. But the present emergency compels me to zing it out once again. I walk a few paces downstream, hoping the bear will remember an appointment or become distracted and I can sneak away.

But a few seconds later she is leaning against me again, raptly watching the stream for any sign of a salmon splash. My luck holds; another fish smacks the withered Wilson, flings sunlight and water in silver jets as it dances its last dance. I implore the salmon's forgiveness: something I had once read revealed that this is the way of all primitive hunters, to take the life reluctantly and to pray for the victim's return. I think my prayer is as urgent as that of any Mashpee or Yoruban, or Tlingit or early Celt, for I not only want the salmon to thrive forever, I want a superabundance of them now, right now, to save my neck. I have an idea this hungry bear, bereft of fish, would waste little time in conducting any prayer ceremonies before she turned me into the main course my salmon were just the appetizer for. When I take up this fish, the bear practically rips it from my hand, and the sight of those teeth so close, and the truly persuasive power of those muscled, pink-rimmed jaws, cause a wave of fear in me so great that I nearly faint.

My vertigo subsides as Ms. Bear munches and destroys the salmon with hearty shakes of her head and I sneak a few more paces downstream, rapidly also with trembling fingers tie on a new Doctor Wilson, observing the utmost care (as you would, too) in making my knots. I cast and stride downstream, wishing I could just plunge into the crystalline water and bowl away like a log. My hope and plan is to wade my way back to the narrow trail a few hundred yards ahead and, when Ms. Bear loses interest or is somehow distracted, make a heroic dash for my camper. I think of the thermos of hot coffee on the front seat, the six-pack of beer in the cooler, the thin rubber mattress with the blue sleeping bag adorning it, warm wool socks in a bag hanging from a window crank, and almost burst into tears, these simple things, given the presence of Ms. Hungry Bear, seem so miraculous, so emblematic of the life I love to live. I promise the gods—American, Indian, African, Oriental—that if I survive I will never complain again, not even if my teenage children leave the caps off the toothpaste tubes or their bicycles in the driveway at home.

"Oh, home," I think, and cast again.

Ms. Bear rejoins me. You may or may not believe me, and perhaps after all it was only my imagination worked up by terror, but two things happened which gave me a particle of hope. The first was that Ms. Bear actually belched—quite noisily and unapologetically, too, like a rude uncle at a Christmas dinner. She showed no signs of having committed any impropriety, and yet it was clear to me that a belching bear is probably also a bear with a pretty-full belly. A few more salmon and perhaps Ms. Bear would wander off in search of a berry dessert.

Now the second thing she did, or that I imagined she did, was to begin—well, not *speaking* to me exactly, but *communicating* somehow. I know it sounds foolish, but if you were in my shoes—my waders, to be more precise—you might have learned bear talk pretty quickly, too. It's not as if the bear were speaking to me in complete sentences and English words such as "Get me another

fish, pal, or you're on the menu," but in a much more indirect and
subtle way, almost in the way a stream talks through its bubbling
and burbling and rattling of rocks and gurgling along.

Believe me, I listened intently, more with my mind than with
my ears, as if the bear were telepathizing, and—I know you're
not going to believe this, but it's true, I am normally not what you
would call an egomaniac with an inflated self-esteem such that I
imagine that every bear which walks out of the woods falls in love
with me—but I really did truly believe now that this Ms. Bear was
expressing feelings of, well, *affection*. Really, I think she kinda
liked me. True or not, the feeling made me less afraid. In fact,
and I don't mean this in any erotic or perverse kind of way, but
I had to admit, once my fear had passed, my feelings were kinda
mutual. Like you might feel for an old pal of a dog. Or a favorite
horse. I only wish she weren't such a big eater. I only wish she
were not a carnivore, and I, carne.

Now she nudges me with her nose.

"All right, all right," I say. "I'm doing the best I can."

Cast in the glide behind that big boulder, the bear telepathizes
me. *There's a couple of whoppers in there.*

I do as I'm told and wham! the bear is right! Instantly I'm tied
into a granddaddy Chinook, a really burly fellow who has no in-
tention of lying down on anybody's platter beneath a blanket of
lemon slices and scallion shoots, let alone make his last wiggle
down a bear's gullet. Even the bear is excited and begins shifting
weight from paw to paw, a little motion for her that nevertheless
has big consequences for me as her body slams against my hip,
then slams again.

Partly because I don't want to lose the fish, but partly also because I want to use the fish as an excuse to move closer to my
getaway trail, I stumble downstream. This fish has my rod bent
into an upside-down *U* and I'm hoping my quick-tied knots are

also strong enough to take this salmon's lurching and his intelligent, broadside swinging into the river current—a very smart fish! Ordinarily I might take a long time with a fish like this, baby it in, but now I'm putting on as much pressure as I dare. When the salmon flips into a little side pool, the bear takes matters into her own hands, clambers over the rocks, pounces, nabs the salmon smartly behind the head and lumbers immediately to the bank. My leader snaps at once and while Ms. Bear attends to the destruction of the fish, I tie on another fly and make some shambling headway downstream. Yes, I worry about the hook still in the fish, but only because I do not want this bear to be irritated by anything. I want her to be replete and smug and doze off in the sun. I try to telepathize as much. Please, Bear, sleep.

Inevitably, the fishing slows down, but Ms. Bear does not seem to mind. Again she belches. Myself, I am getting quite a headache and know that I am fighting exhaustion. On a normal morning of humping along in waders over these slippery softball-sized rocks, I would be tired in any case. The added emergency is foreclosing on my energy reserves. I even find myself getting a little angry, frustrated at least, and I marvel at the bear's persistence, her inexhaustible doggedness. And appetite. I catch fish, I toss them to her. At supermarket prices, I calculate she has eaten about six hundred dollars worth of fish. The calculating gives me something to think about besides my fear.

At last I am immediately across from the opening to the trail which twines back through the woods to where my camper rests in the dapple shade of mighty pines. Still, five hundred yards separate me from this imagined haven. I entertain the notion perhaps someone else will come along and frighten the bear away, maybe someone with a dog or a gun, but I have already spent many days here without seeing another soul, and in fact have chosen to return here for that very reason. I have told myself for many years that I really do love nature, love being among the animals, am restored by wilderness adventure. Considering that right now I would like nothing better than to be nestled beside my wife in front of a blazing fire, this seems to be a sentiment in need of some revision.

Now, as if in answer to my speculations, the bear turns beside me, her rump pushing me into water deeper than I want to be in, where my footing is shaky, and she stares into the woods, ears forward. She has heard something I cannot hear, or smelled something I cannot smell, and while I labor back to shallower water and surer footing, I hope some backpackers or some bear-poaching Indians are about to appear and send Ms. Bear a-galloping away. Automatically, I continue casting, but I also cannot help glancing over my shoulder in hopes of seeing what Ms. Bear sees. And in a moment I do.

It is another bear.

Unconsciously, I release a low moan, but my voice is lost in the guttural warning of Ms. Bear to the trespasser. The new arrival answers with a defiant cough. He—I believe it is a he—can afford to be defiant because he is half again as large as my companion. His fur seems longer and coarser, and though its substance is as golden as that of the bear beside me, the tips are black and this dark surface ripples and undulates over his massive frame. His nostrils are flared and he is staring with profound concentration at me.

Now I am truly confused and afraid. Would it be better to catch another salmon or not? I surely cannot provide for two of these beasts and in any case Mister Bear does not seem the type to be distracted by or made friendly by any measly salmon tribute. His whole bearing—pardon the expression—tells me my intrusion into this bear world is a personal affront to his bear honor. Only Ms. Bear stands between us and, after all, whose side is she really on? By bear standards, I am sure a rather regal and handsome fellow has made his appearance. Why should the fur-covered heart of furry Ms. Bear go out to me? How much love can a few hundred dollars worth of salmon buy? Most likely, this couple even have a history, know and have known each other from other seasons even though for the moment they prefer to pretend to regard each other as total strangers.

How disturbed I am is well illustrated by my next course of action. It is completely irrational, and I cannot account for it, or why it saved me—if indeed it did. I cranked in my line and lay my rod across some rocks, then began the arduous process of pulling myself out of my waders while trying to balance myself on those awkward rocks in that fast water. I tipped and swayed as I tugged at my boots, pushed my waders down, my arms in the foaming, frigid water, then the waders also filling, making it even more difficult to pull my feet free.

I emerged like a nymph from a cocoon, wet and trembling. The bears regarded me with clear stupefaction, as if one of them had casually stepped out of his or her fur. I drained what water I could from the waders, then dropped my fly rod into them, and held them before me. The damned rocks were brutal on my feet, but I marched toward the trail opening, lifting and dropping first one, then the other leg of my waders as if I were operating a giant puppet. The water still in the waders gave each footfall an impressive authority, and I was half thinking that, well, if the big one attacks, maybe he'll be fooled into chomping the waders first and I'll at least now be able to run. I did not relish the idea of pounding down the trail in my nearly bare feet, but it was a damn sight better way to argue with the bear than being sucked from my waders like a snail from its shell. Would you have done differently?

Who knows what the bears thought, but I tried to make myself look as much as possible like a camel or some other extreme and inedible form of four-footedness as I plodded along the trail. The bears looked at each other, then at me as I clomped by, the water in the waders making an odd gurgling sound, and me making an odd sound, too, on remembering just then how the Indians would, staring death in the eye, sing their death song. Having no such melody prepared, and never having been anything but a bathtub singer, I chanted forth the only song I ever committed to memory: "Jingle Bells."

Yes, "Jingle Bells," I sang, "jingle all the way," and I lifted first one, then the other wader leg and dropped it stomping down. "Oh what fun it is to ride in a one-horse open sleigh-ay!"

The exercise was to prove to me just how complicated and various is the nature of the bear. The male reared up, blotting out the sun, bellowed, then twisted on his haunches and crashed off into the woods. The female, head cocked in curiosity, followed at a slight distance, within what still might be called striking distance whether I was out of my waders or not. Truly, I did not appreciate her persistence. Hauling the waders half full of water before me was trying work and the superfluous thought struck me: suppose someone sees me now, plumping along like this, singing "Jingle Bells," a bear in attendance? Vanity, obviously, never sleeps. But as long as the bear kept her distance I saw no reason to change my *modus operandi.*

When I came within about one hundred feet of my camper, its white cap gleaming like a remnant of spring snow and beckoning me, I risked everything, dropped the waders and sped for the cab. The bear broke into a trot, too, I was sure, because although I couldn't see her, had my sights locked on the gleaming handle to the pickup door, I sure enough could hear those big feet slapping the ground behind me in a heavy rhythm, a terrible and elemental beat that sang to me of my own frailty, fragile bones and tender flesh. I plunged on like a madman, grabbed the camper door and hurled myself in.

I lay on the seat panting, curled like a child, shuddered when the bear slammed against the pickup's side. The bear pressed her nose to the window, then curiously, unceremoniously licked the glass with her tongue. I know (and you know) she could have shattered the glass with a single blow, and I tried to imagine what I should do if indeed she resorted to this simple expedient. Fisherman that I am, I had nothing in the cab of the truck to defend myself with except a tire iron, and that not readily accessible behind the seat I was cowering on. My best defense, obviously, was to start the pickup and drive away.

Just as I sat up to the steering wheel and inserted the key, however, Ms. Bear slammed her big paws onto the hood and hoisted herself aboard. The pickup shuddered with the weight of her, and suddenly the windshield was full of her golden fur. I beeped the horn loud and long numerous times, but this had about the same effect as my singing, only caused her to shake her huge head, which vibrated the truck terribly. She stomped around on the hood and then lay down, back against the windshield, which now appeared to have been covered by a huge shag rug.

Could I believe my eyes?

No, I could not believe my eyes. My truck was being smothered in bear. In a moment I also could not believe my ears—Ms. Bear had decided the camper hood was the perfect place for a nap, and she was *snoring,* snoring profoundly, her body twitching like a cat's. Finally, she had responded to my advice and desires, but at the most inappropriate time. I was trapped. Blinded by bear body!

My exhaustion had been doubled by my sprint for the camper, and now that I was not in such a desperate panic, I felt the cold of the water that had soaked my clothes and I began to tremble. It also crossed my mind that perhaps Mister Bear was still in the vicinity, and if Ms. Bear was not smart enough, or cruel enough, to smash my window to get at me, he just might be.

Therefore, I started the engine—which disturbed Ms. Bear not a whit—and rolled down the window enough to stick my head out and see down the rocky, limb-strewn trail. I figured a few jolts in those ruts and Ms. Bear would be off like a shot.

This proved a smug assumption. Ms. Bear did indeed awaken and bestir herself to a sitting position, a bit like an overgrown hood ornament, but quickly grew quite adept at balancing herself against the lurching and jolting of my truck, which, in fact, she seemed to enjoy. Just my luck, I growled, to find the first bear in Alaska who wanted a ride into town. I tried some quick braking and sharp turn maneuvers I thought might send her tumbling off, but her bulk was so massive, her paws so artfully spread, that she was just too stable an entity. She wanted a ride and there was nothing I could do about it.

When I came out of the woods to the gravel road known locally as the Dawson Artery, I had an inspiration. I didn't drive so fast that if Ms. Bear decided to clamber down she would be hurt, but I did head for the main road which led to Buckville and the Buckville Cannery. Ms. Bear swayed happily along the whole ten miles to that intersection and seemed not to bat an eye when first one big logging truck, then another plummeted by. I pulled out onto the highway, and for the safety of both of us—those logging trucks have dubious brakes and their drivers get paid by the trip—I had to accelerate considerably.

I couldn't see much of Ms. Bear except her back and rump as I had to concentrate on the road, some of which is pretty curvy in that coastal area, shadowed also by the giant pines. But from the attitude expressed by her posture, I'd say she was having a whale, or should I say a salmon of a time. I saw a few cars and pickups veering out of the oncoming lane onto the shoulder as we swept

by, but I didn't have time, really, to appreciate the astonishment
of their drivers. In this way, my head out the window, Ms. Bear
perched on the hood, I drove to the Buckville Cannery and turned
into the long driveway.

Ms. Bear knew right away something good was ahead for she
rose on all fours now and stuck her nose straight out like a bird
dog on a pheasant. Her legs quivered with nervous anticipation
as we approached, and as soon as I came out of the trees into the
parking area, she went over the front of the camper like someone
plunging into a pool.

Don't tell me you would have done any differently. I stopped
right there and watched Ms. Bear march down between the rows
of cars and right up the truck ramp into the cannery itself. She
was not the least bit intimidated by all the noise of the machines
and the grinders and stampers in there, or the shouting of the
workers.

Now the Buckville Cannery isn't that big—I imagine about
two dozen people work there on any given day—and since it is so
remote, has no hurricane fence around it, and no security guard.
After all, what's anybody going to steal out of there besides a
few cases of canned salmon or some bags of frozen fish parts that
will soon become some company's cat food? The main building
is up on a little hill and conveyors run down from there to the
docks where the salmon boats pull in—the sea is another half
mile away—and unload their catch.

I would say that in about three minutes after Ms. Bear walked
into the cannery, twenty of the twenty-four workers were climbing out down the conveyors, dropping from open windows, or
charging out the doors. The other four just hadn't got wind of
the event yet, but in a little while they came bounding out, too,
one fellow pulling up his trousers as he ran. They all assembled

on the semicircular drive before the main office and had a union
meeting of some vigor.

Myself, I was too tired to participate, and in any case did not
want to be held liable for the disturbance at the Buckville Cannery, and so I made a U-turn and drove on into Buckville itself
where I took a room above the Buckville Tavern and had a hot
shower and a really nice nap. That night in the Tap and Lounge
I got to hear many an excited story about the she-bear who free-
loaded at the cannery for a couple of hours before she was driven
off by blowing, ironically enough, the lunch whistle loud and
long. I didn't think it was the right time or place to testify to my
part in that historical event, and for once kept my mouth shut.
You don't like trouble any more than I do, and I'm sure you would
have done about the same.

Inside Dope

Gail Galloway Adams

This is a story about being in love with a man named Billy Lee Boaz, only he's called Bisher, don't ask me why. You need to know what he looks like because Bisher is a type, if men don't recognize, at least the women will.

First, a Boaz is not big. Five foot six is about as tall as they get, and they are dark with black hair and eyes, real tanned skin, and bodies just as trim and tight as their lips are wet and loose. They have bandits' faces, with bright shiny eyes that gleam in a dashboard's light, white teeth that do the same, and they are as good in bed as they are at working on the engine of a Pontiac. They don't do sports, except sometimes if the high school is small enough you'll see them on the football line digging in like baby buffalo; stamina and spite keep them there against all odds. They usually aim their every action to rewards, and the mean variety end up in the service yelling at shaved-head recruits and being fussy over lockers. The civilian ones are good-natured boys, then men, who smile a lot. They are the kind who, when they come down to breakfast in clean white T-shirts and starched khaki pants, freshly showered and shaved, come smiling into the kitchen. Their hair is always cut the same, "some off the back and sides, just barely trim the top," and around each ear is pared an arch the color of their palms, their soles, and underneath their underwear.

They're jittery men too, jiggling change as they stand, walking forward lightly on their toes, slumping back hard into their heels, and somehow you are always aware of them from the navel down. Although they do nothing with their hands and arms to indicate their lower parts, still, the itch of lust is in the air. When they love you they are given to coming up and getting push-up placed with you against the wall; then they lean down to lick your throat. Before you gasp they unroll a pack of Luckies tucked like a second bicep in their shirt, and light one in a dramatic way: scratching the match against their thigh, snapping it in two with a nail, or deliberately letting the flame burn into their fingerpads. They are also the kind of men who groan when it feels good, and Bisher, who was my brother-in-law, had all these qualities.

But of course, finally, Bisher is different and that's why I'm telling about him. Bisher was, and is, a genius. Everyone attests to that, even the principal who threw him out of school. Bisher works (where he has for years) at the Standard Shell station and wears a blue blouse with his name embroidered on his chest, an oval with a red satin stitch of *Boaz, Bill* right over his heart. He's the one who taught me to call a work shirt a blouse. "More uniform," he grinned, explaining that in the Army they call them blouses instead of shirts and "no one ever called dogfaces feminine." Then he folded in the sides of cloth like wrappings on a gift and tucked them in his pants. That was the summer I was fifteen, and I sat on the shag rug listening to, watching, and admiring Bisher.

My sister Ellen married Bisher at the end of her junior year in high school, and there's no need to go into what that did to our family. First, everyone almost died; then they cried from March to June, and finally, when my parents realized those two would not give up, they were wed under my father's guiding prayers, and we all gave thanks that one of the two—probably Bisher—had the sense to hold off babies for a while. In towns like ours, as soon as a marriage was announced, countdown began. People bought layettes the same day they bought a plate for the bride's table setting.

After a return from a honeymoon in "Gay Mehico," Ellen and Bisher made our third floor home. The room had been ours—mine and Ellen's, I mean—and was really two rooms with a long hall in between, a sink curtained off at one end and a toilet in a closet near the stair. "Deluxe," Bisher said the day he moved in. "I'll add this to my list of ten best spots to stay from here to Amarillo." Ellen blushed to see him standing there amidst our pink stuffed bears and faded rag rugs. I moved reluctantly down to a room which was used once or twice a year for visiting missionaries, more often for making costumes for the church's plays. With Bisher upstairs, our lives took on new rhythms and new ways.

My dad did not, of course, like Bisher, but being a Christian thought he should, and tried to talk to his new son-in-law each day. "Well, young man . . ." Dad would clear his throat. "Well, Billy Lee."

"Call me Bisher, sir," said Bisher. So Daddy would nod and ask, "Have a good day?"

"Yes, sir," Bisher'd reply as snappy as an ensign in starched pants. Then he'd wink at me and purse his lips at Ellen, which made me giggle and her blush, then both snicker.

My mother always caught these three-way exchanges, saw us, her daughters, as traitors, and would draw her lips together and pale. She absolutely hated, detested, despised Billy Lee. She refused to call him Bisher, forbade our father to, cursed "that Boaz," his family, his pets, and malign chance that put him here in this town when he should have been in Houston getting mugged. "Just trash," she'd mutter, "nothing but trash. I never thought I'd raise my Ellen to marry trash."

I would sit on a high stool in the kitchen waiting for Mamma to finish washing the dishes I was to dry, and listen to her tirades against Bisher, and wonder why he made her feel that way. "It's lust, nothing but lust," she'd said once, then flushed, slapped me on the arm right where I was picking a scab off a mosquito bite, and yelled at me to get upstairs to my room and stop hanging around minding everybody's business, which I thought wasn't fair. But as I moped my way to the room beneath the bed where Ellen and Bisher slept, I knew then, as now, that no matter what my mother said, I was on my sister's side, and Bisher's. And I also knew that I would love that short dark boy until the day I died.

Bisher was able, finally and always, to get around my mother as he got around everyone. He won her over in the end, for all the time she was dying the one person she ever wanted to see was him. "Where is that scamp?" she'd ask. "He worries me to death." She'd pull at the collar of her bed jacket, push at her limp hair, and say, "I wouldn't care to see him again." The door'd creep open and Bisher's face would appear, dark and shiny as mischief. "Got a minute, madame?" he'd whisper, letting his eyes look shyly everywhere except at her until she'd say, "Come on in, you're letting air out to the hall." Then Bisher'd slip into the room so quick if you didn't know better you'd think he made his living as a second-story man, or maybe was a meter man gone bad and gone to bed with the lady of the house.

But like everybody else he touched, he touched our mother, made her do things she'd never dreamed of. He taught her to smoke on her deathbed. We could hear her gasp for breath and laugh between puffs and coughs. "Oh, Lord," she'd say, or pray, with stammering breath, "This is so wrong," and then peer closely at the end of her Camel to see if it would contradict. "Look here," Bisher'd command, and she'd watch him fill the room with smoky rings. She learned that too. It was disconcerting to creak open the door to check and see if she was resting well and catch her lying there, propped up on ruffled pillows, head tilted back to the ceiling, her mouth a perfect "O" as it puffed out those rings until they circled her like Saturn's do. Now I understand that that was one of Bisher's secrets. He's the kind of man who'll take you to a raunchy honky-tonk if you want to go, and all night while you are sipping 3.2 beer his feet will be tapping yours under the table and he'll be winking at you or nudging you as if to say, "Why aren't you bad?" He let you play it fast, but safe, and you were grateful to him for it.

I wouldn't say that Bisher's what they call a good old boy. He's not. At least, I don't think he is. For although he works on cars and engines and loves them, he doesn't care for guns. He has one, everybody does, but his hangs behind the door, forgotten as a worn-out coat. "I never liked hunting much," he said one night in the kitchen when we were helping Mamma skin rabbits a church elder had brought. Dumped out of a gunny sack onto the floor, the rabbits filled the room with their blood-splotched fur. Ellen, pregnant with her first, ran to throw up; Mamma murmured, "Oh, Lord," and even Daddy, who preached of death as a new beginning, looked distressed.

"Let's make them look like meat," Bisher said, "then they won't trouble us as much." He heaped them in a plastic tub where they hung limp as coronation trim to be sewed on, then took them to the porch. After they were skinned and all the leavings but their lucky feet buried, they bubbled pale and shimmering in a black iron pot.

"No, I never cared for hunting," Bisher said thoughtfully when all that had been done. "Because I always thought just before I shot. . ." He paused, looked apologetically at my father. "What if it's true we're born again, and in another body, say, like a deer? Why, I couldn't shoot a deer to save my life, cause every time I'd remember Lewis Moon and how he liked to run before he died. Why, what if Lewis was that deer? Excuse me, sir."

My daddy muttered, "Quite all right," and hurried out to write up a lesson for the Senior Sunday School with two main themes— Number 1: Do we need to hunt our animal friends? and Number 2: Beliefs on coming back to life that Christians should put right on out of their heads.

But what made Bisher unique was that he was a genius, and how he got to be one is legend in our town. Others have tried his trick since, just to end up laughingstocks when they have failed. There has been only one other acknowledged genius in this whole county, and George Shapland was never any fun like Bisher. He was always tucked up in a book, which Bisher said proved he wasn't a natural genius. "Not that there is a thing wrong with books. It's just that they don't have no place." George graduated from high school at age fifteen after having proved the geometry teacher wrong and having put the history teacher down (both were coaches, so shouldn't be blamed for being soft in hard subjects), and then he went to State Tech where he took a double load of everything and made friends with others like himself who cluttered up cafeteria tables with maps and measuring instruments. Later it was rumored he became a monk. But Bisher's genius wasn't like George's ordinary kind, for Bisher's brain was pure, and how he brought it to the attention of the authorities was genius enough.

A new teacher came to teach English and the Romance tongues, and one week into French, Bisher's genius was revealed. Called on to read a page of Lesson II, he balked at his desk, slumped into his heels, and said in French he'd rather not. The rest of the stu-

dents didn't know what he said, thought it was filth and that that
was why the teacher gasped and said, "You read it, you canard."
When Bisher quacked and waddled to the front, the others didn't
know what was going on. They now thought Bisher was making
bathroom gestures, sounds. He jumped on the teacher's desk;
then, barely looking at the text, he read Lesson II, skipped on
to IV, ending up with number XII, and he answered all the questions too. The other students still thought he was Danny Kaye-ing
them, making Frenchy sounds, making fun of French, so they
were laughing at his ooo la la's, but meanwhile the teacher had
caught on to Bisher's brain and stood there listening to him reel
off syllables like de Gaulle.

When Bisher finished a rundown of the hardest, longest words
in the index, translating all of them, a silence fell upon the room.
"Is he right?" whispered a semibright boy, and the teacher numbly
nodded her head. When she did, Bisher, who was still standing
on the desk, now holding the book across his chest in a Napoleon
stance, suddenly, without a sideways glance, hurled that text out
the window, splintering the glass. At the crash, he jumped to flee
the room, the teacher in pursuit, screaming "My boy, my boy, my
dear dear boy" in French.

Bisher got kicked out of school about ten minutes later, even
though the teacher intervened, claiming (it was the first time)
Bisher's genius. The principal would hear none of this. "Don't let
me hear of this boy's genius. I call it fits myself. There's at least
ten idiots in the institute can reel off dates and times better than
this Billy Lee 'Bisher' Boaz boy. And as for this last—this French
episode—why, I don't know." He shook his hands from the wrist
as if that limpness signified Paris and all its decadence. Then he
threw Bisher out, saying the reasons were breaking windows and
the backs of books and disrespect for a foreign land.

Once expelled, Bisher was stripped not only of the lessons he
already knew, but of all the offices he held, which, though many,

were not various. He was the sergeant at arms for every club from Future Nurses to the Lindbergh Boys. He had more pictures in the *Cattle Call* annual than anybody but the Snowball Queen, but that year he was officially excised, and every organization picture had an oblong blank that once was Billy Lee. He signed those anyway with Greek signs.

The second reason he was a genius was inside dope. What that means is that Bisher knew something about everything—he really did. Like all smart men, he claimed to have read the dictionary from *A* to *Z*, and was always threatening to start in on the *Britannica*. In every conversation Bisher had things to add, and always they were interesting. He was like those columns in the newspaper called "Ask Mr. Tweedles" where people write in to ask "What are warts made of?" and "Why are tulips bulbs?" That is what Bisher Boaz could do too—not only explain warts in scientific terms, he could tell you about all the different kinds of warts, from plantars on your feet to venereal on your you-know-where. But, unlike a Tweedles, who had to stop at column's end, Bisher didn't. If you showed the slightest bit of interest, as I did, since my hands were always covered with warts—seed pearls of them ringing my fingers, grits of them on my fingertips—he'd tell you how to make them go away. Every night press half an onion and some lemon juice on your palms, then put your hands in gloves so the acid would start to eat away those knobs. Salt and hot water rags might work, but not as well, and he'd heard from a sailor that in Madagascar the natives called warts "woolies" and smeared them with cornmeal and lard and exposed them to the sun. "Are you sure, Billy Lee," my mamma questioned, "he didn't get that mixed up with cooking techniques?"

"No, ma'am," said Bisher, "no siree. And Old Man Allison— he spits on pennies, then ties them to your hands." I shivered to think of wet copper staining my hands green, melting my flesh.

But warts were just one of the things that Bisher knew, could

do. For instance, he knew names, real names of movie stars—
Bernie Schwartz for Tony Curtis, Judy Garland/Frances Gumm.
"Archie Leach, now that's a laugh," he'd say. "Imagine, Cary
Grant!" He knew the made-up names of every level down to grip,
and watching a movie with Bisher could be a chore. "Bobby Ray-
mond's his real name," he'd whisper when the villain appeared;
"Hers is Susie Moore," when the girlish victim smiled at death.
"Oh boy," he'd crow, then clap his hands. "Old Lyman Harkney's
playing that soda jerk." And even when the story was spoiled by
these outbursts, you didn't mind, but wanted to see old Harkney
make a comeback shake. You wanted to know Norma Jean Baker
by her real name, even when Bisher would argue against that
change. "Now why?" he'd say. "Norma Baker is a good star's
name. Norma Talmadge made it. Baker sounds so clean, so why'd
she change? Brought her nothing but bad luck, poor kid. Did you
know she had a round white bed?" He knew political nicknames
too, and was the first person I ever knew to call FDR "Frankie
Dee." Bisher said, "His own family did that in the confines of
their room. The missus, that's Eleanor, I've heard she called him
F. Dee Dee."

And Bisher knew the names of things like knots. He never tied
a shoelace, his or his kids', without telling you just what it was:
half-splice, granny circle, mariner's wheel, whichever one he'd
chosen for that day. Once he macrameed his oldest boy's laces
halfway down, naming each loop and twist as he taught the child
to tie. It was the same with ties. "Windsor, Crown, Full-Dress, or
Brummel Bunch," he'd say, and later, when my dad was old and
unable to sort out the ends of his own, Bisher was always there
on Sunday mornings "to arrange cravats." "A Fanchon Loop?"
he'd ask. My dad would nod, then watch in the mirror as Bisher,
shorter, hidden behind him, deftly moved the material into wings.

Names of tools, nails, brads, a half-lug screw, a soft-headed
angle iron—all these are in my memory, along with others I never

try to find in hardware stores. All are inside dope and fun to know. You can see why children always loved him, wanted to go with him to the Dairy Queen to hear him order "Dope and Dodos two by two" or "Adam and Eve on a raft with a side of down." My daughter loves her hamburgers "dragged through the garden," and she'll eat almost anything if Uncle Bisher says it is "a meal with a story behind it."

I am married to a man who is as different from a Bisher Boaz as any man can be. My Mel is tall, lean, pale, wears wire-rimmed glasses, and is a chemist with hair thinning at the crown. He was appalled at tales of Bisher until he met him, then fell under his spell as hard as anyone. When those two are together I love my Mel more as he tries to slouch his frame down half a foot and bounce tough in Bisher's stride. It can't be done, but I love him for the trying.

Bisher knows what he's about with Mel, teasing, making frogs on my husband's arm, and laughing, scuffling out a foot to kick Mel in the rear. "Break your behind, my old Max. You ain't nothing but a hoked-up cook." He nicknamed Mel "Max" the second day they met. Because, he said, Mel had "the look of Maximilian Schell, or the Emperor of Mexico." My husband, immensely pleased, laughed, betrayed himself with a blush. He's wanted a nickname all his life, not just Mel; a shortened version of your name is not enough. Years ago, at a summer camp, he'd tried to start a nickname of his own. Tall and awkward at first base, he'd chatted up his teammates, addressed himself as "Stumpy," encouraged the others to do the same, but Stumpy didn't stick. Until Bisher's baptism, my Mel remained just what he was, a two-syllable Jewish boy good at math and "chemicals." As "Max" he expands in blue jeans that fit rather than cling oddly to his waist, and the whole of him is revved up by Bisher. He's sparked. He starts making lists and listing things as "Number 1."

Oh, Bisher's lists . . . he has one for everything: ten famous redheads, five deadly Arizona snakes. When my daughter squeals, tumbles backwards on the grass, hurling her legs over her head to show cotton bloomers with a ruffled hem, I know if Bisher were here he'd have her on a list. "Want to hear a list of five famous women who showed their private pants in public places? Number 1: Marilyn Monroe on a hot-air grate in New York City, 1956." And the names remain, for Bisher nicknamed everyone. Ellen had a dozen or more, but "Mistress Mellow" was the one she liked the best. I was "Grits" because "You love 'em, you're full of 'em, and your warts feel like 'em." Far from being insulted, I loved that name, signed "Grits" to papers until I was married. My mother was "Miz Matty Mustard," my dad was "Mr. Chaps." Every friend that Bisher had was changed, renamed. Frail Danny Sells became "Dan, the Panic Man" who tried feats like hanging from a window ledge at noon, while C. C. Collins, a druggist in his daddy's store, was called "Chuckles Capistrano, that fine chap," and he grew to specialize in oily giggling. Bisher had nicknames for every pet he met. "Here, Wolf," he'd coax and our old collie Fred would try to growl, and then he'd croon, "Hey, Big Rufus Red," as he stroked our orange striped tomcat Sam.

But what I always loved the best was to listen to Bisher talk about all the places that he'd like to have been. He knew those nicknames too, and the way that the natives said them, like Newport News and San Antone. I loved the ones that ended in a liquid *a:* Miama, Cincinnata, Missoura, or when he'd give you a choice of pronunciation, say between Nawlans and New Orleens. My favorites always were the "Sans": Peedro, San Jo, Frisco, San Berdoo.

I have often wondered what it would be like to make love to Bisher, or one of his type, and even, on occasion, have worked myself into a frenzy over this. In those early days I watched Ellen with a discerning eye that only sisters have, to see if what she and Bisher did "showed." On her it did. She was and is a woman who is lush, not fat but full, and her skin glows. A man would have to want those deep wide breasts, those soft round thighs that show you she's a natural blonde. Sometimes I wonder who it was I envied most: Bisher, sinking into her to be subsumed, or Ellen, having him with all life's energy.

But for all my dreaming I am aware that Ellen's not had an easy time of it with Bisher being like he is. It's a funny thing that there are men who zero in on a woman they want, as the only thing in life they'll ever want, and once they've gotten her, they start to roam. My husband sees Bisher's episodes as excess energy or misdirected compassion—Bisher's attempts to help some poor girl out. Beginning with advice, he always ends up in bed.

Ellen realizes that these lapses don't mean anything, that she is secure in her position of Number 1. The problem is that it still hurts. She cries her eyes out over each new blonde, and each year I settle down to write a letter telling her that once again all will be well, that Bisher will behave, realize the error of his ways, not to pack her bags and move out here to us, not to storm the honky-tonk, not, whatever else she does, to go to the hussy's house to fight it out with her. Above all, I write, just be calm, you've been through this before. Take up guitar, I urge. You've always had a pretty voice, you like to sing, Bisher likes to hear you sing (not that that matters, I say with an exclamation mark), and that will turn your thoughts away from what is going on at Ruby's Watering Hole. Just get through it, Ellen, one more time. You know you are his everything. And all my love. Then, because I know Bisher would be hurt—and, oddly enough, so would Ellen if I left it out—I add, P.S. Give our love to Bisher but hold off giving it to him for a while.

It always seemed to me that the love story of my sister and Bisher should have high drama in it: a shooting outside the Broken Spoke with Boaz slumping down, wounded in a limb, to be lifted into the back of a pickup truck and jolted into town to have the lead removed. I've pictured that scene a thousand times: Ellen in a cotton dress, shivering in the air-conditioned corridor, waiting for a word about her man, and, at the other end of that lino-leumed aisle, a swinging door behind which sits the hussy who has caused it all. She's a brassy blonde wearing stretch pants and patent go-go boots, but close up, to complicate things, her eyes are tired and vulnerable. It would be her ex-husband, released from Huntsville on a 2–10, who shot Bisher down, and that man's now cuffed and crying in the city jail.

But even as good a character as Boaz was, he couldn't make his fate a better story, and I always find the ending sad, the way it petered out. Finally, it was just what you'd expect of anyone— not a Bisher Boaz genius with all his sweet teenaged love. It was one blonde too many, and too trashy, and then it wasn't bearable any more. Ellen couldn't laugh, as she'd once done, at the tales of woe they'd tell Bisher and he'd repeat to her as to why he'd got involved. Although he'd hardly aged, had stayed almost as trim as his boyhood self, he was older now and should know better. He should think of the kids, be more considerate of her. By now Ellen was wider, heavier, her tolerance covered over by both knowl-edge and flesh. So they were divorced, like one out of every four, and within the year my sister married a widower, a vet who wore pastel polyester leisure suits and had chains dangling on his ex-posed chest (he is another type who deserves a story of his own). But he seems to love Ellen about as much as he does Samoyeds, and she seems quite content. As for Bisher, within a month he'd married his latest blonde craze, who promptly hung up her danc-ing pumps, let her hair go brown, and started in making meringue pies with too much tartar in the gelatin.

On our first visit home since the divorce, Mel said he wanted to go see Bisher and I could come if I thought Ellen wouldn't mind, but he meant to go anyway. At breakfast Ellen said she didn't mind, that she saw Bisher almost every day or so to discuss the kids, or just to talk. Pouring coffee for us, she flushed, glanced at the empty place where the vet would sit except he had to attend the birth of puppies, and said, "You know that Bisher. He's always got the inside dope on everyone."

We drove out to see Bisher at his station, and I stayed in the car because it was so hot out there on the concrete where Mel and my ex-brother-in-law were sparring, making plans to go fishing on the coming Saturday. Then, suddenly, Bisher was walking over to the car. Smiling, he leaned into the window frame and said, "Give me a kiss, sweet Grits," and offered me his sweet wet lips. I inhaled that old smell of him: sweat and nicotine and gasoline and the lotion of Old Spice and Lava soap, and began to cry. "Oh Bish," I blubbered, and he said, "Now, Grits, don't cry." As he massaged my shoulder blade, I heard him say, "Got a brand-new list of five dark men who married blondes and then went wrong. Number 1: Joe DiMaggio." Then we three laughed. That night in bed beside Mel, knowing Ellen and her new man, whose hands smell of Lysol and dog hair, are down the hall, I wondered again of sex and love and Bisher. How can she bear it? I thought. To know somewhere not far away he is in bed, in love with someone else who listens to his whispering of names like Frisco, Nawlins, San Berdoo?

Leaving town, we swung by the station to beep good-bye to Bisher. As we honked, drove off, and left him standing on the platform next to the pumps, I saw he didn't wave.

"The Arapahoe Indians invented waving bye—did it backwards to their own faces" was the first piece of inside dope he'd ever told me. And so Bisher never waved good-bye. Instead he bobbed his head. Now, this morning, he nodded us away, as if to say it was his energy that moved the engines of our lives.

World Without End

Tony Ardizzone

"*Gloria in excelsis Deo,*" Peter said as he steered his squeaking Chevy down Hampton Boulevard, a Winston bouncing on his lip. Glory be to God on high. It was Sunday morning, Memorial Day weekend, the beginning of the tourist season. Most of Norfolk's residents and visitors were eating breakfast or still in bed, asleep. Lena and August, who had flown in from Chicago on the discount airline the night before, sat next to Peter on the car's blanketed front seat. Lena wore a black hat and was as thin as a bird. Gus was gray and as round as a house cat. "*Et in terra pax hominibus bonae voluntatis.*" And on earth peace to men of good will. The old Chevy groaned and rumbled down the street, tires delving into every pothole. From behind a large cloud the sun tried to shine.

"I'm glad my boy still knows his prayers," Lena said, patting Peter's bony knee. He was wearing blue jeans and an open-necked blue shirt.

"You need new shocks," August announced. His hands firmly gripped the dashboard. "We'll never make it to church in one piece. This is worse than a roller-coaster ride."

Peter glanced at his parents, exhaled a thick stream of smoke, shook his head, and smiled. "*Laudamus te. Benedicimus te. Adoramus te.*" We praise Thee. We bless Thee. We adore Thee. Pleased with himself, Peter downshifted as the car neared a red light. So far the visit was going well. He idled in neutral. And he'd do whatever he could to make things stay that way. "*Confiteor Deo omnipotenti,*" he said, nudging his mother. I confess to almighty God. Then Peter beat his chest three times and said, "*Mea culpa, mea culpa, mea maxima culpa.*" Through my fault, through my fault, through my most grievous fault. The Chevy lurched forward as the light turned to green.

"My Petie," Lena laughed. "He's giving us the whole Mass." She turned from her husband's frown and faced her son. "So you're a regular parishioner at this church, Petie?"

"Sure, Mamma." Peter flicked his cigarette butt out his open window and looked away.

"It's a nice church we're going to, not one of those new ones that look like a gymnasium?"

"Beautiful," Peter said, eyes on the road. "Stained glass everywhere you can see. More statues than a cemetery, even more than Chicago's Holy Name. So gorgeous that when you walk inside it takes your breath away." The Chevy hit another pothole.

"This ride is taking my breath away," Gus said with disgust.

Peter and Lena ignored him. "But not so beautiful as our parish back home," Lena said. A furrow of worry creased her brow.

"Of course not, Mamma. Nothing can ever beat what's back home."

Lena adjusted her hat and beamed.

"A church is a church," Gus said. The blanket beneath his legs had begun to bunch up, revealing the tips of two springs that poked through the upholstery. "What do you think, God cares about the furniture?"

"God cares about furniture," Lena said.

"Yeah, maybe the collection basket." Gus pounded the dash and laughed.

"He cares," Lena said. "Why else did He make Jesus a carpenter?"

"Two points, Mamma." Peter licked two fingers and slashed them in the air.

His father's thighs discovered the exposed springs. "Petie, you got to do something about this car. How can you take a girl out and expect her to sit on this? She'll rip her dress."

"Father Luigi still asks about you," Lena said. She shook her head at August, then pointed out his window at a tall magnolia tree. "He says, 'And how is Petie, good old Petie, my favorite altar boy, how's Petie now that he left his good parents and moved down to the South all because he didn't look hard enough for a job in Chicago or maybe because he just wanted to get away from his poor mamma—'"

"Father Luigi says all that?"

"Every Sunday, Petie. He stops us outside church. And sometimes we see him on Thursday nights after he meets with the parish council."

Peter tried a different street. "You're a deacon now, Papa? Mamma said something about Father Luigi asking you to become a deacon?"

Gus wrestled with the springs, his thumbs trying to push them back beneath the upholstery.

"Eucharistic minister," Lena said. "He doesn't think he's worthy." She smiled at her husband, then tried to stop his hands. "He gets up and reads the Gospel sometimes, but he doesn't want to give out Communion. Why should he, he's no priest."

"Things change, Mamma. That's legal now."

"It used to be a mortal sin and now they even let Nick Guiliani touch the Host." Nick Guiliani owned the neighborhood Shell station. "Whenever I see him passing it out with his greasy hands I change lines. Don't we, August? Holy Communion should come from a priest, not Nick Guiliani."

"Before you open your mouth, Mamma, you could whisper, 'Hey Nick, fill her up!' "

Gus chuckled as Lena said, "You take it in your hand, Petie. I'll do it the old way with Father Luigi, but when I get stuck in a line with an ordinary person I take it in my hand. You don't know if they wash."

"It still goes in your mouth, Mamma."

"Yeah, but I give the germs time to jump off on my hand." Lena nodded and looked at her hand. "We talked all about it one night during parish council. Your papa thinks I'm crazy."

"What did Father Luigi say?"

"He thought she was crazy too," Gus said.

"No he didn't," Lena said. "He changed the subject. Whenever I talk to him, he changes the subject. That was the night he first asked me about you."

Peter turned back toward Hampton Boulevard. Azaleas of all colors bloomed in front of the houses lining the streets. Absently Peter said, "So what did you tell him about me? Good things?"

Lena stared at her hands, her lap, the car's roof, out the windshield, all the time shrugging and looking hurt and sad. Peter realized his mistake. He gave the Chevy gas.

"What could I say, Petie? What can a mother say? That her son doesn't think the upstairs flat is good enough for him, His Royal Highness, so he has to move out into a dangerous neighborhood full of hoodlums and ends up wasting half of his paycheck on rent?"

"Mamma, that was nearly two years ago."

"Let me finish. You asked me a question, so the least you could do is hold your breath until I'm finished." Peter reached across the dash for a cigarette. August's thumbs again fought the springs. Lena nodded her head and smoothed her dress. "That's only the tip of the iceberg, my son. Don't think anything you do ever escapes your mother's eyes."

"Lena," Gus said, "get to the point."

"Don't be in such a hurry, Augusto." Lena called her husband Augusto only during arguments. "You're on vacation now. You unloaded trucks fifty weeks for this. Relax. Remember, the doctor told you you don't have a strong heart." The Chevy bounced over another pothole. "Your son throws away his good money on an opium den on South Halsted and you don't think his mother sees? Then he met that girl— That stewardess— That hussy—"

"Lorraine wasn't a hussy, Mamma."

"She moved in with you, didn't she? You didn't marry her, did you? What do you think, I was born yesterday? I don't want to open old wounds, but you had only one bed in that apartment, Petie."

"You'd actually take a girl out in a car like this?" Gus had succeeded in getting the springs beneath the upholstery, but the last bump popped them out again. "I can't believe it. I wouldn't be caught dead. She'd have to wear a suit of armor."

"*Dominus vobiscum,*" Peter said. The Lord be with you. "*Et cum spiritu tuo.*" And with thy spirit. With his right hand Peter made a broad sign of the cross over the steering wheel.

"But then she got wise," Lena said, "and never came back from a flight to Albuquerque."

"Tucson," Peter said.

"What's the difference?" Lena said. "You gave her some thrills, and the hussy packed her bags. So you had your fun, some pleasure, a little enjoyment."

"Lena," Gus said, "it's a Sunday. Don't describe."

"It's only natural, Augusto. We raised a healthy boy. His blood is red like everyone else's. Just as long as he doesn't get disease. Don't pretend to be such an innocent."

"The church is around here somewhere," Peter said, taking a drag off his cigarette and letting out the clutch.

Gus pointed to his heart. "Me? Pretend to be an innocent? Lena, I'm more faithful than Lassie. You believe too many of Monty's stories."

"I know you served your country, Augusto, but you were stationed in France for two years. I go to movies. I'm a modern woman. I wasn't born with blinders on my eyes."

"Maybe it's the next block." Peter exhaled a line of smoke.

"I've never strayed," Gus said. "Even before I met you I was faithful. I swear to God. Nowadays I don't even look."

"Oh, I could see what Little Miss Airlines was doing to our Petie." Lena turned to her son. "First you grew that ugly mustache. Then you started wearing those stupid clothes. How can you sit down when your pants are that tight? And you wouldn't button all the buttons on your shirts. Was it the thin air up in the clouds that made her think that was sexy? Then you lost so much weight I thought we'd have to put you in the hospital. Didn't she know how to cook? I know you had a stove, I cleaned it with my own hands. But I suppose the kitchen was too far away from the bedroom."

"Lorraine was a vegetarian, Mamma."

"I cook vegetables. August, tell Petie that I cook vegetables."

"Petie, she cooks vegetables."

"What you need is to come back to Chicago where you can meet a good clean Catholic girl. Somebody like Rosamaria D'Agostino."

"Mamma, Rosamaria D'Agostino joined the Carmelites. She teaches kindergarten in South Bend."

"Are you sure you know where this church is?" Gus said.

"She would have married you if you asked her," Lena said. "God was her second choice."

"There's a church," Gus said, pointing beyond the windshield.

"That's a post office," Peter said, "and Rosamaria D'Agostino wouldn't have married the Pope. Even back in second grade she wanted to grow up and become a saint. The rest of the kids talked about being cops or firemen or astronauts, but not Rosamaria D'Agostino. She even had picked out her own feast day." He made a turn at 38th Street and tossed his cigarette out his window.

"Some children are blessed with ambition, Petie," Lena said. "Others need a little time to grow, settle down, mature. You could take a page out of her book, you know."

"But you always told me someday you wanted grandchildren."

"You could make plans, Petie."

"I know. Wake up, smell the coffee."

"The early bird eats the worms."

"Remember the Alamo. Tippecanoe and Tyler too." Peter turned, heading back toward Colley Avenue. *"Benedicamus Domino."* Let us bless the Lord.

"You had such promise, Petie." Lena snapped open her purse. She shook her head sadly. "Three merit badges short of being an Eagle Scout. Second soprano in the fifth-grade choir. Sergeant of the Saint Felicitas patrol boys. Captain altar boy. Then in high school you were president of the Camera Club. We were so proud. And all of your science projects, Petie. Remember how you used to cut up those ugly worms? We still keep your jars and ribbons in your old room." Lena held a round mirror before her face as she spread on a fresh layer of lipstick. "Remember how proud we were when they printed the news in the parish bulletin? We thought maybe you'd get a college scholarship. We thought you'd find the cure to cancer. Work with test tubes and one of those fancy electronic microscopes, go to your job every day wearing

a white coat and a tie. Ah, a mother's hopes and dreams. I knew
they were all down the drain the day you flunked out of junior
college."

"I dropped out, Mamma."

"We're family, Petie. You flunked out. Don't be polite."

"I wear a tie to work, Mamma."

"You wear a tie. The crazy Albanian who runs the fruit stand
up on Clark Street wears a tie." Lena put her mirror and lipstick
back inside her purse. "Whenever the ladies come in he smiles
and pinches the cucumbers." She blotted her lips with a tissue.
"That's all men think of nowadays. I tell you, son, that girl ruined
your life. Just look at you. Why can't you at least shave off your
mustache?"

Peter braked suddenly at a red light on Colley. "Papa, did you
ever feel like giving someone we know and love a little punch?"

"Petie!" Lena said, one hand flying to her breastbone, the other
brushing the top of her black hat.

Gus stared out the window, then turned to Peter and smiled.
"That's a good question. Don't think I was never tempted. But
what good would it do? I'm not a brute. I once knew a man who
hit his wife—remember Sal, Lena? The time he raised a hand to
Sophie? We visited him in the intensive care. He couldn't carry
on a conversation because of all the tubes in his mouth and nose,
so we'd stand by his bed and say, 'Hello, Sal, we hope your bones
set, we hope the doctors can stop the bleeding. The priest is on
his way to give you the Last Rites.'" Gus laughed. "They were
boring visits. All Sal could do was gurgle." He caught Peter's eye,
then nodded at Lena. "A man lives and learns. Are you taking us
to church, Petie?"

"Of course, Papa." Peter revved his engine. "Why?"

"Because unless I'm seeing things we already drove past this
post office." He pointed again beyond the windshield.

The Chevy roared across the intersection. Lena stared straight ahead, her arms folded atop her purse. She seemed made of stone or ice. The engine popped and whined as Peter put it through its gears. "There are an awful lot of post offices down here in the South, Papa. And every one looks alike. I figured I'd take the scenic route and show you some of the sights. We'll get to the church in no time."

"Messenger boy," Lena said finally.

"What?" Peter and Gus said, surprised.

"Messenger boy. Flunky. Lackey. That's what I raised. A stooge. Big deal, so he wears a tie, maybe even a nice pair of dress pants, not that he puts them on when I come a thousand miles to see him. So he has clean hands. But he's still somebody's errand boy."

"I'm a courier, Mamma."

"You're one of the Three Stooges. The stupid fat one they hit all the time in the face. Oh, I never liked that show. And I never liked those Marx Brothers, honking their horns at innocent women and walking all over good furniture and throwing pies in your face." Lena took a deep breath. "So your papa should hit me? I'll show you hit, Petie boy. Pull over. Augusto, hand me your belt. He's not too old to beat."

"The boy didn't mean anything—" Gus began.

"Augusto, he showed disrespect." Lena swallowed. "Take us to the airport. We're going home."

Peter drove, his mother's words falling around him like slaps. In the sky a pair of seagulls squealed and soared. "Mamma," he said, "Mamma, I've always tried to do my best. It wasn't my fault I couldn't find a job in Chicago. I looked. I tried. But when Lorraine didn't come back from Tucson I felt devastated." He glanced at Lena to see if she was softening. "Mamma, I was hurt. I was abandoned. I was lonely and without love."

Gus rolled his eyes. "There's a church. Or is it another post office?"

The Chevy bounced forward, free of stop signs, red lights. "I thought about becoming an alcoholic, Mamma, and then I considered trying marijuana, paint thinner, Coke and aspirin. At night I walked the rainy streets, hoping I'd get mugged. I was broken and shattered, Mamma. I even thought about committing the unforgivable sin of suicide. I figured I'd cross State and Madison in front of a taxicab, or I'd blow out the pilot and put the oven on broil."

"There's one," Gus said. "No, it's Southern Baptist."

"I thought about swallowing razor blades, Mamma. Jumping off the Hancock. Going to a White Sox game and telling everyone I liked the Yankees. But then one night I heard a church bell ring and I thought about your love."

"Go on," Lena waved. She unsnapped her purse, found a tissue.

"Yeah," Peter said, "it was nearly noon and the church bells—"

"You said it was at night."

"Episcopalian," Gus said, "or else a fire station."

"I mean it was midnight, Mamma, and I felt so low I could have gone into a grocery store and eaten a jar of Ragu."

"Ugh!" Lena said. "Cat food! Change the subject before I'm sick."

"Your love saved me, Mamma."

"So that's why you moved away, Petie? You don't make sense."

"No, Mamma, no, I moved to get experience. They told me at all the job interviews I didn't have enough experience. Someday I'll move back."

"Catholic, Petie! Roman Catholic! Look, a crucifix and everything! Stop the car!"

"Petie, why didn't you ever tell me?" Lena dabbed her eyes.

Peter pulled over to the curb, tirewalls scraping the concrete.

"You never asked me, Mamma. You assumed it was because of Lorraine."

Gus had opened his door and was untangling his legs from the blanket, his trousers from the springs. Lena patted her son's head. Even though the engine was shut off, the Chevy knocked and sputtered and coughed.

"She was a nice girl, Petie, maybe a little too thin and too stuck up with her nose in the clouds, but she was a pleasant girl to talk to. Still, she wasn't the right girl for you."

"I know, Mamma. But a man's got to have experience." He helped his mother slide out of the car.

"You'll have to tell us more about your job. You deliver important things, like telegrams and legal contracts?"

"Not telegrams, Mamma. Actually I deliver interoffice communications. But my job requires responsibility and punctuality."

Lena smiled. "Those are nice things, Petie."

"Mass starts in five minutes," Gus said, returning to the car. "Is my hair combed?" He touched his wife's elbow. "Do I look all right?"

Lena licked two of her fingers and smoothed her husband's hair. "It's a nice church, Petie, not one of those new ugly ones?"

Gus walked behind his son, checking his hair in the side mirror.

"It's beautiful, Mamma." Peter had never seen the church before. "I come here every Sunday."

Lena laughed. "Of course you do. Starting today." She pinched his cheek. "Right after Mass we'll introduce ourselves to the pastor and sign you up." She smiled and turned. "August, don't waste so much time. We don't want to walk in late."

Gus wagged his head.

"Walk on this side of me, August."

"Coming, Lena."

"*Introibo ad altare Dei,*" Peter said. I will go unto the altar of

God. "*Ad Deum qui laetificat juventutem meam.*" To God who giveth me joy to my youth.

"And you walk on this side, Peter." Lena was smiling. The bright morning sunshine spilled their long shadows across the sidewalk. "I want us to enter the church together, like one big happy family."

The shadows swam together as Peter took his mother's arm, then kissed her cheek. "*Sicut erat in principio, et nunc, et semper: et in saecula saeculorum.*" As it was in the beginning, is now, and ever shall be. World without end.

Peacock Blue

François Camoin

When I was twelve years old and a good deal more certain about the world than I am now, my father bought me a used three-speed Raleigh bicycle; I took it down to the basement we shared with the Schades and painted it peacock blue.

Schade and his wife were very old now but they had managed to have two children late in life, in a final spurt of fertility before the good times passed forever. Georgia Schade, who later became my wife, was eleven; her brother Joseph, the last of the last, was nine. There had been another child, the product of the Schades' first flowering, but he had died tragically and discouraged them from trying again for a long time. Georgia told me that he'd drowned while sailing a model boat in a public fountain. The then-young Schades had turned to each other on their stone bench and lost themselves in a long kiss; by the time they came back to the world and remembered their child, little Jubal Schade had slipped, hit his head on the stone coping, and was floating irretrievably face down in the doubtful water.

Peacock blue is a color darker than sky, brighter than navy, somewhere this side of electric. I had wrapped the wheels of my bicycle in newspapers to keep paint off the spokes and tires; a picture of Toledo's mayor stared at me through the front fork, transfigured by drops of celestial blue. Summer had been a long time coming, but now, as I laid the paint over the bike's original shabby black, I could feel it at my fingers' ends; I almost had hold of it.

"I think that's going to look dumb," Georgia Schade said. She had come quietly down the basement stairs to stand behind me.

"What's dumb about it?" But I knew what she meant; I was laying on the paint like an amateur and I could tell it would never come smooth. It clung to the tube frame and to the arched fenders, clumsy, brilliant. I didn't care.

"Dumb," she repeated. She was an odd girl; she did things that made me uneasy. The top floor we rented from the Schades had no private entrance; the flight of stairs we took to get to our place passed through the center of the house and we walked by the Schades' closed doors to go home. From time to time, by what I believed then to be coincidence, Georgia would come out of the bathroom without any clothes on just as I was passing by. She squealed and wrapped her arms around herself, but I remember now that it took her a perceptible moment to step back inside the steamy bathroom every time.

"Yeah? Well I don't care—I like it," I said.

Banners of dusty sunlight fell from the high basement windows, cutting the gloom into uneven rectangles and making it darker. In front of us the coal furnace squatted cold and silent, holding up the house in its thick tube arms. My happiness that afternoon was just this side of being unendurable.

"I'm not allowed to wrestle with you any more," Georgia said.

I moved my brush slowly down the front fender; a small drop of blue fell in the mayor's right eye and gave him a shifty look. "All right," I said.

"You know why?"

"No."

"Because."

I stopped painting. "Because what?"

"I can't tell you."

"All right," I said.

"You'd have to promise never to tell anyone I told you."

"I promise," I said.

"It was my dad. He said it wasn't right for us to wrestle because I'm not a girl any more."

"What are you then?" I was puzzled.

"A woman," she said. Her voice took on mysterious harmonies when she said it, and her eyes glazed over as if she was looking at a religious object. The object turned out to be Georgia; a broken storm window leaning against the furnace reflected her image and she stared at herself with awe.

"First of all, that isn't true," I said. "You're only eleven years old. You're not even as old as I am."

"In India some eleven-year-old girls have babies," she said.

I pretended to dip my brush and wipe off the excess paint on the rim of the can, but I studied Georgia out of the corner of my eye. She was wearing a T-shirt, and indisputable breasts no larger than lemons lurked under the fabric, giving strength to her claim.

"Yeah, but this is Ohio; we're not in India," I said.

She turned away from me and favored the old furnace with a superior smile; she threw her shoulders back and stepped slowly through one of the bright banners of sun toward the basement stairs, as if to leave. But she stopped at the bottom and leaned on the banister; one breast just touched the painted wood of the railing.

I knew that at the age of twelve I wasn't nearly ready to be a father—if she could have babies, even if it was in India, it gave her an edge I would never overcome.

"Why are you walking funny?" I said.

"My father said you probably wouldn't understand if I told you," she said. She tossed her hair, glancing at the storm window. "You're not to touch me in certain places any more, either."

"What?"

"When we play. If we play. I'm a woman now, and you have to treat me with respect."

That was the end of my perfect summer before it started, though it took me a while to notice the flaw. When the paint on my bicycle was dry I rode it around and around the little streets that wound back on themselves in self-conscious curves. I loved the machine already: the way a flick of my thumb could shift from one gear to the next, the long easy roll of the front wheel over the minor irregularities of the asphalt, most of all the glory of the peacock-blue paint on frame and fenders. But while I made my swoops and aimless circles all through our neighborhood, a piece of me was back in the basement; I kept seeing in my mind's eye Georgia Schade having babies in India, and her peculiar sashaying walk through the dusty slices of sun that fell through the windows crept into the rhythm of my pedaling.

My parents were serious people, a lot younger than the Schades but no less firm about what they expected from the world and what the world could expect from them—not in return but in the course of the natural sweetness and decorum of existence. My father taught tenth-through-twelfth-grade English and coached the football team at Perrysburg Country Day School; my mother was a secretary at the YMCA. At night she worked off part of our rent by typing for Schade, who relaxed from his university teaching by doing translations of Jules Verne. Among the sounds that mark that summer for me are the clatter of her old Royal, the chime at the end of each line, and the rustle of another clean page being fed into the roller.

Someday my parents planned to buy a house of their own, and

probably they would rent the top floor to another young couple next in line for the serious life. I looked at them with mixed feelings: my dad in his chair underlining *Beowulf,* my mother leaning over to read Schade's difficult handwriting, and I saw that for them life was a progress, skirting pitfalls and avoiding temptations. My pilgrim parents.

Of the two it was my father who talked to me more, but we never stayed with it for more than half a dozen sentences at a time. Not that he was humorless, or lacked a feel for that deep absurdity at the bottom of it all, but he couldn't share it with me easily. One night I walked beside him to the corner drugstore to get cigarettes; on the way back he stopped under a streetlight.

"Women don't always understand," he said. He stood with the pack of Chesterfields in one hand, holding the red strip of cellophane between two fingers.

"Understand what?"

"What I mean is, they don't worry about the same things that men do." He tapped a cigarette out of the pack and lit it. "I'm going to quit," he said. "It's a bad habit. Suicide, if you keep at it." We walked along quietly for a while. It was a warm night and behind open windows people watched their televisions; we could see blue gleams in the dark houses, and hear bits and snatches of programs washed into the street.

"Hemingway had a lot of crazy ideas about the world," my father said. "And naturally there's the fact that he blew off the back of his own head with a shotgun—there isn't any way around that." He threw away the butt of his cigarette; it made a little twisting spark that arched into the gutter and died there. "Women don't like him much," he said. "But he wrote two or three books that you can still count on."

Just before we got to the house he stopped again. "Your mother doesn't like him at all," he said. I wanted to ask why that was

important, but he had already told me as much as he could and
he ran up the front steps to escape.

Which brings me to where I sit now, twenty-three years later,
facing a window which faces a California freeway. I feel as hollow
as a blown egg. In another house a thousand miles up the coast
in Seattle my son is twelve years old and waits for me to say the
words that might have made a difference that long-ago summer
in Toledo if my father had found them to say to me. And following the family tradition I don't have anything better than faith in
Hemingway to offer him. Two or three books he can count on.
And admiration for a man who blew off the back of his own head
with a shotgun, an act I have learned to think of as neither brave
nor cowardly.

"Dear Thomas," I want to write. But I don't know what comes
after that; my memory of my father jinxes me and I want to trot
away from my son even in this letter. "How are you?" I end up
saying. "What are you doing in school? Do you have any friends?"

I am seventy miles south of Los Angeles, stranded on this
cheaply magical coast, and the cars race by on the freeway in front
of my window, toward San Diego and Tijuana, the beaches and
the pretty restaurants of La Jolla. I have many friends but I can't
stand to talk to the closest of them for more than twenty minutes
before a deafening boredom sets in. Like my father I also have
students, though mine are a little older, a little less well treated
by the world. They come to Carlsbad Community College and I
give them, for a gift, grammar and a belief in Standard English to
help them along their pilgrim's way through the serious life.

My father packed his clothes one hot night in August twenty-
two years ago and took a room over a drugstore in Perrysburg.
My mother and I stayed at the Schades' house and every other

weekend I visited my dad in his badly aired room with the brown floors. We sat at the kitchen table and played cribbage, he cooked hamburgers on a two-burner gas range, and we hardly ever talked at all. When I got home early Sunday nights my mother would look up from *De la Terre a la Lune,* Englished in violet ink in Schade's tiny handwriting, and ask me how he was. Our talk about my parents' separation didn't go beyond that.

I have faith in the vigorous life and I run my three miles on the beach every day unless the weather is bad; it hardly ever is. Jets and helicopters from the El Toro Naval Air Station swoop low over me while I jog, and back in the yellow hills the boys from Camp Pendleton practice with their howitzers and mortars. The distant explosions sound like the paper bags I blew into and broke when I was a kid. Their noise makes me feel better. The tourists make me feel better, and so does the far-off rumble of freight trains at night. Even the smog that comes down on us when the Santa Ana winds blow in Los Angeles is a sign that people up there still have an interest in making things that smoke and smell bad.

After my run I go to school and dance through the halls with my students, my colleagues, an occasional dean caught in the rush between classes.

"Dear Thomas," I repeat in my mind while my students bend their heads over examples of clumsy sentences and try to figure out where they went wrong. "Dear Thomas, I would like to explain to you about life, but I don't know very much about it and probably never will. Find your own way without advice from Your Loving Father."

My second run of the day. The flap-flap of my bare feet on the damp sand awakens some of the near-dead dozing on the slight slope to the sea, and they raise their heads to see a youngish man trotting steadily south along the edge of the tide, where the water has retreated, leaving a fringe of sea-sputum, foam, and broken shells.

That September after a flawed summer spent thinking about Georgia Schade, I went back to Perrysburg Country Day School, where my father's position on the faculty entitled me to a place among the sons of Jeep executives, real-estate men, and tool-and-die tycoons. In the long fragrant fall afternoons I worked out with the junior high team and listened to my dad, on the next field, putting the older boys through their paces. He didn't have much to work with; there were twenty-six boys in the senior high, of whom two were cripples and one a resolute intellectual, leaving my old man with twenty-three bodies. But he faced each new season with confidence; he was a believer in strategies, and devised fantastic formations and trick plays to make up for the lack of manpower. During football season his table talk was full of two-eight-one defenses and unbalanced lines. His tackles were often eligible and his guards dreamed of taking the snap from center and running to glory while the quarterback zigzagged in the backfield to lull the defense.

In October Perrysburg won its second football game in three years and my father blew himself up with his two-burner gas range, possibly on purpose. It happened early in the morning. I rode my blue bicycle to school; before I could get it parked I noticed my friends gathering around to stare at me with serious, peculiar faces. The assistant principal, Mr. Rodeheaver, cut through the circle and put his arm around my shoulder. I helped him load the bike into the trunk of his car, where the paint left long blue streaks on the carpeting, and he drove me home. Old

Mrs. Schade was hugging my mother; Mr. Schade, Georgia, and Joseph stood in the dark hall wearing expressions of fascinated gloom, like spectators at a car accident.

Later that afternoon, having learned from my mother how he died, I took a bus to where my dad had lived. The city hadn't had time to clean up very much; his room fronted the street and the power of the explosion had knocked the wall straight outward. Bricks lay in a heap across the sidewalk, full of shiny fragments of window glass; long strips of wallpaper blew from the opening on the second floor like party decorations; a piece of brown linoleum hung down over the drugstore's miraculously undamaged plate-glass window like a dirty dead tongue.

A pretty girl in a red swimsuit comes out of the waves and stops, up to her knees in the rolling water, to stare at me. I smile back and without my willing it at all my stride lengthens, my shoulders square themselves, and something in my head goes to work calculating chances I don't want to take.

Georgia, my wife, writes that Thomas is doing as well as can be expected from a kid with no father. She signed up a University of Washington fraternity man to be his Big Brother, and she tells me in every letter where they went camping together, how this rich man's kid from Delta Kappa Upsilon took my son to the zoo, to the circus, to the rodeo, where a fallen rider was nearly kicked to death by a bull. How did the fraternity man cope with that? I wonder. How did he explain to a twelve-year-old that we all have to bleed?

She is only a year younger than I am, but I think sometimes she has not learned a damn thing since that June afternoon in the Schades' basement when she decided, with her father's word for it, that she was a woman. I have news for her this evening from California: she wasn't a woman then and she isn't now, though we had our child without going to India and her breasts got to be big and she let me hold them when we made love.

A year after my father died my mother and I moved to New York and I lost track of Georgia. We met again by chance at a miserably dull party in Manhattan; we went for a walk, thought we fell in love, got married in good faith, and learned to dislike each other.

I jog down the long stretch of sand, thinking what lucky fools marathon runners are. They run for joy. I run to ease myself out of life and some days I do my three miles before school, again after dinner, and if I can't sleep I get out of bed to come here and run a third time, under the yellow moon. *De la Terre a la Lune:* my mother finished the typing that winter by way of something to do and because she wasn't certain that the insurance company would call my dad's death an accident and pay off his policy. I proofread for her and I remember Jules Verne's characters sailing in their aluminum bullet around this moon, high on pure oxygen, anticipating the twentieth century.

I get to running faster and faster until I'm charging down the silent beach, arms pumping, legs flailing. I'm going as fast as a bicycle, faster. A cloud crosses the sun and shadows the water and I feel myself beginning to cry, though I'm not particularly sad. The sea under the cloud is a peculiar lucid blue, deeper than sky, somewhere this side of electric.

Trinity

Daniel Curley

And then the Andersons met again at the deathbed of their child. Theirs had been a particularly vicious divorce. Every item of property had been the subject of separate and distinct acrimony, each book in the bookcase, each stick in the woodbin, each plastic spoon in the picnic basket. Their lawyers hated them. The judge contemned them and, being merely a human judge, arranged everything with absolute impartiality, the settlement best calculated to infuriate both sides. He arranged custody of the child with a miracle of checks and balances that would have tried the patience of saints. A Solomon would have seen at once that the only thing to do was divide the child. Even then, venom would have flowed over how it was to be done, lengthwise or across.

It must be clearly understood that the death was something for which neither could blame the other. There had been no carelessness, no oversight, no omission on either hand. Nor had the child taken it on herself to punish her parents by sudden death, by happy accident, real or feigned, or by the slow torment of anorexia. No, she was a perfectly happy child of divorce who simply chanced to sicken and die at her summer camp.

He—Lars Anderson—came back from walking in the High-

lands. She—Dolores Anderson, nee Sanchez y Silvera—came
back from skiing in New Zealand. For five days they faced each
other across the child, listening to each heavy breath as if it were
the last and to be remembered always. Long before the end they
prayed an earnest prayer of no faith for a miracle, for life or death,
for release for all of them.

The silence when it came was worse than the labored finality
of each breath. There was now nothing to listen to but each other.
She heard him say, "Are you all right?" He heard her say, "Can
you stand it?" Of course they were neither of them all right. They
could neither of them stand it. They leaned on each other out of
the room and down the corridor and into the elevator.

In the privacy of the elevator she confessed, "I blame myself."

"You mustn't," he said. He was quickly estimating the value
of a similar confession on his part, but he didn't want to get into
a fight over who had the greater sense of guilt. He didn't want to
start up old times.

He was still debating within himself when the elevator stopped
at the next lower floor. They sprang apart as if they had been
seizing a moment of desperate love. The door opened and a priest
strode in. He was red-faced and gray and smelled of after-shave
and deodorant—or perhaps that was the flowers he was carrying. He made them feel disgusting after their long vigil, as if he
were seeing in their clothes and in their eyes the true state of
their souls.

The priest addressed himself to the control panel of the elevator, but with a bowl of flowers in each hand he was unable to
manage the button. He gestured his helplessness with the bowls,
with his shoulders, with his head, with a helpless smile. "Will you
please punch Two for me?" he said.

"Oh," Lars said, "sorry." And while he was saying it, Dolores
pushed the button, barely in time.

The priest began his charge out of the elevator. "Have a good day," he said, managing to add no priestly overtones to the cliché. He looked at neither of them.

"It's not likely," Lars said.

"Our child has just died," Dolores said.

The priest was now out of the elevator. "I'll pray for him," he said without pausing or turning around.

"I'd rather you didn't," Dolores said.

"We don't believe," Lars said.

"We're all the same in God's eyes," the priest said out of the middle of his striding back.

The doors closed. Lars and Dolores fell into each other's arms. It was suddenly real.

That night at Dolores's motel they comforted each other as best they could. Mute despair led to half words. Half words led to tentative pats. Pats led to caresses. Caresses led to embraces. And embraces led to the blind old pantomime of denying death, futile and forever hopeful. They fell asleep to Do you remember? and Do you remember? They woke to a dream of remembering. Dolores remembered First Tooth, First Step, First Word. What Lars remembered chiefly was that earnest hand clutching his forefinger as they walked on Sunday morning through the zoo, communing with the beasts, their careful substitute for Mass.

"We never did find our totem animal," he said.

"It might have helped," she said.

"Please don't start that," he said, retreating all the way to comforting pats—but no further.

"Sorry," she said.

But each lay in the dark and reviewed the dim, massive, fierce shapes in an endless frieze: the hopelessly large and the unimaginably small, mammoth and amoeba, sabertoothed tiger and midget shrew, blue whale and plankton, all raging with assertive life. Lars and Dolores still had the rest of their lives to choose, although the choice was no longer important. They didn't really want to know where they had gone wrong.

"What it comes to," he said, "is that there is no one else, anywhere on earth, who can remember with me."

"Yes," she said. Although her answer was undoubtedly the right one, he had a sense he was talking to a star which might already have been extinct for a thousand years before this present light reached the earth. But that light, he knew, was all he had.

And it was by this light that they decided—no, they decided nothing. They followed the light without knowing or really caring if it was a Star in the East or the very ignis fatuus. They found themselves together again in the old house, which Dolores had never left. The gaps in the bookcase were plugged. The woodbin was replenished. The picnic basket once again had its full complement of spoons. All was as it had been, although everything was different.

Together they burned their child's clothes, her books, her games, and all that was hers. But they made a strict calculation of the value and gave that sum, anonymously, to Goodwill Industries.

"We must keep her picture," Dolores said.

"But not by our bed," Lars said.

"Nor yet isolated as a shrine," Dolores said.

"No," Lars said.

But a shrine was exactly what it did become. No matter how it was moved, from the piano to the bookcase, to an ancient sideboard, it managed to attract bowls of flowers. Its flat metal art deco frame picked up glints of distant candles. It was a focus of gravity and bent Lars and Dolores's straightest lines into orbits (not that at this time any of their lines were particularly straight).

They found themselves on Sunday mornings retracing their

steps in the zoo. They would bring the Sunday papers and sit on a bench upwind of the bears. They had never before noticed the number of parents with children and were surprised because they used to think their solution to the Sunday problem was unique. Now it was clear there were others who couldn't leave Sunday to chance, who needed some dodge, both for the children and themselves.

"For a dodge it's not too bad," Dolores said.

"Better than most," Lars said.

"Name one," Dolores said. There were many things besides Sunday that Dolores was not able to leave alone. In fact, her abstract love of debate was, in Lars's eyes, one of the main reasons their marriage became a shambles. She would demand reasons and then reject them. She would demand better reasons and supply them herself while he was still in shock from her barrage. Her better reasons were usually revolting.

"The zoo was better for us anyway," Lars said. He tended to get stuck on a point that had seemed safe, and safety was what he mainly required. And when he had been bombed out of his shelter and didn't know where to run, when he had no better and better reasons, he was as like as not to smash plates, slowly, deliberately, and without apparent anger. She charged him for the plates in their monthly reckoning, and he was glad to pay for what seemed to him the only adequate rebuttal to her reasons.

"Go on," Dolores said. "Name one."

"As a Sunday dodge," Lars said, "the zoo is better than the Unitarian church." He had been brought up a Unitarian and endlessly resented it.

"And why is that?" she said. This was an old routine. She could take him through more steps than this before he set fire to the paper.

"Unitarianism, like decaffeinated coffee, leads to schizophrenia," he said. He was proud of that. He had lain long awake polishing the epigram. He was ready for her.

"Aha," she said. She was astonished but relentless. "And why is that?"

He had not polished that far, but he had an uncut gem or two he hoped would pass. "The pursuit of form while denying the essence," he said. "The compartmentalized mind." He had run through his hoard and said with only apparent irrelevance, " 'I think I could turn and live with animals.' "

"That's bullshit Walt Whitman," she said. The literary game had always been one of their standbys. It helped disguise the fact that they didn't like each other.

" 'A thousand types are gone,' " he said.

"Tennyson—Tennyson," she said. "*In Memoriam*—'So careful of the type, but, no, a thousand types are gone' blah blah." He was drawing her away from the fight, but she didn't care. Sometimes if he caught her soon enough she didn't care, was glad even. She could never remember why the peacemakers were blessed, but she knew they were—except when they were bastards.

" 'Some keep the Sabbath going to church,' " she said. "How about that?"

"Emily Dickinson," he said piously.

"Cutesy Emily," she said. "What a dimwit. You know, Emily Merton told me that when she was a child she was converted to Ornithology one Sunday morning in that very birdhouse. A man said 'Tyranus tyranus,' and her life was changed." She gestured across the shaded lawn toward the aviary, which they could not see but which they both faced as infallibly as if it had been Mecca.

At once, without a word or a glance exchanged, they got up and began to cross the lawn, abandoning the *Times* to the wind, which riffled the pages impatiently and strewed the sheets about as if the news were very bad indeed. They entered the aviary through the double, bird-proof doors, accompanied by an upwardly mobile sparrow.

The vast interior was shrill with the cries of birds. Other than that it was hot and wet and still. Only the sweep of wings and the flash of color showed what was really there, although the jungle foliage was boiling with life and the very air was fraught with fecundity. Cautiously Lars and Dolores patrolled the limits of the jungle, which was held at bay only by a low glass fence. Gross cockatoos hung from the branches. Gaudy flamingos dozed on one foot in the pools. Lars and Dolores peered into the undergrowth for the hidden birds, caring only for the most secret.

Lars—a word man after all—found himself reading the descriptive cards attached to the fence. "*Mimus polyglottos polyglottos,*" he murmured. "*Ardea herodias.*" He saw Dolores's lips moving as if in prayer.

"*Vermivora peregrina,*" she was saying. "*Megaceryle alcyon alcyon.*"

Once, as he muttered, "*Bombycilla cedorum,*" Lars caught his breath at the rush of wings beside his ear and the sudden appearance out of nowhere of a glorious gem on a branch not a foot from his face. But it was only a hummingbird. The godhead of Ornithology chose not to reveal itself. Lars studied the cards and found the hummingbird. "*Archilochus colubris,*" he said firmly. "Lovely," he added.

Then, on the edge of despair, he drew himself up and said magnificently, "*Riparia riparia riparia,* thrice."

"Perhaps we're too old," Dolores said.

"I never did learn to pronounce Latin," Lars said. "The teacher was only a day ahead of us on the grammar."

"How do you know that?" Dolores said. She didn't intend to start anything, but even here, in the very heart of the jungle, her old reflexes were still in command.

"The teacher was my mother," Lars said as if the question were simply polite. "We did our homework together on the dining room table."

At this time they went to bed each night—and some afternoons—with the greed of newlyweds. They forced skin against skin in hope of a total penetration, trying to drive skin into skin, to mingle their blood, to achieve a more-than-Siamese union. What they wanted was no less than the total permeation of the Trinity. But they succeeded only in mingling sweat. Their surfaces slipped over each other with the long moan of a stone skimming across the ice. They fell asleep to "I remember" and "I remember" and woke to a sense of growing desolation.

The photograph in its art deco frame continued to prowl the room, turning three times around on the mantelpiece before settling darkly down. Even there, however, it contrived to catch the flicker of firelight from a distant mirror. And when it nestled in a corner of the window ledge, the lights of wandering cars caused it to flare out in the night like an alarm.

They never knew what they wanted, but they were not out of touch with their feelings. In fact, their feelings tormented them incessantly. They just didn't know what these feelings commanded. They didn't know if they were to spring at each other's throats or move soundlessly apart or continue in despair, noisy or mute. A child was to be the sign, and there was no child. A child was to be the sign, but Dolores's body refused the penance her mind would impose. Once when her period was three days late they looked at each other in growing horror and saw that their punishment was greater than they could bear.

"It's a second chance," Lars said hopefully, as a battered soul might receive a sentence of ninety-nine half-lives in Purgatory.

"A second chance," Dolores said, "to do the only thing we know how to do: fuck up."

"You don't think we've learned anything?" Lars said.

"A.," Dolores said, even now in full command of her rhetoric, "A., if you mean have we learned something about our capabilities, I think we have, and B., if you mean have we learned how to apply our knowledge for constructive ends, I think we have not."

"I think so, too," Lars said, although actually he had thought nothing of the kind, no matter how deeply he had felt it.

They watched with dismay as the head of their child was turned into the red and swollen moon, half-hidden, half-revealed by the veils of the window-ledge shrine. They knew then that the decision had been taken out of their hands and that they were free once more in their determined fate.

"Bosh," the doctor said. He was a very clever doctor and could speak more Latin than any aviary, but he had to get up his small talk out of Victorian novels where most things are not talked of at all. "Bosh," he said and put an end to the whole idea of her pregnancy. "You must be very anxious." He knew all about them and knew what cause they had to be anxious—or at least he knew as little about them as anybody else who knew all about them. "It will take care of itself in time."

But taking care of itself is exactly what it did not do, nor did it take care of them. They were right back where they started—or farther. Their fate had not accepted them, and now, knowing the awfulness of that fate, they could judge the worse depths to which they had plunged. Still, they kept to such routines as they could contrive. They read their books. They lit their fires. They piously carried their picnic basket into the woods, always avoiding that one spoon exuberantly marked with the prints of tiny teeth.

In a little known park they had their favorite picnic table in a glade few people found, and none at a time when Lars and Dolores were there. Sometimes there were cold ashes in the grill, careful trash in the barrels, but no other sign. They sat side by side with a view, leaf-fringed, over a little pond where kingfishers swooped and dived. They dealt curiously with a familiar raccoon that hung under the edge of their table and found food on top like a magnet sensing a needle even through wood. For the local birds they crumbed more bread than they themselves ate, and they forgot, for the time, that they were cursed and that they didn't like each other.

"Gray-cheeked thrush," Dolores said. They sat side by side with their binoculars focused on an obscure bird rattling among the fallen leaves.

"Olive-backed," Lars said, perhaps incautiously, for the bird flew on into the deep woods.

"Perhaps," they agreed, conceded.

"The horses play in the field," Dolores said suddenly. "A child is swinging."

"That's not literary," Lars said. He felt as if she were breaking some rule, ignoring the umpire's call, or sending forbidden signals in charades.

"I never said it was," Dolores said.

"It's what you said after you fainted at the hospital," Lars said.

"They thought I was crazy," Dolores said.

That was the first day at the hospital when the doctors told them it was only a matter of time. Dolores fainted—perhaps partly from jet lag—after all, New Zealand. She opened her eyes and said, "Horses," said, "Child." She kept on saying it until she slept, and they had indeed thought she was crazy. Lars had seen the looks they exchanged, doctors, nurses, aides, even the woman mopping the tiles outside the door.

They all looked at her and nodded their heads and said, "Horses," said, "Child," while they listened to her heart and examined her eyes. Lars, too, nodded and thought Horses, thought Child.

"Do you know what I meant?" Dolores said.

"Yes," Lars said.

"Did you know immediately?"

"Yes," Lars said.

"Did you think I was crazy?"

Lars said, "No." But he knew he had hung fire. She accepted his answer, however, and they looked at each other strangely and shared a summer's day at a country school in Maine, a picnic table under some trees, horses running in the surrounding field, and a child—unnamed—swinging joyfully in the deserted schoolyard.

But in spite of this moment shared, doubts grew. Had Lars really understood at once? Was Dolores really crazed by grief? The doubts, however, were of self. It was Dolores who feared she might have been driven distracted, and Lars who remembered a blinding flash of blank when Dolores first spoke. The blank perhaps could not have been measured in time, but it was clearly there. And Dolores's mind had made a leap not normally available to the waking, healthy mind.

"It's a question of what we owe ourselves," Dolores said. She rolled off Lars with a sound like adhesive tape pulling loose. Although they no longer believed, they went through the motions of creation.

"I suppose," Lars said, "we owe ourselves whatever we owe her." He didn't know what he meant, but it was minimally comforting.

"That's true enough," Dolores said, "as far as *we* goes, but I mean *I* and I mean *you*."

Lars glanced through the open door into the living room, but the picture was dark. By the simple act of moving it to the other side of the window ledge, they had deprived it of all light—candle, fire, car, moon. "I don't know what I owe you," he said, "and I don't like to think you owe me anything at all."

"I mean, what I owe myself and what you owe yourself," Dolores said, twisting Lars's undershirt about her loins.

"Oh," Lars said. He had never thought of that, his deepest assumption, and it still cast no light at all on what Dolores had called constructive ends. But it opened a gap through which they slipped. They got out of bed—each on his proper side—and went their ways without any plan, constructive or not.

However, sometimes in the cold high places—Lars had taken to exploring Machu Picchu—or in the heart of the sea—Dolores had gone in for skin diving—fingering the texture of carven stone or rapt before bright fish among the ribs of ancient wrecks, they felt a rush by their ears, an immanence.

Wilbur Gray Falls in Love with an Idea

Philip F. Deaver

For my friend Craig Sanderson

When I run, like now, I head down Court Street because of its grassy boulevard. I turn west on Prairie so that I approach the University Park fountain bronze dancing girls with the sun behind them, a vast and holy prism of spray breathing out toward me. Then I face the dark welling up in the north, orange setting sun to my left, and do intervals, fast and slow, two miles uphill to Patterson Springs, the old chautauqua ground.

I've been battling depression this whole summer. It's the price I pay in middle life for living lies and harboring secrets. I've waged the battle with daydreams (I conjure, for instance, Skidmore, waving as he drives by, 1963, in the old Ford Victoria his dad had saved for him). When daydreams don't work, I lapse into the mindless, subvocal recitation of memorized prayers, or I surrender to music. Mainly, though, I've learned to depend on the faddish but nevertheless helpful practice of running six miles a day, rain or shine.

In running, I set my mind to the rhythm of my stride and think of things positive and hopeful. I remember, for instance, Ann Hollander, in church nearly twenty years ago (Father Casey in the pulpit lecturing in gravelly Irish on the topic of fund-raising for the new school)—Ann sat in the stained-glass shadows of her father, his mind on God and democracy, her eyes trained on the statue of the Virgin, his shoulders slouched toughly forward, her back straight, her body new and lovely beneath a pretty cotton dress. This was a sweet, sweet girl—she'd slip away through moonlit backyards to love the neighbor boy, she'd dance through dry shadows, across the driveways of sleeping doctors, lawyers, dentists, through the sleeping flowers of their sleeping wives (I'd see her coming, through speckles of light). Through dry grass and cicadas buzzing she came.

My best memories are from this neighborhood, and the exhaustion from running seems cleansing, but even so, the fear and regret, the wrenching isolation of secrets, they stalk me, and sometimes they prevail over me like the lightning in a hot summer thunderstorm once prevailed over the large belfry crucifix here at St. Paul's, our neighborhood parish.

My friends suggest I marry again, or seek absolution. When I pass this church, I always think of that. Absolution—they're on to something there. In 1957, jerking off was the moral equivalent of murder in the dim light of the confessional. Casey's voice, from behind the plastic mesh screen, made the whole empty church vibrate with his priestly authority. Absolution was grudgingly granted to frightened children whose mistakes were limited to the scale of childhood and whose problems were gloriously solvable—even then none of us ever felt completely forgiven.

I think sometimes of form: raise the knees higher and the speed increases, lengthen the stride to heel-toe and feel the therapy in the hamstring.

I remember 1957 as a clean, well-mothered time, and I wonder sometimes what went wrong later. I remember that year as one long baseball summer—textures of wood and leather, grass stains in cotton; the science of raking the infield dry and raking it wet, waiting for the dew to evaporate, learning to spit and other initiations—watching clouds billow up and get black, checking the sun for lunchtime. Establishing a reputation: good arm, good glove, good power to right; vaulting the fence, good form.

That was years before the nights of parking spots like Black River Road and the Hanging Tree, time-honored lovers' lanes deep in the hills left when the glacier melted. I guess I love this day, red and waning; I guess I love this town, falling down. After the fire at St. Paul's we attended mass for what seemed like years in a forest of gray, towering scaffolding inside the church. These old houses, I know them like familiar faces. These streets, I know where they lead. (Skidmore goes by again—he wants to stop, offer me condolences on my poems, show me his latest metafiction, razz me about my knee.) This town and I have deep, dark confidentialities. I twisted my knee in the steering wheel, 1962, in a glen on the Black River Road while missing basketball practice on an earnest, determined mission to discover what made Carol Canfield tick. Even now I think of 1962 as the long vibrato whine of a car horn echoing through the glacier hills on a cold autumn evening. No regrets. They told me she became a nurse in later life.

I'd left the car to pee and when I got back she wasn't wearing anything. She just sat there, the girl of my dreams, smiling, enjoying my embarrassment—her, a tall feisty senior cheerleader—me, a tangled-up, over-anxious second-string forward, Dad's car. Until the day he died, my dad thought I hurt the knee going to the hoop.

J. Richard Peck Hollander, rest his soul, was president of the draft board, and he told my dad no twisted knee nor allegation of color blindness would defer this doctor's son from his duty.

"If doctors' sons don't serve, then why should anyone else?"
he asked, my question precisely, but my dad was insulted—of
course I would serve. I went and talked to them myself. I asked,
"How is this thing in Asia a threat to our security?"

J. Richard said, "You won't wonder that when the communists
come up Scott Street and rape your sister."

"But these guys, they don't even have a boat. How they going
to get to central Illinois? How they going to get past the Penn-
sylvania National Guard, the Indianapolis police department?"
Forget it. I was drafted.

One afternoon right after I got back, I climbed those steps at
St. Paul's and caught Casey just at the end of confessions when
no one else was there. He opened the little window and waited.
I could see his dim shadow, his profile, waiting. I could see the
Roman collar and the ceremonial stole. I tried to think how to
begin. I was trying to separate sins from duty. He waited several minutes, neither of us saying anything. Finally, he slid the
window closed.

I note my knee almost twenty years later—in recent years the
ankle has twisted several times. Maybe, after the steering wheel
thing, the alignment never got quite right again, hip to toe. No
regrets. I turned the ankle pretty bad in basic training; then I
broke it pretty good in Vietnam in a fall off a personnel carrier
when the dumb shit driving it drove through a small mine crater
at forty miles an hour. A lot of guys were hurt more than me.

I've learned from experience that it takes me a mile and a quarter to break a sweat in reasonable weather, eighty degrees or less.
I can feel myself operate, or I can disengage my mind from it,
closing around the usual daydreams or some comfortable mantra.
Tell you this: I'd never remarry.

I've known people who develop a cold view of things. They
find their passion in a few close friends and come to expect
nothing from the larger world—except blockage and thwartment,

puzzlement and consternation. Close to the ground they huddle. Instinctively they limit themselves, away from wind, experience, people, other natural currents. For them the world is an animation viewed through windows, a home movie run at too slow a speed, existential HBO, silent life except for the clicking projector and the occasional comment from the dark. But I know the world is too complicated to relate to on a part-time basis—we spring from it, we're part of it, it's inside us, any separation from it is artificial and doomed. I know what Skidmore means when he says he's sorry he missed the war. Ann Hollander became an example of those insulated people. She became Sister Ann Rene Hollander, even more deeply conditioned to guilt than I am, shrouded under starch, living in the dark linoleum cloister of the most conservative order of monastic housewives of Christ that J. Richard Peck Hollander could find in a new age.

You hear rumors of those who see auras, ghostly hues like halos around people, suggesting their character and destiny. Sister Ann Rene claimed to see a violet aura over the body of her dead father, J. Richard, gaunt like Lincoln, resting on the coroner's slab. Ann dressed him for the grave in the quiet back room of the Waddington Funeral Home down the street. She wrote notes to him and put them in his casket. That's where I got the idea.

Patterson Springs is my halfway point, a place of solitude these days. It's familiar to me from when I was little—I used to play there, and later Skidmore and I would camp there. I rejoice at the wonderful existence of this forest. I take it personally. I marvel at the patience of these oaks. You imagine their roots, reaching down, holding tight. They are my reward for making it this far— the rich fragrance of hickory, white oak, their rotting leaves and cracking acorns, renewal of sprouts.

The old chautauqua ground is located where a deep-running

network of pure-water springs suddenly wells up out of the earth. The pioneer Virgil Patterson built his place among these oaks and so honored the blessing of cold, pure water that he built a shrine, now dank and moss-covered, back in the trees where the water presents with a deep rippling sound coming straight up out of the black loam.

The hush of the wind here, blended with the windy brushing sound of my footfalls in bent grass, momentarily absolves me from, rids me of, my depression, even though I know this absolution is nothing but the arrival of my second wind, the sudden alignment of energy, circulation, and chemistry that produces a moment of strength and optimism. I've learned from experience it arrives at three and one-half miles, deep in this forest on the path that leads to the fresh-water springs and, beyond that, the chautauqua ground. During this fleeting moment I can hallucinate God and Peace, I can envision my own reincarnation, I can summon a sense of relative innocence and well-being. In this moment I realize that this moment is the whole reason I'm running.

As I come across the flat here, the trees arch high above me and through them I see the navy-blue sky. I'm running in the last light. By fall I'll have to start earlier or change the route; scrub bushes and abrupt gullies occupy this tract without pattern. But now as I run I can see the burr oak, sixty meters to my right across the flat. Struck by lightning one night in July of 1959, its top is shattered and its trunk is split but it still lives. Its arms reach wide and have old men's elbows, and at the ends the limbs suddenly plunge upward into the sky.

Several years ago I got the idea to bury a time capsule under the burr oak. It was a strange notion, I admit, and I thought about it a long time, years, before I actually went through with it, this summer. It was a project that occupied me for several weeks. Already a bed of weeds, dense and yellow, obscures the spot.

Roger. Lost a hand in Vietnam. And I remember him squinting through smoke and green beer, St. Patrick's Day, Pat's Pub, Charlottesville, 1974, complaining about his life and prying into mine. Twelve years ago. Even though Roger has always worked hard at pissing me off, I keep him as a friend because he's the only person I can talk to who has been ambushed and knows how it feels. Sometimes I have to find him and talk about being ambushed, or just talk about anything, knowing he's been ambushed, too. I watch his pulse beat a rhythm in his neck—he's alive and I can see that; therefore we both are.

"How've you been?" he's asking me. He knows I'm in the middle of a divorce, that my wife took the kids and headed south to be a potter, rolled the VW bus outside of Oklahoma City and sent me the bill.

"Fine."

Up at the bar there's a St. Patrick's Day party going on. We talk louder to get above it.

"Good," he says. "That's good." He moves his beer mug between us with his hook. I call it a hook. Really it's more like a steel clamp.

"What's good?" I say.

He stares at me. "Actually," he says after a while, "I hear you're bonkers."

"Then why'd you ask how I am?"

He doesn't answer me, leans back in his chair.

I say to him, "Do I ask, 'So, how's your hand?' "

We're both laughing, but we're pissed.

"So, how've you been?" I ask him after a while.

"Great," he says. Roger says he remembers a marine who could drink more than anyone he's ever seen, says he heard the guy recently barged into a newspaper office in Anderson, Indiana, and held the whole place hostage at shotgun point until he started crying and gave up.

"I know how he felt," Roger says to me. "I was in a hardware store buying some wire. The clerk, an old guy, was showing me where it was, and we walked by this bin with big wrenches in it. For no reason it hit me that I could kill this old guy, I could smash this guy's skull. I pictured myself doing it. I knew what it would look like. I got out of there."

I recognize that feeling. It makes my stomach roll to hear Roger give it words. It comes from knowing how close death can be, an old ambush lesson. I tell Roger that J. Richard Peck Hollander died, president of the draft board back when we were ushered out of town in the dead of night on a Greyhound bus, the modern equivalent of marching off to war. Roger says he's sorry to hear it, he really is.

He says his dad was a veteran of Guadalcanal, and now every year veterans of Guadalcanal come to some great hotel in Dallas or Denver and have a reunion. He says even the Japanese come. "Now goddamn it, Wilbur, I'm telling you that is proof positive that the world has gone completely crazy." His beer spills. Quietly he mops at it.

He says he'll miss J. Richard at our reunion, when we get in the mood to have one.

"Forget it," I say.

"Forget what?" he says, and we laugh.

"What a pitiful son of a bitch you are," he says to me at the end of the laughing, and we laugh again, guzzle a little green beer, and toast the party at the bar. "The worst is over," he says after a while, and then we say nothing, watch the party.

"Gotta girl?" I say. He looks down, keeps looking down. I try to think of something hilarious to say. Can't.

"C'mon," I tell him. "You're a great-looking guy. There's some-body out there for . . . goddamn it, don't hold that thing up. That's not the reason . . . that thing's sexy . . ."

Roger laughs, there's relief in the air. "Seriously," I tell him, "you gotta find some other excuse, not that. Women love a good war wound. Signals a hero."

He's retreating. He's being cordial, but he wants no part of that talk. He'll be out the door in another few seconds. Fast, I try to tell him our conversations never turn out the way I hope they will but I can never think of how to improve them. I tell him I want to be real close friends, confidants, and tell him some of these terrible secrets and shit that give me the clangs when I'm trying to sleep. He's sliding his chair back—he's angling for his jacket on the back of it. He doesn't want that stuff. I think of maybe grabbing him to try to keep him there. His face flushes up in the cheeks—his eyes water. He's afraid, he doesn't know what might be said or if he can handle it, he's running. He doesn't want all that warm friendship and frank talk.

And, getting up to leave, he says, "Wilbur, you know what you need? You need a sophisticated shrink."

And I knew this woman, Erica—my wife. For many years we lived alone together and had children whom she wanted to con-sider gifts from her to me. Whether she has night terrors like mine, I wouldn't know. For me, marriage is under the burr oak, and fatherhood. With them I buried this poster I had of the mush-room cloud over Hiroshima—I had framed it with the caption "The Baby Boom." It hung in our various rented living rooms, later our various rented bathrooms.

That's us, Ann, Skidmore, Roger, Erica—the baby boom. It took us until about 1958 to realize what was happening. For a long time in the fifties we thought we were in the clear because we'd managed to dodge polio.

At this point, I complete a mile loop through the Patterson Springs acreage and am back on the road headed south. I already know I won't sleep well this evening, with Roger and Erica and Skidmore haunting me, with guilt scratching at me inside my chest and stomach. I think I miss my kids. I can see, perhaps a mile ahead, the first lights of the University Park, and I focus right on them, set it to automatic, and move through the dark down the asphalt at 60 percent. I can hear the wind in the drying corn husks in the fields on both sides of me. I try to take my mind into the hush of the drying corn.

Tomorrow we shall die. Or at least we could if we didn't already, not that dying is the enemy necessarily. I guess I didn't like the bomb tests much, the ones on TV in the early fifties, Sunday mornings. Right after mass you got to come home and watch while they showed in slow motion what the hydrogen bomb would do to your house if it was made of straw, if it was made of sticks, and if it was made of brick. It blew harder than the big bad wolf, you figured out, age five.

The time capsule was made from an old and very large footlocker I got at a garage sale. I mixed concrete in a wheelbarrow after I dug the hole, set the footlocker in a foot of wet concrete and pushed it down in it. I had chicken wire in the concrete for reinforcement. I filled the locker with all the stuff, closed it, folded the chicken wire over the top of it, and then poured in the rest of the concrete. I waited a couple of days to be sure there were no cracks. In a few years I'll check on it again. Two thousand years hence, some other life form will bulldoze it up, crack it open, and put it in a museum. Or maybe, a monument to my terror and secrets, it will remain there in the dark for all time, undisturbed, unrevealed, unconfessed, steeping inside the drawn-out ravages of the long haul. Or maybe the doom I've been taught to expect will occur, and that odd rock will hurtle through space as one of the fragments, holding together even though the brick houses did not. Or maybe it too will be emulsified—but at least I tried.

So, what else did I bury? Old newspaper clippings I'd kept in a space behind a false wall in the house I grew up in—a picture of Jackie on the car trunk and Clint Hill jumping aboard, somebody's shoe sticking straight up from the back seat, speaking of ambushes; a picture of Musial, speaking of hero worship, standing on second after his three-thousandth hit; a picture of Laika, the Russian space dog, in a space suit—poor furry little corpse may still be in orbit for all I know; a picture of J. Richard Peck Hollander and his daughter Ann getting a trophy for winning the Kaskaskia Father-Daughter golf tournament; a clipping from the newspaper about the destruction by fire of St. Paul's, struck by lightning—I still remember how high the flames soared, and the helpless flitting through the trees of the red lights of the local volunteers, running and shouting in their red helmets and yellow raincoats, neighborhood dogs howling in the red shower of sparks.

I also buried a photograph of my dad, a doctor, giving TB tests at school, his hands on someone's little white arm. I buried a portable TV, believe it or not—every time capsule should have one. I buried my chess set, from back in the days when I could concentrate, my Selective Service card which I won't be needing anymore, my dad's twelve-gauge automatic (broken into its two principal parts) and a box of shells. I buried some poems I never want to see again; two defunct suicide notes, 1969 and 1974; a dozen eggs in the Styrofoam egg holder (seemed funny at the time); a fading photo of Roger when he was in high school, shooting me the bird, taken in one of those K Mart foto-booths—

he's using the doomed hand; drawings rendered by my boy, of a boat, bike, house with yellow sun. I buried all my Vietnam photographs, the friends living and dead, toasting the camera with Miller's High Life in steel cans, standing next to dark green helicopters whose motors I can hear the thump of this moment; and a plain old white towel—unbelievable story, but I ran a marathon in Louisville several years ago and the route went past the convent, and wouldn't you know, the nuns all came down to watch, and, I swear this happened, there she was, doing what marathon watchers do, holding out drinks and towels for the runners—I took the towel, Veronica Wipes the Face of Jesus—Jesus, I loved that girl.

Maybe it wasn't her, I don't know. Never in one million years would I discuss my life with a shrink.

I buried my briefcase from when I was working, without even checking what was in it. I buried the sad letters my mother received from my dad during Korea—he never got over that one either, and damn sure never went to any conventions—and the manic letters my mother received from me in Vietnam. Naturally I buried the explanatory letters from the VA about the defoliants. Buried in the ground forever.

Sometimes I try to neutralize my thoughts by reciting poems to myself, like "Fern Hill." I feel that people pass through me, through my life, and through their own, like water, like different temperatures of water mixing.

Lately I've been thinking that maybe by burying my past, my lies and secrets and the enormous collection of mundanities and froth I've amassed, maybe instead of escaping from these things, I've preserved them. I guess it was only meant to be ritual anyway—there is no real-life absolution for the frightened and faithless, no grace, no way at all to explain it, or find relief, or to get away.

I also buried my ball glove and my bat, leather and wood all cracked from years of playing in the dew followed by years of no play at all. And, of course, I buried the series of pictures I'd taken of the wonderful center bronze-and-dancing nymphet of the University Park fountain—here she comes now.

When I was working, I would come over to the park at noon to eat. I was unhappy and sleepless, this was 1972 or so, and I couldn't understand anything that was happening to me, so there's no wonder I fell in love with a statue. It reduced the number of variables in love remarkably. Whoever the sculptor was, he loved this one, too. While the others, all of them dancing arm in arm in the center of the falling water, seemed blurred, this one was smiling like stars and like children smile, staring down into Fountain Circle through cascades and spray and attentive pigeons setting their wings to land. Her eyes would always seem to be looking at me. She was perpetually a little girl, as, face it, I'm perpetually a little boy—I never have wanted any of this shit about being grown-up. I'd gladly play an afternoon of Indian ball on one of the overgrown-in-weeds ball diamonds in the park or at the school. I have no illusions about getting ahead. I'd rather have it the way it was: a dancing nymphet forgetting the world, coming across the dark green lawns, and why? To love the neighbor boy, happy and fun.

But Erica had always been nice to me, and we'd had days happy and fun, be sure of that. When the life went out of it, however, it went all the way out and all of it went. You know about marriage, sometimes, especially among children of my generation, whose notion that "happiness must happen today for tomorrow we shall die" is tatooed to the back wall of their brain. How she rolled the bus without hurting anybody, I'll never know.

This would be called the homestretch. I'm now in the neighborhood of my boyhood again, and every front porch along here has had me under it and I've climbed every maple and chestnut, been in the attic of every garage, buried birds and cats in Ball jars and shoe boxes, and secret concoctions in plastic bowls, all along the alleyway. In crannies in the old foundations of all these houses, perhaps there are still notes and secret pocketknives. In this dark, I feel the presence of my past on either side of me— I sense the ghosts of the neighbors long gone and the neighborhood dogs, good companions then and two generations gone by now, the low voices of moms and dads in yard chairs who later grew old and withdrew inside—I see their amber lights in the windows now, and sometimes their shadows moving; I sense the echoes of the wheeting and tooting of little kids, parading down the sidewalk on roller skates and pulling wagons full of kids littler yet, or hiding in the bushes and laughing loud.

An ambush takes about one minute sometimes. The people on both sides of you get killed. They go down like a bale of hay, then maybe they roll around, dead but still terrified. Sometimes the bodies get hit so many times they start to dissolve. The air is electric with the ripping, the snapping, ripping sound of automatic weapons and rounds popping everywhere, and everybody firing wild, branches falling out of the trees. Adrenalin makes you think you can't die—you feel your nerves and blood jump the thin line between your hand and the plastic rifle stock and your actual being goes right down into the weapon to do its business. There's boys yelling and branches falling and the air is black and hot, and there's the ripping, the ripping sound, the cushioned ripping of people and air around you, it's all the same, forget it. Then it's over. You aren't finished—"ambush interruptus," Roger calls it. You're pumped up but there's nothing left to shoot at and it's over to the extent anything like that ever gets over.

I had a daughter born with an open spine. I got a letter from the VA that explained that a bunch of government lawyers had proven in a court of government law that the defoliants aren't why. There were some good doctors in Chicago, and we got her there early. But I don't know. The past is never quite gone, it seems. Steeps inside, for the long haul. I buried, as I said, the VA letters, and my peace-sign belt buckle and my green, nylon-mesh jungle boots. I buried Skidmore's letters, including a fairly recent one:

Dear Wilbur,

I read some of the poems you sent me, and I want you to know they are the most worthless, pitiable utterances I've ever known to be authored by an adult. I get embarrassed just thinking about them. They're abstract and escapist and have very little to do with you. All I want to know about is your pain, Wilbur, and if you can't write about it, then hang it up. I'm telling you pain is all that motivates and everything you write should be an extended paraphrase of the word "Ouch." Stop mulling over abstractions and keep running, is my advice. If it hurts, run faster.

Here's my latest effort at metafiction—"Wilbur Gray Falls in Love with an Idea"—and who knows, you might see a little of yourself in it! I know it's contrived and shitty, so don't send comments. I think I agree with Roger (down here we call him Lefty): You're a real downer. I know it's been rough, but like Lefty says, the worst is over. You know what you need? You need Carol Canfield. Maybe you could catch her between husbands, take a hot bath with her, get her to give you a back rub, hit the road. You need to hit the road, Wilbur. That town will make you nuts. Keep in touch.

Your pal,
Skidmore

It would be nice, I think, to be a little boy again and to see my parents in patio chairs in shadows on the lawn, my mom talking in low tones about the choir, smiling and hoping for the best, my dad just spotting me now and rising up, arm extended, the hand reaching to touch mine. I imagine sometimes that I would talk with them better, given another chance, knowing what I know, discuss for instance Oedipus and why my own dad wouldn't do anything to get me out of what I went through if he was really my dad, and why his didn't either. But Dad and Mom were never any better at talking than I am, and maybe it wouldn't work. I had music, the Stones, the Doors, Joe Cocker; my parents had phrases representing what they believed, and prayers to speak aloud in church in unison with the community of the faithful. They had their war and childhood, I had mine.

The grass boulevard along Court Street here, it's a blessing to the knees. I see the gables on my house in the distance. The job I had, back when I had it, was quite interesting. I was hired by the culture to have and carry a briefcase, wear a dark three-piece suit, and have my hair razor-cut, to rush up and down the street (briefcase in hand), across the mall, to occupy the sidewalks, to have an office and use the phone energetically, carry a busy calendar of meetings and to participate in those meetings to the fullest, to state the obvious emphatically and as often as possible, and in as many ways, all in an effort to give the illusion of quality, productivity, upward movement, the rightness and nonfutility of democratic life in a guns-and-butter economy, action and activity, creativity and motion, motivation and, of course, obedience, go, go, go. I would buy a paper and read the editorials. I would catch the news and read *Time* magazine. I would watch the market, even daydream of buying stocks. I would think of good ideas and route them up the organization. I would make wind and then piss into it.

The lines in my forehead get deeper, I brood without control sometimes, sleepless, like a child in tears, and like all the hard-handed workers, smug patriots, and ordinary men on the street I've known in my life, for whom money, work, women, and the church are all there is and whose hearts these crazy days are breaking.

I have a new pair of running shoes. They cost sixty dollars because of the wing-shaped stripe they have on the side. They are my Sunday best. Hard to believe, but Skidmore and I were camping in the old chautauqua ground the night the burr oak was split by lightning. You could smell the ozone and the heat even after the rain.

Voici! Henri!

Alfred DePew

Now I've done it. I've tossed Henri's things right out the window. The meaning of this will surely not escape Madame DuClos. Christ! The street is strewn with expensive shirts, designer jeans, his precious black bikini briefs.

There's someone at the door downstairs. It might be him. I'll just go and have a look . . . Blast! Damnation! It's Madame. I don't dare lean out the window and say, "Good evening, Madame, I thought you might be Henri," because she'd ask where he was; she'd say she hadn't seen him in weeks—ever since he left on holiday to . . . it was Switzerland, wasn't it? And then she'd laugh that deep down, hearty, malicious laugh she's got when she's having a really good time. She likes to see me suffer. Always has. I don't know why.

Oh she is poisonous, that woman: tiny, menacing, loud. And the pleasure she takes in my present circumstances is out-and-out sadistic. "Monsieur Henri seems to have found himself a new little friend," she says, "and a huge and beautiful car with a chauffeur," she says. "How does it happen that you never go with the young monsieur and his new friend, who is foreign, *n'est-ce pas?*" She thinks she detects a bit of a German or Austrian accent. "Perhaps he is Swiss," she says.

"He is," I say, "a business associate of Monsieur Henri."

"Oh?" she says, and here she raises one eyebrow—I've always envied people who can do that, it's the pinnacle of scorn. "*Comme les autres,* like the others?" she asks.

Ah, she is vicious, *absolument vicieuse.* You see she seems to believe I'm Henri's pimp or something, though she always refers to me as the *intellectuel.* The man of letters, she calls me. She herself is a worker, she describes herself that way, so when we first moved in, as a Marxist, I naturally tried to engage her sympathies, but she would have none of it.

"It's all very well for foreign intellectuals," she says, "but there's nothing in Marx for the workers. I remember the days of *le Front Populaire* and the sit-down strikes. I marched. I sang. It was all very exciting, but they didn't beat the Germans, they didn't stop *les boches,* did they? No! It took the Americans and General Charles de Gaulle to do that! And now. See what we have today. Look at my France, *ma pauvre France:* overrun with foreigners," and she narrows her gaze right at me.

She's out there now, shouting up, "Monsieur Edmond! What are all of these clothes doing in the street?"

I don't see why she assumes they came from our apartment. I mean, we're not the only ones living here. They might have come flying out of any number of other windows.

"*Je sais, Madame,* I know. A little mishap. Cleaning. I got a little overzealous. I'll be right down to fetch them."

"I should hope so," she yells. "I should hope so."

I didn't toss the photograph. I couldn't bear to. It's the one in the Pierre Cardin frame with the mauve mat which sets off Henri's black hair so beautifully. It's not bad of me either.

Voici! Henri! L'homme que j'adore.

The serious student of French will, no doubt, take note of the construction, the man I adore. He might well ask why it is not the other way round, *l'homme qui m'adore,* the man who loves me. But one is never adored by the one one adores. Not ever in the same moment. I think it runs counter to the physical laws of the universe. Though he is, Henri is, really quite fond of me. At least he says he is, usually, or he did, usually, until he went on holiday last summer to one of those fishing villages along the Costa Brava and met—the Baron von.

Henri ne restera pas longtemps chez moi. Henri is not long for this household, I think. Though I'd never chuck him out. Oh no. Not when you're my age, you don't. You wait till he leaves on his own, then you give others to believe it was your idea, but you never say that outright. People would come away thinking . . . something you'd rather they not. At least I wouldn't want them to, you know, think what they usually think—the worst. And there are worse ways, I suppose, for *cher Henri* to take his leave from me than on the arm—though it will most likely be in the backseat of the chauffeur-driven Mercedes—of the Baron von.

Henri is really quite bright. Though he is busy living the unexamined life and has not the sort of intellect that is drawn to books, he is very shrewd. Oh yes, he is. He has what the French call *intelligence du coeur,* which is intelligence of the heart, which is something the French say about the Italians, which is sort of a gentle way of saying they are stupid, which they are not, of course, and neither is Henri. I don't mean it in that sense. I mean he is so generous, one is just naturally inclined to trust him. I love that about Henri. I do. He has this sense about people when they are needing attention, and he gives it to them freely, and often it's just the thing that's wanted. One can tell by their faces, the way they open to receive him.

He has, in addition to this *intelligence du coeur,* he has what you might call *intelligence de la poche,* intelligence of the pocket-book. He has this knack of finding people with enough money to take care of whatever it is he is wanting just then. He's always in the right place at the right time, ready to receive small and not-so-small favors. But that makes him sound like a terrible con, *un mauvais type,* which he is not at all. He's quite the sweetest boy you'd ever want to know. Well, boy, he's twenty-eight, but he's a young twenty-eight, if you know what I mean. Quite lively. Very inventive. Henri is always spontaneous, a real *bon vivant. Comme on rigole quand Henri est là.* The trouble is, he's not often *là.* Not here, that is, not present, so it's difficult to laugh as much, *c'est tellement difficile* to *rigoler,* because these days he is usually off with the Baron von, who is not actually a baron but a baronet, a fact which I would point out to Henri, did it not seem so petty, for it's not the title he's after so much as the . . . well, you see the Baron has quite a bit of money, and Henri has always liked nice things, and it takes me a long time to earn the money to buy them for him. Sometimes I do four translations in a month, arduous ones, from Russian to German to French and then into English— enough to make your head swim, and mine often does, but oh! the pleasure on that beautiful face when I walk through the front door with a cashmere sweater, gold cuff links, or something deli-cious to eat like truffles. But with me, he has to wait. Translations take time. Not everyone is always wanting them done. And with the Baron . . .

Though you mustn't get the wrong idea. Henri works too. When he can find it. In restaurants mostly. To watch him is to see the mere act of waiting tables elevated to High Art. And I'm not joking. He has a certain genius for it. It helps, of course, that he is very handsome, but that's only part of it. He is able to make ugly women feel ravishing and old men feel alive all over.

He models occasionally for one of the men's fashion maga-

zines. And there was that *film,* though it was not a film; it was
pornography without any pretense to art at all. We argued about
it bitterly.

"It's just money," he said.

"No," I said, "when people are forced to degrade themselves
and others to get it, it is not just money but something pernicious."

"What is degrading?" he cried.

And I could never explain it to him, so then he'd change tactics
and call me a Communist, *un euro-communiste,* because I am am-
bivalent about money, I always have been, and so I would quote
the head of the French Communist party at him, you know, "A
Communist can be a good Catholic, there's nothing at all contra-
dictory about that"—Henri despises the Church almost as much
as he despises Marchais and the Communists—and he would say,
"Balls!" or the French equivalent, and I would laugh then because
he is such a *petit bourgeois,* Henri is, and he's the one who sprang
from the loins of the proletariat. Not I. Oh my no. I'm as upper
middle class as they come, which is why I'm a Marxist and he
is not, you see, for I know the upper middle class for what it is,
and Henri only knows it for what it likes to appear to be, and so
he is quite conservative, politically. Every bit as bad as Madame
DuClos. I'm surrounded by Gaullists and Vichy sympathizers!
Why, if General Pétain were alive today, he'd have Henri's un-
equivocal support—or worse, his complete devotion. Well, what
do you expect? He doesn't read. He merely parrots what he hears
from the men who buy him drinks in the bistros. What I can't
fathom is why they seem to talk nothing but politics in bed.

Yes. He goes to bed with them, and if they are rich Henri is
the one who brings home the truffles and a bottle of Château
Neuf du Pape. What can I do? I don't like it, but I can't exactly
tie him to the bedpost—of course I could, one does, one often
hears about it, but it's not the sort of thing that appeals to either

of us. So there is nothing to be done. It makes me jealous. He says they mean nothing to him. He always says that, but it gives me a curious feeling, that they mean nothing to him, and I do, and his going off with them makes me suffer, and yet he does it, though they mean nothing to him, and why would anyone go and do something that meant nothing to him, go and do it again and again? Of course the extra money is quite nice, but we do not, we have not ever seen this in the same way.

It has to do with understanding how delicate, how temporary life is and how in the flick of a wrist it can be snatched away, or it can drain off a little at a time as you stand by and watch, helpless to do anything. Perhaps one has to have come nose to nose with death, one's own, the possibility of one's own, or someone else's. But even then, we all know people who do not see it. I mean surely, once one has had that experience, once one sees life turn from one and start away, one can never say it has no meaning.

What, then, can it mean? That he is not here?

Oh! I long for the old days when we were first getting to know one another, and I knew where he was. I like to think of those days, they give me solace, often they do, but sometimes they do not; they make me feel old and unwanted, used up—cast aside. And for what! For whom! A baronet posing as a baron and simply because he has the money to buy *cher Henri* whatever his little black heart desires. It's the humiliation I can't bear. I've had him— you know, had him around—for eight years. I must be scared to death of losing him. Just look at me. I've broken out all in a sweat. What will I do without him? How shall I live? I've grown so used to him, and now—how can I make room for this grief? For it will take up room, more room than I have here in this apartment that's become so full of associations of *cher Henri.* Or maybe the grief will fill up the space he has left, fill it up nicely, oh yes, and grow, feeding on the furniture, sucking all the oxygen from the rooms, until it heaves, rising up larger and larger to choke me.

Or I could move—far, far away from Madame DuClos—take a smaller flat, sort of squeeze the grief out of my life, but then the grief might fill it up when I'm not looking, might crowd me out of my own home, and I'd have to take all my meals in cafés and go for long walks to keep myself busy, for there'd be no room in my flat for me. Every cubic centimeter of it would be filled with his absence . . . and my own sense of failure.

But wait. He hasn't left yet. There I go jumping to conclusions, when he's not actually left me. Not yet. I must remember that. Yes. That steadies me. He hasn't even mentioned leaving me. Of course he isn't leaving me! How could he? I am his life as much as he is mine. Except that's not quite true. I'm the one who's in danger, not Henri. Never Henri. Even so, I must keep things in perspective. He has not yet announced that he's going off to the Isle of Capri with the baronet—odious little man, he always smokes cigars, with his scarlet cummerbund stretched too tight over his belly full of the world.

Madame DuClos seems to be quite taken with the Baron, despite his German accent. When push comes to shove, she'll go for the title, no matter what its country of origin. She feels that democracy went terribly wrong somewhere along the line and the only thing left to save us is the restoration of the monarchy. "After all," she says, "it's just like what we've got now with this bureaucrat above the next, all the way up to the *président de la république,* but with kings, it's more amusing, we have more interesting people to talk about, as you have in England, Monsieur Edmond"—and she looks at me, as though she were thinking there might be hope for me if only I liked Queen Elizabeth.

So I think she encourages Henri and his friendship with the

Baron. And she flirts with the Baron. She does. I've seen her. She'll notice his car waiting in the street below, and then she runs to put on a dress and one of her old turbans and some rouge, *et voilà*! There she is, hanging out of her window, screeching, "*Bonjour, Monsieur Henri, Monsieur le Baron,* you have such a lovely day for your outing"—that's what she calls them. And anyone can see she's just aching to have a ride in the Mercedes. Anyone, that is, except the Baron, who never offers. He's far too obtuse. Besides, he wants to get Henri away as fast as possible because there I am in another upstairs window, sometimes leaning out to wave, and at others, peering through the partly opened shutters.

I make him a little nervous. I like making him a little nervous, just to remind him that I'm still in the picture. So I wave. "*Bonjour, Monsieur le Baron. Amusez-vous bien.*" Then I ask when they are getting back, or I shout out a time when I'd like Henri to return, and Henri rolls his eyes up at me, the Baron says nothing, and off they go, waving at Madame before they disappear behind the tinted windows—I wonder if they're bulletproof— and Madame waves and shouts after them and then asks me again why it is I never happen to go with them, and then she smiles that awful smile.

But he hasn't left me yet, Madame. The gold-plated razor that was my Christmas gift to him last year still sits on the ledge above the bathroom sink. I wonder how he shaves when he's away.

So we are still together, Henri and I, the only difference being he is never here. This time he's been gone for weeks. I don't know what to think. "Think what you want," he would say. "*Pense ce que tu veut, ça m'est égal,* it's all the same." He might well say that. Isn't it funny, when a lover's gone for a time, and not always a long time either, one forgets what he would say, one almost forgets what he looks like, so one consults the photograph, or one is brought back suddenly to the image of his face by the smell of his shampoo on the pillow. "Oh yes," you say. "I remember, yes, he used to live here, he used to lie right there beside me, and if I close my eyes and concentrate, yes, there is his smile, that particular one, sly, teasing, the one I loved best."

Of course, one cannot hold onto people. It never works. And I suppose I always knew Henri would be, as it were, buggering off one day. Though I ought not to be so callous. I'm quite sure he has some genuine feeling for the Baron, though I personally cannot see why. The man has not made much of an impression on me. Still, it's that Henri has not yet removed his personal effects—the ones I tossed out the window—that gives me reason to believe that this thing, this affair of the heart, this whatever it is with the Baron that is supposed to mean nothing actually does. Mean nothing. I mean that it will come to nothing, and Henri will once again come home to me, though he has not actually left.

If he were coming in tonight, I'd know how much supper to cook. If it's just me, I won't bother. I'm not eating much these days, but if Henri were to walk through the door and he hadn't eaten—why, I can't even think what I've got in the larder. Tinned meats mostly, for emergencies. But if I went out to buy food, I might miss him. He might telephone and, finding me not here, assume I'd gone out, which I would've done, but I'd have been right back and he'd have no way of knowing that. And if I did go out to do the marketing for the both of us, and Henri didn't come home, I'd have endives rotting in the fridge, apples moldering in the bowls, onions decaying in the baskets that hang from the kitchen ceiling.

It's the waiting I hate, the uncertainty. Oh Sweet Mystery of Life at Last I've Found Thee, but I wish you'd call to let me know you're going to be late, telephone or leave me a note when you're

planning to stay away. And yet I dread the note that will read
"Cher Edmond—I've gone off with the Baron forever. Please
send my things. *Je t'embrasse. Grosses bisses! Henri.*"

If I still had friends, they'd say I was a fool. They'd tell me to
get on with my life. They'd insist that I have it out with Henri and
force him to make a choice. But they couldn't know, for I'd never
be able to tell them, how frightened I am he'll make the wrong
one. Leaving me is always the wrong choice, though the ones
who leave never seem to come round to that idea themselves. Off
they go, and all I can ever hope is that they'll regret it some day,
and yet not one has ever come back to tell me that it ruined his
life. In fact, one actually had the temerity to approach me at the
theatre when I saw him again after we had parted ways, and he
said leaving me was the best thing he'd ever done for himself,
and then he thanked me, he embraced me and thanked me, and I
just stood there in the foyer of the Comedie Française: stunned,
dumbfounded—aghast. I couldn't think of anything to say. So I
took Henri by the arm and led him away without introducing him.

Christ! There she is again, caterwauling in the street. All right.
All right. "*Ça va, Madame. Je viens tout de suite.*"

She adores Henri. It's me she can't stand. And so she is always
spying on us and always a little too polite to me and always
giving me veiled threats about Immigration and the authorities:
have I remembered to register with the police again this year?
"You know they are getting very strict," she says. "*À cause des
arabes,*" she says—all of whom she believes to be terrorists. So
we are rather cagey around one another, she and I.

But what am I to say? How shall I explain the clothes in the
street? Well, Madame, Henri is sweet, he's quite the lovely little
morsel, and as he is French he loves the finest things money can
buy, and well, it's evident, isn't it, that the Baron's got money, and
you can see for yourself, *regardes moi,* that Henri's tastes run to

older men. Yet you must remember, *ma chère Madame,* we have, Henri and I, something very special between us. The Baron means nothing to him; Henri says so himself. No, Madame, between me and the *jeune Henri* there is a history, eight years together, an unbreakable bond. Why, I practically raised the boy, Madame, I helped to create him, he could never turn his back on that, now, could he? He will be back, I know Henri, he'll come home, and you'll see, we will be happy again, singing, shaking the rugs out the window, tumbling out of a taxi, home from the bars, drunk and laughing and trying not to wake you, Madame. Surely you understand love. Surely you had in your youth the attentions of some young man, your husband perhaps. And surely you know, Madame, what it is to be no longer young, and how often one's greatest fear is of growing old alone. I don't mean to give offense, Madame, I'm sure you make out quite well on your own, but you see it's something I'd like to avoid myself, so as you may have noticed, I am rather distraught with Henri running off everywhere with the Baron von Deutschemark, the Baron von Mercedes, the Baron von house on Capri. And if this is it, if this is the night he fails to return, if this is the night which marks the onset of a life without love, I doubt, Madame, I shall ever be able to look you straight in the eye again.

Pie Dance

Molly Giles

I don't know what to do about my husband's new wife. She won't come in. She sits on the front porch and smokes. She won't knock or ring the bell, and the only way I know she's there at all is because the dog points in the living room. The minute I see Stray standing with one paw up and his tail straight out I say, "Shhh. It's Pauline." I stroke his coarse fur and lean on the broom and we wait. We hear the creak of a board, the click of a purse, a cigarette being lit, a sad, tiny cough. At last I give up and open the door. "Pauline?" The afternoon light hurts my eyes. "Would you like to come in?"

"No," says Pauline.

Sometimes she sits on the stoop, picking at the paint, and sometimes she sits on the edge of an empty planter box. Today she's perched on the railing. She frowns when she sees me and lifts her small chin. She wears the same black velvet jacket she always wears, the same formal silk blouse, the same huge dark glasses. "Just passing by," she explains.

I nod. Pauline lives thirty miles to the east, in the city, with Konrad. "Passing by" would take her one toll bridge, one freeway, and two backcountry roads from their flat. But lies are the least of our problems, Pauline's and mine, so I nod again, bunch my bathrobe a little tighter around my waist, try to cover one bare foot with the other, and repeat my invitation. She shakes her head so vigorously the railing lurches. "Konrad," she says in her high young voice, "expects me. You know how he is."

I do, or I did—I'm not sure I know now—but I nod, and she flushes, staring so hard at something right behind me that I turn too and tell Stray, who is still posing in the doorway, to cancel the act and come say hello. Stray drops his front paw and pads forward, nose to the ground. Pauline blows cigarette smoke into the wisteria vine and draws her feet close to the railing. "What kind is it?" she asks, looking down.

I tell her we don't know, we think he's part Irish setter and part golden retriever; what happened was someone drove him out here to the country and abandoned him and he howled outside our house until one of the children let him come in. Pauline nods as if this were very interesting and says, "Oh really?" but I stop abruptly; I know I am boring. I am growing dull as Mrs. Dixon, Konrad's mother, who goes on and on about her poodle and who, for a time, actually sent us birthday cards and Christmas presents signed with a poodle paw print. I clasp the broom with both hands and gaze fondly at Stray. I am too young to love a dog; at the same time I am beginning to realize there isn't that much to love in this world. So when Pauline says, "Can it do tricks?" I try to keep the rush of passion from my eyes; I try to keep my voice down.

"He can dance," I admit.

"How great," she says, swaying on the railing. "Truly great."

"Yes," I agree. I do not elaborate. I do not tell Pauline that at night, when the children are asleep, I often dance with him. Nor do I confess that the two of us, Stray and I, have outgrown the waltz and are deep into reggae. Stray is a gay and affable partner, willing to learn, delighted to lead. I could boast about him forever, but Pauline, I see, already looks tired. "And you?" I ask. "How have you been?"

For answer she coughs, flexing her small hand so the big gold wedding ring flashes a lot in the sun; she smiles for the first time and makes a great show of pounding her heart as she coughs. She doesn't look well. She's lost weight since the marriage and seems far too pale. "Water?" I ask. "Or how about tea? We have peppermint, jasmine, mocha, and lemon."

"Oh no!" she cries, choking.

"We've honey. We've cream."

"Oh no! But thank you! So much!"

After a bit she stops coughing and resumes smoking and I realize we both are staring at Stray again. "People," Pauline says with a sigh, "are so cruel. Don't you think?"

I do; I think yes. I tell her Stray was half-starved and mangy when we found him; he had been beaten and kicked, but we gave him raw eggs and corn oil for his coat and had his ear sewn up and took him to the vet's for all the right shots and look at him now. We continue to look at him now. Stray, glad to be noticed, and flattered, immediately trots to the driveway and pees on the wheel of Pauline's new Mustang. "Of course," I complain, "he's worse than a child."

Pauline bows her head and picks one of Stray's hairs off her black velvet jacket. "I guess," she says. She smiles. She really has a very nice smile. It was the first thing I noticed when Konrad introduced us; it's a wide smile, glamorous and trembly, like a movie star's. I once dreamt I had to kiss her and it wasn't bad, I didn't mind. In the dream Konrad held us by the hair with our faces shoved together. It was claustrophobic but not at all disgusting. I remember thinking, when I awoke: Poor Konrad, he doesn't even know how to punish people, and it's a shame, because he wants to so much. Later I noticed that Pauline's lips, when she's not smiling, are exactly like Konrad's, full and loose and purplish, sad. I wonder if when they kiss they feel they're making a mirror; I would. Whether the rest of Pauline mirrors Konrad is anyone's guess. I have never seen her eyes, of course, because of the dark glasses. Her hair is blonde and so fine that the tips of her ears poke through. She is scarcely taller than one of the children, and it is difficult to think of her as Konrad's "executive assistant"; she seems a child, dressed up. She favors what the magazines call the "layered look"—I suspect because she is ashamed of her bottom. She has thin shoulders but a heavy bottom. Well, I want to tell her, who is not ashamed of their bottom? If not their bottom their thighs or their breasts or their wobbly female bellies; who among us is perfect, Pauline?

Instead of saying a word of this, of course, I sigh and say, "Some days it seems all I do is sweep up after that dog." Stray, good boy, rolls in dry leaves and vomits some grass. As if more were needed, as if Stray and I together are conducting an illustrated lecture, I swish the broom several times on the painted porch floor. The straw scrapes my toes. What Pauline doesn't know—because I haven't told her and because she won't come inside—is that I keep the broom by the front door for show. I keep it to show the Moonies, Mormons, and Jehovah's Witnesses who stop by the house that I've no time to be saved, can't be converted. I use it to lean on when I'm listening, lean on when I'm not; I use it to convince prowlers of my prowess and neighbors of my virtue; I use it for everything, in fact, but cleaning house. I feel no need to clean house, and certainly not with a broom. The rooms at my back are stacked to the rafters with dead flowers and song sheets, stuffed bears and bird nests, junk mail and seashells, but to Pauline, perhaps, my house is vast, scoured, and full of light—to Pauline, perhaps, my house is in order. But who knows, with Pauline. She gives me her beautiful smile, then drops her eyes to my bathrobe hem and gives me her faint, formal frown. She pinches the dog hair between her fingers and tries to wipe it behind a leaf on the yellowing vine.

"I don't know how you manage" is what she says. She shakes her head. "Between the dog," she says, grinding her cigarette out on the railing, "and the children . . ." She sits huddled in the wan freckled sunlight with the dead cigarette curled in the palm of her hand, and after a minute, during which neither of us can think of one more thing to say, she lights up another. "It was the children," she says at last, "I really wanted to see."

"They'll be sorry they missed you," I tell her politely.

"Yes," Pauline says. "I'd hoped . . ."

"Had you but phoned," I add, just as politely, dropping my eyes and sweeping my toes. The children are not far away. They said they were going to the end of the lane to pick blackberries for pie, but what they are actually doing is showing their bare bottoms to passing cars and screaming "Hooey hooey." I know this because little Dixie Steadman, who used to baby-sit before she got her Master's Degree in Female Processes, saw them and called me. "Why are you letting your daughters celebrate their feminity in this burlesque?" Dixie asked. Her voice was calm and reasonable and I wanted to answer, but before I could there was a brisk paper rustle and she began to read rape statistics to me, and I had to hold the phone at arm's length and finally I put it to Stray's ear and even he yawned, showing all his large yellow teeth, and then I put the receiver down, very gently, and we tiptoed away. What I'm wondering now is what "hooey" means. I'd ask Pauline, who would be only too glad to look it up for me (her curiosity and industry made her, Konrad said, an invaluable assistant, right from the start), but I'm afraid she'd mention it to Konrad and then he would start threatening to take the children away; he does that; he can't help it; it's like a nervous tic. He loves to go to court. Of course he's a lawyer, he has to. Even so, I think he overdoes it. I never understood the rush to divorce me and marry Pauline; we were fine as we were, but he says my problem is that I have no morals and perhaps he's right, perhaps I don't. Both my divorce and Pauline's wedding were executed in court, and I think both by Judge Benson. The marriage couldn't have been statelier than the dissolution, and if I were Pauline, only twenty-four and getting married for the very first time, I would have been bitter. I would have insisted on white lace or beige anyway and candles and lots of fresh flowers, but Pauline is not one to complain. Perhaps she feels lucky to be married at all; perhaps she feels lucky to be married to Konrad. Her shoulders always droop a little when she's with him, I've noticed, and she listens to him with her chin tucked in and her wrists poised, as if she were waiting to take dictation. Maybe she adores him. But if she does she must learn not to take him too seriously or treat him as if he matters; he hates that; he can't deal with that at all. I should tell her this, but there are some things she'll have to find out for herself. All I tell her is that the girls are gone, up the lane, picking berries.

"How wonderful," she says, exhaling. "Berries."

"Blackberries," I tell her. "They grow wild here. They grow all over."

"In the city," she says, making an effort, "a dinky little carton costs eighty-nine cents." She smiles. "Say you needed three cartons to make one pie," she asks me, "how much would that cost?"

I blink, one hand on my bathrobe collar.

"Two-sixty-seven." Her smile deepens, dimples. "Two-sixty-seven plus tax when you can buy a whole frozen pie for one-fifty-six, giving you a savings of one-eleven at least. They don't call them convenience foods," Pauline says, "for nothing."

"Are you sure," I ask, after a minute, "you don't want some tea?"

"Oh no!"

"Some coffee?"

"Oh no!"

"A fast glass of wine?"

She chuckles, cheerful, but will not answer. I scan the sky. It's close, but cloudless. If there were to be a thunderstorm—and we often have thunderstorms this time of year—Pauline would have to come in. Or would she? I see her, erect and dripping, defiant.

"Mrs. Dixon," I offer, "had a wonderful recipe for blackber . . ."

"Mrs. Dixon?"

For a second I almost see Pauline's eyes. They are small and tired and very angry. Then she tips her head to the sun and the glasses cloud over again.

"Konrad's mother."

"Yes," she says. She lights another cigarette, shakes the match out slowly. "I know."

"A wonderful recipe for blackberry cake. She used to say that Konrad never liked pie."

"I know."

"Just cake."

"I know."

"What I found out, Pauline, is that he likes both."

"We never eat dessert," Pauline says, her lips small and sad again. "It isn't good for us and we just don't have it."

Stray begins to bark and wheel around the garden and a second later the children appear, Letty first, her blonde hair tangled and brambly like mine, then Alicia, brown-eyed like Konrad, and then Sophie, who looks like no one unless—yes—with her small proud head, a bit like Pauline. The children are giggling and they deliberately smash into each other as they zigzag down the

driveway. "Oops," they cry, with elaborate formality, "do forgive
me. My mistake." As they come closer we see that all three are
scratched and bloody with berry juice. One holds a Mason jar half
full and one has a leaky colander and one boasts a ruined pocket.
Pauline closes her eyes tight behind her dark glasses and holds
out her arms. The girls, giggling, jostle toward her. They're wild
for Pauline. She tells them stories about kidnappers and lets them
use her calculator. With each kiss the wooden railing rocks and
lurches; if these visits keep up I will have to rebuild the porch,
renew the insurance. I carry the berries into the kitchen, rinse
them off, and set them to drain. When I come back outside Pauline
stands alone on the porch. Stains bloom on her blouse and along
her out-thrust chin.

"Come in," I urge, "and wash yourself off."

She shakes her head very fast and smiles at the floor. "No," she
says. "You see, I have to go."

The children are turning handsprings on the lawn, calling
"Watch me! me! me!" as Stray dashes between them, licking their
faces. I walk down the driveway to see Pauline off. As I lift my
hand to wave she turns and stares past me, toward the house; I
turn too, see nothing, no one, only an old wooden homestead,
covered with yellowing vines, a curtain aflutter in an upstairs
window, a red door ajar on a dark brown room.

"Thank you," she cries. Then she throws her last cigarette onto
the gravel and grinds it out and gets into her car and backs out
the driveway and down to the street and away.

Once she turns the corner I drop my hand and bite the knuckles,
hard. Then I look back at the house. Konrad steps out, a towel
gripped to his waist. He is scowling; angry, I know, because he's
spent the last half hour hiding in the shower with the cat litter
box and the tortoise. He shouts for his shoes. I find them toed out
in flight, one in the bedroom, one down the hall. As he hurries

to tie them I tell him a strange thing has happened: it seems I've grown morals.

"What?" Konrad snaps. He combs his hair with his fingers when he can't find my brush.

"Us," I say. "You. Me. Pauline. It's a lot of hooey," I tell Konrad. "It is."

Konrad turns his face this way, that way, scrubs a space clear in the mirror. "Do you know what you're saying?" he says to the mirror.

I think. I think, Yes. I know what I'm saying. I'm saying good-bye. I'm saying, Go home.

And when he has gone and the girls are asleep and the house is night-still, I remember the pie. I roll out the rich dough, flute it, and fill it with berries and sugar, lemons and spice. We'll have it for breakfast, the children and I; we'll share it with Stray. "Would you like that?" I ask him. Stray thumps his tail, but he's not look-ing at me; his head is cocked, he's listening to something else. I listen too. A faint beat comes from the radio on the kitchen counter. Even before I turn it up I can tell it's a reggae beat, strong and sassy. I'm not sure I can catch it. Not sure I should try. Still, when Stray bows, I curtsy. And when the song starts, we dance.

What My Mother Knows

Carole L. Glickfeld

Frankie Frangione, standing on the sidewalk, screams up to his ma, up on the second floor in the building across the street from us.

My ma is watching him from the bedroom window. "Scream lazy walk," she says to me. In sign language, cause she's a deaf-mute. Translated means Frankie is screaming up to his ma since he's too lazy to walk upstairs. All the kids scream up to their ma on account of this block having only walk-ups. The elevator buildings are on the next block up Arden Street, across from the church.

We live on the fourth floor. Four double flights, there's nine steps in each half, not counting all the steps in the lobby and the three levels of the stoop. Sixty-six I counted. Which means I have a lot of running up to do if I want something. I can't scream up like the other kids cause my mother can't hear me.

Most of the time my mother's cooking or cleaning. Or ironing. She irons all my pinafores. But if she happens to be hanging out the window, she sees me usually. She leans out, resting her soft, squishy arms on a pillow so that the gravel stuff on the ledge doesn't scrape. If she's looking the other way, though, like toward

99

Nagle Avenue, I just keep waving my arms till she turns back. Then I tell her what I want. In sign. Like, "Throw ball." Meaning please throw down my Spaulding. And she does, in a paper bag, so it doesn't bounce to kingdom come.

I play outside in the mornings and then in the afternoon she takes me to Fort Tryon Park. "For fresh air," she says. The deaf-mutes sit on the benches around the playground sandbox. The way the benches curve is perfect for them because they can see each other across the way to talk. Sometimes they ask me questions in sign language, like what I'm going to be when I grow up. "Teacher," I say. Or they ask if I'm a good girl. I smile and nod. Sometimes they give me a nickel for an ice cream cone. Then I ask my ma for a penny so I can get sprinkles on top, which is extra. She looks at me like she's asking a question and practically kisses her hand, which means did I say thank you for the nickel. I smile and nod.

It's good she has lots of deaf friends she can see in the park. It's a whole other world there from Arden Street, and my mother knows what's going on in both places. All the gossip. More than my big sister thinks she knows, and she can hear, like me.

My ma's the one who told us Frankie Frangione's mother was preg again. The sign for that is done by holding both your hands out in front of your belly, then moving them away from you like your stomach's getting bigger right there on the spot. And she told us that the O'Briens were divorced. "Must," she said, "not see long time." Except she doesn't call them the O'Briens. She says, "Know drunk?" Meaning the guy who's always drunk on Saturday nights. "Unhappy, fight wife, divorce," she said. That just gives you an idea of how my mother's always got her eyes open.

Like when she saw me and Frankie sneak into the alley. We had our eyes on her, too, from across the street. When she looked down toward Nagle, we ran into the alley. Then I told him to touch me. He did. One quick touch down there. He got all red in the face like hives. I said, "Go on, Frankie," but he stopped. Just poked real quick like under my underpants and stopped, getting red. "Nah, I'll have to tell the priest," he said.

"WHAT?" I couldn't believe it. That's when he explained about confession. I used to hear kids on the stoop say they had to go, but I didn't know what it was. Imagine. Going up to a total stranger, even in the dark, and telling that you touched someone under their underpants. You gotta be nuts.

"You don't go to confession?" he asks me.

"I'm Jewish, silly," I said.

"So?"

"So I don't."

"How come?"

"Jews don't."

"Then you're gonna go to hell," he said.

"I'm not."

"Betcha."

"Frankie," I said, "Fran-kie!"

He looked kind of funny, so I said we better get out of the alley in case the super came. It was Frankie's building and all, but still. And then we pretended the super was coming and tried to scare each other, running and screaming for our lives till we hit the sidewalk out in front. First thing I did when we got there was look up across the street to see if my mother was hanging out, but she wasn't. She was coming down the stoop, her slippers with no heels flopping open in back. My mother doesn't wear her slippers in the street like Mrs. Frangione. So I knew I was in trouble.

Frankie took off and I crossed the street and walked up to her at the edge of the bottom landing of the stoop. I crossed my toes.

"You run hide sneak," she said. "Not like."

She wasn't mad. I could tell by looking. Her mouth gets scrunched up when she's upset, like I hurt her feelings.

I didn't say anything.

"True? Tell," she said.

"Sorry," I said. The sign for "sorry" is a fist facing your chest and then you make the fist go in a circle around your chest, like you're washing yourself with a washrag. I uncrossed my toes.

"Bad girl spank," my mother said, but she's never spanked me. Except once, ages ago. I watched her go up the stoop. She turned when she got to the top landing. "Careful you," she said in sign and went in the house. I got into a game of Kings and then I went home for supper.

Afterwards, when she let me eat a slice of Swiss cheese without making me put it on bread, I asked her why she'd gotten upset. Except I said "mad" because I don't know any sign for "upset." "Why mad afternoon?" I asked.

"Dangerous." She spelled it out slowly. "D-a-n-g-e-r-o-u-s." She meant the alley. "S-t-r-a-n-g-e-r n-o play," she added, meaning that a stranger could be there and it wasn't a place to play. You have to spell out s-t-r-a-n-g-e-r because there's no sign for it. It can take a long time to say things in sign language. Which is why you always try to make things as short as possible. Otherwise it takes forever.

"Who d-a-n-g-e-r-o-u-s?" I asked her.

"Any," she said. "Not know. Maybe happen. T-o-o l-a-t-e. Awful." She washed the knife I used to open the cellophane package of Swiss cheese, even though it wasn't dirty. Then she wiped it with the towel I embroidered, not just cross-stitches, either. She taught me how to do stems and leaves, which are my favorite.

"Listen me, sorry," she said. Meaning I'd be sorry if I didn't listen. "Aunt sister r-a-p-e-d."

Sadie, my aunt? RAPED? But I didn't say anything. "Raped" was one of the words I read in the *Daily News* that I didn't know and couldn't ask. The dictionary doesn't explain it good. I just knew it was dirty. I don't know how I knew.

"Sister S-a-d-i-e tell me. Nobody know. Afraid always. Very s-a-d."

I asked her if it happened in the alley.

"N-o n-o n-o." She shook her head and signed both. "Brooklyn, grow up." We lived in Manhattan. "Always remember," she said.

I studied my tooth marks in the crust of the Swiss cheese and then I started to eat the crust.

She shook her head. "Careful sick." But she knew I always ate the crust and never got sick.

It was still light out because it was summer. I didn't want to go to bed but I did. For a while, anyhow. My big sister wasn't home yet from the baby-sitting. I went over and pulled the shade so I could open the window and stick my head out. I couldn't stick it out far since my mother was probably hanging her own head out the window next door and she'd see me.

I stared a long time at Frankie Frangione's windows across the street. All the lights were on and the shades were up. "Waste light," my mother says, if you turn it on before it's dark. The Frangiones always had lights on in all the rooms, at least the ones you could see from our side of the street. Like us, they had windows facing the alley.

I felt sick, but it wasn't the Swiss cheese. I felt like I feel sometimes after I've been on the Whip a few times in Coney Island. Tomorrow I could ask Frankie if I could go to confession because I was scared. But what would happen if I chickened out at the last minute? How could I tell the priest I'm raped? Even in the dark. And then Frankie would get it for sure. They put rapists in jail, that's what the *Daily News* said. Once they said they should electrocute them.

I didn't know it was so terrible when we were doing it. I thought of my Aunt Sadie. "R-a-p-e-d." What if my mother knew

I wanted Frankie to poke me some more but confession stopped him? I'd have to tell the police it was MY FAULT. Frankie didn't even want to. He wanted to play jacks. Oh God, I was the one. My sister says Jews don't go to hell, but there were all kinds of ways God could punish you before you were dead.

A funny noise made me jump. My mother's voice. Deaf-mutes don't have real voices when they try to talk. Sometimes while they're doing signs they make sounds like they're crying, but of course they can't hear themselves. Anyway, my mother made a sound to call me. "Rooh." That's how she says Ruth. "Rooh," she called from behind me. It scared me and made me hit my head on the edge of the window over me. Now it was her turn to say she was sorry. She looked it. "Hurt you?" she said. "Sorry." Her fist kept going round and round her chest.

"No," I fibbed.

"Go sleep," my mother said. "Tomorrow shop."

And then I remembered we were going to Alexander's in the Bronx the next morning on the 207th Street trolley. It's a big store, much bigger than anything on Dyckman Street. I like it, even though I don't know why they've got bells ringing all the time. I mean ALL the time. Ding ding ding. Ding ding ding. It's not something I can ask my mother.

Whenever we go, everyone's always grabbing at the stuff on the counters, but not her. She always opens the drawers under them because she wants things f-r-e-s-h.

I got into bed and watched my mother closing the bedroom door. She did it slowly, and when there was just a little space left she brushed the tips of her fingers over her lips (that means sweet) and made her second finger crooked, going in a line from her head toward the ceiling (that means dreams). "N-o watch window," she added, then closed the door. A second later it opened. "N-o think too much d-o-l-l," she said. She closed the door again.

We were going to get me a doll at Alexander's. For my birthday. I wanted one very bad with blonde hair and real eyelashes. I didn't know yet what I was going to call her. Anna was my favorite name but it was Frankie's big sister's name and I didn't want to think about Frankie. Ever again. His other sisters had those Catholic names—Mary and Catherine and Patricia. I didn't know what they'd call the new baby. "Feel boy s-u-r-e," my mother said. "Another Little Italian." Little Italian is what she calls Frankie instead of his name. But she knows who I mean when I say I'm going to play with F-r-a-n-k. Except now I'd never say it again. Or sign it.

I wouldn't have to see him when summer was over, either. He went to the Catholic school on the next block, like his sisters. On Sundays they went to church there. On Sundays my mother always hangs out the window to see what everyone is wearing when they're dressed up. "How can a-f-f-o-r-d dress many children?" my mother asked. "Shoemaker not wonderful money," she said, about Mr. Frangione. I don't know how she knew he was a shoemaker because Angel's is the shoemaker around the corner from us. She knew Mrs. Frangione had trouble with her feet. "Always tell Little Italian go store," my mother said. Meaning Frankie's mother sent him so she wouldn't have to hurt her feet. I saw Mrs. Frangione when Frankie let me into his apartment to get the jacks. Before we went you know where. Her feet were up on the hassock in the living room.

"See my bird," Frankie said. "Don't put your finger in. Only I can do that."

Then Mrs. Frangione looked me over. I had a red and white pinafore on that my mother just ironed that morning. "You a friend of Frankie's?" she asked. "I seen you," she said. "With your mother, the little deaf-and-dumb lady, right? I really admire the way you talk with your fingers."

"Ma!" said Frankie, and then we got out of there. But he forgot the jacks.

My bedroom was dark finally and my sister Melva wasn't back from baby-sitting. I couldn't tell what my mother was doing because she was so quiet. Maybe looking at the newspaper in the kitchen or ironing. Sometimes at night she hangs out the window, especially when Melva isn't home yet. My mother told me what Frankie's sister Anna and her boyfriend did one night. "Kiss kiss kiss," she said. "Sneak downstairs, can't see, kiss." I could picture them standing in the doorway to Mrs. O'Brien's apartment in the basement. Frankie and I go under there when it rains so Mrs. Frangione can't see us and say Frankie should get upstairs. Anyway, Mrs. Frangione only goes to the window when Frankie calls. It hurts her feet to stand, Frankie says. When they weren't up on the hassock, she was soaking them in Epsom salts. I knew all kinds of things about them that even my mother didn't know.

And then it hit me. I sat straight up in bed in the dark. I knew Frankie had a parakeet and their living room smelled funny and Frankie wasn't so good at jacks. So how could he be a stranger?

I laid down again and watched the lights go across the ceiling from the cars outside until it got too spooky. Then I tried to go to sleep. I pretended my new doll was next to me already. I called her Anna, but just for that night, until I could decide.

I told her that after we came back from Alexander's, her and Frankie and me would go up Arden Street and tell the priest. Just in case. And then we'd go to Fort Tryon. If she was good, she'd get a nickel for an ice cream cone. And I'd teach her to say thank you, in sign language.

She wants me to teach her the whole alphabet. "O-K," I spelled out. The "O" is easy but the "K" is hard. "O-K," I spelled again and then I made the sign for sweet dreams.

A Country Girl

Mary Hood

The Misses Bliss kept store north of the limits, a mile past the FFA sign that said Welcome Back when you were going south and Come Again when you were going north, although if you were to stop and ask them the way to Rydal, the one would be sure to smile in pardon of the question while the other would gently reply, "You're now in town." There was not an uninhabited front porch in all the valley on any summer afternoon, so you could inquire for directions all along if you were lost and someone would be sure to tell you, "Rydal is the center of the universe," and it might be that a barefoot girl with a flat-top guitar would stare coolly past you and her uncle, propped against the post hollowed by carpenter bees, would say nothing, having vowed long before not to speak to anyone, not even kin, till suppertime. The dogs, bellying low on the under-porch shadows, would be saving their energy for moonrise along the river. You could pick up one of the little early apples from the ground and eat it right then without worrying about pesticide.

The most famous local citizen was hanged just that much before a reprieve—a sad, legendary thing; there's a farm named for him, and grandchildren. And the second-most-famous person, the lady writer, is dead nearly as long as the hanged man, and buried in her chapel garden beside her daughter Faith. Not that many pilgrims seek the grave anymore. And the house she loved wears antennae, and a twin-engine fiberglass cruiser on its trailer is parked on the terrace where the doctor, who had a presentiment, told her, taking into account the flowered borders, the wide fields, the view: "You have everything but time."

The barefoot girl by now will have finished her singing, not the impersonal, brave gospel singing, but melodies low and private as lullaby. She will have set the guitar aside with a slight discord. And she will sigh, wanting nothing in the world she can name, free to come and go with no more than a lift of her tanned hand, yet burdened, restless, seeking that one thing to strike out at or from. Soon the afternoon train will track across the valley and the colt in Paul Lilley's pasture will race it, pleasant to see. The girl would go that way. There was no hurry.

But when she got there, there were others.

"I live," said the man with the camera, "where you can hear alligators groaning each night in the tidal mud."

The license plate on the car said Sunshine State, sure enough, but that didn't mean there was no rain in Florida, or liars either. The girl shook her head, slightly, in rebuke, the fair hair swaying and settling into order on her shoulders.

"It's true, every word," his wife corroborated, dabbing a dry brush on her canvas. (But you cannot prove alligators by protestation.) How could they say such things in Paul Lilley's pasture and every cricket and June bug singing born two thousand feet above sea level, thereabouts?

"That's all right," the girl told them kindly.

The woman had painted the colt. The train had been too much for her. So the dappled horse ran alone at the back of her perspective, presentably drawn.

"That's how I like," the girl told her. The man with the camera checked his watch again.

"Mother," he said. The sun was in decline.

"I know, I know," his wife sighed, folding up shop. She released the wet canvas from the easel and admired it briefly. "Oh, well, I guess you got the real action with your camera."

"Two different arts. Two different artists. Two separate truths," he said easily, as though he usually talked that way. He cluttered their picnic things into the hamper and recorked the Pontet-Latour.

"You keep this." The woman handed the girl the painting.

"Oh, no, I caint, I mustn't."

"Whyever not?"

The girl frowned in concentration, seeking the exact ethic being jeopardized. "We don't make uneven exchanges."

The man and woman looked at each other in amusement. He got in the car.

"But I want you to have it," the painter protested. "Find something (quick!) to exchange."

The girl drew a deep breath. "Poor Wayfarer," she said, then announced her name, "Elizabeth Inglish," and began to sing a capella in her low, thrilling way. When she finished, she received the painting from the woman, and they drove away.

"Mercy! I never expected a serenade." The woman snapped her seat belt. Looking back once, she saw the girl still standing there with the painting raised to her eyes as a sunshade.

"Country girl," he said, like a slide caption. Before the dust behind them had settled, they had digested her into anecdote.

The Bliss sisters had directed him here, a stranger. He had their quavering map stuffed in his shirt pocket to keep it from blowing out the window as he rode along. He had no more country sense than to drive on the clay road like a turnpike. His brick-red wake stood tall as a two-story house, slowly settling grit onto whatever laundry happened to be hanging out and seeping into the crevices between the piano keys at the Missionary Baptist Church if Mavis Cole had left it open again after practicing the choir. Anybody who looked could tell some stranger was coming. But May Inglish wasn't looking, she was cooking for the reunion. Horace was at the barbershop swapping lies with the others, and Sophie and Bremen were playing in the branch. Uncle Billy was out in the corn, potting crows. Aunt Lila and them were due in the morning, soon enough. Uncle Cleveland was due any time, and welcome, but at his age you could never be sure. His chair to preside in was already set out in the shade of the beech tree, the sawhorses were aligned to make the picnic tables, and the white sheets for tablecloths were ironed and folded away on the sideboard by the piles of Chi-net platters and bowls. Everybody agreed from the start there was no shame in paper plates so long as you bought the best. It was the same every year: should we or shouldn't we, and where to meet, and what to eat, barbecue, or fry, and every year they arranged themselves under the identical beech tree for the reunion, every year the same with allowances for births and deaths. As the years went on the number of aunts and uncles diminished and the number of cousins increased, but there had never yet in this century been a reunion where Uncle Cleveland wasn't prime mover.

So when Elizabeth looked up from chopping the celery for potato salad and saw two bright tips of a man's shoes (the kitchen was partitioned from the dining room by a fiberglass curtain which was drawn now to fend off the glare from the toolshed roof) she cried, "Oh, it's Uncle Cleveland!" and ran to him. And there stood the stranger with the note pad in his raised hand.

"I knocked and knocked," he apologized. "You didn't hear."

"It's the fan. It lumbers." She nudged it back a bit with her bare toes. The machine rumbled on, ineffectual but soothing. "It's not Uncle Cleveland, Mama," she said over her shoulder to May.

May looked up from her lap of green beans and shook her head. "No, it isn't." May didn't say what is a stranger doing in my house and she didn't say welcome either. She just looked.

"The ladies at the store said here was where to find Cleveland Inglish." He held out the crumpled map as proof.

"You're early, that's all." May dumped another load of bean strings onto the newspaper by her chair. "He owe you?" The remarks were getting down to business now.

"I'm writing a feature on Mrs. Harris—life and works and that."

"Uncle Cleveland did used to work for her some," May grudged. "Off and on."

"But she's dead, years and years!" Elizabeth ran her knife over the whetstone and tested the blade on her thumb.

"She wrote about us," May said. "She got some of it wrong." She bent a bean till its back broke. "She meant well, for all the good it does."

"Are you writing a story story or a true story?" Elizabeth kept her eyes on the knife and guided it gravely through the celery stalks. She never imagined that he might be uncomfortable there, in the doorway, waiting for them to produce Cleveland. She did not realize him at all. She finished chopping and laid the blade aside.

"A true story," he told her gently, as though she were a child. It was the way she listened, yearning for some remark she had never heard, some refutation, some proof.

"I can show you her studio," she offered. He set his tea glass down on the sink apart from theirs so if that made a difference they could tell which was which. "Mama?" she asked in afterthought.

"You're old enough to know better," May said. Maybe she was teasing. Maybe she meant the Posted signs.

"It's not life or death," Elizabeth said.

"Shoes!" May exhorted, but she needn't have, for Elizabeth was already tying on her sneakers.

"If Uncle Cleveland comes in before we're back, ring the dinner bell." She was out of the house and away before the fan had a chance to turn back to her.

The writer's name was Paul Montgomery. She stored it up, but never would call him anything other than sir or mister, though there wasn't a decade between them, just the wide world. They went overland, uphill all the way, and summer had its full go with the trail. "You mustn't resist the brambles," she advised, hearing him tearing himself free, his shirt already picked in a dozen places. "Just back out of them." She demonstrated. He got entangled again. "It's no country for a man with a temper," she agreed as he struggled furiously with the blackberry runner slapped across his back. They could hear Uncle Billy's gun, pop-pop-pop. And the crows laughing. Going under a plum thicket her scarf was torn from her hair. They paused while she retied it. The blueberries were long past prime, but she found a handful and shared with him.

"Almost there," she encouraged. "I can smell the verbena." At the summit they stood undismayed before the fierce sign that proclaimed

KEEP OUT

WHO THIS

MEAN YOU.

"Not us," she said. "Not me." She knew a place where the fence was down. They crossed boldly.

He stood with one arm resting on the warm fieldstone wall that belted the household gardens from the fields. Mint and verbena and lavender and geraniums bloomed pungently at his feet. The last irises were gone to parchment now, and the shasta daisies

were taking their turn. Hollyhocks towered over the iron gate to
the chapel. It was locked. Everything was locked. The place was
like an opera set, and needed moonlight for its true majesty. Even
the graves, as he could see through the gate, looked cute and
common. The stone was baking. An undecided lizard, half green,
half brown, darted past at eye level on the wall, its blue throat
puffing.

"Must be gone fishing," Elizabeth reported, returning empty-
handed from her quest for the keys. "Her workroom's back there.
We can look in the windows." She led the way. Her quick eye
spotted the lizard. She caught him and let him run up her arm and
down her arm and away into the sunstruck flowers. The writer
peered in the window at the lifeless studio, left as it had been
when the enterprise of thought and imagination ceased, decades
since. This was oblivion. The bundled papers were yellowed; he
could catch a whiff of them, a cellar dankness. The table stood
just so in the slant of light, the ink gone to dust in the well. They
moved from pane to pane, staring into obscurity.

"Better it had all burned down than this," she said.

"No." He sounded sure.

"It's like my grandmother: she saved my grandfather's love letters, even after he died; she kept them in a sack under her bed. So
we couldn't ever pry, she cut them into quilt scraps. Now she's
dead and it's Mama saving them and nobody says so but it makes
us sad and ashamed and I'll burn them one day, yes I will!"

"This is different," he assured her at once. It made her think of
the man with the camera who had said, "Two separate truths."

"I thought the bell would have rung by now." She stood listening. "If he doesn't come till tomorrow, will you be back?"

"Is he sharp?"

"You mean Uncle Cleveland?" She laughed. "You'll be pressed
to keep up."

"He must be ninety."

"That don't differ."

"Why did you think I was your uncle? Do I look so old?"

"You're you. Just yourself. Born in God's time and going to last till you're done." She brushed a crumb of moss from her blouse. "It was your shoes. Being new and all, city shoes."

He looked at his unexceptional feet.

"Old folks never wear out their shoes. Not even the bottoms get scratched much. And the tops never crease. *You* know. And so when I saw them—"

"Well, I never noticed."

"It could break your heart. The same as all these things of hers waiting for her to return." She polished a little twig smooth as a chicken bone and broke it in three. She let it drop.

"Have you read any of her books?"

"After sixteen they caint make you," she said.

They were already halfway down the ridge when the farm bell rang and rang.

"That's Bremen," she reckoned. "God never gave him quittin' sense."

Back at the house she sent him round to the front door like company while she slipped into the kitchen. "Only thing," she said in parting, "Uncle Cleveland's slightly deaf." They could hear May and Uncle Billy shouting their welcomes, and the rough monotone of the patriarch's replies.

Uncle Billy told his favorite joke, twice, then went to clean his crow gun. May plumped the pillows behind the old man's granite back and set a glass of tea beside him. Sophie and Bremen, blue jeans damp to the knees from wading in the creek, pressed to the old soul, one on each side of the recliner, showing what they had brought him from the woods, and what had come in the mail, and the oil painting of Paul Lilley's Texas pony the lady had given Elizabeth for a song. The black-and-white cat strolled

in through the wide-open door like family and posed at Cleveland's feet, gazing all the way up those blade-thin legs in their
white trousers to his vest where the gold chain and Masonic fob
rose and fell conversationally. Elizabeth went upstairs and put on
the blue dress he had liked the last time, and brushed the tangles
from her hair. She announced her coming with each step in her
whited shoes from Easter. She curtsied and he called her Priscilla
and asked her to sing.

"With or without?"

"Without? What kind of singing is that?"

So she got her flat-top guitar with the little red hearts painted
around the sounding hole and she sang as loudly as she could bear
to, and he must have heard her. Paul Montgomery did, waiting
on the front porch to be remembered.

"Whose red car is that?" Billy was back with a new joke. The
kids looked out.

" '76 Charger," Bremen said. There was a silence, then May
stepped in.

"Where's your professor?"

And that's when Elizabeth remembered him and asked him in.

"He's writing about Corra Harris, for the Sunday magazine,"
she explained to the old man.

"Ghosts, ghosts, ghosts," Sophie and Bremen chanted. They
once reported having seen a "spectacle" in that tilting barn.

"Behave," May told the kids, but she let them stay. Billy stayed
too, just kept butting in, and Elizabeth, who had heard every
word at least once before, went to peel potatoes. By suppertime
it had been decided that it was no trouble, none at all, and would
Mr. Montgomery stay and eat with them?

He would.

The lady writer got herself mentioned time and again, but
nothing much came of it that Paul Montgomery saw. He kept his

note pad open just in case. He was a city boy all right, speaking
of baby cows and 2% milk. Bremen took it on himself to mimic
Aunt Lilah's boy Bud, spearing his green beans wrong-handed
and nibbling them sideways like a rabbit. He'd been brought up
better, you could tell. It was pure devilment. Aunt Lilah and them
had that effect, even long distance. (One year's reunion Bud shot
out the glass ball on the lightning rod, on the north one, the most
important one by the chimney, and all Lilah Inglish Ames would
say was, "Well, well," and go on chewing chicken salad.) Sophie
thought Montgomery was "weird," having never been that close
to a red-haired man with a mustache. "Vinnie vannie veddy veddy
lou lou lou," she jeered at him, eating pickles right off his plate
without asking. She was seated to his left, and Uncle Cleveland to
his right, so that the writer could shout into the better ear. Elizabeth sat around the table from him while she sat at all. She ate
in a hurry and excused herself. They could hear the porch swing
creaking and her soft voice singing some sad thing, without the
guitar.

"Well, she's just full of summer," Horace said at large.

"Summer don't last long, even in a good year," May said. And
she wasn't looking at the sky.

When Montgomery left to drive to his motel on the interstate,
Sophie and Bremen sprinkled him with goodnights from their
windows upstairs. "Have you heard any news?" Sophie called to
Bremen, silly with sleep. "Not a word. What have you heard?" he
ritually replied. "Welcome back! Come again!" they chorused as
the red Dodge drove off. It was too dark to wave. Only Elizabeth
knew that he had decided to come back to the reunion with a camera, and questions for the others. It was more than his deadline
he was considering when he said, "I need more time."

In the dark Elizabeth sat on the porch and thought about the

colt in Paul Lilley's lower field. She walked out in the moonlight
down across the meadow where the lady painter had laughed at
her scruples. "I brought you apples," she coaxed, but the horse
held aloof, snorting, haughty. "Last chance," she warned, but he
was coy. He trembled all over. He trotted deeper into the shadows. "All right." She flung the apples then and ran up the path
toward home. The lights were on like a funeral was happening,
and those gusts of laughter, and the clatter of pans. She heard
the first tentative scratchings of Cleveland's fiddle, and Horace
calling her to bring her guitar.

It was just like always. The Inglish population had remained stable
during the year so there were no eyes seeking resemblances to the
departed and that bittersweet pang when they were discovered.
Aunt Goldie was meeker than ever. She sat off to the right of
Cleveland's throne, on a kitchen chair; she was neither crumpled
nor crisp, just resigned. She had lived a while at the State Hospital
when she was younger, had started crying one day at breakfast
and couldn't stop; for weeks and weeks she had wept, giving no
reasons. When May spoke to her now she looked up, eyes swimming, but had nothing to say. Aunt Lilah and Big Bud drove in
about eleven-thirty. Little Bud was going for a three-year pin at
Sunday school so they had to hang around home long enough for
him to put in his appearance, then they drove directly on. They
brought watermelons on chipped ice in a galvanized tub. Lilah's
daughter Patty and her groom were already present, joking their
newlywed jokes with Uncle Billy. Grant and Tillie and their five
drove in not long after the watermelons were set to earth from
the back of Big Bud's Buick. And the Bliss sisters arrived, on their
canes, with their cushions and scrapbooks. There were more dogs
than usual and indistinguishable children seen from time to time

dragging first Sophie's Belgian bunny and then Bremen's round and round the springhouse. The elders, in perfect state, arranged themselves by bloodline and years under the beech tree. And all the time there was talk, and renewals, and measurings, and little disputes about what year and just where and wasn't it a Reo and not a Model T? and the tap-tap-tap of May flouring the cake pans and one wife or another running out of the house and setting something on the spread tables and running back in so quick she could almost pass to and fro on one slam of the screen door. The older cousins were stationed along the tables to ward off flies and jaybirds and dogs. Everybody's kind and nobody's kin Johnny Calhoun drove up in his restored Packard after they all had a plateful and a big waxed cup of lemonade and the good hush had fallen where hunger in the open air overcomes sociability. Someone had counted and reckoned there were fifty-four human beings present, or possibly only fifty-three, owing to a confusion about the James twins whose mama, despite psychological advice in *Family Circle,* continued to dress them alike.

"Take out and eat!" they cried to Johnny Calhoun as they'd have cried to anyone venturing into the yard then, friend or foe. But they knew Johnny. He was a chenille manufacturer, forty in a year or so, and wild in the way that made him worth the trouble he caused. He was the best-looking one there for his type, fair and fiery, like Uncle Cleveland when he was a stripling. But Uncle Cleveland had married young and for all time, and Johnny was still free. Mighty free, some said. Patty ran up to him and kissed him right on the mouth and he made faces over her shoulder, brows high and delighted, then winked at Jeff, whose responsibility she was now. Who didn't laugh didn't see. Aunt Goldie eased on up to the house to take her snuff in private. Folks expanded with lunch and love and the elders in their circle nodded

and woke and nodded and spoke. If they noticed how Paul Montgomery was watching everything shrewder than a cousin-in-law,
they just guessed he was Elizabeth's beau and made him welcome.
Welcome all.

It was the custom for Uncle Cleveland as senior to pray over
the food before they ate it and the other brothers and sisters of his
generation to pray afterward. Uncle Tatum began it now, standing upright, four-square, hand on lapel, eyes shut tight against
the distractions of the younguns tearing back and forth like hel-
lions. Elizabeth stood at the outer ring of the connection, near
the childish freedom of the lawn where cartwheels and somer-
sets were underway. It was her wish to escape now, before the
music-making. Once they called on her she couldn't say no, not
to family. She studied her locked fingers, head down, not to mimic
piety but rather to avoid the too-plucking gaze of the aunts. "I'll
never love but one man!" they'd all heard her say since she was a
babe, and they kept watch to see if she had made a fool of herself
yet. Uncle Tatum said, "Amen," and Aunt Goldie stood, shyly, for
her own prayer, lost among picnic debris and her own rollicking
pinafore collar.

"Oh God," Goldie quavered, and her tears, never far off, began
to fall. This was the saddest part of the day, they all feared for her
so. "Goldie's next," they thought, and gazed and gazed, memo-
rizing every living detail. Elizabeth slipped farther away, till she
could hear no childish voices, no ancient piety, and no music at
all. The gray tabby from the hilltop farm crept past her in the
long grass.

Elizabeth lay back on the warm earth and sang so lightly that
the kinglets and phoebes resting in the bower went undisturbed.
She moved her head to the left until the elm shadow lay cool on
her eyes. She watched a great satiny fool of an ant, clown-striped,

race headlong off a blackberry vine above her. The sun outlined everything in silver. The grass looked like cellophane. And there wasn't a breeze in all the world to turn a leaf.

There was something else about Johnny Calhoun: he was quiet as a cat. He nudged her with the toe of his shoe. "Look what I found," he said, as he said every summer to some girl, to Patty, to all of them, that Johnny Calhoun. She stood up too quickly. It took a moment for the landscape to settle in her thoughts. She stamped her tingling foot, dazzled. She could talk and talk among kin, overheard. Now she couldn't even say boo.

"They were calling for you," he reported. He had stripped off his tie long since; it trailed from his coat pocket. There was razor burn on his throat, below his ear. He eased his collar with one finger.

She shook her head, denying all claims. She dusted her fingers on her skirt. "Lilah can play as pretty a bass run as they'll hear, or need to."

He turned her hand palm up and set a little present on it. "For Christmas or the Fourth of July," he said.

"Oh I caint. I mustn't. I don't have anything for you." It was not so heavy; it was not very large.

"It's yours," he said. "It's for you."

"I caint think," she said. "What do you suppose it is!" She un-wrapped it a tag at a time, not to tease him but herself. When she got the ribbon unknotted, she coiled it tidy as a clerk and filed it in his pocket. "Well I don't know," she murmured, filled with exquisite dread. She drew the paper off. A music box gleamed on her upturned palm. It might have been the most precious egg. It took her breath in surmise.

"I'm listening," she said cautiously. He pressed the switch and the melody dripped out, three dozen notes of a nocturne.

"Chopin," he told her.

When it ran down he wound it again.

"Johnny?" she wondered, more to herself than not. Calhoun
lit his cigarette and imperceptibly waited. One old leaf on the
tulip tree was stricken with palsy. It shook and shook. It might
have been any ordinary day since Eden fell. She never did see the
hawk, circling the sun. When she looked at it again, the tulip tree
was motionless, every leaf in place.

"Johnny," she decided.

The music was over, and the melons devoured, and yellow jackets
had come and drunk from the rinds. One of the twins had been
stung so the other had to try it. Sympathy swirled back and forth
between them as everyone gave advice. Most of the food had
been cleared away and the white sheets that covered the plank
tables had to be weighted with stones. In the winding-down part
of the day everyone got more related somehow, and Paul Montgomery, feeling shut out, shut his notebook for good. He locked
his briefcase in the car, then realized that was too citified a thing
to do: heads had turned at the rasping of his key in the car door,
indicting him, and so he left his trappings lying frankly on the
back seat, the windows down, his suit coat on the front seat with
the garnered facts in the black book jutting from the pocket just
the way Uncle Cleveland's Prince Albert showed, like a handkerchief, in its red can. Montgomery swung his camera around his
neck and set off up the hill to the studio for some pictures. He
knew his way well enough, but he looked around for Elizabeth,
hoping she might come along. She had disappeared earlier and
despite several alarms had failed to show. One of the dogs heaved
himself to his feet and volunteered for the hike. They set out in
the best of spirits. There were massing clouds that would make
his camera work more challenging.

He finished the roll of film and, seeing the dogs panting in the shade of the tainted well, he crossed to the spigot at the house and let the animal drink from his cupped hands. He thought he heard the television playing inside; he hallooed and knocked, but no one answered. He paused one last time at the chapel gate and peered through at the graves. Already the first tentative sentences of his article were forming in his thoughts. He turned back down the ridge toward the Inglish farm. The dog suddenly took an interest in something just beyond his view, barked and looked away and did not bark again.

Johnny Calhoun was sitting with his back to a tree, not smoking, not smiling, not speaking. He shook his head to warn Montgomery not to step on Elizabeth's outflung hand still clasping the music box. She lay sleeping, an arm across her eyes to ward off the sun.

Johnny brushed a ladybug from his ear. "We'll be along," he told the writer, neither unnerved nor amiable. Montgomery jogged on past, the camera beating against his pounding heart.

He left without making the entire rounds of all the guests, though he did press the stiff warm hands of the Bliss sisters; he congratulated May on her dinner and nodded to Horace's raised hat, but Uncle Cleveland was asleep again and Goldie was distant.

"Let us hear," someone cried after him from the porch. Uncle Billy already had his chair tipped back against the bee-stuffed post and dozed malevolently. It was Lilah's newlywed Patty who noticed Elizabeth and Johnny Calhoun were both still unaccounted for and when the black-and-white tomcat leaped onto her familiar lap she slapped it away with a remark that made her groom look sharp and Uncle Billy, that impostor, laugh.

The number of tourists driving by and asking after the lady writer's remains increased dramatically in the weeks after Montgomery's article came out. Uncle Billy got so aggravated with the interruptions that he began taking his chair out on the back porch, leaving Horace to direct traffic. Not every Sunday would a literary pilgrim find Elizabeth Inglish on the porch, guitar in hand, waiting for the evening train to pass through Paul Lilley's meadow, but when she was there she stared coolly past the stranger, mute, head held high, as though nothing whether trivial or profound would distract her from her reverie. Some thought she was blind, and walked back to their car to mention it to the others. And some had the impression she was a fool.

The Mouthpiece

Salvatore La Puma

Guido went everywhere with his parents to trans-
late their babble into words others could understand. His father,
Alfredo, and his mother, Sabatina, were both deaf and dumb
from the complications of childhood meningitis. His parents were
brought together as children in the East New York neighborhood
of Brooklyn where they grew up, they became inseparable and
then were married at sixteen.

Alfredo and Sabatina, as children, had learned to read lips, but
never with complete understanding, and they were always too
poor and too ignorant, even as grown-ups, to want to learn signing. So Guido's parents flailed their arms in the air, desperately
trying to say what was stuck on their tongues, and Guido became their mouthpiece almost from the day he said his first word
as a baby. He listened to other people, and then, in a series of
wild noises and gestures, he relayed the message to his father and
mother. They answered him in the same way. Then their thoughts
and feelings came out of his mouth nicely said.

To get results from the hardhearted, Guido could also rave like
a madman in a loudspeaker. He was taught how by St. Finbar's
priests exhorting churchgoers to fill the collection baskets. By the

time Guido was sixteen, no one could ignore his sound and fury. Then his parents were no longer shunted aside by shopkeepers or other customers.

Nearly everyone in Bensonhurst in 1940 half forgot that Alfredo and Sabatina's tongues were as pickled as pork tongues in a jar. Their thoughts were spoken with conviction by Guido. A listener could even be convinced that Alfredo Trapani, squeezed together like a clenched fist, and Sabatina Trapani, thin and shapeless, both with screaming eyes and twisting mouths, were actually speaking Guido's words themselves.

"Science explains everything," said Father Valenti. "But in the end science explains nothing. We must go back to the First Cause. We say a chemical in the body. But why for this one? Not for that one? God wants certain things, in a certain way, whether we like it or not."

"I don't think He's fair," said Guido.

"You can think that," said Father Valenti.

"So I'm never going in the seminary."

"It was *your* idea," said the priest. He was dark, short, broad, and potbellied, with a crew cut and a cigar. He talked out of the side of his mouth like a boxing fan. But his secular love, proven by thorn wounds on his fingers, was the Immaculate Conception rose garden.

"I'm sick of the rosary," said Guido. "Said it a thousand times. Still no miracles. And no call. The novena was a waste."

"You'd be a great priest. Someday even maybe wear the red hat," said Father Valenti. "But I won't talk you into it. In some ways it's a lousy life. I envy your father. And *he's* a caged animal. But he has a wife. And a son. I smoke cigars. Don't shave for days. Drink wine by the bottle. But in the morning I look at the pastor's ugly face."

"What's so good about a wife?" said Guido.

"She warms a man's soul," said Father Valenti.

"No more coming to church either," said Guido. "God's just the plaster statue by the altar. Deaf and dumb. Worse than them. From a novena, He never makes a miracle. I asked people."

"It's okay. Don't become a priest. But you can't fall from grace. I won't let you," said Father Valenti. "If you're not in church, Guido, watch your ass. Some wop priest might give it a kick."

Late on a Friday night when Alfredo received his tiny envelope of a few bills, he was told not to come to the 16th Avenue storefront factory the following Monday to work. When the women on the Singers sewed the few dresses on order, the owner himself, not Alfredo, would press them.

Alfredo and Sabatina had put aside a little money which would buy their food for the next few weeks. But their savings wouldn't cover the rent due in a few days. They needed an extension until Alfredo found other work, or was hired by the WPA, or went on home relief. So Guido was sent up the dark flight of wood stairs, sounding like a soldier with his leather heels, to the front apartment in the four-family house, to ask Mr. Frangano, nicely and with humility, for a few weeks' time.

"We can't pay the rent, but we'll get it. Don't put our stuff out. We're asking nice," said Guido, talking more for himself, his voice making ground meat of the landlord's ears.

One of the worst fears for the Trapanis, and for others on their street, with unemployment like an unwelcome aunt in almost every apartment, was having the marshal come to move out their furniture to the sidewalk, even if it was winter and snow was falling.

"Who pays the mortgage?" said Ugo Frangano, a butcher, who seemed to have acquired the facial features and the body parts of the pigs, calves, and lambs he slaughtered in the yard behind his butcher shop. Those animals were brought in live from New Jersey farms and their blood fertilized his vegetables. "I loose the house," said Ugo, waving his hands, Band-Aids on all the fingers of his left hand.

"Better you *loose* it, said Guido, mimicking the landlord, although Guido knew better.

"I must have the rent," said Ugo.

"And we the rooms," said Guido.

"Two weeks," said Ugo.

"Our furniture goes, your furniture goes," said Guido. "Your door gets smashed down." Guido wasn't sure he would do that, but he would do something. Ugo Frangano shouldn't be allowed to put the Trapanis out on the street.

"One month's," said Ugo, a little worried about Guido's threat, but Guido was only a boy, and not a very big boy at that.

"The old man has the lot. He goes in 6:30," said Tonino. "So we go pick his tomatoes. And peppers. Pick a bushel. Maybe two. Juicy tomatoes."

Older and taller, Tonino Aiello was Guido's best friend. Tonino's first thoughts every morning were of mischief for sport and danger, and often Guido was included. Guido contributed to their friendship his stories, sometimes hammed up for a laugh, of adults he talked to for his parents.

"Stealing ain't fair," said Guido. "In the hot sun the old man pulls weeds. Waters with the can. He can't even stand up straight."

They were sitting on New Utrecht High School's 79th Street steps after dinner. The sun wasn't down yet, but the fresh breeze was cooling their sweat. Opposite the school were the semi-attached red brick houses they lived in. On the house steps and stoops young women had bailed out of their hot kitchens to the fan of outdoors, and kept their eyes peeled on their children on roller skates and tricycles, or hopscotching. Older women, gossiping like secretive nuns, were in black dresses, in mourning for an aunt one year, a parent two, a child three, and a husband five years, and sometimes it all added up to a lifetime in black. The men standing out on the sidewalk talked only to the men and they smoked and they spat in the gutter.

"If he lived to a hundred he couldn't eat all them tomatoes," said Tonino, blowing cigarette smoke in Guido's face because he wouldn't steal the tomatoes.

"His wife makes sauce. Sells it in jars, for the people who don't make it," said Guido. "That's how they live. He grows tomatoes. She cooks them. He's too old to get a job, and they don't have no kids helping out."

"I bet your mother, with your father laid off, would like some fresh tomatoes," said Tonino. "And green peppers. For stuffed peppers."

"You'll go to hell," said Guido.

"Go be a sissy priest," said Tonino. "You ain't got no guts."

Guido took Tonino's cigarette from his two fingers. He puffed it, then gave it back and said, "I might even tell the old man you're the guy who stole his tomatoes. So if I was you, I wouldn't. I hear, to scare the birds, he's got a shotgun."

Alfredo was hindered from getting another job, not only by the Depression and his own lack of skills, but also by his dead ears and useless tongue. After weeks of frantically scrambling all over Brooklyn and into Manhattan's garment district, on subways, buses, and trolleys, he couldn't find any work. Now, in July, even shoveling snow for two or three dollars a day wasn't possible.

In his travels, however, Alfredo had learned from other men that the WPA was hiring pick-and-shovel laborers for road build-

ing on Long Island. Through Guido, he asked in the neighborhood
if anyone drove to Long Island. Very few owned a car and not
one went out there. And since Alfredo couldn't afford the railroad
ticket either, working for the WPA was also out of the question.

When their meager savings ran out, Guido's summer job paid
for their groceries. Guido worked for the Sicilian Social Society
in the storefront under the BMT elevated line on New Utrecht
Avenue. Membership in the club was for men only, mostly grand-
fathers. They sat around and played poker and pinochle, smoked
black cigars, drank black coffee, and talked only in the Sicilian
dialect. Guido's job was to make the coffee and serve it in small
cups, empty the ashtrays, sweep the floor, go out for sandwiches,
and carry messages. When the men wouldn't be going home for
dinner on time, because they were playing and winning, or playing and losing, Guido would explain matters to the wives. Guido
could stand up for the men, and the men knew he wouldn't flirt
with their women.

Some men carried a gun or a knife in their belts. Guido asked
about those things, but the men only laughed, and rumpled
Guido's light brown curly hair. He eavesdropped on their conversations and understood a little, and suspected they did bad things.
But they never revealed themselves. And they were always extremely courteous to him, and Guido needed the money to bring
home to his parents.

The bed was taken apart. The wood pieces were stacked on end,
as was the large mirror, all leaning against the dresser. The day-
bed where Guido slept was piled very high with the clothes from
their closets. Lamps, chests, tables, pots, and dishes were out on
the sidewalk. Books, papers, crucifixes, religious pictures, shoes,
old Christmas cards, palm fronds, forks, spoons, an assortment of
other things were all in a heap in the middle of their faded rug.

Sabatina was crying as an ape would cry if it could, not with sobs and tears but with primitive beastly sounds. When Guido arrived, he immediately understood the meaning of his mother's inhuman noises.

The Trapanis actually had had a month and a half without rent before Ugo and his brother, Felipe, with the marshal lending a hand, moved out the Trapani belongings, on the very day that Alfredo finally accepted the idea of home relief and shamefully went downtown to apply. Their few pieces of furniture, scratched and with coffee rings, and their belongings, rags really, were now blocking the sidewalk, attracting neighborhood children who leered as if a terrible sin were being committed in public.

When the men of the neighborhood arrived home after their own futile or productive efforts to earn a few dollars, streaming down from the elevated at the corner of 79th, their curses and waved fists, and those of their wives who left their apartments, were directed at the Franganos.

To avoid that abuse, Ugo, childless, sent his wife, Tessie, to the double feature at the Hollywood Theater, which gave dishes to women weeknights. Tessie already had a service for five stacked up. Then Ugo and Felipe went to Ugo's butcher shop with two bottles of red wine, salami, and bread.

Guido, as his mother's protector, normal for a boy of his age, but more so for him because he was her voice, fell to his knees, embedded his face in the two slats of her lap, and wept too. His assumed manliness was crumbling into childhood again. Guido felt helpless to comfort his mother, and helpless to haul their belongings back inside, where their apartment door was boarded over to protect against such arrogance, which Ugo believed Guido was certainly capable of.

Then Alfredo came home. So willing to clean toilets or dig ditches, he had believed some lowly job would be his, and his family wouldn't be dispossessed, but every job was coveted like life itself. If only he had applied for relief sooner, he might have the money for the rent, but their first check wouldn't arrive for weeks now. Alfredo couldn't cry. After a dazed moment, he repeatedly struck his head on the headboard to exorcise the devil from his mind before he hurt someone. Then neighbors embraced Alfredo, offering him a room in their apartment for his family for the night.

Guido swept the floor in the men's club as it had seldom been swept before. He even swept down the webs in the corners, previously left undisturbed for the spiders to go on living, but no longer.

Guido's face had long ago lost its adolescent tenderness. His was a young man's face, purposeful, energetic, narrow and sharp-edged like a fish's, with a strong slender nose joining the plane of his pointed chin. In his eyes and mouth ordinarily was a fire, now extinguished, and even his skin was unnaturally ashy. The old men noticed the absence of Guido's voice, pleasurable to them, as evidence that someday he would be one of them, a strong man. Although Guido was there in body, the old men were missing him from their lives.

One of them, Mr. Fazio, the size of a door, who, in a doorway, had to bend his head and go sideways, and was baldheaded with a giant meatball face, said, "You have your life, Guido. Mine is finished. Whatever is bad, tomorrow is better. Spit on the floor. Pick up your head."

"I can't," said Guido.

"You tell me," said Mr. Fazio. "I tell you how to fix."

"Ugo put us out," said Guido. "We have no place to go."

The old man scratched his scalp. "Your father, he has no money?"

"Just what I bring," said Guido.

"I give you the loan. Twenty dollars," said Mr. Fazio. "You pay me back. A nickel a month. No interest. Your father—he gets some rooms for twenty dollars. Take it. Now maybe you sing. Listen to me. Then you *O-sol-e-mi-o sta-nfronte-a-te!*"

The money in his pocket, Guido was on his way to Ugo's butcher shop to talk to Ugo to get the apartment back. He had stayed late at the men's club in order to catch Ugo when he was closing up. Then he could talk to him without customers ordering their veal cutlets and lamb chops. When Guido arrived across the street, he saw through the plate-glass window an old woman still in the shop, so he cooled his heels. When the woman, a shopping bag in each hand, toddled out as if her feet were hurting, Guido went in, leaving his footprints in the sawdust. Behind the counter Ugo was slitting the throats of live chickens taken one by one from their wood dowel cage. Then Ugo threw the birds with their bloodstained feathers upside down in individual pails to drain.

"Get out, kid," said Ugo, putting down the knife and picking up the meat cleaver and waving it at Guido like a knight's weapon of war. "Don't look for no trouble. I have the mortgage. I got to have the rent."

"We have it," said Guido. "Twenty dollars. The rent's twenty-five. So we still owe you. We'll get the other five. But you can let us back in now."

"Let's see the twenty," said Ugo, wiping his bloody hands on the apron. He turned the bill over as if it could be a counterfeit. Then he folded the bill and put it in his pants pocket and picked up the meat cleaver again. "Now get out," he said.

"You took our money," said Guido, so outraged his spittle flew out.

"Your father owes me a month and a half. Thirty-seven fifty. Leaves seventeen fifty," said Ugo.

"You can't take our money and not let us in," said Guido, running behind the counter and grabbing Ugo's wrist in his two hands. Ugo was used to lifting carcasses, sawing bone, and chopping flesh, and he had an animal's chest and muscle, so he easily shook Guido off. Guido fell to the floor where the sawdust got in his mouth, and he spat it out.

"If you don't go, I break your head," said Ugo, fearing a little the bull in the calf daring to reproach him, standing over Guido with the meat cleaver, the flat steel surface catching the overhead electric light.

Guido backed up. He felt betrayed and angry. Fearful too. Of the meat cleaver and the aroused Ugo. For his own protection, Guido was reaching for the knife stained with chicken blood. When Ugo saw the knife in Guido's hand, his face flushed with fury and he charged Guido, the meat cleaver raised. Guido, trembling, went down. In a blinding light he raised the knife. Ugo's weight seemed to suck in the knife, seemed to pull it out of his hand. Then Ugo, smelling of sweat, wine, and chickens, was crashing down on him.

Guido thought to take the money out of Ugo's pocket, but he was too horrified at what he had done. So he hurriedly scuffed his footprints out of the sawdust. Then he ran out as if he were an escaping headless chicken.

"Take the twenty dollars," said Father Valenti, without his collar on, slightly drunk, in the sacristy. "Don't pay me back. I have *no use* for money."

"Thank you, father," said Guido. "And now, for you, I want to do something. Go in the priesthood."

"Don't do it *for me,*" said the priest. "That's a heavy responsibility."

"I thought you'd like the idea," said Guido. "Anyway, I'm doing it."

"I always felt *you* had the calling," said the priest. "But you're still young. Don't say absolutely. It's good you want to. But there's time."

"But who's going to speak for my father and mother when I go to the seminary?" said Guido.

"I will," said Father Valenti, sitting up, wiping his mouth with the soiled napkin, as if to show he would qualify for Guido's job.

"You'll go to the store?" said Guido.

"If they'll have me," said the priest.

"To Dr. Pilo's office?"

"Yes."

"Even at night?"

"I'll go anywhere with them. Any time," said the priest. "And give them absolution. Without confession."

"Make the papers, father. I want to go as soon as possible," said Guido.

"It takes six months, Guido. Maybe more. Maybe you'll change your mind. If you change it, it's okay," said the priest.

"You're an idiot," said Tonino, dancing in the fresh snow as they went to the elevated. "You ain't ever going to get laid. You poor bastard. Means I get yours too."

"I have the calling," said Guido, pulling his moth-eaten woolen hat down over his ears, and wondering how he would look in the cardinal's red hat.

Tonino was carrying Guido's suitcase. Guido had his mother's sandwiches, fruits, and cakes in the grocery's Quaker Oats box knotted with scraps of twine.

"You could take my confession if I rob a bank. And you won't tell. Right?" said Tonino.

"You don't have to tell everything, even if you're supposed to," said Guido. "I wouldn't want to hear you robbed a bank. You can tell God Himself instead. He has ears that can hear."

"I'm going to rob a bank. And get rich," said Tonino. When they reached the turnstiles, he handed over the suitcase. They shook hands. Then Tonino put his cold hands in his pockets. "Maybe I'll rob a hundred banks."

"Just don't kill anybody," said Guido. He dropped in his nickel. Then he went out on the platform and while he waited for the train he prayed for Ugo's soul, Tonino's, and his own.

Jet Stream

T. M. McNally

Betsy, 1980

I don't like to clean the pool, but that's what I'm doing. Norm says people like to swim in clean water; you can tell it's clean, he says, when it's blue. I push the broom along the floor of the pool and watch the dirt stir and whirl like dust devils. Norm is my stepdad.

He's out here on the lawn reading *Time,* backwards, saving the important stuff for last. He looks fat out here: his paunch is really big like he's pregnant, but it's just full of beer and some of Mom's old cooking. I cook for him now, Swansons and Stouffers.

I go over to the engines and set the pool on Backwash, when Norm starts to laugh. The magazine rattles and the chair wobbles; he's really laughing hard. To clean the filter, you have to run the water through backwards, so I turn the handle, flip the switch and listen to the filter whine like the jumbo jets at the airport. The water goes *swoosh* and starts to flood the river-rock behind the putting green. The putting green has nine holes and little red flags.

"What's so funny?" I say, because Norm is still laughing.

"Carter," Norm says. "He's not going to let us go to the Olympics if Russia keeps screwing around in Afghanistan. Now that's what I call effective foreign policy." He says *effective* like he's from a farm, but he's not. "What the hell have you got on?" he says.

He means my shorts: they're really Ruth's and have orange and blue polka dots, and I'm wearing my big white tank top—the one Mom wouldn't let me wear because you can see everything through the armholes. Sometimes I catch Norm taking looks, but this is still my favorite shirt. I like the way it fits so loose. Eric says it's his favorite, but he only wants me to wear it around him. When I graduate, Eric wants to go to New York or Los Angeles with me and become a studio musician.

"Miss Crocker," says Norm, "would you be so kind as to bring me a beer?" He calls me Crocker after the company, Betsy Crocker, but the real name's Betty. My name is Betsy.

"How come the water looks so green?" I say.

"Too many chemicals, that's all. There's some in the vegetable bin."

I leave the water running over the river-rock and go in to get Norm a beer, and he yells, "I hope someone gave you those!"—referring to the shorts. Clyde, my Irish wolfhound, is lying on the floor underneath the kitchen table; his tail sways back and forth to keep him cool. Norm won't run the air-conditioning anymore except at night to sleep. The house is too big, he says, and we don't use enough of it anyway. I go to the garage where he keeps the beer because I know there's only one in the vegetable bin. I open a case and take out eight or nine, the cans on top my arms like sticks. I bring them inside and put them in the freezer so they'll get cold quick. I give Clyde an oatmeal cookie, but he's not hungry. It just sits by his nose while he thinks.

Last night when Eric came over he was still in his ARCO shirt with *Harry* ironed over the pocket. The pockets are always

streaked with ink from his pens going in and out, and he smelled
like mechanic's soap and sweat. The soap smells like plastic and
makes his hands dry. Norm called him Harry, trying to be funny,
and he asked how much for a tune-up.

"I don't know, Norm."

Eric's been working on the corner of Twenty-fourth and Camel-
back for a year waiting for me to finish school. I put the beers
from the vegetable bin in my knapsack and we left. I kept one
out, held it between my legs while I hung on to Eric, while we
cruised on his Kawasaki looking for something. At stoplights I'd
hold the beer up for him and pour. The night was hot and dry,
but you don't notice the heat if you're moving, with the wind
whipping your hair and the steady rumbling of the motorcycle
going beneath you making your legs sweat against the seat.

We went down Central but saw no one we knew: just the
regulars with their hopped-up cars, sometimes their parents' cars.
We drove all the way to South Mountain. From on top of South
Mountain you can see all of Phoenix. The lights spread out into
stars and never stop. You can see them forever up there. We drank
the warm beers and sat on a big rock. There were cars next to us,
some girl was yelling at her boyfriend. The other cars were silent
except for one that was running so its air-conditioning could stay
on. We sat outside and Eric looked at the stars while I looked at
his hands, at the black grease under his fingernails and his leather
knuckles. Inside, the palms are rough and full of calluses. He says
the only way to get them really clean is to use a toothbrush, and I
held his hands with mine and thought about the way they felt so
that later I'd remember it—the feeling with the air and the lights
and the heat, the sound of the car running to keep cool.

When we got home Norm was asleep on the couch, the house
felt cold. Cal Worthington was selling cars with his dog, Spot,

and a beer had spilled from Norm's lap and soaked the carpet. I threw the can away. I took off his shoes and covered him with the sheet he keeps at the end of the couch. I turned the volume down, but left the TV on just in case.

Clyde was waiting for us on my bed, and Eric threw him off.

"Eric," I said, "if you're not nice to Clyde, he won't be nice to you."

And he said, "For Christ's sake, Betsy. It's just a dog."

I put Clyde outside and brushed my teeth while Eric thought about things. Sometimes Eric gets mean when he drinks and wants to fight, but not now. Now he was thinking. He thinks a lot, just lies and stares at the ceiling and thinks. He says thinking is good for musicians, that I should think more. But I don't like to think, I just like to know how things feel.

And then we started doing it, like we usually do, on the big bed Mom gave me when I turned sixteen before I knew Eric. We were going along pretty nice for a while, but then he stopped right in the middle and picked me up so I'd be on top. He didn't even say anything. He just stopped and did that.

I'm at the piano working my way through the second movement of the *Appassionata* when Ruth comes over. I forgot about Norm's beer, but when he came in he said it sounded good. Sometimes he's nice to me to make himself feel better.

"It's in the freezer," I said, "getting cold."

"I'm going to take a shower. Cool off."

Norm showers a lot lately. He doesn't like swimming. The week after the insurance was due, his music store burned down. He said he was busy with other things and forgot. When my brother Kevin got married in Dallas, Mom said that was it. "I've had it," she said. Mom was my teacher, the *Appassionata* my last assign-

ment. She said I wasn't ready for the *Waldstein,* but Norm says
I can do whatever I want: "You know what you want to do," he
says, "and you do it."

"Just like that?"

And he says, "Yes."

Once he told me he wished I really was his daughter, and he
started crying. My real father lives in California. I told Norm it
was okay, and let him hold me while he cried and got my hair
wet. This was after Mom had sent a postcard from New Orleans
where she said it was humid. Later the Arizona Bank sent a letter
to Norm—a notice of foreclosure—and Norm wadded it up into
a ball. He threw it across the putting green for Clyde to fetch,
and Clyde brought it back. Norm kept throwing and Clyde kept
fetching until the wind picked it up and carried the wadded ball
into the pool with Clyde's slobber skimming all around. Clyde
stood on the deck waiting for it to float in reach.

I hear him barking at Ruth's moped, that's how I know it's
her. Today she's wearing white cotton shorts with big pockets
and my red No Nukes T-shirt. Her hair is jet black and she has
these big almond eyes and a wide mouth. Her skin is perfect and
tan, we lie out by the pool a lot with our shirts off. Neither of us
shaves because that's not what they do in Europe. Ruth is really
beautiful.

"You weren't at school," she says.

"Overslept."

We go into the kitchen for iced tea and look out the window
into the yard. The pool is half-empty, the putting green floats
under three or four inches of water: ankle-deep. Norm's lawn
chair lies on its side, the magazine is soaked, the little red flags
with numbers look like they've sunk. Clyde is out there jumping
and splashing in the water looking for fish.

Ruth and I, we just stand and watch. Finally she touches my
hand: tears are leaking out of her almond-shaped eyes filled with

what's inside her—we're never sure what, exactly, but we know it's in there and important like the way things happen in a dream.

"My grandmother wants me to come to L.A.," she says.

And I think this is something I already know how to do, something I'm already getting pretty good at.

Ruth used to sleep with Mr. Fennerstrom, our history teacher. He was still pretty young and wore a beard, and he'd talk to our class as if we really mattered. He told us why Jerry Garcia was important and why John Travolta wasn't. He told us stories about when he was in Ohio protesting the Vietnam war. He told us the Palo Verde nuclear plant would destroy the desert and all of us around it, and he had us write letters to the *Gazette* and the *Republic* instead of reports. They never printed any, but Mr. Fennerstrom said they wouldn't, and he said if people stopped driving there wouldn't be a gas shortage.

Once he took me and Ruth to a Jackson Brown concert at Arcosanti in Cordes Junction. The people had parked their cars in grass and someone's muffler caught it on fire. Cars started blowing up and the concert had to stop. On the way home, we stopped at Ferrells for ice cream. It was a lady's birthday and the hostess banged a drum while a boy with acne and a black garter around his arm honked a brass horn. We all sang happy birthday to the lady, laughing and making shapes with our ice cream, our spoons like big safe chisels. We had a huge mound of Pistachio and Almond Cream in one bowl between us, and this was how we ate it. After Mr. Fennerstrom dropped me off at my house, he drove Ruth to the school parking lot where she left her moped. Ruth says that's when they kissed, in the parking lot outside like he was just another football player or wrestler, though we never go out with jocks. At first it made me jealous.

On one hand he had only three fingers, and he would keep them curled like a loose fist so you wouldn't notice. Once, when he was talking about nuclear energy, he explained what could happen. "It only takes one mistake," he was saying. "One little mistake, one little slip and oops—she'll blow like a whale."

I was thinking about the last movement of the *Appassionata,* how if you slipped up the first arpeggios the whole piece would tumble down inside your head and you'd never find your way out.

"One mistake," he said. "How many of you have ever made a mistake? Just one little mistake?" He stopped pacing and pulled on his beard, looking thoughtful while we all sat and wondered what mistake of ours was the worst, or which one everyone knew the most about. After he and Ruth started it all, he wouldn't look at me in class; he'd get nervous sometimes when I asked questions. But today he looked up, stopped tugging on his beard, with his good hand, and turned right to me. He shrugged his shoulders and said as if he were sad, "I rest my case."

It was strange knowing Mr. Fennerstrom like that. I knew all about him through Ruth, and I know he knew all about me, but it was as if we knew all these things, these secrets, without ever knowing them. They were just there, like air or the mail at your front door each morning waiting to be gone through.

Last December before he killed himself, Mr. Fennerstrom wrote Ruth a letter explaining it wasn't her fault, that it was his own fault and he alone was responsible for him just like Ruth was for her. He said the whole thing had nothing to do with her, but he forgot to mail the letter, or maybe he decided not to mail it and forgot to throw it out. His landlord found the letter in a drawer and gave it to the police, who gave it to the papers. The papers printed it, everything, the stuff about how he thought about her in class, the Jackson Brown concert and me, *the pianist with promise*—even the way he signed it at the end: *Love, Fenny.* Mr. Buckner said he was going to throw Ruth out of school. "For her own sake," Ruth said. But he never did. Miss Williams and some others said she was a strong girl and seemed to be handling the situation okay. Ruth told me Mr. Fennerstrom was wrong, though, that it was everyone's fault—hers, Mr. Buckner's, Miss Williams'. Even mine.

None of the girls at school talk to Ruth anymore because everyone loved Mr. Fennerstrom. The guys all think she's a slut; even Eric tried to hit on her, but he thinks I don't know. The guys at school all know she knows more than any of them, they won't talk to her in front of any of the girls, and now she tells me her grandmother wants her to come live in L.A. Her foster parents think it's a good idea.

"It *was* their idea," she says.

We're outside now, I've shut off the pump. We walk through the water over the prickly grass. Clyde barks and he wants to play. I uncoil the hose, put it in the half-empty pool to fill it up. The metal end scrapes on the sides, and Ruth turns the water on.

"Do you think Norm will be mad?" she says.

The way Mr. Fennerstrom killed himself was: he drove off a cliff north of Phoenix near Camp Verde on Christmas Eve. "So everyone would think it was an accident," Ruth said. "He talked about it once. He didn't want to hurt anybody's feelings."

"Ruth," I say, "let's go somewhere."

She looks at me the way she does sometimes, and I say, "It doesn't matter. I just feel like going."

When you ride with Eric, you feel the bones and muscles inside his back, the long V leading up to his shoulders. Everything feels tight and in place like where it should. But it's different with Ruth, she doesn't feel the same. Her skin feels soft even through my No Nukes T-shirt and I can smell her soap, Dove. Her moped goes slow and putters loud when she tries to go fast. Together we weigh too much for it, but this is the way we go.

The Burger King is first. We drink Tab and look out the window, and you can see our reflection.

"The airport," Ruth says.

She means Sky Harbor where they're building a new terminal. Sometimes we hang out at the airport. We watch people come and go, wave, say hello or hug and cry. In Phoenix all the cowboys except for Norm go to the airport. You never see them on the streets, only in the terminals, with new hats and boots with reptile skin. They're always going home, too. To Minnesota or Milwaukee. At night sometimes we go out on the runway and feel the jets land.

"This was my year for Beethoven," I say. "Mom said she'd finish me off with Liszt, the *Mephisto Waltz*. She said then I'd be ready for anything."

"Who's Liszt?"

"Nineteenth century. When Liszt was little, Beethoven heard him play. After, Beethoven went and picked him up and told him someday he'd be famous."

Mom used to tell me these stories. Mom used to be famous, before she married my dad, when she played everywhere. My dad makes movies and says I don't have to worry about college, that it's all taken care of, even though I haven't seen him since I was six. Ruth doesn't know any of the names but she says she likes to hear me play. She likes Chopin and Brahms. She likes it when I play "Rootbeer Rag" by Billy Joel. Mom said my hands are too small for me to be great. She said it's all in the hands and some people's are smaller than other's. My fingers are too short, but Mom says I use them right. "You know where to put them," she says. "You have your father's hands."

"I hate her," I say, sounding it out.

"Let's go to the airport."

We don't want another Tab, but I still have to fix dinner. I walk over to a pay phone and call Angeleno's. I order Norm a big one with extra cheese, with pepperoni and mushrooms.

Laconic—it's a word Mr. Fennerstrom made me look up. It means quiet and sometimes rude because you don't talk much; it means *terse*. I had to look *terse* up to find out exactly what *laconic* means, and that's what Eric is. He doesn't talk much, he sits and thinks. He broods. Ruth doesn't talk much either, but she's not *laconic*. With Ruth I always know what she's thinking. It doesn't matter if she doesn't talk. Sometimes we both don't talk, we just know and listen to each other. Ruth is more like *pithy,* which sounds worse than it is.

We ride out to the airport, down Twenty-fourth past the ARCO station. Eric's standing outside leaning on one of the pumps with a sign that says *No Unleaded.* He's thinking about something and doesn't see us, and there's a lot of traffic so we don't have to worry about going slow, or not going fast enough. The sun is setting, turning the sky all sorts of colors: purple and green and orange, a little red before it smears into soft thick clouds. In Phoenix you feel like you need an ocean when you watch the sunset. The sky is pretty and it's hot and long green palm trees are everywhere, but there's still no ocean.

A car full of Mexicans speeds up and then slows beside us. They yell something in Spanish and their voices go really high, and Ruth tells them to fuck off! This makes them yell more and we're coming up to a light—yellow. The Mexicans stop and we go on through. A truck carrying dirt with a tractor hooked up behind honks, but you can tell by the look on the guy's face he's not really mad.

It's dark now, the colors in the sky are gone and you can't see any stars. The smog is bad. We climb over a tall chainlink fence with no barbwire, but Ruth hooks the pocket of her shorts at the top. This scares her, and she starts to scramble and shake like she's getting tired of holding herself up there.

"Wait," I say, climbing higher. I reach my hand up to help, but I can't unhook the cloth.

"Rip it," she says, shaking.

That's what I do—I rip it and cut three inches of the pocket. Ruth swings over and climbs down, and I follow. When we're on the ground we both lean against the fence, breathing. My heart is going fast, and Ruth looks at the tear in her shorts. Her legs are tan and make the shorts look white even in the dark.

In front of us is the runway with big arrows and lines painted on in between all the low blue lights. The lights are neon-blue and close to the ground. We walk a while and stop before we get too far. We wait, our arms stretched out with our hands holding onto the warm blue lights. The lights are glowing and color our arms. Between Ruth and me is a light, our fingers overlap while we tense our arms, waiting.

We hear the jet, see the large wings like shadows pulling it down as if gravity really does work, gliding in slow and easy as a goose on water. We feel the pull and heat and feel our legs rise, straight out behind us, hovering like the plane while our bodies get swept up in the afterwash. We're levitating, our fingers touching, with the roar of gas and wind and air blowing through our ears and sucking at us, pulling and making us want to stop because our arms keep shaking. Our legs rise and we float with our eyes closed tight, feeling the jet and the wings, the air making so much noise it almost hurts.

Our ears ring in the silence. We're waiting for another. It's strange the way everything seems so quiet when everything feels so loud.

"This will make you deaf," Ruth says.

"Like Beethoven," I say.

"How'd he do that, anyway?"

It's not really a question, but it was all in his hands. "The Ninth came from his fingertips," I say.

"It'll still make you deaf," Ruth says, but I can't really hear because another plane is coming in from somewhere and we're being sucked up into its space the way it's being sucked into ours. I'm wondering what I'm going to do when Ruth's gone, and she's wondering the same. But we aren't talking about that because we're in a vacuum. We're holding onto blue lights in the dark. We're in the jet stream.

When you fly into Phoenix at night, the first thing you watch is the same lights you see from on top of South Mountain. I've never flown in at night, but Ruth has, and she says the view is the same.

Eric's motorcycle is parked in the driveway and we hear Fleetwood Mac playing. Ruth parks the moped by the gate leading to the backyard where Norm and Eric sit in lawn chairs in the water on the putting green drinking beer. The pool is flooded, filled to the top and running into the water on the grass, and Clyde is lying on top of the diving board where it's dry even though he's all wet. Norm's wearing the Bermudas I gave him last Christmas, Eric's in his jeans, and you can tell they're both pretty drunk and have been swimming or trying to play golf.

"They took the car," Norm says.

"Who?"

"The repossession men, that's who. Didn't even bother to ask for the keys. I would have given them the keys if they asked. But they didn't even ask. They just came and took the car."

"You said that," Eric says. And then, looking at me, "Where have you been?" He looks mean, the way he does when he's worked too long at the station and it's hot, the way he does when other guys look at me.

"Nowhere," I say.

"Goddamnit—"

"Hey," says Norm. "Hey. Just hey—"

"Where the hell have you been?"

Norm stands up and tips over the lawn chair. His shorts are wet and glow under the porch lights. "Eric," he says, "you may very well—" He stops, looks at me. "You may—" Now he's looking for a cigarette. "But I'll not abide your talking to my Betsy that way." He looks serious, even if he is wobbling and digging through his wet pockets.

"Is there any pizza left?" I ask, watching Ruth shut off the hose. I see her go inside before I can tell her not to.

"He gave it to the dog," Eric says.

"Did no such thing."

Eric stands, turns so that he's facing me. "I won't ask you again," he says.

"Does it matter? What does it matter?"

"It matters 'cause I want to know!"

He's not looking at me, he's looking at my shirt. He's looking at me the way he did last night after he threw Clyde off the bed and got tired of thinking.

"Why don't you just leave? Would you please just leave!"

I'm crying and Norm looks at me, then Eric. Then me. He starts to clap, his hands echoing in the dark with the music playing.

"Wish I'd said the same thing," he says.

Now Eric looks confused, like Clyde when you pretend to throw the ball but don't. Clyde's on the diving board, his tail thumping. Above us is the moon, bright as a floodlight, and I'm still crying, wishing Norm had said the same thing. To Mom so she'd know how we really feel.

Mom used to say if you tried to think too much about it, you'd never stretch and everything would come out the way it was on paper and not the way it was in you. Ruth and I sit on the kitchen floor eating Nachos and drinking warm beer from the garage.

Norm has thrown the table into the swimming pool; he's thrown in the chairs and microwave.

He started first by ripping off the speakers from the wall outside and throwing them in the water, one at a time. Fleetwood Mac went from stereo to mono to nothing. Now you hear Norm's panting, sometimes Clyde's bark.

Norm walks by with the television. It's heavy and his face is red, and he says, "You girls gonna help or not?"

I look at Ruth, who can't help laughing. "Sure," I say.

The piano is next. Norm opens up the sliding glass doors and we three get behind to push. The brass wheels stick in the carpet, and Ruth kicks the piano bench over, spilling the music inside. There are some old letters and Christmas cards, a picture of Mom. Norm takes the picture of Mom and sticks it under his arm while we all push.

Outside we have to lift it over the curb of the pool deck, but once over we're ready to go. The piano is a Baldwin baby grand, but out here by the pool under the porch lights and moon it looks like any other baby grand.

We push on *Three*! and the narrow tail falls first. We push again and watch it go. It almost floats before sinking to the bottom with its lid just above the swelling water. Clyde jumps on top and looks over the edge like it's a pier, and Norm throws in the picture of Mom.

Now we do the couch and all the paperbacks from all the bookshelves. I get the weed eater and Ruth takes the vacuum cleaner. We do the lawn furniture and the toilet seat and all the soap and shampoo in the second bathroom. We do the two easy chairs Mom picked out and a lamp.

"Too bad Eric's not—" and Norm stops, remembering why Eric's not here.

"Hey," says Ruth, "it's looking pretty full."

"Wait," says Norm. "I'll get the camera!"

Ruth and I and Clyde sit in front on the piano with our feet wet. Norm is setting the flash and timer, adjusting the tripod and focus. "Okay," he says, and comes running around. He stands on the piano behind us and almost falls in. We smile and Norm says, "Be sure to wave, girls."

We wave, Norm takes the camera off the tripod. "What the hell," he says, and throws the tripod in on top of the couch. He looks it over a while, taking it in. Finally, he fakes a yawn and says, "Think I'm gonna hit the hay."

On his way to the bedroom we see Norm stop in the kitchen and take three beers. Clyde follows, goes into the house; he pauses to shake off the water in his fur. He's going to go to my room and leap on top the brass bed Mom bought me and wait. Norm will have to sleep in his bed tonight because the couch is already in the pool. Next week Ruth will be sleeping in a guest room at her grandmother's house and the bank will have taken ours away. But right now we're sitting cross-legged on the water in a pool full of stuff.

It's really late, after three. We drink more beer and sit on the piano. We smoke and throw the butts in the pool. We keep the beer from getting hot by holding it in the water, though the water's not cold. Sometimes we flick a splash away and listen to the noise.

"Do you miss him?" I ask.

Ruth thinks for a second and sips her beer. "No," she says. "After a while he was just like everyone else. I was just like everyone else, only younger."

Eric tried to hit on Ruth at a party. He wasn't even drunk, and he told her he wanted to know what she'd be like. Ruth said he wanted to compare. Ruth said he was like everyone after Mr. Fennerstrom, even like her uncle, the one in California. She

told Eric she wouldn't tell but she did. We tell each other everything except for the times when we don't have to. For instance, I
know why she doesn't want to go back to California.

"You know you're depressed," I say, "when you think you
aren't but should be."

"Huh?"

"You know, when you think about it too much."

"I'm not going to go," she says. "I'll run away first."

Overhead the stars are brighter than the lights of Phoenix, but
you still can't see them. We used to go swimming a lot: during the
day when Norm wasn't around, or sometimes late at night. It was
always best at night with a bright moon like now. The water felt
more cool and clean and made your hair feel heavier than it really
was. You could feel the sky and if you turned the light on it lit up
the pool from below and you could see your shadow swimming
along beneath. If you dove down and swam near the light, you
could feel the heat from the bulb in the cool water. I remember
once, before Mr. Fennerstrom and everything—I remember us in
the pool. Ruth was glowing in the light under the water because
we still weren't that tan. We didn't even have any lines, and her
skin was white and perfect and she said I looked *luminous,* like
it was me who was making the light. Ruth, she says she's not
going to go, but I already know this. I know this the way I know
it wasn't me making the light. The way I know no one feels like
we feel when the wind is really blowing hard.

The Ponoes

Peter Meinke

When I was ten years old I couldn't sleep because the minute I closed my eyes the ponoes would get me. The ponoes were pale creatures about two feet tall, with pointed heads and malevolent expressions, though they never said anything. What they did was to approach me slowly, silently in order to build up my fear (because I knew what they were going to do); then they would tickle me. I was extremely ticklish in those days. In fact, I could hardly bear to be touched by anybody, and the ponoes would swarm over me like a band of drunken and sadistic uncles, tickling me till I went crazy, till I almost threw up, flinging my legs and arms around in breathless agony. I would wake up soaked, my heart banging in my chest like the bass drum in the school marching band. This lasted almost an entire year, until the Murphy brothers got rid of them for me.

Because the ponoes would come whenever I fell asleep, I hated to go to bed even more than most children. My parents were not sympathetic. Ponoes didn't seem that frightening to them, nor were they sure, for a long time, that I wasn't making them up. Even my best friend, Frankie Hanratty, a curly-haired black-eyed boy of unbounded innocence, was dubious. No one else had ever

heard of them; they seemed like some sort of cross between elves
and dwarfs. But where did I get the name? I think my parents
felt that there was something vaguely sexual about them, and
therefore distasteful.

"Now no more talk about these, um, ponoes, young man. Right
to bed!"

"I'm afraid!" That year—1942—I was always close to tears,
and my bespectacled watery eyes must have been a discouraging
sight, especially for my father, who would take me to the Dodger
games at Ebbett's Field and introduce me to manly players like
Cookie Lavagetto and Dixie Walker. I had a collection of signed
baseballs that my father always showed to our guests.

Because I was terrified, I fought sleep with all my might. I read
through most of the night, by lamplight, flashlight, even moonlight, further straining my already weak eyes. When I *did* fall
asleep, from utter exhaustion, my sleep was so light that when
the ponoes appeared on the horizon—approaching much like the
gangs in *West Side Story,* though of course I didn't know that
then—I could often wake myself up before they reached me. I
can remember wrestling with my eyelids, lifting them, heavy as
the iron covers of manholes we'd try to pry open in the streets,
bit by bit until I could see the teepee-like designs of what I called
my Indian blanket. Sometimes I would get just a glimpse of my
blanket and then my eyelids would clang shut and the ponoes
were upon me. It is possible, I suppose, that I only *dreamed* I was
seeing my blanket, but I don't think so.

Sometimes I would give up trying to open my eyes, give up
saying to myself *This is only a dream,* and turn and run. My one
athletic skill was, and remains still, running. There were few who
could catch me, even at ten, and today, premature white hair flying, I fill our game room with trophies for my age bracket in the
5,000- and 10,000-meter races along the eastern seaboard. Often,

toward the end of a race, I hear footsteps behind me and I remember the ponoes; the adrenalin surges again, and the footsteps
usually fall back. But in my dreams the ponoes would always gain
and my legs would get heavier and heavier and I'd near a cliff that
I would try to throw myself over, but it was like running through
waist-deep water with chains on and I would be dragged down at
the edge. This, I suppose, with variations and without ponoes, is
a common enough dream.

My mother was more compassionate to me because at that time
she too was suffering from a recurring dream. She would find
herself lost in a forest, on a dark path. The ground was soft beneath her bare feet. With a vague but mounting terror she would
begin to run; it soon became clear she was running on a carpet
of toads and frogs. The path ended at a huge pit into which the
frogs were tumbling, pouring. Whatever it was that was pursuing
her approached and she screamed. Sometimes she would scream
only in the dream and sometimes she would scream in actuality
as well. But since her dream only came once a week, or even less
frequently, she didn't have the problem with sleeping that I did.
Even she would lose patience with me, mainly because my school-
work, along with everything else, suffered. Mother was very high
on education and was determined that I was going to be the first
member of our family to go to college. Norman Vincent Peale
preached at a nearby church and the neighborhood was awash
with positive thinking.

During this year, since I scarcely slept in bed, I fell asleep
everywhere else: in the car, at the movies, even at dinner, a true
zombie. In the winter I liked to curl up on the floor near the silver-
painted radiators, whose clanking seemed to keep the ponoes
away. I would drop off at my desk at school, once clattering to
the floor and breaking my glasses, like some pratfall from the

Three Stooges, whom we watched every Saturday afternoon at the Quentin Theater. Eleven cents for a double feature, it was another world! But Miss McDermott was not amused and would rap my knuckles sharply with her chalkboard pointer. She was a stout and formidable old witch, and when she first came at me, aiming her stick like an assassin from *Captain Blood,* I thought she was going to poke my eyes out and leaped from my seat, to the delight of my classmates, who for weeks afterwards liked to charge at me with fingers pointed at my nose.

We had moved from the Irish section of Boston to the Irish section of Brooklyn, and my father, Little Jack Shaughnessy, liked to hang around the tough bars of Red Hook where—he told me—there was a cop on every corner looking for an Irish head to break. My father was Little Jack and I was Little Jim (or Littlejack and Littlejim) because we were both short, but he was husky, a warehouse worker at Floyd Bennett Airport. Though he was not a chronic brawler, he liked an occasional fight and was disappointed in my obvious fear of physical violence.

"Come on, Jimmy, keep the left up." He'd slap me lightly on the face, circling around me. "Straight from the shoulder now!"

I'd flail away, blinking back the tears, the world a blur without my glasses, like a watercolor painting left in the rain. To this day, when I take off my glasses I have the feeling that someone is going to hit me. Oddly enough, it was fighting that made me fall in love with the Murphy brothers, Tom and Kevin, though love may not be exactly the right word.

I was a natural-born hero-worshiper. Perhaps I still am. When I was young, most of my heroes came from books—D'Artagnan, Robin Hood—or movies, characters like the Green Hornet and Zorro, or real actors like Nelson Eddy, whose romantic scenes with Jeanette MacDonald made my classmates whoop and holler.

I would whoop and holler, too, so as not to give myself away, but at night, fending off the ponoes, I would lie in bed in full Royal Canadian Mountie regalia singing, in my soaring tenor, "For I'm falling in love with someone, someone . . ." while Jeanette would stand at the foot of my bed shyly staring down at her tiny feet, or petting my noble horse, which was often in the room with us. This fantasy was particularly ludicrous as I was unable to carry a tune and had been dubbed a "listener" by Miss McDermott in front of the whole music class, after which I spent the term moving my mouth to the words without uttering a sound.

The Murphy brothers were tough, the scourge of P.S. 245. Extorters of lunch money, fistfighters, hitters of home runs during gym class, they towered over most of us because they were older, having been left back several times. Tom was the older and meaner; Kevin was stronger but slow-witted, perhaps even retarded. Tom pushed him around a lot but was careful not to get him too mad, because there was nothing that Kevin would not do when in a rage, which became increasingly evident as they grew older. Pale, lean, black-haired, they wore white shirts with the sleeves rolled up and black pants and shiny black shoes: for brawlers they were very neat dressers, early examples of the Elvis Presley look, though they never looked as soft as Elvis. Most of the rest of us wore corduroy knickers, whistling down the halls as we walked, with our garters dangling and our socks humped around our ankles. Small and weak, I wanted nothing more than to be like the two fighting brothers, who seemed to me to resemble the pictures of tough soldiers, sailors, and marines that were posted everywhere.

The Murphys had strong Brooklyn accents (they called themselves the Moifys), but the whole neighborhood was declining that way and the schools fought valiantly against it: accents were bad in 1942. I still remember the poem we all had to recite:

> There was once a turtle
> Whose first name was Myrtle
> Swam out to the Jersey shore . . .

Tom Murphy would get up in front of the class (like many of the others), grinning insolently, scratching obscenely, ducking spitballs, and mutter:

> Aah dere wunce wuz a toitle
> Whoze foist name wuz Moitle
> Swam out to da Joizey shaw . . .

We would all applaud and Tom would clasp his hands above his head like a winning prizefighter and swagger back to his seat. Miss McDermott never hit the Murphys—she had wise instincts—but tried to minimize their disturbance (distoibance!) by pretending they weren't there.

But there they were: they had cigarettes, they had the playing cards with the photographs that made us queasy, they wrote on the bathroom walls and the schoolyard sidewalks. Of course, they must have written obscenities, but in the fall of 1942 they mainly wrote things like KILL THE KRAUTS and JAPS ARE JERKS: they were patriotic. I thought of the change when I visited my daughter's high school last week. Painted on the handball court was YANKEE GET OUT OF NORTH AMERICA.

And, suddenly, Tom Murphy adopted me. It was like the lion and the mouse, the prince and the pauper. Like a German submarine, he blew me out of the water and I lost all sense of judgment, which was, in 1942, a very small loss. Perhaps it was because I was so sleepy.

On rainy days when we couldn't go outside to play softball or touch football we stayed in the gym and played a vicious game the Murphys loved called dodge ball. We divided into two sides

and fired a soccer-sized ball at each other until one side was elimi-
nated. The Murphys, always on the same side, firing fast balls the
length of the tiny gymnasium, would knock boys over like tin soldiers. I was usually one of the last to go as I was so small and hard
to hit; no one worried about me because I was incapable of hitting
anyone else, and eventually would get picked off. But one rainy
September week while our marines were digging in on Guadalcanal and Rommel was sweeping across Egypt the coach had to
call the game off twice in a row because the Murphys couldn't hit
me before the next class started. They stood on the firing line and
boomed the ball off the wall behind me while I jumped, ducked,
slid in panic, like a rabbit in front of the dogs, sure that the next
throw would splatter my head against the wall. Even when the
coach rolled in a second ball they missed me, throwing two at a
time. The truth was, I suppose, that the Murphys were not very
good athletes, just bigger and stronger than the rest of us.

The next day was a Saturday, and I was out in front of our
house flipping war cards with Frankie, who lived next door, when
the brothers loomed above us, watching. Kevin snatched Frankie's
cap and he and Tom tossed it back and forth while we crouched
there, waiting, not even thinking, looking from one brother to the
other. Finally Tom said, "Littlejim, go get me a licorice stick," and
stuck a penny in my hand. "Fast, now, get a leg on." Mostroni's
Candy Store was three blocks away, and I raced off, gasping with
relief. The thought had crossed my mind that they were going
to break my glasses because I had frustrated them in dodge ball.
I'm sure I set an East 32nd Street record for the three-block run,
returning shortly with the two sticks: two for a penny, weep for
what is lost. Tom took the sticks without thanks and gave one
to his brother, who had pulled the button off Frankie's new cap.
Frankie still squatted there, tears in his eyes, looking at the three

of us now with hatred. He could see I was on the other side. I
sold Frankie down the river and waited for new orders.

"Can you get us some potatoes?"

"No," I said, "I don't think so." Tom glared at me. "Maybe one."

"Make it a big one," he said. "I feel like a mickey." Mickeys were
what we called potatoes baked in open fires. All over Flatbush
you could smell the acrid aroma of charred potatoes.

"My cap," said Frankie. Kevin dropped it in a puddle from
yesterday's rain and stepped on it. Ruined. Frankie picked it up,
blindly, holding it with two fingers, and stumbled up the steps
to his front door. We lived in a row of attached two-story brick
houses, quite respectable, though sliding, with a few steps in
front (on which we played stoop ball) and a handkerchief-patch
of lawn, surrounded by a small hedge. In front of our house was
the lamp post by which I could read at night, and next to it a
slender young maple tree that my father would tie to the lamp
post during strong winds.

I went through the alley to our back entrance and found my
mother working in our Victory Garden of swiss chard, carrots,
radishes, beets. My father went fishing in Sheepshead Bay every
Saturday, a mixed blessing as he would come back loaded with
fish but in a generally unstable condition so we never knew what
to expect. Today I was glad, as it would make my theft easy. My
mother looked up as I passed. "Littlejim, are you all right?" She
has always been able to look right into my heart as if it were
dangling from my nose, a gift for which I frequently wished to
strangle her.

"Of course," I said with scorn in my lying voice, "I'm just
thirsty."

"Well, have a nice glass of milk, sweetheart," she said, wiping
her forehead and peering at me. I trotted into the kitchen and

looked in the potato pail beneath the sink. There were around ten left, so I took a large one and a small one, stuck them in my shirt, and went out the front door. The Murphys were waiting down the street by the vacant lot, the fire already going.

Thus began my life of crime, which lasted almost eight months, well into 1943, for which I showed natural gifts, except temperamentally. I was always trembling but never caught. I graduated from potatoes to my mother's purse, from packs of gum at the candy store ("that Nazi wop," said Tom) to packs of cigarettes at the delicatessen: the owners watched the Murphys while my quick hands stuffed my pockets full of contraband. Under the protection of the Murphy brothers, who beat up a German boy so badly that he was hospitalized, who dropped kittens into the sewers, who slashed the tires of cars owned by parents who tried to chastise them, I collected small sums of money from boys much larger than myself. Like Mercury, god of cheats and thieves, I was the swift messenger for Tom and Kevin Murphy.

I loved them. They needed me, I thought, not reading them well. What they needed was temporary diversion, and for a while I provided that. Kevin was virtually illiterate, so, beginning with the Sunday comics one afternoon, I became his official reader. He read (looked at) nothing but comic books—*Plastic Man, Superman, Captain Marvel, The Katzenjammer Kids. Sheena, Queen of the Jungle* was his particular favorite because of her lush figure and scanty clothing.

"Get a load of that," he'd squeak (Kevin, and to a lesser extent Tom, had a high nasal whine). "What the freak is she saying?"

" 'Stand back,' " I'd read. " 'There's something in there!' "

"Freaking A!" Kevin would shout. He got terrifically excited by these stories.

It was not long before I was talking like the Murphys, in a

high squeaky voice with a strong Brooklyn accent, punctuated
(in school) by swear words and (at home) by half-swear words
that I didn't understand. My mother was horrified.

"What the freak is this?" I'd shrill at some casserole she was
placing on the table.

"Jimmy! Don't use language like that!"

"Freak? What's wrong with that?" I'd say in abysmal igno-
rance. "Freak, freaky, freaking. It doesn't mean *anything*. Everyone says it." This is 1943, remember.

"I don't care what everyone says," my father would shout,
turning red. "You watch your lip around here, and fast!"

On weekends we sat around a fire in the vacant lot, smoking
cigarettes I had stolen (the Murphys favored the Lucky Strike red
bull's-eye pack, which showed through the pockets of their white
shirts) and eating mickeys which I had scooped up from in front
of Tietjen's Grocery. About six of us were generally there—the
Murphys, myself, and two or three of the tougher kids on the
block whose faces have faded from my memory.

One spring day when rains had turned the lot into trenches of
red clay among the weeds and abandoned junk—people dumped
old stoves, broken bicycles, useless trash there—Tom Murphy
had the idea for The Lineup. This was based on a combination
of dodge ball from school and firing squads from the daily news.
The idea was to catch kids from the neighborhood, line them up
like enemy soldiers against the garage that backed on to the lot,
and fire clay balls at them. They would keep score and see who
was the best shot.

"Go get Frankie and his little brother," Tom told me. To Tom,
almost everyone was an enemy. "They're playing Three Steps to
Germany in front of his house. Tell him you want to show him
something."

Since the cap incident, Frankie had become much more alert, darting into his house whenever the Murphys appeared on the block. He often looked at me with reproach during the past months, but never said anything, and I dropped him like a red hot mickey, though he had been my only real friend.

"He won't come," I said. "He won't believe me."

"He'll believe you," Tom said. Kevin stepped on my foot and shoved me into the bushes. It was the first time he had turned on me and I couldn't believe it. I looked at Tom for help.

"Go get Frankie and Billy," he repeated. "We'll hide in the bushes."

I walked miserably down the block, sick at heart. Shouldn't I just duck into my own house? Shouldn't I tell Frankie to run? Somehow these alternatives seemed impossible. I was committed to the Murphy brothers. While my childhood went up in flames, I spoke through the blaze in my head and talked Frankie into coming to the lot for some mickeys. I was bright-eyed with innocence, knowing full well what I was doing, cutting myself off from my parents, my church, selling my friend for the love of the Murphy brothers, whom I wanted to love me back.

"My ma gave me two potatoes, they'll be ready in a couple of minutes. You and Billy can split one."

Frankie wanted to believe me. "Have you seen Tom or Kevin today?"

"They went crabbing," I said, glib with evil. "Their Uncle Jake took them out on the bay. They promised they'd bring me some blue-claws."

The walk down the block to the lot, maybe two hundred yards, was the longest I've ever taken. I babbled inanely to keep Frankie from asking questions. Billy was saved when he decided to go play inside instead—he didn't like mickeys anyway, a heresy ad-

mitted only by the very young. I didn't dare protest, for fear of
making Frankie suspicious. The lot appeared empty and we were
well into it before Kevin stood up from behind a gutted refrigerator; Frankie whirled around right into Tom, who twisted his thin
arm and bent him to the ground.

"Lineup time!" shouted Kevin, "freaking A!" as they carried
the kicking boy over to the wall. There they threw him down and
tore off his shoes, making it difficult for him to run over the rusty
cans, cinders, and thorny bushes. They had made a large pile of
clay balls already, and the three other boys began firing them mer-
cilessly at the cowering figure, their misses making red splotches
on the garage wall. This was the first Lineup in our neighborhood,
a practice that soon escalated so that within a few months boys
were scaling the lethal tin cans their parents flattened to support
the war effort. The Murphy boys held back momentarily, looking
down at me.

"Where's Billy, you little fag?" Tom asked.

"He wouldn't come. He doesn't like mickeys." I was wincing
at Frankie's cries as a clay ball would strike him.

"Maybe you ought to take his place," Tom said. "One target's
not enough." Kevin reached from behind and snatched off my
glasses, plunging me into the shadowy half-world in which I was
always terrified. Without my glasses I could hardly speak, and I
said nothing as they pushed me back and forth like a rag doll.

"You see that hoop there?" one of them said. "Bring it over
to the garage and stand in it, you four-eyed freak." Squinting, I
could barely make out a whitish hoop lying near the fire. I bent
down and grabbed it with my right hand and went down on my
knees with a piercing scream that must have scared even the Murphy brothers. They had heated the metal hoop in the fire until it
was white hot and my hand stuck to it briefly, branding me for

life. The older boys whooped and ran off, firing a few last shots at Frankie, Kevin not forgetting to drop my glasses in the fire, where my father found them the next day.

I knelt doubled up, retching with pain and grief while Africa was falling to the Allies and our soldiers battled through the Solomon Islands: the tide had turned. I went home and had my hand attended to—first degree burns!—and slept dreamless as a baby for the first time in years.

The Source of Trouble

Debra Monroe

I was in eighth grade, reading *Teen Beat,* an article called "Double Dare—What To Do When You Accept Two Dates for Saturday Night," and I threw the magazine down on my ribcord bedspread and looked at myself in the mirror, thinking Geez, counting on my fingers the months until high school, four. My mother says it's short, the time of pale formals covered with net and reinforced with push-up stays that make your cleavage deep, the time between when your date toasts you with his cocktail poured in your shoe and when your husband reads the paper while you pace the floor and the baby pukes. So I hung my red nylon windbreaker over the lamp to make the room dark and I stuck my gum over my teeth to cover my braces, and I thought about how the handyman at school once said to me, "Devita, I think about you every night."

I took my gum off my teeth, put my windbreaker on, picked up my pen and spiral-bound notebook, and went outside and sat on the porch and stared at the lake and made my Popularity Success List Plan: Be nice to boys, all boys, don't make fun of the hair on their chest or legs. Stop saying BALLS. Don't tell that joke about Tarzan's snake being in Jane's cave. Make friends with the

smart and pretty girls at Butternut Consolidated High when you
go there in the fall, but still be nice to Melissy Smith and Laura
Plus (best friends from Glidden).

My mother walked onto the porch and said, "Devita, I got this
letter from Butternut High which says you're going to take the
tour next week so you'll know your way around in the fall." I
threw my notebook down. "I forgot," I said. I'd envisioned myself
in short colorful dresses, wearing makeup and heels, my hair long
and flowing and boys standing next to their lockers and whistling through their teeth. I'd counted on having all summer to
get ready. My mother sat down next to me and stroked my hair.
I smelled her Dove soap smell and my love surged. I can't wait
until I'm a woman. "I'll kill myself," I said. She said, "We'll order
something from Montgomery Wards and it'll be here in time for
the tour."

The next day at school, which in Glidden is a one-room building with kids from first to eighth grade, I passed Melissy a note
which asked what she was going to wear. She put her hair in her
mouth and said, "Depends on what's clean, I guess." So at noon
I asked Laura and she said, "Jeans because if you overdress you'll
look nervous." I'd considered a blue skirt and blouse with shiny
pumps but Laura had a point; I told my mother to order the pale
green shorts ensemble with matching sandals.

It turned cold and rainy that day and when I ran down the
driveway to fetch the paper wearing my bathrobe and flip-flops, I
came back shivering and drenched. My mother said, "Devita, you
can't wear the new outfit." We had a fight and by the time Laura's
dad was there to pick me up my face was puffy, my nose was
running, and I was wearing the shorts outfit but with thick socks
and oxford shoes and I had my windbreaker which I planned to
ditch. Melissy Smith was wearing a wool dress. Laura wore jeans
and sneakers and a sweatshirt that said ANDY'S FISHING LODGE.

Genius, I thought: Butternut High is small potatoes, her clothes seemed to say.

We saw the gymnasium, the cafeteria, boys running lathe in shop class, and Mr. Darby dropped us off at the Home Ec room. "Wait here," he said. He came back a few minutes later with two girls. "Del Rae Thomas and Valerie Verholtz live right here in Butternut," he said, "and they're going to be freshmen next fall too." Mr. Darby left, and Del Rae got a box of vanilla wafers out of the cupboard and Valerie turned to us and said, "Have you met the girl from Fifield yet?" Del Rae rolled her eyes and, wiping cookie crumbs off her mouth, pointed at Valerie and said, "Valerie burns."

Valerie said, "I do not."

I said, "What do you mean, burns?"

Mr. Darby opened the door. "This is Bernice Isabell from Fifield," he said.

Bernice was wearing a Schlitz beer T-shirt and a pair of hip-huggers so low they had only three snaps. She smiled and her corner teeth stuck out. Mr. Darby counted us and said, "Okay, that's all the freshmen girls for next year." He shut the door and Del Rae said, "What about you, Bernice? Do you burn?"

Bernice didn't answer.

Del Rae sniffed the air. "Have you heard that theory that if your shampoo and soap and perfume and talcum don't match, and you use them all at the same time, you smell like dog shit?" Bernice put her hands on her hips and stared at Del Rae. Del Rae said, "And some people just roll in it."

Mr. Darby opened the door. "Have you girls made friends yet?" he said. "It's time for the pep rally."

A few weeks later, after school let out in Glidden, Melissy and Laura and I got the same letter, spidery, slant-forward handwriting on notebook paper: A Get Acquainted Before School Starts Next Year Surprise Party for Bernice Isabell, Bring PJs and Blankets. I took it to the living room to show my mother. She was wearing a wide dress with her crackly slip and pouring cocktails. "You drink too much," she said to my father, "and you fall asleep on the couch at eight o'clock."

He said, "I work hard all day, Arla, and I come home and I want to relax."

She said, "I'm sick of it."

I sat down next to my father and smelled him. I love his silky cheeks where he shaves. I showed him the letter. "Why is that familiar," he said, "that name? Oh. They own that tavern in Fifield." A car pulled up in our driveway. "Arla," he said, "find out who that is and send them away."

My mother opened the door. "It's Jack Burns," she said. Jack Burns lifted her off the floor and twirled her. "Darla," he said. She smiled and straightened her hair. My father stood up and shook Jack's hand. "You're not going to keep us out until dawn drinking and carousing tonight," he said. "I'm tired."

Jack said, "Get me a highball." He smiled at me. "How are you, little girl?" I didn't answer. He said, "Aren't you glad to see me?" Again, I didn't answer. My mother said, "Have some manners, Devita." Jack Burns said, "And after I gave her my swizzle stick collection too."

Laura's dad gave us a ride to Fifield and on the way there I said, "Do you think Bernice is weird?" and Melissy pushed her glasses up her nose and said, "I never thought about it." Laura said, "She is, but Del Rae is mean." Mr. Plus pulled into the parking lot of Isabell's Castle Hill Retreat and pointed at the beer sign. "You girls stay away from the tavern," he said, "you're too young."

He drove away and we stood in the parking lot holding our stuff and no one came so we went inside and a fat lady with piled-up hair who turned out to be Bernice's mom said, "Where did you girls come from?" I said, "We're here for Bernice's Get Acquainted Surprise Party." She said, "Bernice's surprise party?" She wrinkled her nose. "Bernice!" Bernice walked into the bar-room and smiled. "Hi," she said. She said to her mother, "I asked some friends over."

We went outside and across this field, and Bernice opened the door to a small house, knotty pine with checked curtains inside. She said, "This used to be where we lived before we built the bar and put the house on top and now I use it for a clubhouse." She opened the top drawer of a dresser. "Look." There were packs of Marlboro cigarettes, a pint of blackberry brandy, all the makeup you'd ever need. I opened a tube of mascara and used the tip of the wire-coil wand to paint a beauty mark on my chin.

Someone knocked at the door. Bernice looked out the window. "Geez," she said, "I can't believe they came."

"Who?" I asked.

She said, "Those bitches from Butternut." Del Rae Thomas and Valerie Verholtz walked in. Del Rae said, "We're here for your surprise party, Bernice." Bernice said, "You know, I was so surprised. I had no idea. My mother planned it, you know."

We started putting on makeup and Bernice got these slips out and said, "These used to be my mom's when she was thin and they look cool with lipstick." She took her T-shirt off and stood there like she wanted us to see her knockers, and she took her jeans off too and put the slip on. She reached in the drawer for a cigarette and lit it and looked at herself in the mirror. "See what I mean?" she said.

A car pulled up. "Well," Valerie Verholtz said, "that's my cue.

Good-bye."

"Where's she going?" Laura asked Del Rae.

Del Rae said, "With Rocky, her boyfriend, her parents try to keep them apart, it's so sad. But you know they do burn, I know for sure."

Bernice said, "How do you know?"

Del Rae said, "They did it once when she was on her period."

"How do you know that?" I said.

She said, "I just do. Bernice, do you have some snacks?"

Bernice said, "There's that blackberry brandy and me and Devita will go get food." She tucked her slip into a pair of jeans and put a flannel shirt on, unbuttoned and hanging open. We were walking across the field and stars were twinkling and the grass was cool on my feet. Bernice put her arm around me. "We have a lot in common," she said, "like best friends." She opened the door to the bar and said, "Now get all the beef jerky you can and I'll go for potato chips."

We stood in the doorway and she looked around and her face lit up. "Peanut," she said. A tall guy in a plaid jacket walked over and set his beer down. "Bernice," he said, "you look dandy." Above the V her slip made her chest was delicate and pale. She gave me a quarter. "Play the jukebox," she said.

That's where I met Tim Koofall. He was drinking orange pop and playing pinball while his father drank beer, and it turned out we had the same favorite song: "Gentle on My Mind." Bernice and Peanut were standing in the corner between the bathroom and the pay phone and Bernice's mother yelled, "Peanut, I've talked to you about this before, now get the hell out and don't come back unless you can leave Bernice alone." He left and Bernice walked over and said, "I'm meeting him outside. Forget about the snacks."

In the parking lot Bernice and I stood next to Peanut's Clover

Leaf delivery truck and she shoved bags of pretzels under my sweatshirt. "I'll meet you at the house later," she said. I started walking away and the door to the bar opened and Tim Koofall said, "Would you like to go for a walk by the lake?"

We were standing on the pier and looking at the lights on the water, and he told me he was going to be a junior at Butternut High next fall, and he said, "If there was one thing you could change in your life, what would it be?" My hands were in my pockets and I kept my arms close to my sides to keep the snacks in. "I wish my pet rabbit hadn't died," I said. I looked at his profile, and he was wearing a hat with a bill and his nose was one of those fierce-looking ones like I never used to think was handsome. He said, "There's always one incident you can zero down to as the source of trouble and everything bad that happens after it happens because of it."

"An incident?" I said.

He reached for me and the bags of snacks crunched. "What's that noise?" he said. My heart thump-thumped. "Pssst," Bernice said from the bushes. "My mother's on the rampage."

We went back to the house and Del Rae and Laura stood with their hands on their hips. "How dare you leave me here," Laura said. Del Rae said, "I'm starving." Bernice said, "You'll have to wait." She opened the drawer. She reached in my shirt and got the snacks out and threw them in; she ran around picking up cigarettes and ashtrays and lipsticks, and she threw the dresser scarf in too because it had rouge on it. "The blackberry brandy," she said, "where is it?"

Laura handed her the empty bottle. "Melissy drank it," she said.

Bernice's mother walked in as we slid the drawer shut. "There better not be boys here," she said, opening a closet door. "Wasn't there another girl?" No one answered. "Yes," Del Rae said then, "she's sleeping." Bernice's mother walked across the room and pulled the covers back and looked at Melissy. She said, "Does she always wear silver eye shadow to bed?" She leaned closer. "Why are her teeth purple?"

Laura was at my house a few weeks later and we were sitting in the wicker chairs on the porch and she said, "We should keep in mind we're going to have boyfriends soon and we should practice kissing and the things we want to say back when they say they love us."

My parents were in the next room. My mother said, "There's no decent restaurant for three counties." My father said, "So let's stay home." My mother said, "That's hardly the point." She walked away and a door slammed.

"Kiss each other?" I asked Laura. She looked at me. "No," she said, "let's work on our tans." We went down to the boathouse roof, which is flat and overlooks the lake from one direction and the county highway from another. We spread towels and put oil on and laid there, eyes closed, blue-flies buzzing around, and Laura said, "Do you think Melissy is slow?"

I said, "Retarded?"

She said, "About puberty."

Wheels screeched. We sat up. Peanut got out of his Clover Leaf truck. "I thought I recognized you," he said to me. He looked at Laura and all of a sudden it seemed sleazy that she was wearing a halter. She said, "Who's this?" I said, "Bernice's boyfriend." He said, "Nah, Bernice is like a kid sister to me." He tossed a pack of gum to Laura and said, "How about coming for a boat ride?" I said, "How are we going to tell my parents we're going for a boat ride?" He said, "Meet me at the public landing in fifteen minutes."

Laura walked that half-mile to the landing so fast my feet got scuffed, and Peanut was waiting in the boat. Laura sat down next to him and put her hand on his thigh. He gave her a life jacket.

"Don't wear it," he said, "just hang onto it."

I said, "Do we have to jam into these high waves so fast?"

Peanut said, "Have you seen the creek?"

I said, "She has to baby-sit at five."

Peanut slid the rudder to the right, then to the left. Water washed into the boat and suddenly we were in the creek, branches hanging low. He turned the engine off and threw a magazine to me, *The Bass Fisherman.* "I don't feel like reading," I said. He said, "If you wade to shore and walk through the woods for a hundred feet you'll find a road that'll take you home."

I got out and sank to my ankles in mud and when I reached the shore my cutoffs ripped on a brambleberry bush, and I turned around and saw Peanut untying Laura's halter. Sunlight was dribbling down through the trees and her knockers glowed, round and small, pale as snails. "Laura," I said. She said, "What is it?" I said, "If you don't come with me I'll tell." She grabbed her halter and jumped out of the boat. "Balls," she said.

She didn't talk as my father and I drove her home, and she slammed the door when we stopped in front of her house and she got out of the car. My father backed down the driveway and said, "You seem sad, Petunia." I didn't answer. He said, "It's a hard time." I bit my lip and nodded.

"We don't understand her," he said.

"Guess not," I said.

He rubbed his hand through his hair and sighed. "What's her trouble?"

"Who?" I said.

He shook his head and shifted. "It seems like it started as soon as we moved here."

My parents planned my birthday party so they'd take me and my friends across the lake on the pontoon boat to Andy's Fishing

Lodge for dinner. Melissy and Laura arrived first and we were standing in the driveway when Del Rae's dad's car pulled up and she got out and handed me a box of donuts. "For breakfast," she said. "We own Thomas Grocery Emporium, you know. Valerie's not coming." She looked at the three of us. "I have the most dastardly secret."

Jack Burns drove up. "Darla," he yelled as he got out of his car.

My father came outside and said, "Jack, we're having a party for Devita but you're welcome to join us." My mother stood in the doorway. My father said, "Arla, it's Jack Burns." She came outside in a white dress with pink palm trees on it and she was wearing pearls. "Wonderful," she said. She smiled.

My father said, "Are we ready?" I said, "Bernice isn't here yet." He said, "The girl from Fifield?" I said, "I'm not going without her." My mother said, "It's supposed to storm so we better go now. We'll leave a note for Bernice on the door."

We were at the lodge eating chicken, and my father and mother and Jack Burns were at the next table, drinking old-fashioneds, and Bernice burst in the door. "Geez," she said, "I hardly made it. Peanut was going to give me a ride and then my mother wouldn't let him, and finally I got a ride with Tim Koofall and his dad." I looked up and saw Tim. He pushed his cap back and smiled. "Happy birthday," he said.

We finished eating and Tim and I took a walk outside and it was dark and he said, "I have this one dream over and over." We stood on the pier by the moored boats and listened to the faraway, tinkly music, and people in the lodge were laughing. Tim jumped onto our pontoon and gave its steering wheel a twist and the night wind blew his hair back, and he said, "I'm walking through these woods and branches scratch me and bugs bite me and it's humid, and I come to a clearing and you're in front of a house with a little rake. That's all," he said, "but I liked it."

"Devita," my mother called.

"I have to go back," I said.

I walked up the path and the music in the lodge stopped, and I opened the door and my father was standing in front of the pin-ball machine holding Bernice's arm with one hand and Laura's with the other, and they were swinging at each other. "Get the hell out," he yelled at Peanut who was skulking by the side door, "and if I get wind of you poking around fourteen-year-old girls again I'll have you sent up." Peanut got in his truck and drove away, and my father looked at me and shook his head. "And the goddamn Smith girl was trying to get Jack Burns to buy her lime vodka," he said.

My mother said, "It's time to go now."

We walked down to the pier and Bernice said, "I guess I'll ride back to Fifield with Tim Koofall and his dad because I couldn't stand to sleep near Laura." She took off running. "She has a ride home with someone else," I told my mother.

Melissy and Laura and Del Rae and I sat on boat cushions on the front of the pontoon and my father started the engine. Del Rae leaned close and said in a whisper, "Don't tell anyone but Valerie is pregnant and trying to get an abortion, and her parents are Catholic and someone will tell them and she and Rocky will have to get married and I'll be a bridesmaid. That's what I think."

Melissy chewed on her hair. Laura said, "That's interesting."

"You were outside with Tim Koofall," Del Rae said. "It's sad how his father used to be a drunk and then wasn't, and Tim's mother died and his father started drinking again and Tim hardly gets supper now or a place to sleep, and nothing but ugly clothes to wear."

Clouds were rolling across the sky at intervals and in the wake behind us water glimmered. Jack Burns was singing a song about a lady named Mrs. Bliss. "Hush, Jack," my mother said. "As I was saying, my husband and child, their happiness—it's my life."

On the first day of school I was wearing nylons and a new dress and Mr. Darby called us into his office, Laura and Melissy and Bernice and Del Rae and me. We sat in a row. He rubbed his hand over his crew cut and said, "I have something to say."

"It's about Valerie," Del Rae whispered.

He looked at us, his eyebrows wiggly, and he clicked his pencil on the desk. "Valerie Verholtz won't be attending school," he said. "I understand there's going to be a large wedding and many of you will be bridesmaids, punch-servers, whatever. It's an unusual situation for ninth grade and I hope you'll help us maintain a normal atmosphere here. And I urge all of you to make an appointment for the lecture with the school nurse."

A pep rally was going on outside, a bass drum booming, bonfires crackling. Del Rae said, "My father donated those hot dogs." Someone knocked on Mr. Darby's door. "If you'll excuse me," he said. He left the room.

Del Rae turned around. "I talked to Valerie," she said, "and I'm maid of honor and I get to wear a pink dress. Laura and Devita, you're bridesmaids, with pink dresses too. You pass the guestbook, Melissy, and wear a blue dress. Bernice, you can wear anything you want."

Laura said, "A T-shirt. Or, for a formal look, a slip."

Del Rae said, "The dance is at your mother's tavern, Bernice, because no other place would let Valerie or any of us in."

Mr. Darby walked back into the office. "These are precisely the sorts of conversations I hope you'll avoid at school. Now go to the pep rally. Devita, I want to see you." I waited while the others left. He closed the door and folded his arms and sat on the desk. "If something's wrong at home," he said, "we'd like to help."

My father had his suitcase out. "It's a short trip," he said, "and I deserve it." My mother paced the floor and she was wringing her hands. "Our daughter is in the next room putting on her first formal, and for what? Prom? A party? No. A wedding for one of her pregnant school friends. I tell you I won't stay here. If you leave on this trip tonight you'll be surprised when you come home."

I knocked on the doorframe. "How do I look?" I said.

My father's tie was untied. He ran his hand through his hair and smiled. "Like a grown-up," he said.

My mother said, "You should borrow my new earrings, honey." She opened her dresser drawer and I turned to my father and said, "How long will you be gone?" He said, "Not long. You two will be fine." I said, "Will you be fine, Mother?" She waved her rattail comb in the air and smiled. "Of course," she said, "I'll curl up with a book."

It rained hard during the wedding, and afterwards we ran down the sidewalk in front of the St. Francis de Sales and got in a car and Rocky's friend, the best man, drove us to Fifield. The jukebox played a waltz, and we drank punch. I said, "Rocky was crying during the vows." Del Rae shrugged. Laura said, "How do we ditch these bouquets so we can dance?"

Tim Koofall tapped me on the shoulder. He was wearing a suit coat and a white shirt. "May I have the honor?" he said. I said, "I don't know how to dance." He said, "Then let me get you a fresh drink."

He walked away and I watched Rocky and Valerie kissing

under a paper wedding bell and I thought how she was a woman now, her husband and new-coming baby the center of her life. "Melissy had her first date last night," Laura said, "with the handyman from Glidden School." Bernice's mother walked past, setting mint cups on tables. "Have you seen Bernice?" I asked Laura and Del Rae.

Laura said, "Let's go to the bathroom."

We went into the bathroom, which is a storage room with a toilet and a sink, and I held Laura's sash off the floor while she peed and I said, "The handyman from Glidden used to have a crush on me." Laura said, "You're not jealous, are you?"

Del Rae said, "You're interested in Tim Koofall now."

Laura said, "I hate his suit coat. What does he talk about?"

I said, "Nothing."

Laura said, "That night at Andy's Fishing Lodge?"

I said, "About a dream he had."

She stood up and looked at herself in the mirror. "His suit coat wouldn't be bad in the dark," she said, "if you were squinting."

"A wet dream," Del Rae said. "Do you know what that is?"

Laura said, "His nose is ugly."

I threw my punch in her face and it ran in pink streams down it, and she blinked and licked her lips. I went outside then and ran around and went down to the lake and stopped in front of the pier and took my sash off and tied it around my head and walked back and forth and thought about Tim's suit, how he just needed a tie. A branch above my head creaked and Bernice slid to the ground. "Geronimo," she said. "I thought you were Laura and I was going to kill you." I said, "I need a ride home."

So I was in the front seat of Peanut's Clover Leaf truck, barreling down the road, and he downshifted and said, "I don't know what it is about you but I've never had the urge." He pulled into my driveway and said, "God, I hope that's not your old man's car." Rain was falling hard and I couldn't see. I fumbled for my key and a single light burned, and I heard my mother singing. I opened the door. She was on the couch in her yellow dress with the ribbons and she was holding a glass.

"Is Dad home?" I said.

She shook her head.

I pointed to some shoes. "Whose are those?" In the next room, the toilet flushed. "Jack Burns," my mother said. He walked in.

My mother said, "Now get out of those wet clothes, Devita, and I'll bring you the hot-water bottle." I went into my bedroom and threw my dress on the floor and got under the blankets and waited for her. I listened to her laughter, its avalanches and slides, Jack Burns's bass echo, ice cubes clinking in glasses and the tall spoon scraping the pitcher. "So free, so free, so free," she said. I thought about my father rubbing his hand in his hair, Tim standing beside me on the pier, the one incident you zero down to, and the wind ripped through trees outside and the light through my window was spastic and my walls swelled and wriggled, and then it was dawn. And Jack Burns got in his car and drove away.

The Expendables

Antonya Nelson

At one end of the block a funeral was being held and at the other end a wedding would begin in an hour. It was ironic: at our house people were arriving dressed like ice cream cones, pastels and sorbets (the tuxedo I'd rented was called Chocolate), bearing gifts wrapped in silver and lavender, while down the street you never saw so much navy and black. Beginnings and endings. This corner and that.

My sister Yvonne was marrying Chris the Sicilian. Our family had its doubts. Only a month ago Chris had sold one of my brothers a Cadillac for a song. Mint condition, 1964, black interior of leather. Well, not quite mint; there were the holes along the side—bullet holes or repair holes, depending on who told the story. And the fact that the test drive took place at three in the morning, around the graveyard at St. Augustino's. But my sister had been married before; everyone fell back on that for reassurance: this time she knew what she was doing. Her first husband, Mark, modeled and waited tables, and would have been perfect except that he was better looking than Yvonne. I think he weighed less, too, by the time they divorced, though they were still friendly. He was here today, helping my mother with the buffet; she didn't

know what to do with some of the unattractive dishes Yvonne's
roommates had contributed to the party. Mark told her he had a
feeling for aesthetics. He would find some way to "elegantize"
the eggplant and squash.

My beat was car parking, which I got by saying I wanted to
serve drinks. My brother Leon, who'd begged to park cars, now
circulated, asking guests to name their poison. We'd worked this
out last night. Every time we met we slugged down a Kamikaze
each. Our Uncle Cy was mixing everything in plastic champagne
glasses, and the Kamikaze, served in a glass with such circumference, carried a powerful nose.

A good many of the guests were neighbors. Our family, whom
my father called "Catholic only in theory and size," had lived here
twenty-six years. We knew everybody, including the Gypsies on
the corner, the ones having the funeral. There'd been a large debate about inviting them. They hadn't lived in the neighborhood
long enough to be automatic guests. Plus, they insisted on painting their house Pepto-Bismol pink every spring. It's embarrassing
to have to admit that my family would discriminate on such a
basis, but it's dishonest to say that they didn't. It wasn't just the
paint (every spring, for God's sake). A year, even in Chicago,
couldn't do enough damage to merit a painting that often. It was
the furniture on the lawn, or what used to be the lawn.

One of the first things the Gypsies did when they moved in
was pave their front yard in big concrete squares. Then they set
up a sofa and a bunch of chairs and a table. They spent a great
deal of time out there, not really talking, not socializing exactly,
just sitting and watching the street. The men stood on the corner,
also not talking, most of the day. I'd see them when I went to
school; they'd be there when I got back. They broke for dinner
around six, then reassembled, toothpicks in their mouths, about
seven. The Gypsies had become a neighborhood landmark now,

something I pointed out to friends I brought home for the first time. I'd show them the house with the swastikas in the rock work, explaining that before Hitler they meant good luck, then the Gypsies' pink house, the clan out front relaxing on their furniture as if a TV game show was on in front of them, pleasantly numbed and distracted.

But today I saw no one on the furniture; in fact, the couch had disappeared altogether. The men, however, still stood on the corner, all in their suits and bow ties. One of them was tuning a violin, the nee-no, nee-no of catgut on catgut carrying down the block. The oldest man, I guess the grandfather, and I had a waving relationship so I waved today, smiling slightly at both of us in our monkey suits. He just nodded in my direction, his head heavy, it seemed.

The car I was waiting for was my Cousin Gerita's. She drove an orange Spitfire that I was dying to park. We'd already used up the curbs on both sides of the street, so I would have to take it to St. Augustino's and park in their lot. Two blocks; out of sight of the house; me and the Spitfire. I'd take Leon if he was convenient. I was only sorry we had to have the wedding at our house. If this had been Yvonne's first wedding, we'd be at St. Augustino's and nobody'd notice if I was there or not. Me and the Spitfire and an hour to kill.

But it was my father's business partner, Mr. Payton, who showed up next. His tie, though he was old and infirm, was thin and leather and silver. His wife wore a silk turquoise pantsuit that washed around her like so many scarves in a breeze. "Daniel," Mr. Payton coughed out to me, as if proving he could so remember names, bowing his head once while he pressed the warm key to his Lincoln in my hand. He'd separated it from his fat ring of other keys, as if I'd race over and rob his house, given the chance. He didn't even break stride. He was doing crooked things with money from his and my father's hotel business, but nobody'd been able to prove anything. The whole affair gave my father ulcers. As I navigated the Paytons' tub of a car to the church, I remembered it was at one of Mr. Payton's hotel functions that Yvonne had met Chris-the-probable-Mafioso.

When I got back, there were three other cars double-parked outside our house, the third one Gerita's. She'd washed it for the occasion. Its eyeball headlights shone. Gerita was leaning on the car she'd parked in front of, thin legs crossed at the ankles. Her dress was a silly bright yellow, but she looked great anyway.

"Hey, Cruiser. Nice tie." She reached up as if to straighten it and I looked down. She flipped me on the nose. "Gotcha."

"Leon's serving drinks," I told her.

"And doing a damn fine job." She nodded to the hood of the car she leaned on. Three Kamikazes waited. "Do me a favor and park my baby before you belt these down, huh Danny?"

"Who came in the other two cars?" I said.

Sighing, she waved a finger in the air. "A fart. His mother. Her sister. Another fart. Several brats. You think Yvonne will stay married this time?"

"Why not?"

"Good enough. Hope springs eternal. By the way, did I mention I like your tie?" She smiled and I made as if to look down again, nodding my head up in time for her to miss my nose. "I think you're quicker drunk than not," she said, heading with an exaggerated swagger for the house.

St. Augustino's lot was filling with our party's cars. Some people didn't wait for me to park them, just drove over themselves. I watched the people I didn't know unload, but they didn't look like Mafia to me. They looked, if it was possible, duller even than my relatives. Whenever I got in a group like that, a group of sort of middle-aged people with little kids, all wearing basi-

cally the same thing, I started thinking, *This group is expendable.*
I don't even know where it came from. I would get it riding the El
or standing around in a department store or in the waiting room
at the doctor's. A group like that could vanish from the face of the
earth and nobody'd notice. That's what I'd think. The problem,
of course, is that there I was, trapped among the expendables.

I ran back to the house, dying to get into the Spitfire, but cars
were starting to pile up. My heart dropped when I saw my mother
standing at the curb looking up and down the block, I presumed
for me.

"Let Leon help me," I told her, but she scowled, as if I'd addressed her in German.

"What's going on over there?" she said, aiming her glare down
the block.

"Funeral."

"Whose?"

I shrugged. "Where's Leon?"

"How do you know it's a funeral?"

"I saw the casket."

"They got a casket there? In the house? What do they mean
having a funeral at home?" She hardly paused before lighting into
me. "What are these drinks doing on Cy's car? Did you put these
here, Daniel? Alcohol can ruin a car's finish. You should know
that. I see Princess Gerita made it."

"Be nice."

"*You* be nice—you don't touch those drinks." She stared at
them evilly, tempted, I could tell, to dump them. This wedding
would give her ulcers. She and my father would have a matched
set. She loved Yvonne's first husband. She'd adopted him, hoping
for a reconciliation, a reprieve at the last minute. Yvonne hadn't
told her that Mark was gay, that he'd already found a new lover.
My mother is a person you can't imagine breaking this sort of

news to. So Yvonne told her they didn't spark. Period. With Chris, there was spark. There was lightning. That was probably what my mother objected to, all the electricity the two of them set off.

Yvonne's roommates pulled up and I cringed along with my mother, though we'd both seen their car plenty of times. They'd hand-painted an old Falcon purple and gold. Over the hood was an enormous silver cross. Other identifiable shapes dotted a landscape of gold clouds and purple hills. A rainbow broke in half when the passenger door opened. Neither of my sister's roommates had a driver's license or insurance, and whenever they parked they always left the key in the ignition. They'd once told me they believed responsibility had to come from within.

"You put that car somewhere out of sight," my mother hissed, turning for the house before Jennifer or Cleo stepped out.

Jennifer, tall and humorless, didn't say a word to me as she passed. It was because I refused to call her Cassandra, which was her witch name. No joke—she thought she was a witch. But Cleo gave me a pat on the shoulder. "It's very exciting, isn't it? I love weddings." She had flowers pinned all over her.

After I parked their car and the four others that had kept me from the Spitfire, I looked around to make sure neither Gerita nor my mother was in sight, and shot the Kamikazes down. I'd made Gerita promise me that if, God forbid, she died, she'd leave me her car. She'd told me that if she died, God willing, it would be *in* her car and she wouldn't leave anything recognizable for the living.

As I was adjusting the seat and the radio and the window and the gearshift and finally the rearview, I saw the Gypsies. They were coming down the street, lined up like a parade, the coffin rolling along on a wagon. I turned in the seat, willing them to disappear. They were coming my way, to St. Augustino's, of course, but that isn't what I thought of immediately. My first impression was that they were descending on me like an army, slowly but inevitably. When I was a kid, that's how Yvonne would chase me, not fast, but terribly slow, her feet falling like thuds of doom behind me.

I revved the Spitfire and took off with a squeal. I didn't mean to, it wasn't to show off. I just wanted to get away from the Gypsies. I didn't want to ruin their procession; I didn't want them to ruin my drive. But before I got to the end of the next block, there was Chris, sauntering with his groomsmen toward our house. Their silver tux jackets flapped in the wind and they passed a bottle among them. Chris was football-player big and so were his friends. Dressed alike, as they were, they looked like a team headed for victory. I honked and, after some confusion on Chris's part about where the noise had come from—for an instant his face had taken on a hard, aggressive, fuck-you kind of look before he saw who it was—he waved me down.

I checked the rearview again. Sure enough, there, reaching the end of our block, were the Gypsies, a bigger but less authoritative team, making their way our way. This was the end of my Spitfire ride, cut short before I'd even lost sight of my house. To make things worse, curb space had opened not ten yards in front of me. I made the best of parallel parking—shifting the full pattern each time between reverse and first—and then climbed reluctantly out, remembering to leave the radio at full force for Gerita to ignite to.

"Dan-*yell*!" Chris hooted. "What's the story with these yahoos?"

"Funeral," I said. My encounters with Chris were always tinged with my fear that he would find something to dislike about me and then punch me in the nose for it. Not that he'd ever touched me. Not even that he wouldn't recover quickly—the next time he saw me, he'd have completely forgotten what he'd disliked before.

We'd start fresh. Clean slate. But then I'd be just as likely to show
my flaw again, get punched once more.

"What?"

"A funeral. Someone has passed on." The procession waited
at the corner for the cross traffic to clear. They didn't pile up, but
instead stayed in parade formation. I heard violins.

"Passed on what?" his best man said. They all laughed, stomping around one another and wiping their mouths. My mother's
new ulcers had a hard day to look forward to. The bottle they
drank from was cherry vodka. Cherry vodka! I almost laughed.
He probably *was* Mafia; who else could be seen in public with
such a dopey drink.

The Gypsies crossed the street, one man on either side of the
procession holding a flat, no-nonsense hand up to stop traffic.
Please God, I prayed, don't let this become a scene. Though I fell
back on it frequently, prayer had never done me any good. Today
it failed, as always. Chris's gang of tuxedoed hoodlums began
whooping.

"Come on guys," I said in the direction of the Gypsy grandfather. He was close enough that I could see his right eyelid
twitter; he'd heard me. And, lucky me, Chris had not. I'd separated myself from him and his friends by staring, perplexed, at the
houses on the other side of the street, as if trying to remember an
address.

"Nice duds, dude," one of Chris's team said.

"Which one's the corpse?"

"Don't you guys know 'Beer Belly Polka'?"

The Gypsies, with the exception of the grandfather's eyelid,
showed no sign of having heard them. They faced St. Augustino's
and plodded on as if they wore blinders. The coffin seemed small
to me, the way the mummies at the Field Museum seemed small:

it was hard to imagine a human fitting the confines. Obviously, someone in the group had made the coffin: its grain was rough and there were knotholes, like two big brown misaligned eyes, facing me. At the rear of the group were the musicians, two violins and a huge bass. The music was weepy and too slow; I imagined baying hounds and tearful women. Chris's friends extended their left arms at their chins and sawed—air violins. Two little boys carried the bass, stooped over and scooting backwards like crabs, while a fat woman played, her arms circling the instrument. They were admirably coordinated.

"What a fucking blimp," Chris said, as the woman passed. She was the end of the parade. Her buttocks rolled under her faded black dress like the haunches of a rhino. I sighed, relieved they'd gotten by without incident.

"I'm about to become a married man!" Chris yelled at their backs. "Let's not have any more dying today, got it?"

Back at the party, Yvonne was explaining her philosophy to Gerita. "Every few years you have to change your life," she said. "I think about who I was the last time I got married—it's like a whole nother person. Remember? I was blond." Yvonne now had wiglike black hair, dry and frazzled, cut in the shape of Cleopatra's.

"But it's not just hair," Yvonne told Gerita. "One day I woke up and decided I wasn't happy being who I was. So I changed." She'd dropped out of college, begun steadily gaining weight, divorced Mark, moved in with the witch and the midwife. "You just have to set your mind and change," she told Gerita, wide-eyed with wonder at the simplicity of it.

"I change my life every day," Gerita said. "You think I would have worn something this subdued to a wedding yesterday?" She looked around at the pastels, rolling her eyes at me.

"Yvonne," I said. "Your husband and his henchmen hath arrived." Chris and the group had gotten sidetracked at the door, slapping backs with the rest of the men relatives, but I still felt responsible for delivering them into someone else's jurisdiction.

"Oh," Yvonne said, leaving us.

"If he's Mafia," Gerita said, "why didn't his family throw the party? Now, *that* would have been interesting."

Leon joined us, a silver tray of empty plastic glasses on his up-turned palm. "If they don't start this soon, Uncle Cy will embarrass us badly. You can bet on it. He's looped." Leon's voice broke and he giggled. "More looped than even me. What's the delay?"

"It's the damned harpist," my mother said, from behind Gerita. My mother was always sneaking up on people. She liked to pretend she was all-knowing. "Yvonne's damned harpist is over forty-five minutes late."

"Pardon her French," I said to Gerita.

My mother smacked me on the arm. "Go get your sister in here. I'm tired of entertaining her friends." I looked around at the people surrounding us. None of them were Yvonne's friends; they were neighbors, strangers, relatives. They weren't anybody's friends. Expendables.

Gerita and Leon and I found Yvonne in the grape arbor out back. It was badly overgrown with dead vines and weeds, and its floor was covered with fallen paint chips. We used to have two porch swings hung facing each other in the arbor. Our family used to eat dessert there in the summer. I'd had enough to drink to be nostalgic about it, back when Leon's feet couldn't reach the ground and when Milo was still on speaking terms with my father. Yvonne had been a quiet brown-haired girl with a clever sense of humor. She always knew exactly what you meant when you said something. She'd let you know when she caught your eye.

She and her bridesmaids, Jennifer and Cleo, and her ex-husband Mark, sat cross-legged on the dirty floor. A fake-antique Pears

Soap tray was in front of them, complete with gold tube, razor, and coke-filled Baggie. Yvonne looked up at us and smiled. Was it possible that her eyes had slid farther apart on her face since she was little? For a moment I couldn't reconcile the two girls, the sister from my childhood and the sister of today's wedding. "Tootsky?" she said.

"Yeah!" Leon dropped immediately to the floor.

"Pass," Gerita said, though she also sat down.

"Mother wants to know where your harpist is," I said.

"Your *damned* harpist," Gerita corrected.

Leon giggled again. He was leaning over the tray trying to manipulate a line up his nose.

"Sit," Mark said to me. "You're so tall when you're standing." I squatted next to Cleo, who immediately reached out and patted my penny loafer. She was a person who just naturally touched everyone around her. It was very reassuring. I thought suddenly, If we could just get rid of Jennifer, I wouldn't mind living with these five people. We could be very happy. How lucky I was, to know five people I liked well enough to live with.

"That's better," Mark said, smiling dreamily.

"Wouldn't it be nice if we could just sit out here all afternoon, just the bunch of us?" Yvonne said, looking at me. It was as if she'd read my mind. I felt better, believing she might have something left of her childhood self in her somewhere.

"Mm hmm," Cleo said.

Only Jennifer seemed to disagree. She was scowling down at the part in Leon's hair as he took a second line. It was probably her coke and now she saw it going to waste on my little brother.

"You look awfully pale," Mark said to Yvonne.

"It's true," Cleo said. "Have you been taking your potassium?"

"She's getting married," Gerita said. "She's got a right to be pale."

"To sing the blues," Leon sang.

"It's her hair," I said. "It's so black she looks pasty. But good."

"We'll rouge you before the big event," Mark told Yvonne. "We'll rouge you good."

"My mother wishes you were marrying me again," she said, sighing, dropping her plump hands into her lap.

"I'll tell her I'm sterile. That'll set her straight."

"You are?" Leon sat back, his eyes blinking slowly, like a doll's. If we weren't careful, he would pass out. "You aren't?"

"Only the Shadow knows." Mark pulled the tray from Leon. "Talk to me, Miss Pears."

"That's my line," Leon whined.

"No, your line is, 'RA hah hah hah hah.'"

Leon rolled onto his back laughing and then stayed that way, staring absently up at the twisted vines of the arbor roof.

Yvonne turned to her roommate. "I wish you had your Runes, Cassandra. I'd like to know how today will be."

"I always have my Runes." Jennifer said, glumly. She pulled a red velvet bag from a larger mesh bag beside her and began shaking it. Rocks rattled inside. Yvonne pulled one out.

"Well?"

"A portentous day to wed," Jennifer said, turning the rock over in her hand.

"Portentous," Leon echoed thoughtfully.

"Oh, good," Yvonne said, smiling brightly. Mark and I exchanged glances.

"Will she stay married?" Gerita asked. "Ask if she'll stay married."

"Will I stay married?" Yvonne turned her hopeful, over-made-up eyes to Jennifer. Another stone was extracted.

"Neither yes nor no."

"How can that be?"

Jennifer shrugged. She reached into the bag herself and pulled out three rocks, laying them before her quickly. "There's a dark element involved in this wedding. I'm sorry, Yvonne, but that's what the stones say." She didn't look sorry. Bad news seemed to brighten her.

"It's the Gypsy funeral," I said. "They marched by our house and left a shadow."

"Ask it will Wrigley Field ever get lights," Leon said, still on his back. "Wouldn't you love a night game?"

Eventually we had to drift in. We heard harp music.

The harpist was a woman in her fifties who worked with Yvonne at the bar. She had a big happy mouth that moved along with the music she was playing. I missed most of the ceremony because I was in charge of Leon, who kept insisting we were in heaven. He tottered around the foyer, signing the guest list now and then. I had too many sets of car keys in my pockets to be comfortable sitting anyway. When the first relatives emerged weeping from the living room, I hustled Leon out the front door. It was time for a spin in the Spitfire.

The sun was behind St. Augustino's now, casting a peculiar burnt orange shadow down the length of the block. The day had cooled since I'd last been out.

Leon waited until I'd opened his door and helped him aim his long legs into the passenger side footspace before he told me he couldn't possibly go for a ride.

"Why not? We'll roll down the window, cool your jets."

He shook his head emphatically. "I'll be ill," he said somberly, then belched. "Very ill."

I leaned back in the seat and hit the steering wheel with my palms. "You won't be ill," I said.

"I'll retch," he said. "Just smelling the inside of the car is making me queasy."

"How about around the cemetery? I won't go fast."

"I warned you," he said, raising his hands in a shrug.

I shouldn't have, but I started the engine anyway. We had only a little while before we'd be missed. I'd forgotten about leaving the radio on and it screamed out at us, making my heart jump.

"Don't think about your stomach," I yelled to Leon, over the engine and rushing air. We whizzed around the side and back lot of St. Augustino's and into the graveyard. Thousands of black crows took flight at the sound of the engine and thousands more when I began honking the horn. Because I'd learned to drive in the cemetery, with and without permission, I could have driven it with my eyes closed. The roadway was one lane and curved through the various sections of dead people the way I imagined the German autobahn cutting through that country. Everywhere we drove, crows flew out in waves before us, as if from the sheer power of the Spitfire's engine. It was dark enough to turn on the headlights, but I liked driving in the dusk. I felt I could actually be headed somewhere instead of only in a long convoluted circle.

"What?" I yelled over to Leon. "What'd you say?" But it was clear from his face what he'd said. I screeched to a halt and reached over to open his door. He threw up on the running board, on the side of the seat, on his own tuxedo leg, on the pavement. In sight of the Gypsies, whose faces, once the crows cleared, were set like so many frozen white masks in my direction.

We got the hell out of there.

Back at home my father's partner, Mr. Payton, was having a fit. He wanted to leave and I had his car key.

"Where have you been?" my father said. He never really got

furious with us. He was too tired. He let my mother handle fury.

"Leon wasn't feeling well. We went on a walk," I said. Leon, to his credit, looked terrible. He had bags under his eyes like bruises. Plus, I'd made him drink from the backyard hose before we went in and his tie was soaked.

"Mr. Payton would like his car," my father said.

Mr. Payton shook. Spit flew when he spoke. "Where've you put it? I was ready to leave fifteen minutes ago." For a moment I could only be amazed at how angry he was.

"We have a party," his wife said. She actually used a cigarette holder.

I volunteered to get the car, but Mr. Payton stuck his hand in my face. "Give me the key, boy." And when I'd pulled it from the tangle of other keys, he added, "I hope you remembered to lock the doors."

"What an ass," I said to my father as we watched them walk down the street, Mr. Payton still ranting.

"A real ass," Leon amended.

"Boys," my father said to us, as if to preamble a long speech, but then didn't go on. He rubbed his cummerbund, soothing his ulcers.

From nowhere, my mother appeared. "Gifts are being opened in there. I expect you'll want to see what they get?" She didn't wait for an answer. This was how she ordered us around.

But we went in. Leon in particular wanted to see how Yvonne liked her gift from him. The first time around, he'd given her wine glasses, all of which had been shattered during one of her fights with Mark.

"I like it," Yvonne said, holding up the Swiss Army knife.

Leon beamed. "It has a plastic toothpick," he told her. To me, it seemed a more dangerous present than the wine glasses.

They got crock pots and coasters and wall-hangings and pot holders and towels and bottles of wine. The best gift was from my Uncle Cy, a fifty-pound fruit basket he'd made himself, packed with everything that would qualify. Sitting on the table, it was taller than Yvonne. To keep the fruit upright, it was wrapped in plastic and tied with a red bow. Pineapple leaves sprouted from the top like a palm tree.

The real action of the day, the event no one would forget, I missed because I stole that fruit basket. While pretending to take all the gifts to Yvonne's room upstairs, I smuggled the fruit basket out the side door. It really did weigh fifty pounds, and I couldn't see over it as I tottered down the block.

The Gypsies' house was also lighted, though not with white light, like ours, but in a sort of murky orange light, like old streetlights. For once, none of them was outside. I had imagined simply setting the basket down at the grandfather's feet, bowing or something in sympathy, and then scurrying off. I could have left the basket on the doorstep, rung the bell, and run, but somehow it didn't seem the right gesture on the night of a funeral.

The one blond child in the family opened the front door. Her skull was too small for her eyes, which bugged out even farther when she saw the fruit. I was struck with momentary dumbness. I had no etiquette to fall back on; I'd never made a sympathy call before.

"Come in," someone said, from a hall door. I stepped in. Their house had a floor plan similar to ours, something you wouldn't have guessed from the outside. The foyer, like ours, had doors leading to all the other rooms of the downstairs, with a stairway at the end.

"I've brought fruit," I said, unnecessary as that was.

"Thank you," the voice said. "Mimi, help him set down his

fruit." The little girl led me to a white sideboard and patted its top. I set the basket down and looked at it, completely embarrassed. It was really such a monstrosity.

"I'm sorry," I said, hoping the apology covered everything— their loss (whoever it was), our family's not inviting the Gypsies to the wedding, my new brother-in-law's behavior, Leon's puking at the gravesite, my ugly gift—but the more I thought about it, the less likely it seemed. Outside, tires screamed around the corner. Of course, that would be one of *our* guests.

The voice, which I thought belonged to the grandfather, but which I now saw belonged to one of the younger men, again said, "Thank you." He stood with his arms crossed over his suit, his eyes burning dark holes in my chest. Even Mimi had retreated from my side and stood behind him. I backed out their front door, sweating in my monkey suit, glad to be outside.

Down the block, hysteria had broken out. People were running in and out, joining and leaving a clump of others on the lawn. Our front door slammed open and shut. I thought rice-throwing must be going on, some last-minute crying and hugging, but when I approached the clump broke open and there was Chris on the lawn, face and suit black with blood. I thought, *The Gypsies have killed my brother-in-law.*

He got shot in the head. Grazed, I guess you'd say. We couldn't call the police. Before he passed out, he'd made that clear, grabbing at Yvonne's dress with his bloody hands. They were not to find out. "I used to know him," he told Yvonne of the gunman, smiling like it was some kid from his first-grade class he'd just met again. Chris's guests, relatives and others, had already begun making preparations, phoning a private ambulance, phoning a private hospital. The private doctor, it turned out, was already among us, attending the wedding. My sister's second wedding ended with her husband being driven to the hospital. Yvonne couldn't even go with him. She would be called.

His guests left soon after, thanking my father for the party. The women, including my mother, Yvonne, Gerita, the harpist, and the roommates, were upstairs. We men took the front stoop.

"Is it Gotto?" my Uncle Cy asked. "Gotto or Gambolini or something like that? Was Chris one of them?"

"Maybe he wasn't but he wanted to be," Leon said. "I was thinking they had to shoot at him to initiate him."

"Who knows? What if they missed and killed him instead? I never heard of such a thing, but who the hell knows?" Cy leaned back on his elbows. "I was beginning to like him," he said. "He was a snook but I liked him anyway."

"That's the past tense," Leon pointed out.

"So it is," Cy said, nodding. He'd pulled off his suspenders and unbuttoned the top button of his pants. Men in our family develop a certain sagginess in their old age.

My father watched the street and I took my cue from him. What was there? Our neighbors' new cyclone fence, ugly enough on its own, but now made uglier by a threatening sign from the sheriff's department on the gate. I could almost read the words from where we sat. They'd been among the first to leave after the shooting, though I knew they were peeking out from their curtains to keep posted. Or maybe my father was remembering when we were all little children, three boys and a girl, a brown-haired, shy, sensitive girl who never seemed to be the one who'd cause trouble. I tried to imagine what worries must be specific to fathers concerning daughters, but how could I?

I said, "Yvonne says you have to change your life every now and then."

"Yeah?" Cy said. "Yeah?" He appeared to think about it. "Hunh," he said. "Today must count for something."

"Yvonne has been reincarnated as a lunatic," Leon said.

But my father said nothing. He wiped his hand through his slick, thin hair. I thought through all the parts of his life I knew about: my mother, his business partner Mr. Payton, my brother Milo in California, now Yvonne's new husband, Yvonne herself. It suddenly seemed to me, sitting there next to him, that I *was* him, I was my father and his life was happening to me, sitting on my house's front stoop, defeated. I was a man who'd somehow ended up here, married to a woman I no longer felt sparks with, working with a man I couldn't trust, ashamed for having lost my oldest son, so weak as to have allowed my daughter her foolish marriage, looking out a neighborhood gone not bad, but askew, with cyclone fences and Gypsies and shootings at weddings.

"How does she propose to do such a thing?" my father said. "How does she exactly change her life?" He was tired and sad and beaten. Yes, I thought, tired and sad and beaten myself, how does this miracle come about?

When there wasn't anything left of the evening, when we'd made as much sense of the senseless as we could, we left the scene of today's crime, the bloodstained patch of dirt by the front walk, the plastic champagne glasses upended like futuristic mushrooms grown out of some futuristic mulchy rain, the hulking shadow of the pink Gypsy house on the corner—we left it and entered our well-lit house, where soon we would be joined by the women. By then, my father would be his unfathomable self once again and I would be me, sent to retrieve my Cousin Gerita's Spitfire.

Banquet

Susan Neville

Alma sits alone at the table, watching her family line up for food. She will go last when the line is shorter. A daughter complains to her husband that every Oktoberfest banquet is the same, that it takes weeks to rid her clothes of the sour odor of kraut. The husband laughs, squeezes the daughter, and whispers something. Alma's sure, about humoring the old woman. Eat the sweet sausage, he's saying, buy the children cloth toys stuffed with some old lady's hose, cast-off shoes covered with macaroni sprayed gold. Alma says nothing, knows they care for her really, these older ones who feel the relationship, knows they're frightened and sometimes angry at what she might have passed on to them. Lately they give her pats instead of hugs. She has lived the last twenty-five years of her life with only one breast. It has been months since anyone kissed her on the mouth.

A great-grandson sits to her left, gives her an extra roll he's picked up in line, a sweet sticky roll with the fresh taste of yeast. Across the table a younger great-grandson's first scribblings dig through the paper cloth in places to the wood, drawn with his grandmother's pen, another of her daughters. Soon the table will be filled, a whole tableful of people there because of her. She never did, finally, teach school but she did something, didn't she? A granddaughter standing in line wears blue jeans, a flannel shirt. Alma never at church without white gloves, tight between the fingers. But doesn't say anything, remembers her mother saying *Change with the times, grow old with grace.* Earlier that same granddaughter bragged of how she would remain single until she was thirty-five, love a thousand men, and backpack in Europe, then become a mother and a nuclear physicist, said, Grandma, why did you never teach? Looked at her condescendingly, thinking, you could have done all this and you did nothing, poor woman. Alma explained again, the old story, about World War I, about German being taken from the schools as she was coming home on the train, filled with stories of school chums to tell her brothers, a degree from the small-town Indiana college in her lap, wrapped in leather, the degree that would allow her to teach children to speak her mother's language. And then rolling bandages, making socks, John back from the war, marriage, children, but the granddaughter didn't really listen—thought, years have passed between then and now, you could have done something.

This granddaughter wants to move away—to Paris, San Francisco, New York—says there is no continuity, only her freedom, will waste much time fighting her own mistakes, mistakes that Alma could point out. What are generations for if not for that? Alma, amazed, wonders how you face death alone in New York, her own father having told her that the family is like the revolving spokes on a wheel, that you see the spokes rising up behind you and falling in front of you, and when it's your turn to fall you're not afraid because more spokes are rising and the rest of the wheel keeps revolving.

The granddaughter walks over from the line, gives Alma an extra roll, then sits at the other end of the table, afraid to be like her. Can't be helped. And maybe she doesn't remember as much about being young as she thinks she does. Earlier, at the bazaar, she called the eleven-year-old grandson *Schnikelfritz* and kissed him as he stood talking baseball with a friend. He blushed and said, Oh Grandma, and now he comes and sits near her, red at the neck. Like the granddaughter, he spends much time deciding what he will be, though not in as much turmoil, knows everyone will expect him to be something. He talks of space shuttles, atomic power, thinks she knows nothing but memories of tin pails of beer carried to her father in the summer, ice carts pulled by horses. Alma thinks, no, too much emphasis on style, not substance. Widows eating the noon meal after church on Sunday. One had been a doctor, one a secretary, one a housewife. One had been crazy. All talk about the ocean, a pain in the joints, the color yellow, the taste of coffee. It comes down to that. There is that connection between friends. Alma watches her family ladling kraut from the huge kettles to their plates. All of the grandchildren standing unaware of the things that have come from her, a gift. A certain twist of a certain chemical causes the reddish hair, they know that. But there are things that they don't know.

She takes one of the sweet rolls from the pleated and waxed container. The amber liquid sugar settles in a pool at the bottom. Some sticks to her fingers. A grandson has a bead on the tip of his nose, the Reverend stands by the banquet table and smiles, a bit of caramel on his tooth. She smiles back. Clean German Protestant, enormous thighs, she's heard he sweeps the snow off the driveway of the manse every twenty minutes as it falls, and never has to shovel. She had a crush on him once, before the fat covered him like mounds of potatoes. Of course she never told him and never told John, decided not to feel guilty about it as long as it didn't hurt anyone. They were her thoughts and she had a right to them. It made her happy for a whole summer when she was twenty-four and John was thirty and working too hard.

She would come into the cool dark church in the afternoons to cut out pictures from picture books for the bulletin board in the cradle room, hoping she might catch a sight of him pacing at the end of a high-ceilinged hall, working on his sermon. She wore a cotton print dress and sat on the cool green linoleum by a crib, very aware of herself. She often laughed at this, knowing that he wasn't aware at all, and glad of it. She would see him in one of the dark halls, first a blur of dark suit and light brown hair, then her eyes would become used to the dark and she could see the serious features of his face in the same way, she thought, that the babies in the cradle room would see the picture of Mary she was cutting out for them, first as a blur of blue that was part of the brown corkboard, then as something separate and finally, at the end of two years, as something resembling a real person.

That was many years ago but she still thought of him with gratitude, could sometimes see the young man in the old. He helped her in the years after John died, told her to look for a sign, and she began to sit long hours in the sanctuary washed by the light from outside dyed deep blood colors as it filtered through the stained glass windows. A ray of royal blue that had once been white warmed her hand as she sat in her pew all that spring after John's death. The sign was this: things change form with ease, with abandon. There was much comfort in that.

Another granddaughter comes to the table, brings Alma a square of dark red Jell-O, half a pear trapped in the bottom like a small white turtle. Alma thanks her, wants to give her a gift also, points out the steam in the kitchen, a gas that had once been liquid, crowding against the window in the swinging door which leads into the banquet hall, leaving a film of moisture on the glass. But the granddaughter says, That's nice, accustomed to her excesses, doesn't know that Alma's trying to save her years of searching, goes down to the other end of the table and sits by the granddaughter in the man's shirt.

Other grandchildren and great-grandchildren come to the table. Some bring her Jell-O, others bring her rolls. One laughs, says, We're the Jell-O brigade. Alma knows she will remember that phrase forever, that that grandson will always be the leader of the Jell-O brigade. Never one to think of a phrase, she is always the one to make it stick. One of the women at Sunday dinner looked at the table of widows and said, We're the go-go grannies. From that point on, Alma had never issued an invitation to coffee or games of Manipulation or chicken dinners at the Hollyhock Hill without saying, It's the go-go grannies, We're the go-go grannies, The go-go grannies are getting together. Long after the rest of the women had forgotten where the phrase came from, Alma could have told who said it and where, on what Sunday of what month of what year.

Another grandchild comes with a roll for her. He sits and wraps a transparent ribbon of kraut around the tines of his fork, doesn't want to eat it. A son sits across from her and begins telling her how much he's always loved her music cabinet with the hand-painted picture of a man playing a lute on the front. He guesses it must be worth hundreds, a real antique. Sometimes Alma welcomes these comments, wants her things to go to those that want them. At other times she's resentful, thinks they pay much more attention to her things than they used to. She grows suspicious that they're all waiting for her to die, holding their breath. On days like this it seems that they're all talking at once, saying Grandma, I like your monkeypod tray from Hawaii, I like your cloisonné lamp, but you didn't really sell the Tiffany, did you, you do still have the humidor and the cranberry glass? When this happens she can feel her lips getting tight and thin, her eyes getting narrow,

and she hears herself ask in a scratchy voice that can't be hers,
Why do you want to know? There are things she can't bear for
anyone to have. And they're not the important things—her Bible,
her pictures of John, the china and cut glass. It's silly things like
her rolling pin, the mammy and pappy salt shakers, a metal coffee
can where she keeps her saltines, a cotton slip. She knows they
won't fare well. She can picture her daughter saying, Of course
these things we can throw away. She can see them looking at her
earrings—how tasteless, how quaint, how old-fashioned. She can
see them laughing at her supply of wine that the doctor told her
to drink to build up her blood, a joke almost slapstick, the old
lady drinking wine for medicinal purposes. She's told them often
enough that she enjoys the wine, has had it for dinner all her life,
that the doctor only told her not to *stop,* that it was good for her.
The one son who loved to make jokes found her wine the richest
material he'd had in years. It was this same son who, when he
was twelve and obsessed with being pure and wanted to become
a saint, when he stopped eating for a week, had thought her wine
was wicked and wild and poured a bottle out in the gravel driveway to save her soul. Alma thinks that she hasn't changed, that if
her wine has to be interpreted she would rather be thought of as
slightly wicked than as feeble and silly.

And last week in the middle of the night she suddenly couldn't
bear the thought of someone throwing away the tiny clear glass
bird with the air bubble in one wing and the broken wire sticking
out of its breast that John brought her as a peace offering at the
end of that same awful summer when she had the crush on the
pastor. When he brought it into the dark entry hall, the wire was
longer and embedded in a piece of driftwood. They knelt in the
hall to put the driftwood on the floor and a thin wedge of light
through the letter slot in the door lit only the glass bird, the round
glasses on John's face, a lock of his blonde hair, and the diamond

on her hand as she touched the bird's left wing. And filled with white light, the wire hidden in the dark and bending, the bird looked as if it flew away from her on its own power, then back to her hand. And she decided that she loved him again, through that bird. Then John placed the bird on her dresser where two days later one of the children, she'd forgotten which one, snapped the wire and left the bird lying in an ashtray. She told everyone she'd thrown it away then, but she kept it in an embroidered handkerchief in her nightstand, ashamed of being so foolish. Then last week she started thinking about it, and she put the bird and the handkerchief in a velvet-lined ring box and went outside in her nightgown to bury the box in the yard. When she came back into the kitchen and poured herself some wine and sat at the table she started to giggle, couldn't stop, wondered how she'd become exactly what they expected of her, a crazy old woman drinking medicinal wine, going outside at night in her gown with a shovel, burying things in her back yard.

The table fills. Everyone eats, the younger ones push the kraut to one side of their plates, wrinkle their noses. One great-granddaughter takes a napkin and dries the kraut juice from the knockwurst she chose instead of sausage, because it tasted the most like hot dogs. One granddaughter, the dancer, taps a tune on her plate with a knife. A son wolfs down his sausage, spears his wife's uneaten sausage with a fork, finishes that, and looks around for more. Alma eats a roll, some Jell-O, wonders if any of her married children will notice that she doesn't have anything else, decides she'll wait to get more food until someone mentions that she doesn't have any. Before her illness they would have noticed, now they're afraid to look at her too closely. They talk to her of things around her, look at that car, at that photograph, and that's where their eyes rest. A four-year-old great-grandson sitting on her right leans over and says, Grandma, are you sick? and his mother, putting her arm around him says, No, of course Great-grandma's not sick, she's fine, she'll live forever, and Alma wants to stand up, make a speech, say, Listen it's true and today I'm not all that afraid, things change form, why are you all ignoring it? But she doesn't say anything, because she knows it's hard not to be afraid. She wants to say that it's only something about cells growing too fast. She knows enough to sound scientific about it, she can talk knowledgeably of organs and glands, but she doesn't know enough to stop it from feeling like black magic. And it hasn't been that easy to live with it. A few cells having a grand old time at the expense of her body, not just her body, but her self and everything she saw through her eyes in her own way. One consolation there. Revenge if she wanted it. The earth would lose one way of looking at it. No one would ever listen to her back yard quite the way she did. And that's all the earth has required of her after all—a pair of eyes, ears, a nose, nerve endings in the skin, another organism to sense that it all exists. God required more of her, her husband even more, or sometimes it seemed that way. But the earth required only that she touch, and the earth contained the cell in her that was going wild. For a while she tried thinking of it in another way, that those cells in her throat were life, growth in a knot. The only recourse, she decided, was to feel herself as the cancer, to become the cells, cheer as she felt the explosions in her neck, as each cell lit a new cell, eating a vacuum through her body. The grandson in the khaki coat back from Vietnam, short hair he wouldn't grow so he wouldn't forget, talked about lighting up an enemy, not death. That lighting up was real to her, but she couldn't carry it off. She was wherever the cancer wasn't, it was as simple as that. She couldn't contain it. She couldn't ignore it. She wants to tell her children that, that she didn't will it, that she doesn't want it to happen to them, but that if it does, they can stand it, that things change form with ease, that they should remember the family. She wants to tell them that, but they don't want to talk about it, each one of them positive that he is the one human being in the history of the earth who will never ever die.

The great-grandson on her right leans over to her, blonde hair like John's brushing her arm, and says, Grandma, I'll trade you this hot dog for that Jell-O, and he pushes a plate of kraut and applesauce and a hot sausage with one bite missing toward her. She gives him two red Jell-O salads and a sweet roll, saying Take this sweet roll and remember that yeast is an animal that causes flour to rise, and the grandson laughs, Funny Grandma, and takes a bite of the roll, dripping caramel on his clean white shirt.

La Bête:
A Figure Study

Melissa Pritchard

Beginning with . . .

Jeanne-Marie, an abnormally fat child of sixteen who works as a laundress at Madame Lutte's and has the afternoon off. Cook has given her a custard pie as a treat, and Jeanne-Marie has carried it all the way to the meadow outside of the village where a shallow stream runs through. She has taken off her black shoes, her black cotton stockings, and put her reddened, swollen feet into the water. Propping her elbows on her knees, she holds the pie and begins methodically to eat, her whole being occupied with the sensations in her mouth. A small splash lands in the stream near her, then another, and another. All at once she is pelted with stones that sting her neck and back. She turns, tries to get up, custard smearing her mouth, when a gang of village boys, ten or eleven years old, descend on her, grab the pie away.

"Come and get it, fatty . . ."

"Run for it, run and you can have it, here fatty, have a taste of pie."

They smash the half-pie onto the ground and surround her.

She tries to push out but they are sturdy, won't let her. She cries from humiliation and that goads them further. Dragging her to the ground, one holds her head, one her legs, while the rest unfasten her clothing until she lies there, a young, naked girl, exposed before their glinting, taunting eyes. Her primitive femaleness shocks them, then one spits and says she is a pig, a sow, a cow. They tie up her clothes and fling them into the uppermost branches of the tallest tree.

When they have gone, she tries to climb the tree and scratches herself. She gives up and decides she must wait for nightfall to return home. At the door, her father accuses her, her mother weeps; Jeanne-Marie will tell nothing of what happened to her. They agree she has been raped. Her father ends by thrashing her with the hearth broom while her mother wails absurdly that she is surely pregnant and will be a disgrace.

Jeanne puts on her blue and white striped dress, her white cotton apron, and goes out early in the morning with a long stick, back to the meadow. She pokes at the bundle until it drops to the ground. At Madame Lutte's house, she will spend more than enough time scrubbing the soiled cloth of her skirt, the cloth of her soiled blouse . . .

Jeanne-Marie interrupts . . .

The woman stopped in our village, found me at Madame Lutte's, scrubbing out my clothes, and asked if I would pose for a portrait. Madame, hoping to have her own conceited self painted for a reasonable fee, by way of ingratiating herself, let me go without protest. So, my apron still wet, I found myself seated in the woman's carriage, driven at an eager pace to her summer chateau.

I cannot say she was unfriendly to me, but my character held little interest for her, nor anything I might have had to say. My figure had always brought great unhappiness to me, but here was an artist from Paris who would find it worthy of intense, if cold study. Into her *salon de peinture,* as she named it, with the northern window opened wide, cherry and quince blossoms jutting awkwardly from pale crocks set upon bare floors, whitewashed walls with sketches pinned here and there, she brought me. Dressed in an elegant smock of white crêpe de Chine, she asked that I remove all my clothing and mount the model's stand in the center of the room. I dropped my clothes upon a plain chair and like some ponderous creature climbed onto the model's stand. I began wringing my hands and sweating from nervousness, comforting myself with the idea of the money I was to be paid.

"Hair down. Please, unbraid your hair for me. We'll set these blossoms here, lean forward, not so much, there, fine, fine, look sideways towards me, yes, now throw the hair over one shoulder so we have the blossoms here and the hair here, yes, that's perfect. Lovely. It is essential not to move, Jeanne-Marie, until I give you permission."

My breasts hung shamelessly out before me, and my coppery hair pulled like a weight to one side of my head. The studio felt as full of warm and cold currents as a lake.

"Unbelievable laziness . . . models in Paris nowadays are utter lazybones, not wishing to strain a muscle, refusing to take positions which are too difficult."

So she talked as she worked, full of complaints, as my limbs grew heavier and heavier. I must have moved slightly, for she reprimanded me and I was afraid, and thought I would faint with fatigue.

She brought a shawl and allowed me a few minutes' rest. The immense effort of staying motionless as a chair or a dish dazed me.

A platter of cold chicken and fruit was brought in, and I twisted my greasy fingers shyly through the ends of my hair and sucked the juice delicately off my fingers. When some of the violet juice dribbled down between my breasts, she told me to leave it.

After the portrait was finished, I returned to Madame Lutte's, where I quickly became discontent. I wanted to model. I quit Madame's and with this woman's references and a list of names I took a carriage to Paris, where I sought out the artists' quarters. My first employment there was so unfortunate that I nearly turned back to the life of laundress, tormented by stupid boys, in my dull country village.

The figure study class was deserted except for fifty chairs, easels, drawing boards, and the model's platform with an unlit stove near it. The russet walls were littered with caricatures and scrapings of paint from numerous palettes. I ascended the model's stand and sat in the small chair with a black fringed shawl wrapped around me. The chair bit into my thighs and I stuffed the last bit of bread I had brought into my mouth; it was dry in my mouth and I thought I could not swallow.

At last the students, all young men, herded noisily into the room. One whistled when he saw me, and joked that he must have stumbled into landscape class; he couldn't possibly be in figure study—all he saw before him was an impressive mountain of flesh.

The master arrived, establishing an air of false discipline, and asked that I assume a strange sitting posture, hands on my hips, head arched back, mouth slackly open. With a black cane, he tapped my legs apart.

Their eyes wandered over me, biting like stable flies. The studio stunk of tobacco and unwashed bodies and oil paints. I closed my eyes, imagined I was in the woman's studio with her benign eye upon me. I had no money left except what I would be paid for this day's modeling.

After an hour of brief poisonous criticisms, the master excused himself. I had taken a short break, drunk from the pitcher of water he had handed me, and now resumed my pose, my neck aching horribly from the strain. The atmosphere in the studio became loose and unrestrained. There were lighthearted denunciations of one another's work, much gossip and talk of lunch and cafés.

Unexpectedly, yet as if it were ritual, five or six of the students dragged their chairs over to the model's stand. Sitting backwards, they galloped in a circle around me, shouting obscene songs, singing the *Marseillaise,* which was forbidden by the Empire in those days. I held myself rigid, but when one of them reached up and pinched me, asking the others if they thought I could feel anything, I stood up, knocking over the slight chair, and left the studio. With enough experience, I would grow accustomed to the bizarre spirits of my art students, even playfully grabbing at the handsomer ones as they rode by me, fresh-cheeked boys on hobbyhorses. But that first day, when I complained of my treatment to the master, he asked if I would not prefer instead modeling privately for him.

This man was soon escorting me to cheap theaters, to cafés, introducing me to friends, reading from Verlaine and Baudelaire, after which he would bite my arms, muttering that I was the most delectably corpulent beast in all Paris. Sometimes he would feed me and, fascinated, watch me chew and swallow what he had placed in my mouth. I lived with him for some months, and finally prospered when he did, by a series of sketches he sold of me on brown paper.

Posing for this, for any artist, I was no longer the village freak, tormented and shunned, but was instead a figure of challenge to be studied in different positions, in varying angles of light. I was fed and given shelter in numerous garrets and studios. I wore men's clothing because it was a joke, because it was comfortable. I began to smoke tobacco and to drink wine. I laughed and no one objected, I raged and they drew out their sketchbooks. In short, the more extreme a character I displayed, the more sought after I found myself. In exchange for hams and sausage and breads, I goaded the incessant appetites of artists. I was an overnight fad in Paris, one of those meteors with a high, swift rise . . . I had become La Bête.

Not everyone liked me. One man, very fastidious, confessed that the thick petals of my flesh disgusted him, that excess such as mine revolted him. He took me one afternoon to a morgue and insisted I stare at the tables of cadavers laid out as if for some tainted feast. He explained that he had spent five years of his life drawing these gray, foul creatures.

"Look, will you, idiot! That is where someday you will be, upon a table like that one!"

I bowed and said, "And if you should arrive here before me, may I bring my knife and fork?"

At cafés among my new friends I began ordering very little food. I wished my companions to believe that La Bête ate next to nothing, that fat increased upon her like a Catholic miracle. In private, I gorged myself. I had the idea of pasting little stars of silver and gold in my red hair, and did so.

In early August I rode one evening with a group of students from the art school into the countryside. The master brought a white linen tablecloth and a pale blue oval dish with smoked salmon heaped upon it. We ended up in a meadow where the moon was bloated and discolored and the crickets howled fiendishly among the grasses. The cloth was unfolded and, shimmering like a bolt of water, was laid upon the meadow. The young men observed the effect of moonlight upon the cloth, where shadows

The latest man, this silly artist, he presses the juices from me. He says the water overflows the jug and I am the jug. I have posed over three weeks in this same attitude, stepping out from a tub, my buttocks toward him, my eyes looking straight into the bathtub. Yes, there's a little scum of water in it, stale as any water that sits. He waits until the light comes through the windows at the correct exposure, heaves a bucket of water over me, orders me to step into the tub, then feverishly rushes back to his easel. He has me hold until my ass trembles from the effort to be still.

Sometimes, with my one foot splayed out in the water, I begin to sing bawdy verses to pique him. On occasion I fart and say, "Put that onto your canvas, you fool!" This man is very famous, not used to insult, so I am glad to give it.

I sit on the edge of the tub or lie on the bed to smoke one of the cigarettes I've rolled for myself. Funny, this one tells me that I have grace. My flesh is full of lights, he says. Nothing about me disgusts him. He goes outside while I eat my meal of sausage and cold potato; he returns in exactly five minutes.

Do I care anymore what they put on the canvas? Not much. I come over and blow smoke at the buttocks he has drawn and daubs with greenish-white.

"What horse apples," I snort and go, breathlessly, back to the bathtub.

Peculiar man. He likes to paint my huge bulk in erotic common postures, yet he never approaches me except with the bucket of water, then stabs in queer, caressing ways at the canvas with his brushes!

He calls me his mule, heaving the damn water over me, making me hunch for hours over this cracked porcelain until I cry out. Remorseful, he apologizes by throwing sausage and bread at me and turning his back.

I tear into the meat, huge mouthfuls, my pubic hair staring up at me, a reproachful orange mouth. When the picture is finished, I am given money, and I stare hard at the painting.

"Well, my mule, what do you think? It's perfect, is it not?"

"It stinks," I say, and he never hires me again.

Descent of La Bête . . .

Oh, when was it that my boys, my creators, began to neglect me? They lost their imaginations, that's what, sneaking into their garrets and studios such ordinary, slender grisettes . . . I tore up one lover's drawings during the night he did not return home. He went off with a bony nag who did nothing but crochet from her little basket and snub me. My temper grew worse; not one had the courage or the patience to risk using me. One newly arrived painter who had no money but offered to share his food used me, and I violently attacked his work, saying, "You call this a work of art?"

"And you," he screamed back, sweeping his pastels off the table onto the floor, "do you call yourself a work of nature—you are one of her aberrations!"

I abandoned that young fool in the middle of his work.

They had no more use for me, they could find no more art in me. Acquaintances in cafés vanished, or turned away their faces, and miserable La Bête came at last to selling flowers and matches on the hard steps of the Luxembourg, though she kept stars in her hair, as always.

One morning I sold more than enough flowers to pay my way into the museum. I moved through a hushed, churchlike maze of pictures and busts, until I found myself . . . enormously fat and red with a small head, reclining in a wet, blurred orchard like some rotting, overripe fruit. I had been uncovered like this, before the world, and now they had no more use for me. I sat on the floor and wept and beat my fists upon the floor, tried to scratch the picture, until two, then three guards took me out. I told them who I was and as I was pushed out I spat into the fountain, hoping to pollute the false, fickle waters of art.

But the sickness never left me. I needed them, however much I disliked their results. Creeping back to the ateliers, I asked, then begged for work. I reformed my temper, but my poor health . . . I had begun with little fits of sleep, narcolepsy. On the model's stand, not even a poor student wanted me. La Bête was broken-winded.

La Bête and the recluse

An endless monotony of rain ran off the black slate roofs. It was gray and chill as only Paris can be in October, when even bread is damp. It became too cold to sit on the museum steps any longer.

> Oh, sweet fall of the rain
> Upon the earth and roof
> Unto a heart in pain,
> O music of the rain.

The houseboat was tied up beside others of its type, broken down, peeling, bleached, ruined. I knocked, opened the small red door, and went in sideways.

"No, I have little need of a model like yourself. I have no need of anyone or anything but paint and God."

He was willfully blind to anything outside his tiny, cramped houseboat. Boxes, papers, broken furniture, garbage stacked to the ceiling, narrow snakelike paths from his bed to his easel, from his easel to his stove. He stank vilely, but insisted that his layers of clothing ventilated him. And his canvases, strewn about like blowing litter on a street, some propped up, others lying face down, to ripen with the movement of the water, he said. He painted me standing in the middle of a salmon-colored river with black skies. He painted me wading in a choppy cobalt sea with no features on my face. I cleared away some of his boxes and furniture to make a bed for myself and a small toilette. I cooked on his small filthy stove, but since he often neglected to eat I learned to eat his portion before it grew cold. I smoked outside and regarded the ramshackle wharf. Odd, that an artist for whom only beauty mattered would choose such grim clutter.

We suffered that winter; snow drifted through unclosed windows. I found two cheap rooms in Paris and we left the houseboat. Strange to be in open, ill-favored space with this man. Wallpaper dangling in faded, defeated strips, plaster crumbling off the ceiling. The view from our two windows was of a tiny stamp of courtyard with arthritic burls of chestnut trees staring indifferently back at us.

His paintings were washed in half-light, phosphorescent, devoid of sunlight. He was a creature of dampness and night and perverse conversations. There was a benefactor who infrequently purchased his paintings, and on this, but mainly on donation, we existed.

When he became unwell, medicines made their way into our rooms, and the place where he slept was blatant with suggestions of a sickroom: a spoon in a tumbler of clouded water, a mortar and pestle, packets of white powder, stained rags by the pillows. A cat lived with us, an old calico who sat in his lap when he dozed upright in a chair. Late in the spring he began complaining of cold and went about in a shabby brown fur-lined overcoat, a white nightshirt, and black trousers, with a short black coat over all this.

We had enough money from the sale of a painting to hire a carriage for an evening's ride into the country. My friend was in some nocturnal reverie, walking through groves of birch, stepping across streambeds, leaning against a small limestone cliff, while I cursed and swore, trying to keep up with him. I also remembered the glorious night when I had been a feast of inspiration for young artists, reclined upon a white tablecloth.

He painted my head, took it off with the palette knife, began a second time, allowed it to dry, scraped again, in this way building up form, refining the drawing; after each scraping there would be a subtle layer of paint left. Being too feverish to go and purchase proper paint, at one point he seized the candle off its dish and used the grease from it to paint with. Fasting and improvised prayers over his work went on hour after hour. He had no use for my once-famous body, painting only my head, with a green scarf concealing my famous hair, tobacco smoke like a fine, hissing aureole around me. I was to be laughing, some of my teeth missing, my cheeks mapped with broken veins. But the sitting went badly. I kept dropping off to sleep, and he was exhausted, able to work for only a quarter of an hour at a time.

The cat would hunch upon a broken arm of a couch, delicately washing itself. We worked only at night, the glowing tongues of many lamps and candles wagging wastefully around us.

He told me, "In darkness the trivial is unwelcome. In an absence of light, first the face, then the shadows around the face."

I grunted, half-asleep.

"So it is among common people that you will find grace."

I woke up. "Oh, crap. Common people fling rocks at the backs of common people." I coughed and spat phlegm onto the floor.

"You call that grace, you idiot, you beloved idiot of mine?"

"Oh, yes," he said, his eyes on mine like a priest's.

When I awoke from another of my sick little naps, the lamps and candles guttered weakly in the morning sunlight, and I found my artist, who needed nothing but God and paint and me to cook for him, me to grind up his medicines for him, me to sit for him, had gone, his head fallen over into the wet oils of my open-mouthed portrait.

Looking as if he had fed himself to the devil.

La Bête had devoured him, it seemed.

As it turns out . . .

After feeding and bathing her mother, Jeanne-Marie walks to the other end of the village, where old Madame Lutte still lives. In her basket she has rolled up the white cloth from Paris. When she gets inside the laundry room lined with its dark, cool stone, she fills the metal tubs, one with hot water, the other with cool. Disregarding the baskets of soiled linens and dresses, Jeanne-Marie takes out the white cloth, feeds it into the steaming water, takes the tallow bar of soap, and begins scrubbing. Her hands work among the cloth and the water, like red fish they move, quick and chapped. The cool water accepts the cloth, and a grayish scum of soap rings the metal tub. Wringing out the tablecloth, she stretches it across a rope to dry in the summer sunlight. It floats, a square unnatural cloud, against the blue seamless heaven.

Jeanne-Marie returns to the laundry room, pours out the fouled water, and begins the tedious, ordinary job of washing out Madame Lutte's expensive dresses and linens.

By noon the tablecloth is hanging stiffly across the rope, smelling of sunlight, and Jeanne-Marie's work is finished. She rolls the cloth into her basket along with the cold joint of meat and slice of cake given her by the cook.

In the familiar patch of meadow, she shakes out the snowy tablecloth, sets down the plate of meat and pie. Removing her blue and white striped dress, her apron, her heavy shoes and black stockings, Jeanne-Marie sits crosslegged upon the cloth, unbraiding her hair until it drops in a coppery sheet around her.

The poplar trees at the edge of the meadow clamor and flash silver in the strong afternoon breeze. She chews, sensuously and deliberately, wiping her fingers in her hair. Abruptly, she drops into sleep; the sun bleaches out her flanks, sets dull fire to her hair, sparkles against the sharp-edged white cloth in the sour grasses.

The village boys peer through a particularly dense stand of poplar trees; having discovered the habits of this queer laundress, they have snuck out from their chores to ogle her, in a kind of nervous dread of her enormity. There is something of an ogress in her raw pose, something of a folktale in the way her huge fans of flesh lie open before them. Their fathers and mothers only know Jeanne-Marie as Madame Lutte's ugly, disgraced laundress, in her shabby dress with her red chafed hands and broken chatter. But these boys know the awful enchantment of her naked body, set out as if for a feast upon an immaculate white square in the sunny meadow.

La Bête, even asleep, feels the boys out there, their pale, unripened faces shifting among the green leaves, their whispers like a shaking of wind through the poplars. She allows them, for she is worthy of study. Her figure commands attention. La Bête knows that her boys, her artists, can never have enough of her. She is that good.

Horror Show

Sandra Thompson

My brother, soft palms and knees moving silently across the carpet, approaches me lying above him on the bed, unsuspecting. It is his favorite game, "Ribs." He is the character Ribs, and I am me. He raises himself to the height of the bed, rests his chin on it, level with my body, and as he makes his ascent up the side of the bed, the trip from the foot of the bed to where I am lying near the pillows, he mutters, "I am going to kill you." At five his enunciation is crisp and he knows how to raise his voice on "kill" and drag that word out slowly, through his teeth. Ten years later, the walls of his room are covered with posters: of the Wolf Man, Dracula, the Frankenstein monster, whom he affectionately calls Frankie. The Thing. He has a fake rubber hand that can be left protruding from a closed closet door. Coming home from school, I look up at my second-floor bedroom window to see my brother's body hanging there by a rope, but it's his pants and shirt stuffed with laundry.

At night, on the far side of the bed, I see a hand made of flesh. I ease out of the sheets, holding my breath, tiptoe down the stairs to my father's bed. We lie together like spoons. My father jokes about his free arm, that he doesn't know where to put it.

It all changes when I'm seventeen and the Big Goof arrives. He is my first lover. My father pouts and sulks in his big chair. "Tell him you love him," the Big Goof advises. "When you go in tonight, wake him up and tell him you love him." "I love you," I say, crouched on the blanket at the foot of his bed. "What?" my father growls. "I love you." His eyes narrow. "What do you want now?"

The Big Goof, so named by my brother because he is big and his last name is Goff, wears Old Spice and has a fake I.D. He smokes and swears (he says everything but "fuck") and he drinks Scotch. He is a 230-pound All-State tackle. He has friends who wear wide-collared shirts that don't button down and who go out with showgirls. I wear sleek Schiaparelli hose and high heels, and for my eighteenth birthday he gives me a giant stuffed panda and takes me to a motel.

Fifteen years later, when my father hears his name, he grunts. "That son of a bitch!" Fifteen years later, my brother still calls him the Big Goof.

"I promise I won't get into your pants until you're eighteen," he says, but he doesn't make it. It's at a party on Lake Shore Drive, in the bedroom, my black silk Chinese dress with salmon lining pushed up above my waist. The room throbs. I lie on the bed, unsuspecting. The blood. He is pleased at the blood. Where the blood has spread to my dress, the shine has gone out of the silk. He walks to the window; along the torn barbed-wire edge of the screen he rakes his hand until it bleeds. With drama, he reenters the party, blood dripping from his hand, to explain my dress.

Now I am "his" virgin. He buys the most expensive rubbers, the kind that are already wet and have ribs along the sides. We will get married, of course.

Lying on the living room sectional underneath the Big Goof, I hear a noise, a rustle. I follow it around a corner, up the stairs, into the bathroom. My brother is standing, in his size 10 sneakers, fully clothed, behind the shower curtain.

Why doesn't somebody stop it, I don't want to go to college, I have to be under or beside the Big Goof. He wants me to be a Pi Phi. The day I leave him I feel as though my hands have been cut off at the wrists.

On my purple bedspread there is a flesh-colored pool of vomit, its pieces diffuse and undigested. My brother walks silently across the room, his face deadpan; with his thumb and forefinger he picks up the vomit. "Rubber," he says. His lips curl up over his incisors, only the soft corners of his lips participating in the smile.

The Big Goof phones me in the dorm after the switchboard has closed for the night. The housemother, in haircurlers and robe, raps on my door and announces "the emergency." It's Dr. Goff, a routine bed check. Do I belong to him, or am I a whore? For Christmas vacation someone in knee socks and loafers comes home in my place; on St. Patrick's Day we meet secretly and drink champagne for breakfast in the hotel, but I want orange juice. I don't love him, he's not magic. I have to love him. "I'm not a virgin," I'll have to say to someone, sometime, and it will be unacceptable and I don't want to be a nun.

"I don't love you," I say anyway that second summer in his Mercury with no shock absorbers, parked in the Forest Preserves, and he throws himself out of the car, throws himself on the ground, and writhes in the wet leaves, groaning, choking, gasping. "I never told you, a rare disease, the doctor said at any moment I—" His breathing stops, he clutches his throat and his face turns red and swollen, and I stand above him, my arms at my side. I deserve it all, and worse.

And get it. So much later, lying underneath some other lover on the floor, a carpet tack scrapes the skin of my back when he puts his weight on me, pushing me up the rough carpet. Afterwards, there is a round raw spot on the surface of my backbone, bleeding and open, and I have to wrench my body around to admire it in the bathroom mirror. It will heal up, form a scab, and disappear.

In the dark room the yellow light funnels from the television screen. My brother and I are watching Shock Theater. Marvin, the host, is a ghoul dressed in black turtleneck, black pants, and sneakers. Each week he has conversations with Dear, his wife. Week after week, Dear is seated, tied to her chair, her back to the camera, and she is gagged. "Isn't that right, Dear?" Marvin asks, and she mumbles "Help" through her gag, but it comes out like a muffled thud. My brother, his hair cut short in blonde spikes, laughs, throwing his head back, the contours of his face forming upward V's in the dim light.

The first time the Big Goof meets my father, he offers him a light. (He has a gold Dunhill lighter like the one Elizabeth Taylor gives Laurence Harvey in *Butterfield 8*.)

My father rises from his chair and it is settled: the Big Goof must
go. So I meet him on corners. My father sets his clock radio every
hour on the hour after midnight: Patti Page at two, he checks my
bed, Dean Martin at three. At four, he is standing on the porch,
fully dressed, smoking Lucky Strikes, his number 5 iron leaning
against the screen door. The Big Goof drives over his lawn, leaves
tire tracks on his sod.

The Mercury parked in a deserted cul-de-sac, the beam of the
policeman's flashlight falls on my chest where the Big Goof's
head has been. He flashes his I.D. and says, "This is my fiancee."
The wind is cool on our damp skin as we drive naked through
the suburban town, the only car on the road.

At the kitchen table, under the bare light, my father offers me
$1,000 not to see the Big Goof for one year. My brother hulks,
unseen, behind the sliding door.

The Big Goof tells me he will love me no matter what, he will
love me if my arms are amputated or my body paralyzed below
the waist. He will love me, no matter what—except, maybe, if
something happened to my face— (I sit in a gleaming wheelchair,
the useless silver armrests kept shining by the Big Goof's muscle,
my sleeves empty, my legs hanging from my body like rag dolls,
my beautiful face waiting for its own collapse.)

And I will love him because I smell him and breathe him and am
surrounded and inundated by him, and I have no choice: if he
were a hangnail soaked in Old Spice, if he were a toe—

So what happened? To the beach blankets, their smell of sweat and wool roasting in the sun, turning damp and salty in the evening, so full of us I want to shove them down my throat, and still, and still— The matching yellow monogrammed pajamas we kept hidden in the trunk of his car. The hot leather seat covers steam under my thighs: we are moving. He slams me up against the refrigerator, presses his hands around my neck. I yell "Help" like a muffled thud.

The Night Monster is the worst because he is human, and, better, crippled. His dead legs hidden under a plaid blanket, he rises from his wheelchair into the mist; his legs, stiff as cylinders, move him forward. "Come on, Night, baby!" My brother grins into the TV screen, slices through the center of a kernel of popcorn held tentatively between his front teeth.

I hated seeing him that last time in his Corvette Sting Ray with fuel injection, he is still smelling—reeking—of Old Spice, and I almost reeled, almost. In the motel the sheets are stretched tight across the bed, cool and crisp from the air conditioning; we get that far, then I bolt. Feeling sorry for the money he's spent, sorry he, sorry— He was big, but his muscles had turned, he was so much meat.

What am I supposed to do about them? The brother who loved Frankie, my father with his big bucks and narrowed eyes, the Big Goof who went soft? The scab, you can't see a trace of it, but I remember its red amoeba-like shape, circled in pale yellow, the hint of infection, a sore, a badge.

Skin and Bone

David Walton

You take my skin,
I take your bone.
You take my bone,
I take your life.
—precept of Shotokan Karate

Tuesdays they practiced upstairs in the women's gym, and sometimes there he felt it, if he'd done particularly well that night, into April and May after it started staying light later and the windows could be open—the oneness with the stance you were supposed to feel, a loosening of muscles and easing of the pain, not a diminishing of it exactly, but going beyond it, into an almost druggy transcendence where colors, shapes, the surfaces of things became abstractions of themselves. Thursdays, and Saturday mornings during wrestling season, they practiced downstairs in the fencing/volleyball room, where there were score markers and notices all over the walls, and street sounds coming through the windows, high, frosted-glass windows flush up to the ceiling, with chicken wire embedded in the glass and some

elaborate crank mechanism for opening and closing them that ran
down the side of the wall. Upstairs they were at the back of the
building, looking out onto a wooded hillside, with stretch bars
and full-length mirrors, and enough floor space for separating the
beginners from the advanced groups.

Tuesday, ironically, was the night Emil led practice—ironic
because Emil was the one Tim considered the most rootbound of
the blackbelts, a stocky, and for all his conditioning, somewhat
chunky graduate student in either mathematics or physics, with
a bright, unflagging smile and a sparse tuft of sandy hair curling
out of the hollow of his throat. "I *want* you to improve," he would
tell them as he went around correcting postures. It had been Emil
the winter before who, with the flu and a temperature of 102,
came in anyway, just to prove he could overcome it, running four
miles outside barefoot by himself before practice, and then leading the club through five hundred side-thrust kicks, five hundred
side-snap, at least a thousand roundhouse kicks, ending the evening with fifteen minutes in *kibadach*—all low leg exercises, Tim
noted. This was just about the time Tim was starting to get over
the trouble he'd been having with his knees.

"This is crazy," he told Dietz.

"This is what you gotta do," Dietz told him, "if you want to
be ready for special training."

The special trainings were a recent innovation, weekend-long
retreats held bi-yearly on the campus of a community college outside the city, three and four intensive two-hour practices a day,
with special surprise sessions thrown in at five in the morning—a
little like hell week in the fraternity, Tim was thinking, watching
it all from a detached perspective, the mounting enthusiasm, the
growing rigor of the practices as the big time drew near, the pressure on everybody to sign up, go along. "If anybody doesn't have
the twenty dollars," Emil told them after two separate practices,

"I'll give him the money out of my own wallet." And then afterward, the esprit, the camaraderie, the casual ostracism of those
who hadn't gone by those that had.

(Around this time, too, a move was on to federate the different clubs around the country, accompanied by a five-dollar raise
of dues and, by the appearance, at fifteen dollars a copy, of the
English translation by the American head of the school of the
founder's autobiography, which required all the stances to be re-
vised downward, and for the last three months the brownbelts
were every five minutes breaking off practice to run over to the
coatracks to consult a copy on some point of dispute.)

It was a Tuesday, three weeks before spring special training,
that Esther appeared. She walked in five minutes before time for
practice to start, crossing the floor with solemn, self-contained
steps, her brown belt over her shoulder. She put her bag down by
a pillar, tied on her belt, and stretched, walked out to the middle
of the floor and breathed and stretched, sank down into a full
split, turned left, and then right, and then over into a plow, which
she held, unmoving, until the call came for bowing in.

A nice sense of theater, Tim thought.

She wore a *gi* of a lighter fabric, a couple of shades whiter
than those of the club, the jacket loose fitting, accentuating the
slimness and narrowness of her line. She was around twenty-four
or -five, tall, around five-nine or five-ten, with brown hair parted
down the center and clipped behind her ears with bow barrettes
of red and yellow molded plastic. Sparring, she went through
some stylized breathing routine, giving out a growl every time
she made a punch. The first time Tim stood up to her, he broke
up, which infuriated her. After each set of punches, she rehearsed
back over the final one to herself, as if to imprint its deficiencies
on her mind.

Mr. Shuri was there to supervise that evening, a distinction in itself, and after bowing out, he raised a hand for further courtesy.

"Tonight back from former Europe pretemper Esther Hardy."

He heard later that she was a remote descendant of British novelist Thomas Hardy, another nice touch, Tim thought. She was a past member of the club returning after two years in Europe, where she'd trained with Didier, who was a former fellow or esteemed former pupil of Mr. Shuri's. Every eight or ten words Mr. Shuri lapsed into a shrugging inarticulacy, a little gathering in and back that was more expressive, more lucid finally than any words could be. What came across most was the *gentilesse* of the man, a sense of good meaning and design—though a certain part of that Tim had concluded had to be written off to simple inscrutability. For a long time he'd been thinking he was telling them to "Excel! Excel!", a suitable enough exhortation, he'd thought, until he realized that what he really was saying was, "Exhale! Exhale!"

Called upon herself to describe her experiences abroad, Esther was similarly inaudible, speaking out of a modesty that confined itself to whispers. Tim passed the time scanning the new beginners' group, sprawled out across the lower end of the floor, gaping at her as if a berserk had been set down into their midst—figuring out which of this assorted rape bait and bully fodder would be the ones most likely to stick it through, which ones would prove the real *aficionados,* measuring the distance between them and his own beginners' class of two years ago, many of whom, and of the three or four classes since then, had long since passed him by. She was a carpenter, had apprenticed to a cabinet maker in Belgium.

"She's trained in France," Dietz told him afterward in the showers, "she trained in Spain, she's trained all over Europe. She trained with Didier." Dietz's tone said that while he recognized that her commitment was strong, he could never take any woman's commitment fully seriously. "They wouldn't let her apprentice here so she went over and did her apprenticeship there and now she's suing the union." His tone said he thought she was a troublemaker.

"The training in Spain is mostly overcoming the pain," Tim suggested—but Dietz had his head under the shower and probably didn't hear that. Dietz wasn't large but he was powerfully built, and he worked exceptionally hard. He could bring his leg up and hold it alongside his head, and was the only one of the brownbelts Tim considered really able to do the roundhouse—although the fact that he could see him doing it probably suggested that he wasn't doing it properly, the true level of technique, the blackbelt's level of technique, being always undetectable. A fringe of dark hair, smoothed down by the water, outlined the curve of his buttocks, hard, almost grotesquely rounded buttocks, his whole body firm and sharply articulated, as if he'd been conceived on a heroic scale and then reduced down to everyday size. He snapped his head back and shook it side to side doggy style, spraying water the width of the enclosure.

Tim said, "I had this dream last night where there was this temple on the beach, a training school, and all the rocks were painted, and the principal design was this big mouth eating pussy. And all the acolytes were ambulatories, cripples."

Dietz, taking this for a confidence, returned it with one of his own, "I've been going without sleep lately, just to see how long I can do it. You know, if you don't sleep you don't need to sleep at all. It's just a habit people get into. I've made it four days so far."

In the past he'd confided similar projects to Tim, like his method for curing a fear of heights by climbing a 40-foot stepladder a step at a time while reading Descartes' *Rules for the Regulation of the Mind,* or his conviction that old age and death are the products merely of inattention, the toxins entering the body at the first age of maturity, twenty-one, twenty-two, the age he was coming into now, and the thing to do was never to let your guard down and allow them to get in in the first place. He was convinced he was going to live forever, he was a fanatic, that one element of fanaticism, Tim recognized, recognizing it as what was missing in himself, the feature that led him to excel.

He took his time dressing, taking slow pleasure in the buttoning of a button, the tying on of a shoe, waiting until now, until he was about to leave the building, to make his visit to the water fountain. Ten short sips and no more. Not to put too much cold water on the stomach so shortly after practice. Just inside the door the three Buckley kids were waiting for their father to come get them, the younger of the girls, Little Eva, the infant prodigy and sweetheart of the club, a brownbelt at age nine—and it was said that Mr. Shuri was holding her back for fear of advancing her too early. Under the shadow of her example the other girl and the younger brother, both of them bespectacled and hopelessly awkward on the floor, were taking on more and more of a whipped appearance, hanging listlessly against the sides of the Coke machine, while she stood up straight and tall at the door, bidding a smiling good-night to each person as they went out.

"Good practice."

"Good practice."

Outside there were still a few people sitting on the railing and on the wall along the bottom of the steps waiting for their rides. As he came down the steps, Tim could hear Oster describing someone, apparently from another school, who "held his fist against his chest, and just turned it like that, and he was flat out on his ass." There was an active cornball element running through the club, evidenced in a lot of breathless stories about men wrestling the horns out of live bulls with their bare hands, and a lot of sly little jokes with shindigs in the punch line. It was still light, still mild outside, the evening carrying over into it something of

the balminess of the day, the first good day almost of the season. A slow April and chill rains the first week of the month
had retarded the budding, and now it was as if the whole world
was in bloom simultaneously, the evening fragrant with surrep-
titious possibility, the kind of evening where opportunity has its
thumb out on every street corner. From behind a building on the
other side of the street a voice called out and another answered,
not quite coalesced into voices yet, more still manifestations of
a mood, the row of maples across the street, each with the bulb
of a streetlamp in back of its shrub, a trail of glittering starbursts
leading in even diminution into the darkness of the park.

He'd left his car at the bottom of the park next to the coal
memorial, but took a more roundabout route up the golf course
and over the ridge, along the rim of a wooded hillside that paral-
leled Cornwallis Avenue. Just over the crest of the ridge was an
old estate that for the past several years had served as an arts
and handicraft center, and in the summers as headquarters for the
park mimes. The main building had recently been torn down, but
the foundation walls and a section of formal gardens were still in-
tact, bordered on the right by a line of five semiruined archways,
in the intervals of which were mock arches in which there were
stone benches. In the shadow of the second of these there was a
figure, a pair of figures were standing. Automatically he shifted
his bag around to his back and angled out to the left, mediating
a course between the arches and a clump of lilacs on his other
side, gauging as he moved how many steps it would take to land
a lunge punch into that evergreen, a side-snap to the trunk of that
tree, elbows close, arms loose at his sides, taking quick, purposeful steps. Just beyond the arches was the opening of a drive that
led down the hillside to the street. It was here he was making for.

Halfway down the hill, where the drive made a sharp turn just before dropping to the street, a figure in a blue jersey, that he hadn't spotted until he was right on top of him, turned out of the bushes zipping up his fly.

"Hey, good lookin," Tim said as he was going by, "whatcha got cookin?"

That slowed him down. He was a young guy, about twenty-two or -three, not too tall but nice built, slim built, with dark hair and a bushy mustache.

"Hey, what's happening, hey, you got a match? You live around here? Say, you wouldn't happen to have the time, would you?"

The young guy laughed and said, "Na, hey, I'm down here waiting for my bus, I just came up to take a leak is all."

Tim took a step in, then back.

"Hey, you need a ride? hey, come on over here a minute, I'll give you the world tour."

"Na, hey," the young guy said, "that's all right, I'm too busy right now." He took a couple of steps down the hill, but didn't quite break away.

"Hey, hey, nice arms, umm, like those big arms. Hey, hey, walk over here a minute, take a walk over here, I've got something I want to ask you."

"Na, hey." The young guy laughed and rubbed his stomach under his jersey, but in the end said, "That's okay, I gotta meet my bus," and went on down the hill.

For a while Tim hung around the edge of the streetlight—once he looked around and saw him standing there, and then didn't look around again. He let two buses go by. Perhaps neither one of them was his. Tim walked back to the top of the hill, where the same two figures were still standing in the shadow of the arches, and another one now along the side of the foundation wall, which he reconnoitered, and as he returned to the head of the drive he caught sight of a figure in a blue jersey cutting up into the trees just this side of the turn. Tim was right behind him.

Afterwards they sat on the trunk of a fallen tree sharing a smoke.

"How come you're like that?" the young guy wanted to know now.

"It's my nature," Tim told him. "It's how I am."

"I mean, were you always that way? Didn't you ever try it with a girl?"

Tim started to give a very exact answer to that, but he wasn't waiting for that. "You know I'm not putting it down. I figure for everyone's fair pair. I'm just wondering how it started is all. Was it something went wrong with a girl? Or what?"

"It's how I am," Tim told him. "It's what I am."

He knew what was called for, though—if it was in you, you'd have known it by this time, if it was coming out, it would have shown itself by now. People can be all sorts of things, do all kinds of things, without it affecting what you basically are.

"I just can't figure it," the young guy said, and went back down the hill shaking his head.

Still, it wasn't a response Tim minded necessarily, as responses go, himself as the exceptional, the unprecedented encounter, the gratification of such basic requirements, the craftsmanship of gratification, his own special satisfaction. He walked taller now, up the hill and across the gardens, where the same three figures were still situated

cho-cho-chuckala
with a rink-link-rucklaba

over the crest of the ridge, the tips of the downtown buildings just visible above the top of the next hill, half the width and half the height of its plane, and that half again the width and slant of the slope spread out below him, the silhouette of the clubhouse on his right matched with some shrubbery on his left, a tree a little past that with two smaller trees a little farther down on the other side, mass for line, ground with sky, his steps in perfect pace with the evening.

Esther's return prefigured a series of changes in the club, most of them coinciding with the close of the school term, when the three university clubs telescoped down to one to practice together for the summer. The third weekend of May was spring special training, followed in ten days by the spring *qu* test, in which Oster and Little Eva again failed to receive blackbelts, after which came a series of year-end parties, opulent potluck spreads heavy on zucchini and bulgur, where everybody stood around flexing their fingers back and trading stories of favorite practices.

(About this same time, too, the move to federate the clubs necessitated a permanent *dojo* in the city, which, once found, had to be cleared out, sanded down, and revarnished, and this in turn necessitated a closer affiliation with the black club, the one fee-paying, non-university branch of the school in the city, which resulted in some talk—though subdued, since the university clubs had their own black members—that the clubs were being taken in by the blacks, the clubs providing the material and better part of the labor so that the blacks could have their own place to practice in their own part of the city. In short, a politics began to develop, which Tim, who cared no more about it than to avoid any impression of avoiding it, relished as yet another dimension in the substratum absurdity of the whole enterprise.)

Three days before the start of special training, Esther cut off the tip of her finger on a band saw and was told by her doctor that she wouldn't be able to practice for at least three weeks.

"These things are brought to us," Tim suggested, "as a way of keeping us from taking our commitments too seriously"—but she failed to find any merit in that point of view.

In the summertime they practiced outdoors on the Tech lawn, a long grassy concourse set inside a neat symmetry of buildings and walks. At the lower end the lawn dropped off into a deep wooded ravine, on the far side of which rose three squat cylindrical towers, the A, B, and C dorms of the St. Vincent's campus, dubbed by the students Ajax, Babo, and Comet, and it was possible to chart the progress of the second hour of practice by the passage of the sun, nudging the upper righthand corner of the lefthand tower, down a steep trajectory to a point about a third of the way from the bottom of the center tower, to disappear, about the time they were finishing sparring and starting *kata,* into a blaze of amber refraction. The lawn for those final fifteen or twenty minutes was a network of chartreuse highlights against a field of verdant black, the shadows of their maneuvers stretching fifty, sixty yards, almost to the row of hedges that ran across the front of the porch of the Architecture Building.

Tim hated it, though. However deserted the campus might be, there was always a steady stream of stragglers filing by, each one of which invariably had to stop and ponder and point. He had living room muscles, calisthenics muscles, a thick trunk and arms and then spindle legs and something of a paunch. Moreover he always sweat a lot. Even before warm-ups were through, his *gi* would be marked down the back with damp spots, and after every sequence he'd be having to be pulling up and retying. One night a little black kid's dog, excited by all the shouting, bit him on the back of the thigh.

A week before special training, a couple of weeks after Esther had returned, another former member, a blackbelt named Paul, came back to the club after two years in the army, where he'd been stationed in Salt Lake City and for a time had trained at the central *dojo* in Oakland.

It intrigued Tim, once he discovered they had both started in the same beginners' group, had left the club at around the same time, and now were returning within a couple of weeks of each other, how little apparent attention they paid each other. At first he thought it was some buried competitiveness, a case of some long-standing antagonism, but there was no real evidence of that, their dealings were all cordial, just uninterested; rather, he decided finally, a typical example of like oblivious to like.

Paul was around twenty-four, not tall, about five-eight or five-nine, with straw blond hair cropped close and parted straight back the side; the army looked superimposed over a face that was basically boyish and fair, apple cheeks, a few light speckles of beard dotting the mustache line and around the point of the chin—all of which made the ferocity of his approach that much more intimidating. At first Tim thought he was only extending himself as a way of regratiating himself back into the group, or of setting an example for special training, but after a week had passed since special training, after two and then three weeks had gone by, and after he heard that it wasn't after Paul got out of the army that he'd trained in Oakland, but while he was still stationed in Salt Lake City, driving 500 miles each way every weekend to sleep on the bare floor of the practice room, he knew he was in the presence of a true believer.

The first of June Emil left to work for 3M in Connecticut for the summer, and Paul took over the Tuesday night practice. June was muggy and hot, and around the middle of the month there was a four-day stagnation alert. "Take it little easy tonight," Paul would tell them, "air's bad tonight, work more for form than strength tonight"—but so provocative were these words leaving his lips, so anathema even the idea of giving anything less than the fullest effort, that before the first half hour was out he was calling for deeper punches, higher kicks—"Faster! Harder!"—the brown-belts at his instigation going around with their belts off, swatting ass—"Lower there! Try there!"

Tim stopped going to Tuesday night practice. He'd been having trouble with his knees in February and March, with the wrap bandages and the needles into the kneecaps. He started spending Tuesday evening on the living room floor, the same span of time, the full two hours, stretching, limbering, form-building exercises.

By this time, though, Paul's spirit had so permeated the club that it colored even those practices he didn't personally lead. Here the ethic was to extend yourself, to push beyond your capabilities. By ignoring the pain of your body, you overcame your weakness; by being master over yourself, you became master over your opponent. He simply stood for the established creed.

"Suppose you're standing at the bus stop some night," Paul would tell them at the end of a practice, "you're walking down a dark alley and five guys jump you"—throwing little grins back over his shoulder, as if to choruses of accolades called to him from the shrubbery and the trees.

It was a function, finally, of it being summertime. Emil was away, Dietz was away, for the last two weeks of June Esther was in Nova Scotia, Ed Able was busy getting married, the brown-belts were in a rapture of dedication anyway. Amoto, who made a career of inscrutability, also made a career of letting things go by him.

One night Tim saw him kick Sominex, who nobody else even bothered with anymore, just casually as he was going by him, like you'd kick a piece of cardboard out of your way on the street.

"You kicked him," Tim said.

"No talking in line. Down there."

"You kicked him. You kick your students?"

"He was cheating. Mr. Shuri kicks his students when they don't try hard enough. No talking in line." With three quick maneuvers he circled around Tim, swatting shoulder, rump, thigh—"Lower stance! Down there! Try there!"—and continued on down the line.

Cheating—it was a moral issue with him. What Tim thought afterward that he should have told him was that a gentleman doesn't need coercion to lead, a gentleman leads by quiet persuasion and example. But he could see a direct confrontation wasn't going to be the way to deal with him.

For the final fifteen or twenty minutes they did *kata,* ritualized combat routines designed for countering four, six, or eight opponents, three lines of eight spread across the grass, each member in turn counting out the steps. Most of the others counted in Japanese, "*Ich . . . nee . . . sun . . . chee . . .,*" but Tim considered this an affectation.

"One . . . two . . ."

"Louder."

"Three . . ."

"More forceful, louder."

Tim stopped counting.

"You put into your voice the force you expect your body to show. Go through again." Paul was at the end of the first row facing front, and hadn't yet looked around.

Timing his pause, Tim said, "I don't understand. You'll have to show me."

Without a moment's hesitation, Paul was around and back through the lines. "You put into your voice . . ." He gave Tim a shove hard with both hands against the chest, sending him back a step or two, "the spirit you want the others to show in their movements," turned and walked back to place. "Go through again."

That was the last time for three weeks Tim went to practice.

He counted through again, no louder really than before, and this might have been seen as having held his ground, and at the end neglected to give the command *yasume* to return to natural stance, which might be construed as a further act of defiance, though the fact was he'd simply forgot. He spent some considerable time afterward thinking through all he might have done or might have said—while feeling pretty much that the fact that he was thinking this much about it at all was reason in itself to be pulling back for a while.

It was not, he felt fairly convinced, any added element here, any case of the repressed impulse acting itself out as aggression. No Prussian officers hiding here. Paul was attractive, insofar as peak conditioning and an unassailable self-esteem in the prime of life could make any man attractive, though a little too clipped, a bit too close-chiseled for Tim's taste. It was in fact because he felt free of any motive in the case that he felt free in challenging him at all—at the same time recognizing that any move he made at this point would have to be construed as a challenge, that to opposing him there was no alternative except to be pulling back.

Lacking the customary male incentives, he lacked too the traditional masculine regard for stamina and will, and with it, any feeling of shame at not doing any more than he absolutely cared to do. Knowing perhaps better than any of them here the practical value of these skills—the virtue, for instance, of knowing how to deal with four or six opponents in a tight place—he valued still more his own right of choice, the right to choose the exact extent and nature of his commitment. It was a matter, simply, of whether he could let himself be pushed.

There was more certainly to it than that, and he did see that nevertheless he would be backing down, and that there might be consequences to that more debilitating, more overriding finally than any action he might take, but it was because he did see that

that he saw the futility of taking any action at all. Driving through Singer Oval one afternoon, he spotted Paul ahead of him on his motorcycle, stopped at a red light. He was over a lane and right up to the light, his *gi* strapped in a tight, anonymous bundle on the rack behind him. It was Wednesday, Tim remembered there was a special blackbelt practice on Wednesday afternoons, and for as long as they sat there, for maybe a full half minute, he never looked around or saw Tim, and the moment the light changed started immediately up, looking neither right nor left—and it occurred to Tim that he wouldn't see, that in his mind there was probably no antagonism even existing. So confident was he of the integrity of his every move, that he would interpret any opposition merely as a sign of weakness, and out of tolerance, perhaps, out of his own idea of generosity, simply overlook it.

Tim set out as soon as it was getting dark, coming in on the river road through Elco, a swing around Riverside Park and past the Elco bluffs, where sometimes hitchhikers stood along the catch-fences hunting rides out to the dance bars in Dithridge and Clarksville. It was the Sunday after Fourth of July. The Fourth had fallen on a Tuesday this year, at the pinnacle of a week of mild and cloudless days, but three or four days ago the weather had turned hot, and the air started piling up and piling up until now it was a tangible factor in all transactions, shrouding any object larger than a fire hydrant in a stale grayish mist, blurring the lines of movement—through the market strip, where the fork-lift operators were working barechested tonight, a right on Calley and down Carlson a couple of blocks onto the Eight, a diagonal overlapping of two long rectangles of blocks looping the bus station at one end and Schwabb Park at the other, with the lower end of Alliance and part of Ninth forming the long-bar, and two or three blocks along the river end of Oriel the crossbar, across

Alliance and up Liting past the two churches and around the park, with an optional cut down the alleyway back of the Sholes, and then back down Philadelphia and the upper end of Alliance, a circuit of maybe twenty or twenty-five blocks in all.

On the newspaper stand at Philadelphia and Alliance two guys with their shirts off and beer cans in their hands were harassing the traffic, and it was a sign of the evening that there were some who were taking this for an invitation and were slowing down and hurriedly turning around for another pass by.

In the doorway of Guiding Light the Elastic Trick, a tall, scrawny, unattractive kid, so named for his propensity to mold into whatever contour he leaned against, who he didn't think anyone ever picked up, was standing horribly beaten and bandaged, the whole left side of his face swollen and discolored, but still out at his accustomed spot as usual, as if in warning, as if in some obscure form of reproach.

At Ninth and Philadelphia the man next to him at the light was rubbernecking all around—though at what or after what he wasn't sure. A good part of this same route was shared by the downtown hookers and their trade, and at two or three points crossed the stadium and the Hoit Hall traffic, and this time of night there was always a line of cars along the farther side of the park waiting for the bookkeeping shift at Dollar Bank to let out, and it was one of his recurring fantasies of these travels that he might one night make a chance turn and lock in with one of these, end up in some new part of the city with a new life, new habits and drives.

As he drove along he caught, as he frequently did, a perceptual tic, certain dominant features, certain doorways and sections of block standing out, like a stage set made up from a few representative props, or more, like a computer enhancement in which all background irrelevancies have been bled out. For a long time he'd been hearing people talk about Pancherello's, going down to Da Paunch, and always wondered where this Pancherello's was, until one night he found out it was on Alliance next to where he would have had to go by it probably a hundred different times, and it was another one of his recurring fantasies that he passed over these routes invisible, a life that left no tracks, a foolish and, he knew, finally just careless point of view.

For a while he followed a station wagon with the license I-DAD—#1 dad?—and then another one with a bumper sticker that read HELP ENSHRINE USS LAFFEY DD 729. He cut down the alleyway back of the bus station, where sometimes under the streetlights at the little cross-streets that connected to Oriel there would be somebody waiting, or along the fence that ran around the bus lot. These were the badlands now, a dismantled badlands, tucked into three or four vacant lots, a row of loading docks at the rear of three or four adjacent buildings, the field of derelict box-cars on the other side of the bus lot. There was a gap between the two fences just wide enough to squeeze through ("No chubbies, please," somebody had written down the side of one of the poles in fingernail polish), and one by one the last summer the cars had been broken into, until there had been one point in August it had been possible to walk across boards spread between the doorways of five of these, with a short leap into the sixth, into an absolute blackness where you'd never know what you might encounter, or had encountered. Coming back from here one night, he had met a skinny black man standing at the opening with a knife in his hand, and just shifted a little to one side, his feet a shoulder width apart and hands open and out a little from his sides, looked straight at him and said, "You come at me holding that knife, best you be sure that knife isn't holding onto you"—and it'd worked, either that had been too complicated for this guy to comprehend, or he'd comprehended it well enough, because he didn't make a

move, just stood there as if he was under an enchantment, while
Tim edged around him and out the opening.

But tonight there was nobody there, nobody on the steps of
the two churches on Liting, no one on the wall in front of the bus
station pretending to be between buses.

He parked around the corner from the all-night McDonald's on
Litchfield. The movie houses on Alliance were newer and better
attended, but he preferred this one just after Litchfield turned one-
way, where you could be stopping off a minute on your way back
from the bars in Duquesne Square, on your way back to your car,
on your way to pick up coffee at McDonald's.

A bell jangled on the door as you came in. There was nobody
behind the change counter, and inside all the lights were on, the
booths were being swept out—Tim turned around and walked
back out again. With the blacklights on, these places had a kind
of gutter romanticism that was almost appealing, but with real
lights on it was totally impossible.

He walked up to the corner and down the other side of the
street, pausing to examine the store windows. Every so often
somebody would come by and stop outside the theater, as if trying to figure out what this could be, and then, with a kind of
investigative resolve, march on inside, or go a few steps by and
then suddenly, as if an invisible giant hand had reached out and
plucked them up, wheel around and dart inside.

He waited about ten minutes and then went back inside. The
blacklights were on now, the coin man back behind his counter,
the doorbell jingled as he came through the door. You entered
through a small foyer done all in red and black, red shag carpet
and red flock wallpaper, and a pair of black leatherette couches,
the change counter a basement bar with alternating diamonds of
red and black—"Her," the counter man was saying to somebody
on the phone, "I wouldn't fuck her with your dick"—through a

bead curtain into a long, high-ceilinged room that might at one time have been an actual theater: the walls were needlessly high, almost as high again as the height of the booths, and up near the ceiling on the farther wall were a couple of what looked like projection slots. The walls, ceiling, the ducts and pipes running along the ceiling were all painted black, the floor black tile. Whatever the broom had swept up had left a few damp stains up the middle of the aisle.

Four of the booths had lights on, and Tim stood sorting through his change until their occupants emerged, two of them men he'd seen come in while he was standing outside, and a businessman type with an attache case and a newspaper folded up under his arm, and then a pudgy black kid who took a slow time deliberating between booths and after two or three went on out the door.

The doorbell jingled, and Dubonnet, who he'd known from the old Troy Hill days when he first came to town, walked in all smiles, in white shoes and a pair of light pants that showed butter yellow under the blacklights.

"How do?"

"How do."

He went around and checked the peepholes, then came over and joined Tim.

"Aren't we looking spiffy this evening," Tim told him.

Bonnie, pleased, went into a little flurry of revelations, "I was having dinner over at my sister's and we were having stuffed pork chops, and um-*um* I-want-to-tell-you, and they were all sitting down to play cards but I was feeling kinna sleepy, so I thought I'd just stop off a minute here on my way home, what is it, dead?"

"Dead," Tim nodded.

"It was dead the other night in here. They're all going up now to that new place on Gower, you know the one with the double booths and the cushion seats, you been up there yet?"

Tim hadn't.

"Um-*um*. This in here anymore, you know the other night in here some guy jumps out of the booth at Ron while he's coming around checking the booths, slugs him on the head with a pipe rolled up in a newspaper, and runs out the door. And cops in here, maybe you noticed those two in the station wagon along the side of the building when you came in, that's why I never come in here anymore."

This came out in bits while he was strolling up and down the aisle, but when he saw that Tim wasn't going to be encouraged to leave, he settled down beside him.

"It's dead."

"Dead," Tim nodded.

"Oh, then. And have you seen this new one they have now with the battery that goes inside your pocket, and when you get wet, the current—"

"Shocking," Tim said.

The doorbell jingled, and they separated and drifted down to opposite ends of the aisle. The curtain parted and a young kid with a wispy mustache walked in, not bad but a little soft looking, with a giveaway fussiness—looking all around, like he'd always wondered what one of these places could be like.

"It's dead."

"Dead."

"Last week I'm driving home from here, and I see these two young guys, well, you know I don't usually stop for a hitchhiker, least of all when there's two at a time, but these ones were dressed nice, though you could tell they'd been drinking—"

His fingers fluttered around the corners of his mouth, the nails with their clear lacquer yellow and luminous in the blacklight.

"And this one says to me, You mind if we light this joint? And I say, Go right ahead, as a matter of fact I might even try some myself, and the one that's in back kind of has his knee up against the back of the seat, so that when I reach back with the joint I figure if he doesn't—"

The doorbell jingled and a middle-aged man wearing a slicker raincoat buttoned to his neck came in carrying a shopping bag. Tim had wandered down to the far end of the aisle, and as he was turning to walk back, the young kid, who he'd almost forgotten about, motioned to him from inside the doorway of one of the booths. He moved aside to let Tim past him, easing up onto the stool and leaning back until his head came to rest against the wall. He dropped a quarter into the slot.

A black plumber working under the sink in coveralls was being pestered by a negligeed housewife. He was only trying to do his job, but she just wouldn't leave him be. The young kid edged in to get a closer look.

"Where're you from?" he asked Tim.

"Ah, Spillway, Spillway." Tim slipped his hand around the back of his neck, tracing a fingertip along his hair line.

"And did you go to school in Spillway?"

"School in Spillway? Ah, yeah, yeah, school in Spillway."

"And when you were in school, did you ever play hookey from school?"

About this time Tim started to remember he'd met this particular kid before.

"And when you played hookey from school, and you got caught, what did they do to you?"

"Scusez."

Tim squeezed by him and back out of the booth, and a minute later, when he emerged and walked by Tim, neither of them showed the least sign of recognition.

The doorbell jingled and an incredibly tall, incredibly skinny, incredibly black boy in scarlet basketball silks and stripe-matched

socks and one of these strap-on beaks that all the black queens
were liking this year walked in, walked all the way down to the
end of the aisle, turned around, and walked back out again, followed almost immediately by another, shorter, very muscular, and
equally dark number in skin-close white jeans and a white temp-
tation top, who did likewise. It was show night tonight. Up at
the head of the aisle an old man was standing coughing, and had
maybe been standing coughing for as long as he'd been there,
single, dry, dislocated coughs, one every ten or fifteen seconds,
while the man in the slicker raincoat, who had what looked like
three or four more coats buttoned up underneath that, was going
around very conscientiously reading all the signs and munching
on something crunchy that he had to dig around for in the bottom
of his bag.

The signs were of three varieties: commercial blacklight posters
tacked up around the walls just under the ceiling, cosmic space-
girls and copulating abstracts; next to the doors of the booths
one or two small denominational signs, 2 BOYS 1 GIRL, TWO +
ONE = FUN, FUN WITH BLACK & WHITE; and accompanying
these, handpainted title signs that Arthur the nightshift man made,
BIG BANANA and MAGIC MOUTHS, HUMAN SANDWICH sub-
titled DOUBLE JOINTED, BAR TEND HER and COCKTAILS FOR
TWO, COCK and TAILS in different colored letters, with little beds
and WOW signs painted in the corners. These last apparently were
thought to have talismanic powers, because there were as many
as nine or ten of them tacked around some of the doors. He was
leaning against the side of one of the booths picking at the corner
of one of these, and as the doorbell jingled just lifted his head, as
Paul came through the curtain.

Just inside he paused, and there was a second or two before
his eyes started to pick out details, when Tim could have slipped
inside one of the booths and been passed by unseen, and that he

didn't afterwards had to seem, in however dim a way, to have been deliberate.

"What's good in here, anything?"

"There's a couple over here that aren't bad, this one here was okay—want to try one?"

"No, that's all right, I was just seeing what it's like"—and he turned and walked back out the door.

Tim was right behind him. He hadn't meant to make a move, rather the opportunity not to make a move, to turn the encounter casual and unmemorable, but he immediately saw that if he left it at this it could only have an opposite effect; so in each step that followed the crucial thing was to avoid the break coming at that particular point, and the only way of avoiding that to push ahead to the next possible step.

Outside the door Paul turned left, Tim alongside him now, and started up the block, neither of them looking at each other or saying a word, not matching each other exactly, they weren't moving in step, for example, but at a pace too rapid for nonchalance—up ahead he saw a man coming the other way shift out toward the curb. At the corner they both swung another left, and immediately around the corner Paul's motorcycle was parked, and directly in front of it was Tim's car. He hadn't identified the car as Tim's, and betrayed some surprise when Tim walked over and unlocked it.

Tim smiled blandly and said, "Looks like our paths are crossed this evening."

Paul nodded, more of a shrug than a nod, and said something about having just come back from the Blue Marble—"except you know that's really just a neighborhood bar."

Tim said, "I was just going to say maybe you'd care to stop off and have a beer."

"You know some places around here that are good?"

"Probably this late on a Sunday night there might not be too many open. But I have some back at my place, we could stop off there."

Paul had been fitting on his helmet, but now he took it off again and held it under his arm while he deliberated. He was a person who would always give that second or two of consideration to any question he was asked, however trivial. He had a way when he was being serious of pulling down the corners of his mouth and looking over to the side—that was the look he'd wear at thirty or thirty-five. That's the way our faces change, Tim was thinking, the way we form our faces as much as our faces form us.

Or he'd grow out of it, maybe, grow into his authority, more trusting of the immediacy of his own responses.

"You go on, I'll follow you."

It was a fifteen- or twenty-minute drive, across the broad end of downtown and up the Streets Run through a long succession of lights, at each intersection having to slow down and check back, Paul lagging perpetually behind, until after a while Tim stopped worrying about him, for long stretches almost forgetting he was back there, thinking no more about it than to think that whatever happenstance would bring him, happenstance was guaranteed to make right.

Then when they reached the house, as he was kicking down his stands and pulling off his gloves, Paul pointed over the rooftops in the direction of Wilmer, which was only a couple of blocks away, and said, "Twenty-two months ago, and I'd have been sitting over there in one of those desks."

"Twenty-two months? How old are you now?"

"I'll be twenty-one in twenty-three more days. I'm in one of these new forty-nine-month programs, where they have you in for seven months and then you're out for seven months, and the government pays for your training. I start an internship down at Rolinar tomorrow morning."

Immediately Tim's whole impression of him changed—his actual appearance seemed to change—what had seemed the man's too-earnest self-regard revealing itself as the promising boy's tight-held apprehension at not being taken entirely seriously.

Climbing the walk, mounting the steps to the porch, his eyes were constantly in motion, measuring, checking out. Though still fairly young, he carried in him already the habits of a man of knowledge. He would never walk into any place where danger waited him.

Tim bustled ahead of him—"I've had this place for almost two years now, I used to have another place up on Sussman that was bigger than this, I've had three places since I've lived in the city. This one is really only two rooms, but they're on two different floors, so you don't really feel it's such a tiny place. It's a two-room duplex, you know?"

Inside the door Paul picked up and dropped one foot and then the other, the remnant of some wintertime stomping gesture, looked around, and said, "Hey, nice place."

"What can I offer you? Beer? Juice? Something stronger?"

"What d'you have?"

"I have apple juice, grapefruit juice, sorry no orange juice. Bourbon, scotch, a little tequila. Vodka with tonic, white wine. Encino."

"Bourbon's fine for me. Ice, little water."

He went over and sat down on the couch. Tim mixed him his drink and took it over—he was sitting hunched up on the edge of the couch, and reached up to take the glass without lifting his head—and then went around and did the things he did, lit a couple of candles, lit a stick of incense and stuck it into one of the plant pots, put a record on, and as he was passing the couch noticed that Paul's glass was almost empty and offered him a re-fill, which he accepted. Then he made a quick trip upstairs, and apparently that was a mistake, because when he came back down and sat down on the couch next to him, he was all clenched up, and his glass was already two-thirds of the way empty, and what he thought was there was something that was bothering him, he'd come here with something on his mind and maybe he could help.

"Is something the matter?" Tim asked him. "Is there anything I can do?"

This triggered off an excited and jumbled response—"Now, I don't want you to think I've been jagging you"—jumping up and immediately sitting back down again—"don't mean to be, don't want you to think I'd be jagging you"—the gist of it being that when he'd heard Tim ask him over, what he heard was himself asking girls the same question.

"Well," Tim said, "you never know what'll bring 'em."

Paul leapt to his feet and started pacing the floor. "My mind's not straight, I've had these drinks, I can't make decisions when my mind's not straight, I've got to have time and think this over, I'm not trying to jag you, though."

"Don't mean to be jagging you," he kept saying. What he was saying was, I'm getting out of here.

"But I don't want you to think I've been jagging you."

"Wait a minute, wait, wait, wait a minute now, just wait a minute here, what're you saying, you're saying you're walking out of here now?"

"My mind's not straight, I can't make these decisions while my mind's not straight, I've had these couple of drinks, I've got to have some time to think this over."

"All right, all right, now, let's just slow down here a minute now."

They were both on their feet now, circling each other around the middle of the floor. At a certain point Tim could feel him drawing into himself, consciously taking command of himself, a watchful and then inquisitive look coming into his eyes.

He gave Tim a sidelong look and said, "Do you always talk like that? Take a line like that?"

"Oh, yeah, the quick lip, yeah, yeah, story of my life right there."

"I mean take a line with someone like that."

"Oh. Well. Well, see—you see, you put something out in front of somebody and see how they react. As a way of finding out what they are."

Paul nodded. He'd only been interested in how it worked.

"Don't you like women at all?" was the next thing he wanted to know.

"I wouldn't put it like that," Tim said.

"I'm not putting it down, you understand. Was it something that went wrong with a woman? Or have you always been that way?"

"It's my nature," Tim told him. "It's what I am."

From that point on though he could see there would be no getting through to him at all. Still there was the actual business of getting him out the door, Paul wanting to recount some incidents that had happened to him hitchhiking in the desert in Utah and Nevada, and then to leave on the note that he was only going to think things over and maybe later on would be back to talk some more, Tim going over to the end of the couch sitting with his knees drawn up, going "I see, yes, that's right," and "No, no, that's all right, no, that's all right"—until suddenly he just turned and bolted out the door, an abrupt, awkward parting.

For a long time he didn't make a move, but just sat where he was, on the couch. Paul had been there at the most fifteen, maybe

twenty minutes. He'd left the door into the hall a little ajar, and he
didn't think had fully secured the bottom door, either—leaving
himself, if only symbolically, a way back in—and Tim knew he
ought, as a first step toward putting this whole episode out of his
mind, to go down and lock them, but for a long time he didn't, just
sat, his mind empty and lax. He'd been through episodes like this
before, situations where he'd supposed too much, where something he'd assumed to be tacit had later been withdrawn, and each
time they left him the same way, drained, depleted of all reserves.
Unmanned, he thought of it. He told himself that it was only a
principle involved here, and not necessarily an indictment of himself personally, or alternately, was only personal, some error of
approach, a misstep on his part, that needn't be read as an entire
life judgment, and in any case he'd been honest, had concealed
nothing.

Eventually he did go downstairs and locked up, climbed the
stairs to the upper floor and undressed and turned down the bed,
leaving the light on over the kitchen sink and the stairway light
on, in case Paul should come back by looking to see a light, and
even after he was in bed was still half listening—keeping alive
as long as possible the possibility he might still be back and this
cleared up, deferring as long as possible the official start of his
unhappiness, on the chance that some of it might slip by him sub-
liminally. He knew what was in store for him now. It was a two-
or three-day process, in which he would have to rehearse back
through line for line everything that had been said, or might have
been said, or might still be said—for fairly early on he recognized
that now he would have to start back to practice again, and that
raised a whole new series of contingencies and doubts, so that it
wasn't for another full week that he actually went back, and by
then Paul had been dead for nine days. He'd run his motorcycle
off a turn on a backcountry road the other side of Clydedale, killed

instantly. By this time, details had cooled, and interest shifted to more prodigious aspects, such as him having been killed "instantly," and having been just twenty-two days short of turning twenty-one, so that Tim was never sure afterward how he'd even determined it was that same night it had happened. He was in the locker room getting dressed for practice, and Mike Houser was describing how he'd driven over there the day before on his bike, and the dumpster, it was a dumpster he'd crashed into, wasn't even set straight but on an angle with the turn, and "if he'd been just fifteen degrees shorter, or fifteen degrees wider coming around there—"

He'd gone out that night in the state he was in and killed himself.

Tim had killed him—and because he thought that first, before he even knew any particulars of the case, always led him afterwards to feel that he could to some measure discount it in his mind.

At the same time he recognized that this was to be an event totally without consequence, that no connection was likely ever to be drawn to himself, that whatever penalties were to be extracted here were to be entirely out of his own mind.

His immediate thought was only to make it through practice, to show nothing, lining up, bowing in, running through warm-ups, having to follow the others to perform the simplest of moves, down the floor and back, a turn and then back, slipping into a lulling of routine, an easing forgetfulness out of which each second he would have to encounter it, and the next second again fresh from the start—this was what shock is, he was thinking, the confrontation with the thing greater than our capacity to absorb it, so that we must re-encounter and re-encounter it full until the quota can be filled; crossing the floor and picking up his bag and down to the showers and out to his car, climbing the stairs to the upper floor, pausing to spread his *gi* out over the shower rod to dry, to settle down finally into the spot he'd reserved for himself in his mind, on the floor next to the window in the alcove off the bed.

It was nearly dark, only the water tower on top of the next hill and a low flat building next to it that might be either a hospital or a school all that was still distinguishable against the sky. The window swung in, coming between his back and the wall, so that he had to lean in, his forehead against the sidebar of the frame, his hand gripping the sill. The feeling was of things moving very fast all around him, and he had to hold very tight, and keep very still, if he was to keep track of even a fraction of it all.

It was a thing that was unassailable, there was going to be this thing now in his life that he was going to have to deal with, that by its very nature he was going to have no way at all of being able to deal with. It was like a border he was unable to cross, or more properly a territory he was confined to, where no matter what direction he set out in he was unable to go more than a few steps before he was stumbling and faltering.

At some point in his life he'd come to realize that ordinary rules of conduct were inapplicable in his case, and had turned his back on them, wandering off the common path into an antinomian wilderness, a dark wood from which reason was no guide.

After around midnight the street began to quiet, and from then on each occasional arrival and stir along the block took on a disproportionate significance, the night becoming a perpetual series of accusations and alarms. Around four o'clock he went over and lay down on the bed, on his back with his knees drawn up and the heels of his hands pressed into his eyes, until around six, when he went back to the window to watch the water tower and the buildings around it take shape in the morning light, until it was time to get ready for work, and as soon as he returned home that evening returned to that same spot, to the window, giving himself over to a schedule of remorse, to certain designated postures and hours of the day (so much so that after three or four days the bar of the windowframe had printed a permanent crease across his forehead, and several people remarked on it), giving himself over, almost unwittingly, to endurance, to recovery, to— as he came increasingly to feel it—a blunting, a smoothing over, a compromise, cutting himself off from his ordinary ties and obligations and noting, not for the first time, how easy it is to lapse into the background, how widely our lives may veer and nobody even notice.

One of the curious aspects of the thing for him was a peripheral sharpening—of vision, feeling—for the play of light on the bricks of the sidestreet below, for subtle variations in the changing aspect of the water tower against the sky, as if all the emotion were being squeezed out around the edges. At work he was more deliberate, more painstaking, his judgments surer and more rapidly formed, at practice (for through all of this he continued diligently to attend practice) he felt himself coming nearer the stance, his concentration sharper, his endurance lengthened. After a week or ten days had gone by, he hadn't so much assimilated as exhausted the feeling, and from then on had to be especially on guard against some casual reference to it slipping out in conversation. At night he encountered it in grossly literal symbolizations in his dreams, giant pointing fingers and crowds that turned their backs on him in the street.

And at times a bitter hilarity seized him—for what was he to think, finally, that so repugnant was his love that even the thought of it was enough to drive strong men to their deaths?

One night as he was coming down the steps after practice, he heard Burger King, one of the St. Vincent brownbelts, talking about going down to Tantoni's with Paul after practice and shooting burners, more of an intonation than any actual remark, but enough to send him on a chance to Ed Able.

He said, "That's a little unusual, isn't it, a blackbelt and a drinker?"—and saw from the response the extent to which this was true.

"There was never anyone more dedicated than Paul Hough," Ed Able told him. "Paul and I used to live on Frew Street together, and three or four in the morning sometimes, if we couldn't get to sleep, we'd get up and do two or three hundred front kicks together—"

After that Tim started sorting back through again, certain inconsistencies he'd let slip by him before, those five-hundred-mile-every-weekend drives, and the strange intensity of his whole style. So maybe their paths had been more than crossed that evening after all. If so, it wouldn't be the first time he'd borne the burden of another man's demon.

Those three and four a.m. kicking sessions were especially revealing, the two of them tossing on their respective pillows. *Hey, Ed. Huhh? Hey, wanna do some front kicks?*

After a while he began to feel even angry over it, seeing that whatever the case, it was going to have its change on him anyway, coming in the end to feel, as he had on so many occasions earlier in his life, himself the victim of the affair.

He was lying downstairs on the couch, his arms hanging back over the arm. There had been a shower of sunspots playing over the top of the coffee table and the back of the couch when he first lay down, but now, though an impression of daylight was still hanging in the air, all around the surfaces of the room were black. He scooped up his wallet and keys, turned over some papers that had been lying out on the coffee table—the buzzer sounded twice more before he could reach the bottom of the stairs. He pulled aside the curtain, and saw Esther Hardy standing outside. She had moved a couple of steps back from the door and was looking away to one side. She'd never been here before, and he hadn't even known she had known where he lived, but different times they'd talked, and a couple of times had gone out to eat with some other people after practice, and he wasn't entirely surprised to find her here now.

"I didn't see any light on, I was afraid you probably weren't going to be here."

"Oh, no, no, not at all, in fact I'm glad you rang, I sleep this early and then I can't get any sleep later on. Can I offer you something? I have wine, I could heat water for instant coffee or tea, I have apple juice, grapefruit juice."

"No, just apple juice's fine for me."

First she had to go around and comment on everything. She had a wide, bright, wondering gaze, and listened carefully to everything that was said to her. A bit of this came over as slow-wittedness, a kind of warrior pose—the buffoon manqué—the male counterpart of which he'd encountered various times in the past. She was wearing loose pleated pants, belled all the way up like a *gi,* and a loose sleeveless sweater. A narrow stripe of suntan ran the length of the back of her arms, arms that were long and uniformly thin, the wrists disconcertingly frail. Her hair was parted down the center and pinned behind the ears in a practical style, emphasizing still more the wideness and directness of her gaze. She was right to emphasize the eyes, they were fine, clear, untroubled eyes, a pale gray with tiny chips of amber and deeper gray sprinkled around the pupils.

She sat on a low hassock, smiling and rolling a glass of apple juice on her knee.

"So, and you live all alone here?"

"Oh, yes, all alone."

"That must get lonely sometimes, I imagine you'd get very lonely here sometimes."

"Oh, well, but you know everybody's got to find their own way."

She nodded, examined something on her left, something on her right.

She said, "You know, I've been watching you lately at practice."

"Oh? You think I show any future?"

She had to think a minute about that.

"You're not bad. There are ways you could be very good. There are things you have that you could build on."

He'd found on these occasions that a direct declaration is always best, that the less angling is done early on, the better chances later for an accommodation.

He said, "You know, I probably ought to tell you, I'm strictly one of the guys."

"What does that mean?"

"It means I'm gay."

She said, "I thought probably you might be. That was one of the things I wanted to find out."

He waited to see where she would take this now.

"You know, I actually live very close to here, on the top of Castlemaine near Dobbs. I go by here when I'm going to pick up my lumber, though I doubt if you've ever noticed me in my van."

Still he was waiting to see where she was going with this.

"One of the funny things, I felt, one of the things that always stuck out with me about Paul and me in the club, is while we had almost the same history in the club, we started in the same beginner group, and left the club almost at the same time, and were away almost exactly the same time—we even returned with some of the same moves—we were never really friends. Though I always felt there was some special understanding that we had, like there were things about him that I could know that nobody else would ever know, and vice versa."

In a way he was almost relieved. He'd gone into the kitchen section to put on water or take something out of the refrigerator, but now came back and sat down on the couch facing her, leaning in until his eyes were level with her own.

"I can't know," he said to her, "I can't ever say for certain what extent something I might have said, something he could have interpreted out of anything that happened here might have contributed to what he did that night, but I am certain that nothing I intentionally said, nothing that could have happened here in any way outright figured, on that much I am sure."

She gazed at him unjudgingly, saying nothing.

"I don't know to what extent I'm the contributor to, was only the bystander of what was going on inside him, I think in all honesty fairly little. I've asked myself the hard questions that I can, and I don't believe that I am. I don't in any honesty feel that I am."

"But you have these doubts," she said.

"I think I'll always have doubts, and pay a penalty as high for them as if I were to be sure. But I don't believe that I am. As far as I can ever know, as truly as I can ever feel, I don't believe I am."

"But still you have these doubts."

"I have these doubts—if I didn't have doubts, if I was positive, wouldn't that tell you something there? What better answer could I give you?"

He didn't quite catch what she said to that.

"You're heavier," she said, "but I'm more advanced. My speed up against your strength. We're about even matched."

"You want to fight me?"

"In overcoming me, you overcome my suspicions, and vanish your own doubts. Though neither of us can know the truth, the truth will make one or the other of us stronger."

A second or two went by in which he tried to gauge just how serious she might be—and in which he wasn't fully able to repress a smile.

"We'll go over to the new *dojo*. I have a key."

"I just have to get my *gi*."

He'd left the *gi* over the shower rod to dry, and first it would have to be ironed. He didn't have a proper ironing board, and had to clear off one of the tables to use instead. He never quite got around to putting things away, and there were piles of canned goods and packages of light bulbs scattered over the furniture, and little stacks of magazines and correspondence planted around the floor. She shifted back into the easy chair, relocating onto the floor a pile of new, variously colored socks on top of a crumpled store bag that had been sitting on the arm.

He started rinsing out some dishes, "I don't like to leave my place unless everything's just the way I want it."

She nodded, "I must spend twenty minutes on my bench before I start in the morning, and again before I walk away at night."

He wiped the sink, did some business with the blinds, straightened out a few things on the shelves, all the time keeping up a running dissertation on the virtues of steam cooking, "It's only lately I've been doing almost all my cooking by steamer. It keeps in flavor and cuts vitamin loss. You know, you can cook more ears if you steam your corn instead of boil it, plus you eliminate the danger of splashing. Or squash, I wash 'em, scrape 'em, slice, sprinkle with a little white pepper and grated parmesan cheese. And string beans. And dry fruit—you can save the liquid for a brew with a little brown sugar and powdered cloves."

She nodded, taking it all in, showing no impatience. She was giving her evening to this.

"How do you feel about women, then?" she finally asked.

"Women, then?"

"You were saying you go for guys, how do you feel about women, then?"

"I like women." He came back over and sat on the couch. "I don't dislike women, or resent women. I don't see myself in any kind of competition with a woman. I think I have an understanding of the kind of conflicts a woman has to deal with, conflicts that probably she is prepared more efficiently to resolve."

"And have you always felt like this? Was there ever a—"

"Actually," Tim said, "actually I think it's the thing I lack that I crave, the essence of a man. Something of a transubstantiation idea in that for sure. In a way, I think it's a way of making myself more a man." The forthrightness of this he could see was going a long way toward turning her around, and he wasn't able to resist adding: "Actually, I think it's probably even more quantitative than that, a certain quota—a certain yardage I feel I have to cover each month."

It took her a second or two for the implications of this to begin to settle in, and then he could feel her straightening up in her chair; he could see that as usual he would be paying high dividends for scoring these points. Now she was only waiting for him. After a couple of more minutes of stalling, he gathered up his *gi* and stuffed it into his bag, and said, "All set!"

Her van was parked out front, a big, anonymous looking Dodge van painted telephone-truck green. She opened up the back for him to see inside—a complete living unit, kitchenette, bunk bed, a table with two fold-down chairs, the joints so painstakingly worked they seemed to be budding from the grain. "This has two burners, this is insulated but not refrigerated, I believe if you're going to be more than two days away from processed foods, you'd best be prepared to live off the land, this folds down, this opens out." Fire extinguisher, flares, tools and sundries behind the side panels, blankets, towels, and clothing in tight tubular bundles in back of the ceiling slats—"for added insulation"— a drop-down ironing board that locked into a slot on the back of one of the chairs, even a tiny aquarium built into one wall, all surprisingly frilly and feminine, the bedspread, curtains, and tablecloth a matched gingham check. Her manner, too, was softer now, more easygoing. He realized she'd taken all that business upstairs as confessional, and this was her way of returning it.

"I'll drive over, you can follow me."

The new *dojo* was inside Singer Oval, a four-lane traffic bypass set down around the old east-end shopping district, marooning it from access on every side. After dark it was all but deserted in here, except for an occasional bewildered derelict and a few scattered clumps of bus transfers, grouped tight together like vigils, the long rows of darkened shops, the broad stretches of mall paving, the three churches on one intersection with the rust-concept fountain in the middle, lighted by special crime-deterrent lamps, having the overclarification of a stage set, on which every actual encounter was made muddled and scary.

The *dojo* was above a florist's, in a tall green frame building that connected at the rear with a lower, longer gray-shingled building with a slanted roof and no windows. She let them in by a door almost at the end of the other building, leading the way up a steep flight of stairs and down a narrow hallway, and then up four more steps to another locked door, not putting on any lights—"There'll be enough light from the windows once we get inside to see by." It occurred to him she must come here regularly, probably every night like this.

They came in the back way, picking their way down a long hallway past stacks of plasterboard and big cans of something, past a couple of small offices and two smaller practice rooms that had been partitioned out of a larger space, through a curtained doorway into the *dojo* proper, a wide, high-ceilinged room with bare varnished floors and rows of high windows across the left and front walls, that let in, as promised, plenty of light to maneuver by. Around the sides of the room were areas of deep shadow, a pair of hanging ferns silhouetted above the sloping line of the partition, the right wall alternating mirrors with exercise bars. The floorboards were edged with fine lines of light, but inside the mirrors the floor was a solid dark space, blacker than black.

She put her bag down next to the partition and started undressing, fragments of silhouetted elbow and hunched-up back popping out and being quickly reabsorbed back into the darkness behind her. He took his bag over to the end of the row of mirrors and set it down. As she reached her arms back into her jacket, the light caught a bright keyboard of ribs, a narrow, practically flat chest. She was too thin, too tall, her center of gravity would be high, probably too high.

He'd just gotten a new *gi,* and it hadn't quite shrunk down yet. The belt was one of these new wear-resistant fabrics that appeared to be knot-resistant as well.

She walked out to the middle of the floor, stretched and bent, brought her elbows then her head to the floor, tried a few practice kicks. He wandered around for a while, as if hunting for just the right place, pushed up onto tiptoes a couple of times, then bent down, brushing his knuckles to the floor.

"We bow in."

They faced each other and brought their feet together, bowing from the waist.

"*Ra.*"

"*Ra.*"

They started circling, easing in and out of stance, moving in a
few steps, and then back, keeping always just a step or two outside of striking range, a quick thrust in, and then quickly back,
in, and back, the slant of the partition, the silhouettes of the two
hanging plants, the left wall of windows passing behind her, then
the front wall, the right wall of mirrors, the curtained doorway,
and back around to the partition again, the lower of the two plants
momentarily situated behind her head like a fantastical bonnet—
and it came as a distinct surprise as the first blow struck him, a
quick jab to the solar plexus, and immediately she was back and
out and circling, hips low, body turned, offering the narrowest
possible target of retaliation.

He'd never been hit before. At practice the standard was to
deliver the blow with maximum force to a point just short of con-
tact. The two times he'd ever hit anyone himself, one time the
Sominex wholly by accident, and once Ed Able in free spar after
he'd had his guard down, he'd been led to feel it was tantamount
to disgrace, fully half of the club coming up to him afterward
to assure him he needn't feel bad about it. That blow was followed immediately by another a little lower, both of them quick,
deliberate lunge punches.

He'd been knocked out of stance and taken a couple of steps
to the side, and as she came in again he continued his sideways
movement another step or two, caught hold of her wrist and spun
her around, as he let go giving her a side-thrust kick to the rump
that sent her sprawling.

Then he went over and tried a technique that Emil had shown
them one time, offering her a hand up saying, "Hey, you know
you could hurt yourself doing that," and making a joke out of it.
But either he'd kicked her too hard, or, as he was beginning more
and more to suspect, she was just void of any sense of humor,
because she came up with a side-snap kick to the groin that he
just barely blocked, followed by a hard slap across the face.

Immediately she was back and out, circling, her eyes fixed on his—coming immediately back in with another lunge punch. He came up with a counterpunch, more a block than punch, that stopped just short of her nose.

"Don't hold back. Don't be holding back."

She moved in with another slap across the other side of his face, then quickly back and out, circled half around, and then back, her shield arm loose and bobbing, as if teasing an invisible line.

"Come on. Come on."

Her movements were more economical now—as he made a thrust she moved only a single step aside, quickly returning in with another slap to the other side of his face, then taking only a step or two back, her breathing controlled, her eyes never varying from his own.

"Come on, come on."

A wearied melancholy began to spread over him, his face burning and streaming sweat, his eyes tearing. He moved toward the center of the floor—twice again she was in, with another slap and then a lunge punch, blows he more acknowledged than fended—taking a position at the center of the floor facing the left wall of windows, his head tilted back, his arms slack at his sides. He could never know if this punishment was merited, but perhaps the only way to lift himself of the burden of it was to endure it to the full.

"Come on."

He fixed his eyes on the second window from the front, on one of the lower spires of the nearer of the two churches, that had a crescent of rust-sculpture superimposed over its lower half.

"You have to fight me, come on."

She hit him with a side-thrust kick to the right buttock, knocking him momentarily out of stance. He repositioned his legs a little wider apart, knees slightly bent.

"You have to fight me, you have to fight me."

She gave him another side-thrust kick hard as she could directly from behind, this time failing to budge him, and then circled around front, pantomiming blows to his face, then gave him several hard slaps back and forth across his face, and then a sharp back-knuckle strike to each nipple that made his *gi* crack.

"Come on, you have to fight me, come on, you have to fight me."

At a certain point he began to feel her bringing her anger under control. She was in back of him, had been aiming little nip-kicks at his buttocks and the backs of his thighs, and then for a minute or two there was a gradual slowing down, a barely discernible slackening of blows, and after that he could feel a pattern beginning to develop. She began to scatter her blows, aiming higher, to the shoulders and upper arms, tracing a jersey line along his collarbone, working exclusively with side-snap and roundhouse kicks now, quick, sharp strikes with the stinging edge of the foot, moving around his body in a generally counterclockwise and downward progression to a point just below the knees, a blow to the right side counterbalanced a minute or two later by one to the left, one to the shoulder complemented a few blows later by one to the wrist or hip on the other side. He saw she was going to cover his whole body with blows. Nothing less than that would satisfy her now.

After several minutes of this his entire body was stinging and burning, exquisitely sensitized, radiating specific layers of heat like a thermographic portrait. He began where he could feel precisely where the next blow would fall, could feel her circulating in the darkness, and the exact spot where she would emerge, could feel the spot where the blow would strike, cooling in anticipation, and the corresponding part of her body glowing as she began to make her move, as if she were in orbit, assembling in slow rotation around him.

An opposite succession of shapes, the curtained doorway, the wall of mirrors, the two walls of windows passed behind her, the slant of the partition, her feet gathering in the little threads of light that lined the floorboards, and as she stepped back dispensing them out again, in and back, the two of them closer and then back, as if trying to fit into a single outline, into a mutual stance.

There was a moment's awkwardness when they first went to touch, where they had to figure out how first to touch, and what they did was to grab elbows and give a shake, and she laughed, for which he was grateful, his prime fear at this point being of it proving all too ethereal. He'd lost his belt and she had shed her jacket somewhere along the way, and for the first time he noticed how flushed she was, her face and neck streaked with sweat.

They took turns holding each other's shoulder as they stepped out of their *gi*'s. Then they had to work out a position where neither of them would be dominant, that is to say, neither one of them subordinated, trying it first on their side, but they weren't able to work their legs out that way, then sitting up face to face— while he could feel the momentum siphoning off, the moment drifting off, and he turned her onto her back and quickly mounted her, fucking her and fucking her and fucking her until the point was effectively moot.

She exuded a faint workmanly odor, that he'd previously associated exclusively as a masculine odor, and there was a certain sense—a certain lack of rhythm in the frenzied parts, where she had the feel of a man. As she turned over on top of him, her arms braced behind his head, breasts pulled almost flat against her chest, her hips taut and almost fleshless under his hands, he could almost imagine her a boy—but they were beyond that now, beyond differences now, it could as easily be her inside him now.

At one point he heard her speak and lifting his head thought he could hear her counting, "*Ich . . . nee . . .*" and felt the laughter welling up, but he suppressed that, pushed beyond that, out into a lengthening clarity where each isolatable shape in the room lay on a separate plane, each at an assigned distance with an absolute value from the next, fanning out in a backward progression counterclockwise around the room. Just as he was beginning to settle into that feeling, he felt himself start to draw over—pulled back, but a moment too late, so that he experienced the moment as a stumble and a loss. She urged him on, responding with a reserve of energy that he wouldn't have expected, that was hardly sexual—for she made no effort to pretend that this was her moment, too—drawing him closer, tighter, every part of her body that touched his body in motion, no motion at all required of him, drawing him down to a refinement of stillness where even pleasure seemed to lie in suspension.

At the peak, the very sweetest moment, she bent her head and lightly touched her lips to his eyelid, the corner of his mouth, the side of his nose.

Then for a long time they just lay, he on his back with her lying half on top of him, her head inside the crook of his neck. The skin across the top of his thigh was pinched up where she was sliding off him, and her wrist had gotten wedged up under his chin, but he focused on the discomfort of that as a way of fixing the moment, his head back, his eyes open, empty of any motive or idea.

Then gradually over the space of a minute or two, as in these speed-action films where the figure of Adam is formed out of bare dust, or a beautiful woman reverts to a wrinkled crone, the different sections of the room began to align themselves, and without either of them having moved, he could begin to distinguish her body from his own. Then she stirred, lifting up to readjust the position of her leg, and pushed back her hair. He'd gotten his ankle tangled up in one of the *gi*'s. He tried to shake it loose, then bent down to free it, and when he lay back again, the two of them side by side now, he could feel them matching breaths, aware now of the rhythm and tone of her breathing.

Then they were both up—

"Did you see a—"

"Did you try over by the—"

His whole head and chest were radiating and tender like a sunburn. He'd wear this evening's entertainments for a few days to come. He wandered out into the hallway to look for a water fountain, and found a utility sink in one of the closets, letting his head and arms hang under the faucet, and then drip for a minute or two, and when he came back, she'd finished dressing and packing her *gi* into her bag. Seeing him standing there, she gave him a smile, an easy, contented smile, and it occurred to him, for the first time in a number of minutes, that for her all of this had been a combat, and that in her mind she'd probably won. He stood for a moment in the doorway trying to gauge the extent to which this was true, and to what extent it mattered to him.

"You see," she said as they were coming down the stairs, "it's just a matter of finding your own way of doing it."

He had just been thinking that if this was the only way he could do it, that only proved the impracticality of doing it at all.

They came out the front way—there was a push bar on the front door that locked automatically behind you—and just as they were stepping out the door there was a rush and bustle from around the corner. Instinctively they took a step back and began to lower into stance, their shield arm raising—but it was only a couple of black kids, a boyfriend chasing his girlfriend, she pumping high-kneed and shrieking over her shoulder, he loping comically along behind, down the block and around the next corner. They looked at each other and laughed, a little embarrassed, and the easing up of that carried them the rest of the way down the block, but he could see an uncertain moment coming up here when they reached the cars and it came time to separate. But as they came around the corner—swinging wide, in case any vagrant should be lurking around the other side—he decided maybe not. Across the street, through a narrow gap in a low line of hedges, the van and car sat parked, in the nearest, lightest section of the lot, parked two or three spaces apart, so that even as they approached them their paths were diverging, and from here it was only a matter of a few more steps, a smile perhaps, a word or two, and then good-night.

South of the Border

Leigh Allison Wilson

In a car, headed point-blank down an interstate, there is a sanity akin to recurring dreams: you feel as if every moment has been lived and will be lived exactly according to plan. Landscapes and peripheral realities blur and rush headlong backwards through the windows like the soft edges of sleep. And the road ahead and behind you becomes a straight line, framed in the perfect arc of a dashboard.

My sister sits hunkered against the side of the car and fiddles with the radio, careful not to touch my right leg. On a Sunday morning in the midlands of South Carolina all radio stations play either gospel music or black church services. Jane Anne chooses a church service and claps her hands, eyes closed, to the hiccupping rhythm of the preacher, both his voice and her percussion sounding disembodied in the smallness of the Volkswagen. "Take Jesus, oh Lord take Jesus," the preacher says, "take Jesus for New Year's." Clap clap clap goes my sister, clap clap. "Jesus is my friend" clap "Jesus is your friend" clap "Friends, accept Jesus" clap clap. Deep in her bowels she is a fundamentalist, a lover of simple truths and literal facts; her resolution for the coming year is "to see things more clearly." In this she is resolute, commenting often on points of interest as we careen northward through cotton fields and marshy bottomland and stark-colored advertisements.

I have no such resolution. While driving I develop an acute myopia and it is all I can do to concentrate on the pavement that blears and dashes like water underneath the car. Outside the world flashes by as if switched on and off in a two-dimensional slide show, one frame at a time, the whole universe condensed to a television screen.

"Look at that!" Jane Anne cries and points frantically somewhere outside. "Look, look!"

"What was it?"

"You didn't even look," she says. She claps her hands together with a violence that means she wishes one of them was mine. "Didn't even goddamn look at what I saw. You probably had something more important on your mind, I'm sure, probably aren't even interested in that cow I just saw with the human face."

"You just saw a cow with a human face?"

"No," she says, almost happily, "I didn't see a thing," and then she stares sullenly out her window.

Just last night my father and stepmother engaged in a domestic catfight over this kind of optical delusion. During a television football game, the Gator Bowl in Florida, they break out in an almost-brawl over forces beyond their control, forces five hundred miles to their south. Clemson, a South Carolina school, and Ohio State are playing and my father perversely roots for Ohio, a state that exists for him only during television football and basketball games. My stepmother was raised in the thick of Clemson patriotism, a twitch at the corner of one eye blossoming into a full-blown spasm, possibly hindering her vision, at every Clemson penalty and first down.

By the end of the game tension is extreme, my stepmother's eye winks rapidly, my father's mien settles like concrete as he stares at a commercial. Clemson is winning, my palms are sweating and slick, my stepmother is exultant, and my father steadily slips into a familiar attitude. Once, eight years ago, he almost hit me when I won a Monopoly game. His is a competitive madness that operates at a slow boil until all is lost, then his expression explodes into a kind of pseudo-apocalyptic blitz. So when a Clemson player intercepts a key Ohio State pass and Woody Hayes, ex-coach of Ohio State, smacks the Clemson player in the face, my father blitzes out, saying "Kill him, kill the bastard, Woody." My stepmother blithers to her feet (they sit in identical easy chairs, separated by a coffee table), winks and gasps, arms akimbo and shivering, shouting now: "You might as well say 'kill me,' that's what you mean!"

Blitz over, my father settles back into concreteness while my stepmother marches, footstep-echoes beating into the walls against one another, into their bedroom. An hour later everyone is sleeping heavily and even the television has sunk into a blank stupor. Today she poked her head in my bedroom doorway, flashing a smile birthed and bred in South Carolina and cultivated like white cotton, and told me goodbye before she left for church. She plays the organ for the Methodist Church of Fort Motte.

Jane Anne points out advertisements for the South of the Border tourist complex still an hour and a half in the future. CONFEDERATE FOOD YANKEE STYLE, BEST IN THIS NECK OF THE WOODS one sign reads. So frequent are these advertisements that they serve as punctuation along the sameness of the interstate and I begin to despise them because I feel my utter dependence on their familiarity. I come South twice a year, once at Christmas, once in the summer, each time more of an amnesiac experience than the visit before. I am fearful that after another few visits I may go home and never be able to leave, my present and future eradicated by the vicious tenacity of the past. But, truly, I am hypnotized

home by the staid reality of what I remember—a somnambula-
tory reality so familiar and so unchanging that it appears to be
the only true god in my life.

"I'd be a fool to stick around," Jane Tressel sings from the
radio. My sister has found an AM station. Lips taut and round,
she sings along with her mouth forming the words as if molded
around an ice-cream cone. The way she sings turns the words
into nonsensical baby-noise, but this is also a special function of
AM radio, this ablution of meaning into a catchy anonymity. Jane
Anne carefully reads several beauty magazines, pining over the
structured perfection of the models, always running out to buy
new beauty products although she is as frugal with her money as
a squirrel in autumn. A stranger, she sits so close to her door that
no place in the car could be equally far from me and she eyes the
side of my face with the wariness of a stray dog. She could be a
nervous hitchhiker, except that she controls the radio. This trip is
the first time we have been together alone in eight years. She is
a stranger, stranger still because for thirteen years we slept in the
same bedroom and now she resembles a kewpie doll rather than
a younger sister.

With her left hand, when it is not spiraling around the radio
tuner, Jane Anne tosses boiled peanuts between her lips. They
look like a pile of swelled ticks, gray-skinned and blood-bloated,
in the palm of her hand, and she is soberly emptying a paper sack
full of them. I have noticed that she eats in a dazed trance, similar
to the manner in which she sings to the radio, as if eating were a
habitual duty. She was always a dutiful child, and now she weighs
one hundred and seventy-five pounds, has a prematurely stooped
back, and the corners of her mouth pucker down in a perpetual
expression of bad humor. An unhappy kewpie doll.

Fifteen years ago she was a beautiful, dutiful child. Fifteen
years ago I would bring her red and purple ribbons, watch her

thread them through her hair. It looked like miniature maypoles, and when she tossed a braid I wanted to grab one and swing out. Today she wears a mud-colored scarf tied tightly at the nape of her neck.

"Why don't you ever talk seriously to me?" she asks and I grip the wheel, staring hard at the car in front of me, abruptly aware of the scores of vehicles swarming the interstate ahead and behind me. Each one is a possible fatal accident.

"What do you want to talk about?" I say warily, my thighs beginning to feel cramped in the immobile space-time of the traveling Volkswagen interior. In the event of an accident, all is lost in a Volkswagen.

"What do you want to talk about?" Jane Anne mimics in a voice that, remarkably, is more like my own than my own sounds to me. She is full of surprises, this sister of mine whom I do not know. "I'll tell you one damn thing," she says, really angry this time, her tongue flailing against a stray peanut, "you may be smart, but I have all the common sense in this family." Snorting, she clings to the side of her door.

This is true. She does have the common sense in our family, a fact uttered and re-uttered by my paternal grandmother who likens me to my Uncle George Wilkins. My Uncle George was so smart, she says, that he was almost an idiot. He died with a moonshine-ruined liver and a cancer that ate from his breast right through to his back, and Grandmother said it would have gone on through the bed and into the hospital linoleum if his heart hadn't stopped first.

He was a geologist and forever poking rocks with his cane, head bent forward, arm flicking, cane flicking, eyes pouncing toward the ground to examine and file away every square inch of land that his feet passed over. Once he broke his nose against a haybaler, never saw it, saw only the gray-black pieces of sedimentary rock that flipped over and under the tip of his cane. But he was a smart one, my Uncle George, and twice a year scientists from Washington came down to sober him up and fetch him back to a laboratory where he performed penetrating geological studies. They wanted him to fly up there, but he always said he did his traveling on the ground. Now he's his own specimen, buried under six feet of sand and sedimentary rock in Calhoun County, South Carolina, and he's not going anywhere.

"I'll tell you another damn thing," Jane Anne says and warms up to one of our childhood wrangles, the kind where neither of us is aware of the reason but both of us will stake our lives on a resolution in our favor. It is our father's blood that swells up at these times, bubbles of madness that break at the mouth. "I'll miss your sweet, sweet eyes," Willie Neal croaks from the radio, "I told you when I left, I couldn't live with your lies."

"I'm sick and tired of you making me feel stupid. You act like I'm still eleven years old, like I'm still your devoted and moronic pawn. I'm nineteen, damn you, I've read Sartre and Camus." She utilizes her French education in all arguments, since I have studied only Latin and vaguely remember it anyway—French is her code language through which she can curse me to my ignorant face. "I've seen Chicago and New York, I've seen Paris and *you* don't even have a passport."

"A passport isn't exactly a rite of passage, Jane Anne."

"Not," she says, "if you don't even have one." Furious now, she sputters like a cat and is just seconds away from a serious assault. Sometimes when we were younger we'd forget what we were angry about in the middle of a wrangle, and so kept on with it anyway, only louder and with more passion.

"Not," she says, "if you travel with your heart incognito like a goddamn ghost. You've been just a barrel of laughs for two weeks."

"Didn't come down here," I say, grim as a soldier, "in order to entertain my family." There is a white Pontiac endangering my rear bumper.

"Then why, in God's name, did you come at all?" Jane Anne kicks the peanut sack; the Pontiac veers to the left and passes safely, though in a glance I can tell that the man inside it is a lunatic.

"I know one thing and don't you forget it: I am as educated as you are, I am as competently conversive as you are."

This, too, is true. In fact, Jane Anne can shift facilely between Sunday dinner chatter at my grandmother's and mournful sympathetico at my aunt's where my first cousin, Jonathan, is dying of cancer. Both situations strike me dumb.

At my grandmother's Christmas dinner, I deaf-mute my way through the awkward vacuum during which butt-pinching uncles watch football games and bouffant-headed aunts question me as to how many boyfriends I have and my grandmother pounces at odd moments to bark in my ear, "Can't go to school forever!" Normally I wink and grin like a demon, offer condolences for my slovenly personality, giggle madly while my butt is tweaked, and create countless football players who appear and disappear as boyfriends according to my whim. Once I created a rather bookish law student who was poorly received and he disappeared during the course of dessert, an hour later reappearing as a dashing quarterback who was a well-received pre-med. This time, however, I sleepwalk, staring maniacally at each relative until they leave me alone.

"Time to eat!" Grandmother cries, pertly, her presence in its element and as relentless as a Mack truck. Fourteen grown men and women rise as one and throng into the kitchen where dishes of food, festive-colored and bubbling, are lined in perfect rows to be picked over, placed on china plates and retired to the dining room, there to be consumed in dutiful silence. But first comes the continuum in which fourteen grown men and women hang back, hem-haw, pluck at their sleeves or pick their noses, succumb to the cowardliness of not being first in line though for five hours their appetites have been titillated to the peak of a savage desire. For a few seconds we stand like tame vultures and just peer, ravenous, at the untouched food. I believe I will faint from hunger, until I finally find myself at the table, slapping mashed potatoes onto crisply cool china.

"Jane Anne," Grandmother says in her grand commandeering tone, a tone reminiscent of both grade-school teachers and Methodist preachers, "would you please say grace." Jane Anne positively glistens with glee, jubilant while all eyes pin me against the profaned table, potatoes puffed and accusing on my plate.

"For these Thy gifts, Oh Lord let us be thankful," Jane Anne croons, in a strangerly fashion. The surge is on now, compliments and condiments fly across the table, and I sleepwalk through dinner, an attendant to disapproval.

FREE IN-ROOM MOVIES: TWENTY HONEYMOON SUITES I read on a huge sign. In twenty minutes we will pass through the middle of South of the Border, almost into North Carolina. The peanuts have risen once more into Jane Anne's lap, and she nimbly eats them. "It's my last night in town, I'd be a fool to stick around," the radio says. I do not know the performer although his song is appealing in its drowsy insistence. At South of the Border Jane Anne will meet a boyfriend from her school and I will continue north to my school alone. Both of us are hyper-aware of the advertisements, as if they are motes of sand trickling time away. She wants to get out of my presence as badly as I do hers; we are both morbidly afraid of each other. FREE—ADVICE, AIR, WATER. EVERYTHING ELSE REASONABLE.

"Another thing," she says, wrapping up her side of the dialectic before handing the floor to me, "you have been nothing but rude and ill-mannered this whole vacation, to me, to Daddy, even to Aunt Louise. You lack discrimination, that's what you lack."

"Jonathan . . . how is he?" Jane Anne whispers to my aunt. I perch on the lips of a couch, finger wringing finger, my tongue thick as a marble tombstone.

"Dying," my aunt chokes, "dy—ing."

"How long?" Jane Anne looks absolutely engrossed, a dutiful child.

"Days, weeks, God knows when he'll be free from the pain." Solemnly Jane Anne acknowledges the mercy of God with a slow, dazed nodding of her chin. She is gathering momentum for the predictable eventuality wherein my aunt will begin to sob and she can console with a firm and warm arm across the heaving back. But—surprise—my aunt visibly marshals her circumference and pulls herself together with a prolonged sigh. My palms are clammy with the dead and the living.

"Sarah Louise is home," my aunt says, giddy with recovered strength, but poised along some precipice of mental breakdown. Sarah Louise is also my first cousin. "She's in the back bedroom getting dressed." Sarah Louise is in the back bedroom getting dressed, Jonathan is in the front bedroom, blinds drawn, dying. For a while we sit in an uncomfortably loud silence until Sarah Louise comes into the living room. Like her mother, Sarah Louise has reddish-brown hair and a pointed face that articulates itself at the breach of the nose. She looks like a rumpled domesticated animal, exhaustion whitening her cheeks in random places like frostbite. She is looking directly into my eyes.

"He wants to see you, Bo."

"Me?"

"He's asking for you."

Jane Anne shivers and recoils, I recoil, a creeping nausea deep inside my throat; I wish to hell I was somewhere, anywhere, somebody someplace else. When I was two, Jonathan christened me into the family by nicknaming me Bo, a name used only by blood relatives and, to them, a name coincidental with my very existence. Only recently has Jane Anne begun to call me Jennifer, her statement of self-determination. Nomenclature is her forte.

I remember Jonathan in two ways: first, the way he looked at eleven, knobby-kneed and skinny as a fence post, my best friend and comrade. Like rabid dogs we chased the cows on his father's farm until they ran idiotically into their pond water and grouped together up to their buttocks in sludge and cattails. The days I spent with him were always warm and cloudless and kinetic with revelry. We played doctor inside the very room where he now lies dying; he was the first man I ever studied. Once my father found us together and beat me with a leather belt until welts crisscrossed my bare legs and back like textile woof. Afterwards, since we lived in different towns, he grew out of revelry and into proms and long-legged cheerleaders. I saw him last two years ago, a young man so handsome he could send pangs of romance down the back of Ayn Rand herself. Blond hair feathered and long around his neck, the face of a beautiful woman made a little rough at the edges, an unaware body oozing casual strength and grace, the man was unbearably pretty. I believe the mythic Christ, aided by centuries of imagination, could never approach the fullness of reality in Jonathan's splendor.

I stand and rub my hands together and they slide against their own moisture. In times of stress I enter into a semicomatose state like an instinct-driven opossum. Automatically my brain begins to decline a Latin noun, a ae ae am a, ae arum is as is. The room is shadowed and unlit, a thickly-queer smell of medicine and urine and *sweet Jesus* the smell of life itself condensed into a pungent and rancid death-room, without light and without hope. I feel an acute hatred for myself, sweat trickling—an endless beading health—under my armpits: da ta ta ta, a ae am a, this is the way the world ends. Across the room the bed seems to rest against the far wall but surely to God he is not in it, there is no indentation under the quilt, there is only a skull resting on the pillow, a yellow hairless sunken skull.

"Bo," he says, a muffled, anonymous sound, drugged, removed, a physical impossibility save in nightmare. Dipping strangely, the lines of the room combat with a nausea, and I realize my mouth is whimpering and salivating. This nausea moves around the throat like unconscious prayer. The sting is for the da ta ta ta, arum is as is.

"Bo," he whispers, "I wanted to tell you . . ."

"Tell me."

"It's not so bad."

"Tell me quick."

He coughs without coughing, resting. Two more minutes and I will go mad and this thought is comforting. Someone is whimpering somewhere.

"Are you still my friend?"

("Fucking Jesus!" Jonathan yells and punches the air with his fist. The cowshed blows up in slow motion, splinters of wood fall like dust on his hair and shoulders. Large pieces of board fly over the fence, landing with dull thuds in the pasture. Down below, huddled up and frightened, Bo studies the delicate white hairs on the back of his right leg.)

"I wanted to tell you goodbye," he says.

(The others said, "Don't tiddle in the pond," but they pay no attention. They are full, with the warm brown water pressing against them, and they pay no attention. Across the water, stabbed by erect cattails, the cows stand knee-deep and black near the pond's edge, tails slapping onto their backs, heads browsing onto the surface then easing back up to stare at pine trees. Bo and Jonathan know that they think of great things, standing there in the water, staring. They tiddle freely and silently into the pond.)

"It's not so bad," he says.

I pretend I haven't heard.

"It leaves."

"Jonathan . . ."

"Goodbye," he says. "I loved you, yes," and then he starts to doze.

"Goodbye."

I return to the living room and begin to cry. My aunt and Sarah Louise begin to cry. Jane Anne stares at me with narrow eyes, her mouth puckered in distaste, then she pats and coos and comforts Sarah Louise. Uncontrollably I want to punch her in the nose, kiss her on the mouth, dash outside to the car, and get the hell out of South Carolina. A past is dying out from under my feet and I notice for the first time the blinking red lights on my aunt's Christmas tree. One two three, one two three they waltz, immobile, on the outskirts of the fir needles. I picture my sister wrapped in red lights, clapping her hands—one two three. When we get into the Volkswagen, she says: "You should have controlled yourself, you shouldn't have cried in front of them. We were guests in their house."

Ramona Stewart sings: "The sun's falling from the sky and night ain't far behind." Jane Anne waits for my defensive remarks, contemplating her retort through a wriggling at the lips, the worrying to death of a boiled peanut at the tip of her tongue. "Sun's falling," Ramona goes on, "night ain't far behind."

"Listen, Jane Anne," I say, glancing briefly in her direction, then staring straight ahead, a cheap power play although my hands and eyes are truly busy. She is filing away the information, noting the brevity and attributing it to arrogance.

"Can't we part as friends, can't we please just forget our old roles and part as friends? Please?"

Up ahead a huge sombrero sits atop a five-story tower. We have arrived at our connection, South of the Border. My sister sits in complete silence, one of her half-dutiful trances, and I pull off at the exit and enter the parking lot of a coffee house that is partly Mexican, partly southern, and mostly middle-American slough. Jane Anne's friend slumps manfully against the wheel of a red Datsun hatchback with Wisconsin plates and, suddenly business-like, Jane Anne is out of the car, suitcase in hand, pocketbook slung in a noose around her neck.

"Goodbye," she says and is gone. I watch while she situates herself in the Datsun, then I pull out of the parking lot, drive up the entrance ramp to the interstate, alone inside the throb-bing, hurtling Volkswagen, then insert myself into the welter of anonymous northbound vehicles.

I can go home again, again and again, each episode like a snow-flake that sticks to your eyelashes. They melt and mingle with your tears. Take a memory, any memory, and it becomes an in-violable god, a sanity exactly according to plan. But those soft edges—those peripheral realities that blur, those landscapes that shift and rush past—those are the crucibles of emotion, and they flow headlong backwards beneath your feet. I come South only twice a year, once at Christmas, once in the summer. Each time is a possible fatal accident.

The Metal Shredders

Nancy Zafris

When I describe my job, I put on a bit of an act. I'm not completely honest about it. But dishonesty works, I've discovered, especially at these get-togethers where everyone shows up with a six-pack. Guys throw out a "So what do you do?" feeler as they sit down with hands tight around a beer bottle. Bored, nervous, with accusatory glances toward the spouse who made them come, they nod lifelessly at the responses.

This is where I enter the scene. I start talking about my managerial position at the Metal Shredders. Within minutes, the white knuckles are gone; the hands start to relax. Pretty soon they're leaning back enjoying it. The wife is off the hook.

"You're kidding!" they say after I relate a few job anecdotes. They're laughing. I'm apt to laugh myself. Somehow it doesn't seem so bad from the safe distance of a Saturday night. But the fact is I hate my job. Every morning I bury my head under the pillow until my wife drags me out. I'd rather die than go to work. But I'd rather go to work than tell my father I quit. "I'm quitting John Bonner & Son Metal Shredders, Dad. I'm not working for you anymore. I'm leaving you. Yes, Dad, I'm betraying you."

I'd rather die than say it. In fact, I'd rather go to work. Every morning it's the same vicious circle.

But at parties I weave a few tales, all of them true enough, though you tend to embellish after a few beers. If I find the details getting out of control, I look over at my wife, staring at me with that stoic disgust she saves for when I'm naked (gaining weight recently), and it reins me back in somewhat. Besides, with this job even the truth is serviceable. And it's certainly true from my point of view that my employees form the crudest, most mal-formed group of men on earth—half Dirty Dozen and half Three Stooges. Yet these men I claim to despise are the very swine that string the pearls of my anecdotes. Even the dead employees liven things up. Listeners' eyes grow wide with half-drunk amusement. First I get them with the story of the human shredding. Then I follow it up with the wild dogs. After that, anything I say is funny. But people who are drinking have no taste. Though they may appear to be sloppily attentive, their minds are actually a blank.

The truth is that my job is excruciatingly dull. During the course of the day I have the time and appetite to eat about four brown bags of lunch. On occasion the workers have thrown their lunch pails into the small refrigerator near my desk, and I have been driven to furtive acts of theft, greedily opening their trea-sure chests and wolfing down tidbits that wouldn't be missed. I haven't reached thirty, yet I'm growing fat. Being a redhead, that means pudgy thighs and a stomach that's excessively white. At night I suffer pains after supper. My wife thinks it's an ulcer from working so hard, but it's just from eating everything in sight and washing it down with cups and cups of burnt coffee. Because if it's one thing men can't do when they're left on their own, it's make a decent cup of coffee or keep their toilets clean. When you face the kind of toilet I do every day, what's a rancid cup of coffee to that?

Besides, I don't work hard enough to warrant an ulcer. I sit at my desk. I sit at my desk. Am I repeating myself? I do, every day. Sometimes I stare out the window at the metal waste surrounding me. Other times I take both fists, slam them to the desk top, and exhort myself with a cleansing "Okay, let's do it!" Then I throw myself into work. Once in a while my wife calls; having twisted herself into a knot, she's unraveling fast. It's not just my ulcer she's frantic about. She's convinced my ulcer is responsible for her lack of pregnancy. I don't have an ulcer, yet I feel telling her this might not be entirely welcomed news.

At any rate I sit here at the Metal Shredders, wishing instead I was scurrying about to important meetings in some I. M. Pei office building, running down marbled hallways, silk tie flying, briefcase swinging, slapping the elevator door as it closes in my face. Not the wildest fantasy perhaps, but it's better than the yellow and pink carbons that have stained my hands the color of a lifelong smoker's.

Right now I'm going over Accounts Receivable. The books are a mess. I'm not keeping up my end. The debits don't equal the credits, not that they ever have, and now I have to send out the bills again. Bonner Senior says I don't need a secretary, but I do. Someone to address envelopes. Put stamps on them. Find a mailbox. Make a decent cup of coffee and throw a PowerBoy into the toilet. I can't stand it. I'm planning to go nights for an MBA. An MBA should rocket me out of here. With offers storming in even my dad, Bonner Senior, won't want to hold me back.

I look out the window. It's depressing here. The office is a prefab aluminum box with a flat roof that frightens me during snowfalls. In the summer I worry about frying like an egg. Even with a fan turned on my face, my insides boil so bad I might pop. I could go outside, but that means having something specific to do. The office is built on stilts, and I would look pretty stupid

walking down the steps and standing at the bottom doing nothing until I was so embarrassed I simply walked back up. I know
this because I've done it. So I'm stuck up here. Thus, the four
brown bags for lunch.

Presumably I'm up here on stilts so I can see what's going
on. This means I have a panoramic view of stacks and stacks of
wrecked cars. I feel like a demented air-traffic controller madly
conducting crashes. And what is going on under my watchful eye?
My workers hide out during the day and emerge at night when it's
time to go home. Working, sleeping, or drinking, I don't know.
When they want to hide, even binoculars can't find them. During
lunch I might see them playing Mad Max with Uzi water pistols.
They're very much into these kinds of games. Man against scrap
metal. One feeds the other, it's a symbiotic relationship between
workplace and futuristic metal movies.

The Shredders, with its high rises of scrap as the buildings
and the greasy apron as our future farmland, displays a nuclear
winter already in progress—bizarre metal appendages, fossils of
Skylarks and Chryslers from the twentieth century. Man-eating
machines. It's the new classic confrontation. It's true that one time
a machine really did eat someone; we had an accident and he
slipped right through the tunnel of the shredder with barely time
to scream. The shredder is fast and powerful. It hardly does to
say it wasn't a pretty sight. It was hardly a sight at all. But that's
another story. A story, I'm sad to say, I tell to friends whose usual
reaction is to laugh their heads off.

And during the rest of the day when the workers aren't playing
Mad Max? If I see them at all, they're under the hoods of their own
cars, then under the hoods of their co-workers' cars. To a man
they drive horrible bombs, disgusting big hunks pieced together
with junk from the even more disgusting cars we've shredded, and

after barely making it to work only to break down at the entrance, they spend all day fixing them so they can barely make it home. The paycheck never makes a round trip either. Overseeing them is not what I envisioned as a career. That is, a Business Career. You think:

People who take taxis

People who know what checkbooks are

You don't think:

Squished cars

Men who squish cars

Stealing their lunches

Being within a hundred miles of them

I go back to Accounts Receivable and try to bear down. But my eyes keep wandering to Accounts Payable and all these invoices that don't sound familiar. There's a bunch from Laskow's U-Pullem. Who's been pulling what? I'll have to ask Bonner Senior about this. He often does things without telling me.

It's quiet now at my desk. Outside, the noise is stopping. The machines are powering down. The shriek of metal slows to a high scratch; I shiver until it's over. There's no traffic beyond the fences. Suddenly it's very quiet and it's like one of those things, a hammer bashing you over the head. It feels so good when it stops. The silence is wonderful. I lean back and listen to it. It feels good. I put my feet up on the desk. I'm in charge of the place. Just great. And I close my eyes.

The door is kicked open. Tony, our arc welder, walks into the office and strides over to the time cards as if he owns the place. He picks up the cards and shuffles through them. I barely, just barely, open my eyes and glare at him. A thick fur runs up his forearms, onto his upper arms and into the sleeves where it burrows under his T-shirt in a buoyant layer. Even through the hair

I can see the speckles of welding burns on his skin.

Tony stands by the time clock. "Hello Tony," I say in a mono-tone. There's no answer. I think longingly of my MBA.

From the deck of time sheets Tony selects a card. He looks at his watch and makes an obvious gesture of checking it against the clock. "Mr. Greenjeans is late again," he says.

This time I don't answer.

"More than his usual half hour."

"Those seats have to be welded in," I tell him.

"I got some nice cream-colored upholstery," he says.

"Well slap it in. Do some welding for a change."

"Jesus it stinks. You'll never get that smell out. I can't even go near it."

We picked up a car declared unsalvageable by the county attorney because of the odor (some corpses stored in the trunk). My dad has a friend, Mike Charny, who works at the county attorney's, and we get a lot of interesting junk coming our way from their office. This one is a good deal. An '86 LTD. Mechanically it's perfect, but the interior has been ruined. We're going to throw in some new seats and a bunch of air fresheners and put it in our auction.

"Well go near it anyway," I tell him.

"Go near it anyway, he says." Tony picks up the beaker from the Bunn machine and swirls the coffee. "You got a cup? And I tell you another thing," he says, grabbing the mug from my hand and thrusting it in my face. "Them dawgs going to come around. That's dead meat they're smelling."

"Well clean it up for Crissakes."

"Listen to him. What'd I just tell you? I put a bandana around my mouth. I still can't go near there. It looks like Greenjeans to the rescue."

"Leave him alone, Tony. He's just our night watchman. He's an old man."

"The smelling section of his brain is gone."

"How do you know?" I ask. This kind of interests me.

"He had an operation knocked it out."

"What operation when?"

"Brain surgery. I don't know!"

My legs are still plopped up on the desk. Tony walks over to me and looks down at my crotch. "I need in," he says. He drives his hand between my legs—I barely avoid clocking him on the jaw with my boot as I jerk down my legs—and fiddles inside the drawer of my desk.

"Don't get nervous," he says.

"What are you doing, Tony?"

"I need the key to the tow truck."

I fling his hand aside and dip my fingers into the well that holds the tow truck keys. They're gone. "What do you need them for?"

"Your old man has a job for me."

I lift the tray and search the rest of my desk drawer. "Where the hell are they, Tony?"

"Anybody sign out?"

We start scattering papers for the clipboard that's not hanging on the nail where it should be. Tony finds it by the coffee machine. The last entry is not only coffee-stained, it's over six months old. Tony shrugs, brushes and straightens the top page like it's a wrinkled shirt, and hangs it back on the nail. Coffee-yellowed, it seems as ancient and discarded as the concept of organization behind it. Tony reads the page. "Supposedly Thompson was the last person to use it."

"That helps," I say. I lean back and laugh. Thompson is dead. Tony grabs a chair, swivels it around, and hikes a leg over it. "You've got a great sense of humor," he mumbles. Then he plops his chin on the backrest while he stares into space with the rubbery-faced intensity of a bulldog. Thompson was a friend of his—not a great friend, but a friend. He and Tony succeeded in transforming the Metal Shredders into a brewery and personal car repair shop. Too much of the first and not enough of the second led to his demise.

For years there's been talk of a pack of wild dogs in the area, and Thompson proved it wasn't just myth. He broke down not too far from here after going with Tony to one of those desolate bars that always manage to spring up in desolate places. Thompson knew about the dogs of course. They were legend, often talked about but never quite seen directly except by the friend of a friend. A lot of people didn't buy their existence at all, but Thompson must have believed it enough not to start walking but not enough to stay locked in his car. He stood out on the hardtop and worked under the hood, and I suppose being drunk destroyed his reflexes or his hearing. It scared us all when we found out, but there was a certain thrill to it too. Frankly, it was the first time I was glad the office was built on stilts. If Tony knew the story I told about it, prefaced by a hilarious description of his friend (extremely short with arms as long as an oragutan's), I don't know what he would do to me. Well, now I can add a punch line to the story: at least Thompson did one thing right before he died. He signed out the tow truck.

"Tony," I say, "it suddenly occurs to me that you used the tow truck the day before yesterday."

"I put the keys back," Tony mumbles. Now he's staring at the floor and his mouth is open and sucking the back of his hand.

I hold up the invoice from Laskow's U-Pullem. "So is this you?"

Tony raises his head long enough to give me this look, this

look that says, How stupid can you be? Then his face, smooth from stretching toward me, plops back on his hand and is instantly mushed into oatmeal.

I reach down to my bottom drawer, try to open it, kick it, remember to crack the top drawer to unhinge it, and reach down for the rest of my food. I'm reluctant to bring it out because I'll have to offer some to Tony and I want it all for myself. But I have to have something. I've got to eat.

I bring out half of a turkey and cheese submarine from Lawson's and pick off the cellophane. (My lunch is augmented in pit stops at several stores during my morning commute—I'm even embarrassed to tell my wife how much I'm eating and too embarrassed to buy it all in one place.) The guts of the sub have gotten nice and soggy, the way I like it, and I grab a bite before reluctantly holding it out to Tony, who shakes his head no. Just as I'm inwardly celebrating his refusal he asks, "What else you got in there?" I make an elaborate show of looking down in my drawer to find him something good. My hand brushes aside a Drake's apple pie and I resurface with a rock-hard, skinny cigar of jerky. "Slim Jim?" I ask.

"Un-uh," Tony says. "I'm in the mood for something sweet. You got anything sweet?"

At first I'm convinced that Tony, having heard the telltale crinkle of cellophane when my hand hit the Drake's pie, is just being a sadist. When I toss him the pastry, he rips off the wrapping without even bothering to check what fruit flavor he's received (unless he has package colors memorized, green for apple), breaks the crescent pie in half, and devours it in a continuous gulp with three spasms of his throat that pass as bites. To my complete surprise he hands the other half back to me, having some notion of fairness after all, and appears to give the pie no further thought.

I don't think he even noticed what he was eating, and just as briefly as he savored the taste, he now seems to have forgotten completely about it. This is like sex, I think. This is how a man is supposed to be. This is how I'm not. Ask my wife, no don't.

My wife. Thinking about her does me no good. I squirm in my seat and my face grows hot. Tony's face is still mashed into the back of his chair. It's about time to go home. But I have a few minutes. I reach into my drawer and pull out my Slim Jim. When I hear rattling on the metal stairway, I chomp quickly and throw it back into its hiding place.

The slow-climbing footsteps have a crisp hollowness that reminds me of autumn. Tony is about to say something smart about the footspeed of our night watchman when the window reveals the bold gray hair of my father. Tony jumps up as soon as he notices him. His lower body is an empty pyramid where he's standing over his chair, his upper body a masquerade of attentiveness.

My father opens the door and does a stomping routine as though it's winter out (it's late spring). "Been welded to that chair since yesterday," he says.

I watch as Tony goes from at-ease to attention. He swings his leg over the backrest and brings his thighs together. He fusses with the chair, rolling it on its casters until he has it arranged under a table. But he makes no response. After all, Bonner Senior could have been addressing me.

My father takes off his jacket with excruciating precision. We wait silently. Then he turns and fixes a neutral gaze on Tony. All I feel is relief.

"What?" Tony finally says, shrugging. He quickly twists up his palms. Bonner Senior doesn't answer and Tony gets nervous. Having nowhere to go, he walks in a circle. With all his hair he looks like a caged animal.

Bonner Senior doesn't bother with any niceties. He just says,

"Why were you sitting down?"

"Well, Mr. Bonner . . ."

"Do I pay you to sit down?"

"I was trying to discuss the time card situation with Mr. Bonner. I mean . . . not you, I mean your son."

It takes a lot to make Tony call me Mr. Bonner. Watching him squirm isn't pleasant. I know how he feels. My stomach starts to burn. I feel a flush creep up my chest.

Bonner Senior straddles the corner of my desk and aims his crotch directly at Tony. "I guess this means the car's all done?"

"I have located the problem," Tony says. This is his answer to a yes-or-no question.

"And?" Bonner Senior throws out his hand like a friendly politician fielding questions.

Tony responds by looking at me. His glance is followed by my father's.

"The car's outside," I say.

"And?"

"And? And nothing. The car from Mike. It's outside. Tony's in the middle of putting in new seats." I try to sound casually dismissive, but by now the traitorous flush has attacked my neck and face.

"Your son is right," Tony says.

"Well, this should have been completed by now."

Quick, clumping footsteps sound a brief reprieve. In a second the door opens and men move quickly to the time clock. Bonner Senior takes advantage of the noisy flow. "Why didn't you get on this earlier?" he enunciates, facing me in an exaggerated way so that Tony can't read his lips. "We have an auction on Monday, remember?" His eyes attempt to pull a comprehending nod out of me.

My own eyes want to oblige, but they're suddenly riveted to

a spot on the desk. Looking at it from my father's point of view, I can imagine how he feels. My blank sockets must resemble a stalled slot machine; no doubt the butt of his hand is twitching with the urge to unjam me.

But he regards me impassively. Control is his only expression. "You didn't forget that, did you?" It's a question, but it's asked in the imperative voice.

I look up at him, completely lost. It's like one of those school amnesia dreams. My skin is a mess. I imagine by now there's a violet tinge to the redness. "Is this ringing a bell?" my father finally asks.

Yeah, it's ringing a bell. A school bell. And I'm getting one of those school sweats. MBA classes don't look so good right now. I pretend to watch the men clocking out, check to see they're doing it right. As they pass my desk, they nod respectfully but wordlessly to my father and sneak a quick eyeful of me.

Bonner Senior's eyes and mouth clamp shut, vents closing down to prevent steam from escaping. He's aware of the presence of these men, so he begins a soft explanation about the auction on Monday.

Men are still beating a path by our desk. Bonner Senior keeps his back to them as he talks to me. But he can feel their glances lingering longer than necessary, and once in a while he turns around to face them. This is enough to shoosh them away. Tony stays in the corner, rocking stiffly on his bowlegs.

"Okay," I say after the explanation. "I'm up to speed now."

Bonner Senior sits down slowly and gives me a sorrowful look. I can't stand to meet his gaze. I turn to Accounts Payable and flop through the bills. "It's here somewhere," I say, though I haven't a clue what I'm referring to. I scatter some invoices around, I check my bottom drawer, which contains nothing but food. I do anything to avoid looking up into his face. Bowlegged Tony is standing like a wishbone, taking it all in. "Okay, so . . ." I mumble. I stand up. "I guess we'd better get started."

Bonner Senior pushes back his chair in obvious relief.

"There's a problem of odor," Tony says.

"You heard the man, Tony." Bonner Senior's already at the door.

Outside, I see that our night watchman has arrived. Mr. Joe Greenslade is talking with Marcus, the only other worker who hasn't scattered homeward.

"Joe," my dad acknowledges.

Mr. Greenslade bows. He's old, and he has slow, elaborate manners.

"I've got something I want you to do," Tony tells him. Greenslade bows deeply. Tony motions for him to follow but Greenslade heads for the stairs, oblivious. Tony is forced to pull him off the bottom step to make his point. Greenslade hangs onto the railing and stands for a few seconds to get his bearings. He's an old man. Balance is a problem with him. But he's not annoyed. There's a big smile on his face.

Meanwhile, Bonner Senior is pointing Tony toward the car. "Come here," Tony says to all of us. Marcus, at least, is willing to edge closer. I throw my support to Marcus and leave Bonner Senior standing alone. "I want to show you something," Tony says. "Just come here."

We get closer to the car. An odd smell creeps into the edges.

"That can be taken care of," Bonner Senior informs us when he sees our faces cringing.

Tony hides his nose inside the collar of his shirt. He stands as far from the trunk as possible. With his left foot poised to run, he uses his right arm to flip open the trunk.

"Jesus! God!" The smell is overpowering. We immediately run in the opposite direction, stumbling over Greenslade, who's still shuffling toward the car. At a safe distance we turn around.

"Guess I'll head home now, Mr. Bonner," Marcus says.

Mr. Greenslade is the only one who doesn't want to escape. He steers himself back on course after being run into, and slowly makes his way through the dizzy landmines of middle and inner ear disturbances until he's next to the car.

"See I told you!" Tony shouts with excitement. "His smeller's gone."

"I got vertigo is all," Greenslade says, leaning on the car.

"Look at him! It doesn't bother him. He's perfect for the job."

Once his balance is restored, Greenslade looks into the trunk and smiles. His old body is built like a stepladder, straight but on a slant. At one time he must have been a strong man. His pelvis is wide for a male, though with no flesh on his buttocks, and his back, shrunken from arthritis, is now planted in his hip bed at a size too small. Though he's officially our night watchman, his main job is to dial 911 if something goes wrong enough to wake him. I'm not sure he can even handle that. He talks with a stutter, whether from excitement, old age, or a speech impediment I haven't a clue. Yes we tried getting younger ones, but they have a problem called not showing up. We were thinking of just bagging it and getting a guard dog instead, a Doberman or a German Shepherd, but the wild dogs put an end to that notion. The theory of the wild dogs is that they used to be respectable pets that somehow "turned." Apparently they're now like a gang of hoodlums on a rampage, corrupting other innocent canines in their path, their numbers ever growing. Nobody wants a guard dog that might become one of their new recruits.

Greenslade removes his head from the trunk of the car. "S-s-s-ome . . . went on here," he remarks. He turns to Bonner Senior with a dry laugh.

"There were a couple of bodies in there for a while," the Senior says. Mr. Greenslade lifts his head. "I say there was a corpse in there."

Greenslade nods knowingly. "Thought so," he says. He starts his shuffle over toward my dad. Marcus's ears perk up at the mention of corpses, and he shuts the door to his pickup and slides over.

Greenslade's got his thumb jerking over his shoulder, and his head bouncing away to the rhythm of his stutter. But he can't get the words out.

"What bodies?" Marcus asks.

Tony's flipping his hands at everyone. "I know this story already." He puts his face down to Mr. Greenslade's. "A *man* body and a *girl* body." He intertwines his fingers and thrusts them up to the old man's eyes.

Greenslade rubs his kidneys while he considers this. "W-w-w they engaged to be married?"

"They were either engaged, Joe, or they were married already." Bonner Senior shrugs soberly, the best answer he can give to a good question. I watch him as he tells the story to the group. He's a man in charge with a studied version of the common touch. Physically he looks like the type who always plays the sheriff on TV westerns like *The Big Valley* or *Bonanza*—thick whitish hair, stately, retirement handsome, authoritative but deferential to the right people, the Barkeleys, the Cartwrights, and Mike Charny at the county attorney's.

The story, as the sheriff relates it, is that a man and a woman from North Carolina were going to buy some marijuana. They were dealers. "Do you believe it?" Tony interrupts. "Small time." But for having heard it all before, Tony remains pressed to my father's side for the rest of the story. In no time his tough face inherits the look of a child.

"Anyway, the woman was driving," the Senior continues. "The

man was in the passenger seat with a briefcase of money. The supplier told him to come back into the garage. When he did, somebody with an Uzi was waiting for him."

"Was he a, a . . ." Greenslade starts to ask but spots Marcus, who is black, and stops.

"A Mexican," my dad says.

"Yeah," Greenslade agrees happily. He grins reassuringly at Marcus.

"He opened fire and killed the guy. The woman of course had no chance to escape. She knew she was done for."

"Yeah," Tony chuckles. They're coming to his favorite part.

"What happened?"

"Shot her up right in the car. About sixteen bullets."

Greenslade has to bend over, his delight is so great. He gets dizzy again and Marcus helps him straighten up.

"They caught the men, by the way," my father adds. "And listen to this explanation. The guy claims he didn't mean to shoot them. His finger kept slipping."

"Yeah right . . . ," Tony agrees.

Marcus stretches out his chin to ask something.

"They hid them in the trunk, Marcus," my dad preempts. "A couple of weeks at least."

Marcus, satisfied, retracts his neck.

"Oh," my dad remarks, "here's something interesting. When they did the autopsy on the woman, guess what they found? An old bullet in her from a previous run-in. An old bullet, Joe. She'd been shot before."

With this, Greenslade—barely recovered from his last jag of laughter—is forced to sputter anew.

"He likes hearing about dead girls," Tony says. He stares at Greenslade's shaking body. Then he pokes him.

"Don't poke," my dad says.

Greenslade waves him off, still laughing. "It's all right. W-w-w-where was that bullet located?"

"Turns you on, don't it?" Tony's saying.

"I don't know, Joe," my dad answers. "Near the heart, I imagine. Too dangerous to remove."

"In the chest," Mr. Greenslade observes.

I decide to put an end to this. "Well, this is an interesting story, it's all well and good, but the fact remains that you'll never get the stink out."

"It smells?" Greenslade asks.

Tony rolls his thumb toward the old man. "I told you!"

"I don't mind driving it," the old man offers.

"I'll keep that in mind, Joe." My dad accords him a weighty nod.

"We don't need anyone to *drive* it, dingbat!" Tony yells.

Greenslade shakes his head, thoroughly amused. "Dingbat . . ." he mutters.

I leave the group to their merriment and head for the stairs. Once inside the office I call Sharon and tell her I'll be a little late. I'll just meet her and the others at the fern bar she's got picked out. She says okay. Is she withdrawn or simply unannoyed? It's not like her to be calm. "Are you alone?" I ask. She hangs up on me. She's probably alone wishing she weren't. It's my fault. She wants a baby that looks like Bonner Senior. Strong planed features, unethnic but nicely tanned, no freckles. Dark brown hair. But I tell her, Look at my mother and that's what you're going to get. You're going to get a redhead, it's like a tungsten gene, it's strong, it'll burst through anything.

Bonner Senior opens the door and goes through his midwinter stomping routine again. "I've got them fixed up with some industrial-strength cleaner. That should keep them busy." He takes a seat across from me. "It's true. Old Joe Greenslade doesn't smell a thing. It's mighty peculiar." This sounds kind of like *Bonanza* talk. He crosses his legs; then his arms. "Marcus has gone home," he adds. "You'll have to get some lime to deodorize it."

I poke my chin toward the phone. "Had to call Sharon."

He leans quickly over my desk. "Can you do that?" His eyes flicker at me, accusatory, searching, long-suffering. "The lime?" He fastens me with another look, the kind of look aching to be topped off with a cowboy hat. "Don't put Tony in charge of it. Do it yourself. Tony's a welder. End of story." He falls back in his chair.

"You don't have him on a welding job right now," I say, a real edge of anger in my voice. "But you don't seem to mind that." I try to control the heat in my face by flipping through a gift catalog. A Master Desk Appointment Log bespeaks my position in the world with its aura of authority. It promises a quantum leap forward.

I can feel my dad's eyes burning through me as I try to appear engrossed in the World Holiday Labels, an easy way to remember important holidays in different countries. Of course, the red blotches have started and it's clear I'm not engrossed in anything.

"Look," my dad begins. "If you're not happy in your job . . ."

"If you're not happy with the job I'm doing," I retort.

His back and arms push the chair to its maximum give. "I'm happy with the job you're doing." He holds up his hands to stop me from butting in. "For the most part. I just think you need"— the chair squeaks up and down—"a little more management skill."

Have Chris set up NY appointment. Study ad campaign of Sloane. Set up executive vacation schedule. I read from the list of sample entries on the Master Desk Appointment Log. They've even got them handwritten. This is management skill. I close the catalog and toss it aside.

"Enough of that kind of talk," Bonner Senior announces. "We'll get you straightened out. Any news on the home front?" His chin indicates the phone.

"No," I say. "Sharon's fine."

"But no new news to report?"

"No new news."

"Okaaay." He stretches and stands up. "Any plans on the docket tonight?"

"Going out with some friends. Nothing major."

"Well, according to your mother, she has something planned for me. Dinner, I guess. Or a movie. We'll see. Got to keep them happy, right? I'm willing to go along with it."

This is what I hate most, I want to tell him. Because you have good things to tell me about metal shredding doesn't mean you have good things to tell me about life.

He opens the door and waves without turning around. I get up, watch him go down the steps and into his car. He backs the car up to Tony and Mr. Greenslade, hangs out the window with his instructions, then gives them the same kind of blind wave as he drives off.

I stand at the top of the stairs. Greenslade's got the hose out and is spraying into the trunk. "Are you guys almost finished?" I yell. They don't hear me so I clamber down the steps. A piece of paper floats in the air and I clamp it down with my foot. When I stoop to pick it up, I retrieve a hundred-dollar bill. The first thing I do is stuff it in my pocket, stand up straight, check to see if anyone saw me, and run back up the stairs. I lean against the office wall and huff from nerves and exertion. I am seriously out of shape. I take out the hundred-dollar bill and examine it. It's Benjamin Franklin and he's staring right at me. Is this Uncle Sam's way of keeping you honest—aren't the lower denominations kind of profiles? I put the bill back in my pocket, but then I can't help myself. I slip it out again and bring it up to my nose. It smells. It smells bad.

A clod of gravel sprays against the office window. Tony's outside hollering. I open the door. "Come here! Come here!" he's screaming. "Jesus, come here!"

Money is flying in all directions from the trunk. "Get it out, man!" Tony is yelling to Greenslade, who's frantically unearthing the trunk's bowels. Even all that money can't bring Tony closer to the trunk. He runs up to the office and flies back down with a trash bag. "Get it all!" he orders Greenslade, whose inept clawing is annoyingly ineffective. Yet neither of us can help. The smell has drawn a hostile border around the car. "Thank God for no brains," Tony says. He jogs up and down with nerves as he watches Greenslade from a safe distance.

By the time we get all the money collected, it's twilight. We rush up to the office, Greenslade a few minutes behind, and Tony looks in the bag like a kid looking at his Halloween candy. "How're we going to count all this? Man, it stinks. Greenjeans is going to have to do it. In the meantime . . ." Greenslade opens the door, out of breath. "You're going to have to count this, old man, it's too stinky for us. Okay? In the meantime, we'll divide it up." Tony disappears into the toilet. He comes out with two more plastic bags. "Anybody have any objections?" He cocks his head in a question mark.

Greenslade and I keep quiet.

"Fine," Tony shrugs. He hands the two empty garbage bags to Mr. Greenslade, dumps the third bag upside down. We watch as tens, twenties, and hundreds come streaming out. Tony looks down at it and up at Greenslade. "You're not busy this evening, are you, Greenjeans?" The old man chokes on his laughter. "Here. You're the only one can stand to touch the stuff."

"W-w-w-w-w."

"Count," Tony says.

"Oh yeah," Mr. Greenslade mutters. He bends laboriously and struggles after a hundred-dollar bill.

"Not now. Never mind, go ahead."

A bubble of snot starts to fall from Greenslade's nose. He wipes it off with the bill. "God," I mutter and roll my eyes at Tony.

"Yeah, just mix it up with the dead meat, old man."

"What?" Greenslade asks.

"I said, Think you'll finish by morning at that pace?"

Greenslade bounces his head in amusement. He slaps Tony the jokester on the shoulder. Tony backs off. "Please," he says. "I got to get home and take a shower. Hey, I should pull out a couple of these hundreds for my date tonight. Man, I liked the part about the extra bullet in that girl's tit. Do you think it's true?"

"I imagine," I say.

"It kind of turns me on. Doesn't it turn you on, your old lady with a bullet in her tit? Hey! Greenjeans! Does Mrs. Greenjeans have an old bullet in her tit?"

"I w-w-wish." He chuckles and again goes for Tony's shoulder, but Tony's too quick for him. He heads for the door and I follow. Greenslade's bent body chases us like a slave. "Hey hey, Tony. M-m-my w-wife hasn't got an old bullet, she's just g-g-g an old tit."

"Ha ha that's great, Mr. Greenjeans, tell it to Captain Kangaroo. Don't forget to count the money."

Greenslade stands at the top of the stairs and watches us go down. All of a sudden he rears back and laughs as loud as his old dry throat will allow him.

"Are we leaving?" I ask Tony at the bottom of the stairs.

"Yeah."

"But what are we going to do?"

"Get back here early in the morning. It's Saturday, nobody'll be here."

"Then what?"

"Then. Then nothing. Then it's our money."

"But," I say. But, I want to scream, how do we do it? What if we get caught? How do we get rid of hundred-dollar bills? Where do we go? How much at a time?

So instead I say, "What about the old man? Can we trust him?" I recognize the line from a TV show the night before.

Tony waves me off. "Hey, Greenjeans, no cheating up there. Don't let that money start talking to you."

Greenjeans lifts his head and emits a dry sound. His hands are on his hips. He looks happy.

"And don't tell anyone!"

Very deliberately Greenslade draws a line across his lips. "M-m-my l-lip . . ."

"Yeah we get it. Look, what can I tell you? He doesn't have a brain. Who knows if he can even count."

"That's what I'm worried about," I say.

"When the stink dies down, you count yours and I'll count mine. It can't be that much. It's just dope money for Christ's sake. That's been out for years. Figures somebody from North Carolina would be into marijuana in 1987. Wearing bell-bottoms, right . . . I hated hippies, man, but now I'm one myself. Still running against the wind." Tony begins to sing.

"Has this happened to you before?" I ask. "I mean, it's not really the counting I'm worried about. I mean . . ."

Don't make me do it, Tony, I think. Don't make me whimper.

"Everything will be all right," Tony answers. "Tomorrow we'll get here real early, we'll go about it very logic-minded. We won't do anything in a hurry. We'll send Greenjeans on his way, and then you and me will pour some after-shave on our money and figure out what to do. You can't count on Greenjeans anyway, he'll walk into a store and stink it up to high heaven, we just got to hope they think he's been stuffing it under his mattress."

"But don't you think we should do it tonight?"

"We can't do anything until we get rid of some of that smell. Are you willing to touch it?"

I shake my head.

"Besides . . . it's late."

A dog howls in the distance.

Tony jerks around. "Did you hear that?"

The dog howls again, followed by a chorus. The sound razors the back of my neck.

Tony rubs himself nervously. "They smell it. Shit, man, this is like a werewolf movie. They're after my meat, man. Hey, Greenjeans! Them dogs is out. Stay inside. We'll close the gate."

Greenslade stays locked in his stance, that of a happy witless housewife admiring her laundry line.

"Get back inside! I said. Them dogs is out. We'll shut the gate."

Finally Greenslade throws back his head in a rasp of comprehension. His chuckle saws the quiet night air. Another dog howls.

Tony's bouncing up and down. "I'm waiting for you, Bonner. I got the smell all over my jeans. Oh Jesus, let's go."

Tony jumps in his car. He pulls out of the gate and parks across the street. I pull in front of him. We both hop out and run across the street to the main gate, swinging it out onto the road before shutting it. "I can feel those dogs," Tony's saying. His hands are shaking as he fiddles with the gate chain. "They're after me," he says.

"Calm down, Tony."

A rustle in the bushes propels us into the air. We twirl and come down frozen, backs pressed into the fence. When nothing happens, my hand unglues itself from the wire mesh and clamps the lock. I keep my eyes ahead. "Do you really think the dogs are coming?"

"Yes, man! They're smelling the meat. They got Thompson, didn't they? They got a taste for humans."

Even Tony pauses at this last remark. Then we take off running for our cars, laughing hysterically. When I get inside and lock the door, the hysteria turns to hyperventilation. Without thinking, I take out my hundred-dollar bill and bring it up to my nose like smelling salts. The fumes clear my head. They really clear my head. My mind is working now, it's watching Tony strut into the bank and give himself away with his hairy welding-speckled arms. A guy like that wouldn't have money, they'll know it, the bank'll know it, the bank's been trained, they know the way money smells when its been festering with a corpse. A chimera suddenly flits through the night; it sends me to the floor. It couldn't get any worse. Now I'm dog meat. The car is rocking. I tell myself: The car may be rocking but the door is locked, calm down. When I resurface, Tony's face is pressed against the windshield. For a moment we stare at each other's distorted features.

"Can't you start your car?" he's yelling.

I roll down the window. "How are we going to cash it?" I ask.

"It's cash. Cash. It's already cashed."

"But you can't . . ."

"After the scent dies down. Don't worry. We'll talk tomorrow." Tony looks around fearfully. "What's wrong with your car? Please, man, don't make me stand here any longer."

"Nothing's wrong. I'll start it up. Let's go."

"I'll follow you home. I'm right behind." He jogs toward his car. "Do you have after-shave?" I call to him. *I got after-shave* I hear echoed back to me. "Would you pick up some lime too for the car?" I yell. In the dark I see his body pumping.

No stories tonight, I tell myself. Sit quietly at the fern bar and don't turn red. No spinning yarns about the Shredders. Let your friends do the talking. Don't start on the dogs. It'll lead to other things, a taste for humans—don't even start. Stay sober. Talk about adoption.

I turn on the engine and pull out. Now and then I look up to see if Tony's still behind me. His headlights bounce off the rearview mirror and catch me in the eyes. He's got his brights on but I don't mind. It keeps me running smoothly, steady on the road.

Contributors

ROBERT H. ABEL, Flannery O'Connor Award winner in 1989 for *Ghost Traps,* is also the author of two previous collections of short stories and two novels. An alumnus of the University of Massachusetts writers program, he is currently Visiting Writer at Trinity College in Hartford, Connecticut.

GAIL GALLOWAY ADAMS lives in Morgantown, West Virginia, where she is Writer-in-Residence at West Virginia University. Several of her stories have been anthologized, and she has won fiction scholarships to Duke University and Bread Loaf Writers' Conference. Her novel *The Notebooks of Madame Eye* is now circulating.

TONY ARDIZZONE is the author of two novels, *In the Name of the Father* (1978) and *Heart of the Order* (1986) and has recently completed an interconnected collection titled *Larabi's Ox: Stories of Morocco.* A native of Chicago, he teaches at Indiana University and in the MFA program at Vermont College.

FRANÇOIS CAMOIN teaches creative writing at the University of Utah. The Flannery O'Connor Award volume *Why Men Are Afraid of Women* was his second book of short fiction. A new collection of his stories, *Like Love But Not Exactly,* is scheduled for publication by the University of Missouri Press in 1992.

DANIEL CURLEY was one of the editors of *Accent* and founded and edited its offspring *Ascent* from 1974 until his death in 1988. In addition to three novels and several collections of short stories, he wrote criticism, poetry, plays, and three books for children. A posthumous collection, *The Curandero,* was published in 1991.

PHILIP F. DEAVER, winner of the Flannery O'Connor Award in 1986 for *Silent Retreats,* lives in Longwood, Florida. In 1989 he received a fellowship from the National Endowment for the Arts and in 1990 a fellowship from Bread Loaf. He has recently completed a novel and a second collection of stories.

ALFRED DEPEW lives in Portland, Maine, and teaches writing and literature at the Portland School of Art. A native of St. Louis, he has taught in France, Spain, England, the Soviet Union, and, closer to home, the University of Vermont, the University of Southern Maine, and the University of New Hampshire.

MOLLY GILES teaches creative writing at San Francisco State University. After winning the Flannery O'Connor Award, her first collection, *Rough Translations,* went on to win the Bay Area Book Reviewers Award and the *Boston Globe* Award. She also won the 1990 National Book Critics Circle Citation for Excellence in Book Reviewing and a 1991 Marin Artists Grant.

CAROLE L. GLICKFELD grew up in New York City, the setting for most of the stories in *Useful Gifts,* her award-winning collection. She was the recipient of a 1991 National Endowment for the Arts fellowship as well as the Governor's Arts Award in Washington State, where she is a freelance writer. A fellow of both the MacDowell Colony and the Bread Loaf Writers' Conference, she is at work on a novel.

MARY HOOD won the Flannery O'Connor Award and the 1984 *Southern Review* / Louisiana State University Short Fiction Prize for *How Far She Went,* her first collection of stories. Her second collection, *And Venus Is Blue,* was published by Ticknor & Fields in 1986, and she has a novel forthcoming from Alfred A. Knopf. She lives in Woodstock, Georgia.

SALVATORE LA PUMA, author of *The Boys of Bensonhurst,* which won the Flannery O'Connor Award in 1985, grew up in Brooklyn but now lives in Santa Barbara, California. His first novel, *A Time for Wedding Cake,* was published in 1991. A second collection of his stories, *Where*

Angels Learn to Fly, is scheduled for publication by W. W. Norton in 1992.

T. M. MCNALLY grew up in Chicago and in Phoenix, Arizona. He now teaches at Murray State University in Kentucky. He has been Writer-in-Residence at the Hotchkiss School Summer Program since 1989. McNally has new stories appearing in the *Hudson Review,* the *Gettysburg Review,* and the *Denver Quarterly*.

PETER MEINKE is a poet and short story writer living in St. Petersburg, Florida, where he directs the Writing Workshop at Eckerd College. His stories and poems have appeared in the *New Yorker,* the *Atlantic,* the *Georgia Review,* and other magazines. His latest book is *Liquid Paper: New and Selected Poems* (1991), published by the University of Pittsburgh Press.

DEBRA MONROE, author of the Flannery O'Connor Award–winning collection *The Source of Trouble,* has lived in Wisconsin, Kansas, Utah, and North Carolina. She now teaches in the MFA program at the University of North Carolina–Greensboro and is at work on a collection of six novellas entitled *A Wild, Cold State.*

ANTONYA NELSON won the Flannery O'Connor Award in 1988 for *The Expendables.* A second collection of her stories, *In the Land of Men,* was subsequently published by William Morrow, and she has had recent work published in the *New Yorker* and *Redbook.* She teaches at New Mexico State University in Las Cruces.

SUSAN NEVILLE, author of *The Invention of Flight,* has a book of essays forthcoming from Indiana University Press. Her second collection of stories, *Tornado Watch,* was a finalist in last year's Drue Heinz Literature Prize competition. She lives in Indianapolis, where she is the director of Butler University Writers Studio.

MELISSA PRITCHARD received the Flannery O'Connor Award, the Carl Sandburg Literary Arts Award, and the PEN/Nelson Algren honorary citation for *Spirit Seizures,* her first collection of short fiction. Currently director of the Santa Fe Writers Conference and author of the recently published novel *Phoenix,* she has completed a second book of stories and is at work on a new novel.

SANDRA THOMPSON, whose collection of stories *Close-Ups* won the Flannery O'Connor Award in 1982, published a novel, *Wild Bananas,* with Atlantic Monthly Press in 1985. A native of Chicago, she now lives in Tampa, Florida, and is the assistant managing editor for Newsfeatures for the *St. Petersburg Times.*

DAVID WALTON lives in Pittsburgh. His collection of stories *Evening Out* was the first of the books to be published in the Flannery O'Connor Award series. Walton teaches classes in fiction and poetry at the University of Pittsburgh and reviews books for several newspapers. His novella "Public Lives," which appeared in *Quarterly West* in 1989, will be the title story of his next collection.

LEIGH ALLISON WILSON grew up in Tennessee and now teaches in the State University of New York College at Oswego. Her most recent collection of stories, *Wind,* was published by William Morrow in 1989. She has been anthologized widely, and her work has recently been in *Harper's, Grand Street,* and the *Kenyon Review.*

NANCY ZAFRIS lived in the Boston area for several years before returning to her native Columbus, Ohio, in 1989. *The People I Know,* her collection of stories that won the Flannery O'Connor Award in 1988, also won the Ohioana Award the year it was published. She has written a novel based on "The Metal Shredders."